TWISTED KICKS

Tom Carson is one of America's foremost writers on the current music scene whose work regularly appears in the *Village Voice, Rolling Stone* and the *New York Rocker*. TWISTED KICKS is his first novel.

Tom Carson

TWISTED KICKS

An Arena Book
Published by Arrow Books Limited
17-21 Conway Street, London W1P 6JD

An imprint of the Hutchinson Publishing Group

London Melbourne Sydney Auckland
Johannesburg and agencies throughout the world

First published in Great Britain 1983

Made and printed in Great Britain
by The Guernsey Press Co Ltd
Guernsey, C.I.

ISBN 0 09 931580 7

FOR PHYLLIS AND ROBERT
AND FOR MY FRIEND PHIL MCDERMOTT

ONE

CHAPTER ONE

Three days after Erica slashed her wrists with a piece of glass from the mirror she'd smashed in the psycho ward of the hospital where they had pumped her stomach and put her under observation after her previous attempt, Dan Lang came back to town.

He was twenty-one, and soon to have a birthday. Thin, slightly built, he seemed brittle and easily broken. Yet among those who knew him, in certain places in New York, he had a reputation as a fighter. When you looked more carefully, a wiry strength showed in the bunched tension of his body. His face had the deep and permanent pallor of a man who lives underground—all his features were screwed tight to his bones, as if the wheel that formed them had turned one time too many. He wore white stovepipe jeans, ripped at the knee, and battered gray sneakers. A well-worn leather jacket lay coiled in his lap. He looked more like a black-and-white photograph than like a living thing.

He was the last person left on the bus when it pulled into the stop. The driver stood up and walked down the aisle to him.

"Icarus, Virginia," he said. "End of the line."

Lang yawned. "I guess that means I have to get off, then," he said without moving.

"You live around here?"

"I used to."

1

Self-consciously, the driver ran a thumb over his chin. He had a creased Southern face, a boiled and pitted neck.

"Listen," he said. "You look to me like a fairly interesting dude, one who knows his pleasures."

Lang looked up. His eyes were a pale gray, bright and lucid, set deep in their sockets. There were heavy shadows of exhaustion beneath the lids.

"Oh man," he said. "You going to put me on to something?"

"If you want it, I know where you can get it. What's your game?"

Lang pondered.

"Tell me what's around," he said.

"I like that," the driver said. "I was right about you. I got an instinct."

"Everybody does."

"Yeah," the driver said. Nailheads of rain spotted the window behind him, gleaming in the streetlamps' light. "But in my line of work, I see a lot of people, and you know, on this route especially, I get a lot of guys like you—and I figure that if I can put something in their way, there's no harm." He gave a grin that was meant to be cool, but a queasiness in his upper lip gave it away.

"So what can you do for me?" Lang said. There was a dry edge in his voice, as if he did not believe the words he spoke were actual, and was impatient to be rid of them. His eyes never stopped moving, straying beyond the driver's shoulder to the rain-spotted night outside the windows.

"Well, say . . . If you wanted something to smoke, or sniff, or maybe even you wanted to meet a chick or two, then I could point you to the action. Don't get me wrong. I just like to be a good Samaritan like they say."

Lang lifted an eyebrow. "Say I was looking for some uppers," he suggested.

"Man, you hit it on the nose. There's a dude, name of Malone—"

"Jacker Malone?"

"Yeah, that's him. He can take care of you."

"Not too well," Lang said. "He's dead."

"What? Ah, I hadn't heard. Malone, that is a real shame. How'd it happen?"

"He got shot by a connection, in the city." Lang paused, deliberately, and then added: "Two years ago."

The driver's face collapsed, then tried to pull its pieces back together. "No, man, you must have him mixed up. I talked to him last week—scored some good shit off him."

"No mixup," Lang said. He swung his duffel bag off the baggage rack; he moved with a spare, lithe precision, like a man afraid of losing control. But his voice was easy. "I knew the Jacker real well." He laughed. "We were in the drama department together," he said, "in high school."

The driver had lost all his gregariousness. His face sagged. His fragile link to glamour was gone, and he was nothing but himself again.

"Do you know why they called Malone the Jacker?" Lang asked.

The driver shook his head.

"Cause when he shot up, he couldn't wait for the rush, he was greedy, and he'd jack the shit, like this"—Lang made his hand a fist, and pumped it rhythmically from the elbow—"to get it moving faster. So all the dealers called him the Jacker. They disapproved of him actually—it was bad politics to use what you were selling. That's one reason he got killed."

"I guess you did live here once."

"Yeah," Lang said, "and I left once too." He saw the driver's face, and added quickly: "Don't worry. I don't work for anybody."

The driver nodded.

"But listen. The next time you hear some kids talking, make sure it's up to date before you pass it on. You coulda gotten into trouble."

"Yeah, I *coulda*," the driver said. Lang saw that it was no use. He liked the idea.

"Stay loose," the driver called out, as Lang stepped down onto the road. Lang watched the bus roll away, its yellow windows swaying back and forth.

He felt sick.

It was nearly two A.M. and the life of the town had contracted, like a school of moths, to its few points of remaining light. Walking, Lang saw the glowing island of an all-night fast-food joint. Cars and motorcycles were tangled all around it, and drunken laughter scraped against beercans and rusted chrome. All the night people of Icarus would be gathering there, as they had done for years, as they would probably do forever. There would be bright-eyed bobbing girls, Lang knew, who looked at you in cold mockery and said "Crazy. Wanna come?" when you asked where they were going. There would be high-school football players at the end of their last season, gone on a beer bust. And rednecks and old freaks in an uneasy truce on the asphalt of no man's land. There would be giddy kids throwing up their first high, and ageless teenagers who had been hanging out for years and were already without knowing it in mourning for their middle age . . .

And, he remembered too, there would be Erica, somehow shimmering inside that bright confusion of shouts and cars—leaning against a big black Merc with her fingertips tucked in the front pockets of her jeans—alone and private, arrogant, and infinitely sad, with rock 'n' roll blasting from the cassette on her dashboard. That was how she looked the first time he saw her, in just such a place, on just such a rain-filled night—two years ago, when he and his crowd had gone dancing in Suffragette City and come ganging back across the river in their cars for something to eat before dawn. A sadness blew over him as he thought of it now. He had almost forgotten that she was dead. He had been a part of all this once, just as much as Erica had; and might be again, for having chosen to return.

But it wasn't a return at first, he thought; first it was flight. He hadn't come back because of Erica. As it happened it was only by coincidence that he had heard she was dead, at a time when he had already decided in his heart, though his mind didn't know it yet, to come home. The street turned as he walked—his thoughts turned from Erica to the last date he and his band had played, before he left New York.

It was the last night of a three-night gig at the same club that had given them their first job, a rat's hole of a place which yet had a reputation as the birthplace of many bands, Lang's own the most recent candidate among them, that had used it as a jump-off point for various kinds of notoriety and fame. Its air mixed the odors of the hospital and the morgue, of sweat, and smoke, and the whine of unchannelled heat. Down the long tunnel of its interior, hung all along its length with neon-tubed advertisements for every brand of beer, you could find a junkie from the greasiest pots of Avenue C sitting next to the most fashionable couple of the social season, or a gang of leather-jacketed young toughs a table away from a movie star and her entourage, or a bearded Hell's Angel, amphetamine gleaming in his eye, making gnomic conversation with the shiny young men from every record company, who still kept their blank contracts folded away inside their jackets while they applauded—for the music that was played here had been decided by their experts to be too brutal for consumption in other, sunnier parts of the country.

When Lang first moved to New York, he had come to this place—

first as a spectator, crowded into the back with the one beer he was able to afford from the part-time jobs that kept him alive. Then, after months of preparation and rehearsal, he had come back at the head of his own band. In the beginning, like so many others, they were thrown in as an opening act on midweek nights, playing to empty seats and the ringing bells of the pinball machine next to the door. Then they had begun to attract a following; the critics came to see them and pronounced them good. They were headliners now. At the club, people had started wearing T-shirts emblazoned with the band's name.

On that last night, Lang and the band were halfway through the second set, and Lang was in the middle of introducing a new song called "The Map," when someone at the side of the stage, where all the standing-room showoffs were jammed together in bright hot confusion, lurched forward and shouted "Twisted Kicks!"

"We don't play Twisted Kicks any more," Lang said.

"Twisted Kicks!" a girl with forked purple hair and green eyes called out in agreement from the bar. Behind Lang, Billy the bass player fingered his frets. Slow looping notes uncurled behind the sudden spaces in the air. His amp buzzed. Rim shots off the snare drum fell through walls of smoke.

"Ah, I don't even remember the words to that one . . ."

"Twisted Kicks!" the first voice insisted, stumbling all over itself. It was a New York voice—the sound of a hyena in its high nasal keen. From the end of the tunnel came a sound of breaking glass. A few other people yelled, somewhere out there in the dark. The drummer pumped his foot-pedal; his sticks smacked the tom-tom.

"You wanna come up on stage?" Lang said to the voice. His own, vibrating over the P.A., was no longer his. "You wanna come up? Cause we can write some new words for ya, fuckface."

A woman laughed. Through the smoke and the glare of the footlights, Lang saw some people trying to hold back the guy who was yelling. He caught a glimpse of a pale, rabid face, a crucifix swinging on a ripped black T-shirt. Billy hit the top string of his bass impatiently. The drummer hit the snare again.

"Cocksucker! I'll kill you, motherfuck—"

"Okay," Lang said. He looked back at the band. Billy nodded. Lang counted off the beat, his guitar pick poised for the first chord.

"One, two, three, four—*Let's go*—"

> *I made a map of your mind,* he sang into the mike—
> *I drew a path—to all the things you left behind—*

I drew an arrow to mark—all the things that you cared for
In the dark—but isn't that what we
were—there—for—

But the unsung song came back to him, later. The voice in the
alley. The sheen of iron, in the rain, there.
. . . Play Twisted Kicks, he had said.

The second set ended at three. Lang got back to the band's loft
at five. Sally—his sometime girlfriend, or at any rate a girl, who had
lived in the loft and shared Lang's bed (and sometimes that of the
other band members too) from the time when they had first begun
to rehearse—was up waiting for him, and she threw him off. He came
in with his hands trembling—he didn't want to see anybody.

"You're awfully late," Sally said in her reedy voice. "Everybody
else is already asleep. What happened to you?"

"Nothing. Just business."

She stood up, so suddenly that involuntarily he took a step back.
"Are you back on stuff again?" she demanded. "God, Danny—you
look like you are. But you're not, are you?"

It took everything he had, then, to keep hold of himself. He
was ready to crack apart.

"Do you want to look at my arms?" Lang asked. "No—I'm not."

"Your eyes are all right," Sally said, thoughtfully. "But you still
look awful."

"It's raining," Lang said.

"You had a phone call," she told him.

"Not a label—not this late . . ."

Sally shook her head. "No. Some guy named Richard. He
sounded very spaced. He said he called to tell you that some girl—
some singer you used to know—committed suicide this morning . . ."

At first he couldn't get hold of the meaning of her words. Then
he understood. "A singer . . ." He was frozen, unable to think.

"He didn't say who, or where. He didn't name names—except
his own."

"It doesn't matter," Lang said. "I know who—I know where . . ."

"Hey, you all right?"

Lang came to Uncle Lou's Pub, which had opened the week after
Virginia legalized beer for eighteen-year-olds. He hesitated at the door,
like a man about to re-enter the church of a lapsed faith, before going
inside. It was a naugahyde kingdom in there. The booths were full of

people who looked rooted to their seats; the long bar was crowded with bikers having a chugging contest. One stood on a chair, neck arched, a pitcher lifted to his lips. The others clapped him along. Fear gleamed off the braces of the giggling girls standing against the wall.

Lang got a beer and sat down at a booth near the jukebox. The music leaped from the speakers, circled past the faces at the bar, flirted with the rim of a glass, and curled around his cigarette. A girl in the next booth was blowing smoke rings. The boy beside her poked a finger through each one just before it dissolved, and they laughed together as Lang watched. A pair of pitchers stood on the table before them like machine guns.

A year ago, before he had left for New York, this place was the choice hangout of his old crowd. Here he'd gotten drunk on gin and tonic countless times, surrounded by familiar faces, familiar jokes—here at four A.M. he and Erica had marched the length of the empty bar singing "Over There." Here, too, she and Richard had had their last fight, the one that ended the romance for good, only a week before Lang's departure. It hadn't occurred to him until now that it was also the last time he had seen Erica alive.

All of them had been there that night. It was Richard's choice to fight in public; Erica would never have permitted herself anything so sloppy. Lang passed the faces in review, as if he were clicking snapshots through a projector. He remembered how one time he'd said that they were all Richard's friends because they were the only people in Icarus who hadn't slept with Erica—"yet, anyway," he'd added, wasted that night and no longer caring what damage the words did. And how Richard's anger had made him care still less, and only Erica's cool questioning glance had cut him to shame.

Brewer had been there, slumped and morbid. Odell had too, flung on his chair in an imperious sulk, no one paying him any attention. Lorraine had been there, her quick mouth moving in unabashed fascination as she watched the fight, ignoring the patient unhappiness poor lovelorn Brewer cocked her way like a monocle, his round face tense and miserable. And Lang too, in a corner, drawn to watch in spite of himself, no longer wanting to be drawn and yet, like all the others, unable to keep his eyes from the far end of the table; not even watching Richard, although he was doing most of the talking, but fixed instead on Erica's glittering green eyes, her angular cheekbones, her harsh, silent lips.

It was painful to remember; but Lang let himself rest on the pain as he sat in Uncle Lou's, sipping his beer only a few chairs away

from the chair she sat in that night. Just beyond the memory of
Erica was a street in New York, a face in the rain, a voice calling out—
then a gunshot. Lang could not face that street, that face, that had
followed him all through the long trip down. He started toward the
jukebox to look for a song instead, when a voice above him said
quietly:

"Hey. Ain't it Lang?"

Lang looked up in relief. "Yeah, it is. How's business?"

"Slow," Carmel said, with his quirky, interior smile, sliding into
the bench opposite Lang. "Half my friends are turning religious on
me. One girl I thought was regular—I mean, she was mainlining, and I
usually don't touch that, but it was a special favor—then I see her
last week, selling flowers for Hare Krishna. I almost got violent. But
you know I'm not a violent guy, so I bought a flower instead. You
can't just write them off—she might come back to it."

"Uh huh."

"Just like you, see? No one ever thought you'd come back,
either. What happened? Big Apple too much for you?"

"Oh, no. New York is the greatest anaesthetic in the world.
You should check it out if you ever need a new territory. But you
know what happened to me on the way in? Bus driver tried to
hustle me."

"Shit." Carmel lit a cigarette with delicate movements of his
long white fingers. "Everybody wants in on the act. There's no class
left, it's gotten so bourgeois. I wouldn't go to New York," he added.
"This is the town for me."

"You for it, it for you."

"What did this bus driver look like?"

Lang laughed. "Oh, don't worry about him," he said. "He told
me to ask for Jacker Malone."

"The Jacker? He sure was up on his data, wasn't he?" Carmel
grinned. As with everything he did, there was no waste in the grin.
"That idiot. I haven't thought of him in years. There wasn't a dealer
in the area who was complaining when they totalled him."

Carmel was dressed for business. Whenever he was out on
his regular rounds, he always wore clean corduroy slacks, a newly-
pressed work shirt and sports jacket. His narrow face was always
clean-shaven, his blond hair neatly cut and combed. That was
standard procedure for all the area dealers. Carmel took it a step
further by never passing the goods at the same time he made
the contact. All deliveries were made separately, by Carmel or

his partner, in a second-hand U.S. Mail truck.

Professional courtesy shadowed Carmel's face now. "I guess you heard about Erica," he said.

"I heard that it happened."

Carmel beat a riff with his nails on the formica. He always had one or two telephone numbers written down in magic marker on the back of his hand.

"Well—I was around, the time they took her to the hospital, but I had some business of my own, and I wasn't watching the nuances too carefully." He coughed. "And that kind of thing is getting to be such a drag, anyway. How're you making out up North?"

"All right. I've got a band, we're getting a few dates. We might be doing an album."

Play Twisted Kicks. Yes, it was a gun.

"Not bad," Carmel said, pursing his lips appreciatively. He was only being polite. Other people's failures and successes meant nothing to him; envy and commiseration were both equally foreign to Carmel. Within his universe, he was complete.

"How long are you in for?" he asked.

"I don't know."

"And staying where?"

"I'm not sure. I thought I'd try Hoffentlichs'."

"I could take you," Carmel said. "I'm going that way. I've got to talk to Alice—the daughter, you remember her."

"Yeah. She still doing acid?"

"No, downers. Downers are very big these days." Carmel glanced over at the next booth. The smoke-ring girl caught his look and saluted him with her glass. He gave her a pontifical wave in return. "Just an old friend of mine," he said. Friend was Carmel's term for a client.

"I thought it might be love," Lang said.

"You know me better. No chance."

"I know."

"What's love? What can it get you? No peace of mind," Carmel said, "and I like peace of mind."

"Don't be so sentimental."

Carmel gave him a blank smile. He was a psychologist, of necessity, but in a limited field. He understood people only by their needs, never their desires. "I never know how to take you, Lang," he said.

"It's because I don't have a hustle."

"Of course you do," Carmel said, smiling. "Of course you do.

Why, you want to be an artist, don't you? That's the worst hustle of all." He stood up, leaving his drink unfinished. "Come on," he said. "Let's go."

Even if he had not remembered the house, it still would have been easy to recognize. No other on the street would have its lights on at this hour. As they walked up to the driveway, Carmel said, "Remember how it used to be? You couldn't come here of an evening without finding the court full of cars. People passed out in the bushes—all kinds of noise from inside."

Lang had been thinking the same thing. He nodded.

"The scene's changing," Carmel said. "If it wasn't for the perks, I'd get out. Everyone's just sunk in their heads. They've gotten to be like moles. They dig underground, and they're blind in light."

"It's not like you to talk like that."

"I'm getting old. I turned twenty last week." Carmel smiled in the darkness. "I'm changing, too." He opened the door without knocking. "Myra?" he called out.

"Here," a woman's rough, husky voice answered him; then, apparently talking to someone else: "Damn you. You said you'd be back by seven. If you'd just tell me—if you'd say, Myra, I'm going out to get smashed, and I will call you from some unknown place at an ungodly hour, I'd say fine, but—" She propped the telephone against her cheek, shifted her cigarette to the other hand, and motioned for Carmel and Lang to come in. "Oh, you pig, you can't even talk. Why don't you just pass out? Just fall over . . ."

She would, Lang knew, be talking to Andrew, Andrew Hoffentlich, her husband, who had spent twenty years with the CIA, and half of eternity with Myra, and was drunk in some bar, as usual, with the memories. Lang had heard the same conversation many times before —in a way it was reassuring to find it still going on a year later, with only the calendar on the wall behind Myra changed. Then he looked closer, and saw even that wasn't changed. Over Carmel's shoulder he could hear the deep, slurring rasp of Andrew's voice emerging from the phone.

The TV set above the refrigerator was on, soundlessly; its reflection flickered on the varnish of a table so crosshatched and scarred with cigarette burns that it looked like some impressively modernistic design. The refrigerator was covered with shopping lists, phone numbers, news clippings, bills, and bright rags of anonymous paper, held together by small plastic-topped magnets in many colors. A high-school yearbook lay open on the stove. Cans, glasses, and ashtrays pocked the room like acne; magazines and newspapers were piled everywhere.

In the center of it all was Myra. She sat as if she were her own throne, ajangle with jewels at wrists and throat, her clothes a spangled network of straps and beads, buttons and pins, her hair piled on her head; her force seized the air around her. She was big too, but it didn't look like fat, only another part of her massive ornamentation. In the old days, when Lang was still living in Icarus, Myra had been the mistress of a salon, half-matron and half-confidante to all the drunken, brilliant children of the town, who had come there first because of her daughter, and then because of her—the Ex-Prodigy club, Lang had named it once. They would come to drink and talk from midnight until dawn in the hot months of summer, while Myra chain-smoked her way through an endless round of gossip and dirty jokes, and Andrew her husband mumbled long, intricate stories of life in the CIA over his pipe, between covert visits to the basement where he kept a bottle hidden from Myra's eyes. Lang had taken Erica there once, but she hadn't liked it—"It's just like playing Chopsticks in there," she said, contemptuously. "Everybody already knows all their lines by heart."

As a girl, Myra Hoffentlich had been beautiful; Lang had seen pictures of her wedding day, and he would have known even without that, for she often spoke of her years as a teenage queen in the post-war suburbs of northern Virginia—"before I met the drunken bastard," she would invariably say, puffing hard on her cigarette and nodding toward Andrew's slumped inert form on the sofa. Now she filled the spaces of her loss with cigarettes and talk, and her face was royal with twenty years' realizing that being beautiful did not mean the world before her would also be.

She hung up the phone and stared heavily at Lang. "Well," she drawled. "We all figured you were dead in some gutter, up there."

There was a pause. "Not quite," Lang said. "It sounds like you're all way ahead of me."

Myra gave her cackling laugh, and gestured toward the phone. "Oh, yeah. Isn't it wonderful?" She snapped the ash from her cigarette. "You know," she said, "I'm going to divorce him, I swear. The only way I survive is by planning that divorce."

"You were saying that when I left."

Myra nodded. "You were smart to leave," she said, and sucked deeply on her cigarette. "You were an asshole to come back," she added, through a cloud of smoke. "Why'd you come back?"

"I was at loose ends, and I followed one of them here."

"Not good enough," Myra said.

"Give him the evil eye, Myra," Carmel said.

"Yes," she answered, "he deserves the evil eye." She covered one of her eyes. The other stared at Lang expressionlessly, cold, devoid of life.

"How do you do it?"

"It's false," Carmel explained. "You don't know it so much when she's got both open."

"Yeah . . . I got a cancer in my eye—right after you left, as a matter of fact. So they took it out. Did you know that cancer always moves on a spiral? Thank God this one went forward. If it had gone back, into the brain—well, it would have been interesting. But I was lucky, if you call it luck." She grinned. "Now if I could just lose twenty pounds, and get some new teeth, I'd be all set. The fake eye is actually prettier. Less bloodshot anyway."

"The first one they gave her was the wrong color."

"Didn't fit too well, either," Myra said moodily. "They had to make me a new one. And I know why you brought it up, too, Carmel—you're perverse. Did you notice?" she asked Lang.

"Notice what?"

Carmel held out his spread hand. From the middle finger, a cold blank eye stared into Lang's eyes, set in a heavy brass ring.

"Myra gave me the first one," Carmel said. "What else can you do with a homeless false eye? This way I can see behind myself."

Lang was still looking at the ring. The eye seemed huge.

"More chicks comment on it," Carmel said. "Erica liked it, though—she was always askin' me if she could try it on."

"She was insane, that girl," Myra said. "I only met her once, but I said to myself, That girl's going to commit suicide some day. She's got what it takes."

"Nice of you to keep her secret," Carmel said.

"Well, she was rude," Myra remembered. "She didn't say hardly a word."

"Is Alice around?" Carmel asked. "I've got to talk to her."

"You know the way." Myra jerked her head toward the stairs. "Don't bother to knock. She'll have the headphones on."

Carmel nodded and went out. He carried himself with a trim, well-knit elegance.

"You look terrible," Myra told Lang.

"I've been drunk for two days, and hungry six months. What can you say?"

"I'd say I never knew you were so romantic. Coming to the wake of an old girlfriend."

"Not girlfriend. We were never together."

"You must be one in a million then."

"She was a friend of mine. That's all."

"Still, you come back right after she knocks herself off." Myra cackled, lighting a fresh cigarette. "That's very suspicious—I'm not one to judge, but you do have to admit that is very suspicious."

"I'm not planning to resurrect her."

"Ugh," Myra said. "Don't. Have you seen any of the gang?"

"Not yet."

"Neither have I. Carmel's about the only one of them who stops by anymore—he and Alice seem to be getting on very well, which pleases me, except I don't know him as well as I should."

"He wouldn't let you," Lang murmured; but Myra had been living in a monologue for so long that she no longer noticed interruptions. Fully launched now, she went on:

"Richard, now, I haven't seen him—I don't think anyone has—and he used to come here all the time. I heard he was shacked up with a fourteen-year-old girl, and not doing much of anything except screw away what's left of his brains. . . . And Lorraine—you remember Lorraine—I heard she was doing some theater work."

"Oh?"

"As an usherette."

"An usherette," Lang said, smiling. "Poor Lorraine."

"It's still a taste, I guess." Myra leaned forward. "And she also happens to be living with the man upstairs."

"God, or Carmel? . . . He's done stranger things."

"Yeah—they both have. And . . . Let's see . . . Brewer, I don't know anything about, really, but Alice saw him. In the city. He was coming out of Sunset—you know the place."

"You mean the gay bar, down near the river?" Lang was startled. "That doesn't sound like Brewer."

"Stick around, you'll find out—nobody sounds much like anybody these days."

Lang shook his head. "I guess that means he got over Lorraine at least."

"I guess it does."

"What about Odell?"

"Oh, Jesus. You don't know. Odell is the coming thing. He's wearing leather pants, and mirror shades, and talks about nothing but Nazis. He's got a gang of kids who follow him around—just the way he used to follow all of you. . . . The pattern's come full circle, don't you see? I don't know, Lang. You, your crowd—they're done. It's all over. You lost something, somewhere along the way. Erica knocking herself off like that, just puts a period to it all."

"Maybe," Lang said, "except it's not my crowd any more."

"Sure it is. It always will be."

"What do you mean?"

"You came back, didn't you?"

Carmel's voice came floating through the door: "I'll be in touch. . . . Take care, Alice."

He came back into the kitchen. The trail of his cigarette smoke crossed Myra's and they mingled as they disappeared. "Well," he said, "I've got to go. It's time to get to work."

"You're working nights? That's awful," Myra said.

"True," Carmel said. "So true. Are you all set here?"

"I was wondering if I could crash with you," Lang explained.

"Oh, sure. Of course. One more body can't hurt."

"Good," Carmel said. "I might give you a call tomorrow, Lang."

"I wonder what he wanted to see Alice about," Myra said, as the door shut softly behind him. "That was a short conversation."

"I wonder what he wants to talk to me about," Lang said. "He's a busy man."

"Where does he work?"

"I think he operates a switchboard."

"Terrible job," Myra said.

"Uh huh."

Myra gazed into her ashtray, as if reading entrails. "You made a mistake coming back," she said. "There isn't anything left here any more."

"There never was," Lang said.

"Just because nothing's changed, don't think that means things aren't getting worse." Myra sighed. "I'm trying to think of any other gossip I can tell you, but there isn't even too much of that either. . . . Oh, shit. Wait a minute. There was something, I know you reminded me, but we got to talking and oh, where is it?" She hunted through the gaudy racks of paper on the refrigerator door. "Here. She mailed it to us because she didn't know where you were."

"Who?"

"Johanna. She's living somewhere down South now."

"Johanna? She's not in Icarus any more?"

"No. She left right after you did, last year—she was the only other one who left." Myra handed him the letter.

"Mind if I read it now?"

"Mind? I'll kill you if you don't. I've been dying to open it. None of us has heard a word from her."

Lang opened the letter with more anticipation than he'd expected, or would reveal to Myra. But he hadn't expected, either, the sudden quickening in his blood when Myra spoke Johanna's name, or when he saw her cool, precise handwriting on the envelope. He hurried to finish the letter, while Myra squinted impatiently beside him.

"Well?"

"She's working at a radio station in south Virginia," Lang said.

"What else?"

"She wants me to come visit her. That's all."

Lang folded Johanna's letter and put it back in the envelope. Its real message was the fact that she had written it. She really didn't need to say more.

"Are you going to go down there?"

"I don't know."

"Lang! You have to."

Lang stood up, the letter held carefully in his hand. "I just got here," he said. "We can argue about it tomorrow if you want. I haven't slept in three days."

Myra looked at him dourly. "All right. Crap. Take the couch down in the rec room."

"Thanks."

"Welcome home," Myra said.

But when he was lying on the couch and the lights were off, and the house was silent, and he thought that at last he was ready for sleep, sleep didn't come. The walls were covered with masks and paintings from three continents, the souvenirs of Andrew Hoffentlich's government career. Lang's mind roved beneath the shapes of their shadows. When he was young, he had thought that the shifting patterns made by passing lights in his window were the shapes of his thoughts as they drifted; when he was young, too, he had the fantasy that if he could only empty out his body in one long breath, he would find a sweet oblivion at the end, beyond dreams, beyond thinking, and the shadows would stop. Now the hot breath of memory breathed on him. His mind would not stop, and he lay trapped beneath it. For the first time in months, he found himself aching for a fix.

Because he had done that too. Lost and footloose in New York, the shadows of Icarus riding hard on his shoulder, he had pushed and forced himself into every hole, driven by the impossible desire to obliterate all that he had been and done before; he had gotten Sally too, and fucked her the same night he met her, because he couldn't afford to wait; he had made every scene, and whipped his body along the way to a cold and furious grace, until the little girls clinging to the rim of the stage each night had come to speak of him (in all ser-iousness—their seriousness) as evil. And with every aching breath he had taunted the void in his wake, appealed to that backward-glancing darkness: *Can you match this. Could you do this. I am going to beat you*

"Are you back on stuff again?" Sally had asked him, when he came back to the loft that night. And for a moment he had thought that what he had just done—in those two hours between the end of the set and the time he finally got back—must be plain as blood on his face, wondered even if perhaps there was real blood on his face, and Sally was right, dead right, because it felt exactly like heroin: not that first green and phosphorescent rush of joy, but later, when you had fixed four times in a day and your flesh smelled like dead rubber, your circuits were dead. What a need to forget there was by the time you got to the fourth shot—what a sense that your brain was burning, literally burning up its cells, and he wanted that, liked that, then.

In an after-hours joint in the West Village, he remembered, he had once had an argument with Sally. She said she could never under-stand how killing yourself could be glorified, it was a coward's way— "Life is such a precious gift," she said, and her eyes lifted from the table to the junkies huddling in their Bolshevik coats against the cold inside their skin, and the tired call girls in their furs in the shadowless light that gave their nicotine faces a garish energy, and the blond and pasty-drunk college boys staring vacuously at the aging female imper-sonator mouthing the words of a popular song on stage. That was his version of New York, a city of exiles, allowing him to be one of them, and he liked that too, then.

"No," he said to Sally, "there's more to it than that. There's a lot more to it than that."

He had been thinking of Erica. At the time he hadn't heard the news, because of course she hadn't done it yet, she was still alive; but her love affair with her own death was hardly Lang's or anybody's secret. She was a live wire that would find satisfaction only in being extinguished. Standing in the rain the night they met, she told him that she was a singer, and they spoke of Lou Reed and Bessie Smith—*ain't nobody's business if I do*—and he had gone to hear her sing, a week later, in a dreary little bar out on I-95, the same highway he had traveled tonight when he made his escape from New York.

"You came back," Myra had said. Yes, he had come back—but standing in the hallucinatory light of the terminal, in the evening of this same day, he had not made any choice: when he came face to face with the clerk behind the glass, the words "Icarus. Virginia" came spilling out from numb dazed lips without his willing them, as he stood there sweating in a trance with the gleam of a pistol still flashing in his eye. He had only known then that he had to escape. It was later, much later, when dark 95 parted and fled like a deer before the hunting headlights of the bus, riding South, that he remembered Erica—and Richard, and Brewer, and mad furtive Odell, and all the rest, all those names that had come tumbling like flecks of dried blood, like bright red rust, from Myra's mouth—and realized that he was coming home.

And maybe in that same moment—although he hadn't realized it yet, hadn't even remembered her name until Myra had handed him her letter—maybe then he had also thought of Johanna—imperiled Johanna, who was tempted to sterility as Erica was tempted to dying. What had the letter said? She was working at a radio station, somewhere in the South. She knew too, Lang thought. She got out too. But she hadn't had to come back.

Johanna didn't like Erica. Erica didn't mind because Johanna disliked her for all the right reasons. Erica said it was like having a conscience locked up behind glass, where everyone could see it, but no one had to touch it, and no one had to pay. Lang remembered how, in the middle of those awful, endless Icarus nights, when they had all gotten so wasted and wrecked that the horror had congealed into a dull and comatose stillness, and people lay like cracked eggshells all around (those entertainments they had devised to while away a summer night) Johanna would still be sitting quietly in the center of the wreckage—Erica having gone off with her squire, or swain, or whatever horn she had chosen for the night, hours before—her grave face melancholy, and aloof, and strangely peaceful, as if she knew, Johanna knew, that this was the way it was meant to be, had to be, for all of them.

That slow death had ended for him a long time before Erica's death; but the exile he had chosen instead had also ended with a death. "Are you looking for some kicks, kid?" he had said—that face suddenly remembered from the club, the black T-shirt soaked in sweat and grime and now rain too, as he advanced toward Lang in the rain and said, "Are you looking for some kicks, kid?" with a white glow of madness in his face and the flash of a gun in his hand. . . . And Lang had fled to the apartment, and heard the news of Erica—and run from New York then too, as he had once run from Icarus, with the memory of the boy in his black T-shirt slumped against the wall with the dull rain washing his sightless eyes—only to come back to another history, and another corpse.

He had stopped playing the song "Twisted Kicks" because it was his song from Icarus, and he had come to hate it the same as he hated all of Icarus by then—because he had made himself believe that he was free, that he wouldn't ever look back. He was adrift in a bright new world, in love with its false brightness, false newness because that gave him sanctuary. And if, once in a while, stray word drifted to him from Virginia that Richard was doing more drugs, or Brewer was still desperately messed up over Lorraine, or that Erica had a new band, or that Carmel was expanding his operations, he paid them no mind, because that part of his life was over. Now, imprisoned on the couch in the Hoffentlich basement, as the night wore on toward dawn, he knew that there were never parts in anyone's life, he knew none of it had ever been over.

The last time he had sung "Twisted Kicks" was when the band taped their demo for the record companies, two months ago. In a mood of drunken exhilaration, he had mailed a copy of the tape to Richard. He had never received an answer, but by the next morning, sober, he hadn't expected one.

Maybe Erica had heard it.

Once, they had all been at a party, and Carmel had opened his stock to all of them for free. They danced all night and then fell down, as couples came together and solitary figures quit their searching to sprawl on the wine-stained rug—Odell put "My Generation" on the stereo and then passed out beneath the speakers while the song played over and over. Richard and Lorraine were necking on a couch; Lang sat, stupid on pills, and watched them both. Then he turned, and saw Erica beside him.

"Do you know what we're all doing here?" she asked.

"No. What?"

Her face was impassive. "Everybody's trying to decide how long they're going to live."

Of course that would just have been one of Erica's jokes. Because she never had to make up her mind. She knew; she knew all along, that the others could only provide the smoke around her. She was expected to provide the fire. He could imagine her, dutifully, regretfully, casting about for an appropriate flame.

He thought again of his last glimpse of her, a year ago at Uncle Lou's. Richard had finally said something unforgivable—or done something unforgivable—or maybe she had just suddenly gotten tired of the whole charade, but she got up and turned to go. Richard, in despair, the despair he always held in reserve until the time was right to spring it, had dropped all masks, of anger and indifference, and lunged after her. When his fingers touched her arm, she looked back— Lang had never seen such a face. In her proud features were mingled all her grief and wisdom, all the knowledge she'd salvaged from her thousand sleepless nights.

They stood like that for a long moment. Then Erica said to him: "You know, I just can't do this any more." She pushed his hand away and left.

So she had known, then; not necessarily that she was doomed (although she was, certainly, in that she had been forced to use herself up like fuel to build that fire, and she must have figured it out at least that the supply would have to give out sooner or later), but that her destruction was the only act that would make her life mean what she wanted it to mean. It was Lang, who was still alive, who did not want to know—who did not want to say, even to himself, as he lay there between suffocating sheets in the hard dawn, fighting off the memories engulfing his head, that Erica's suicide, and all of Icarus with it, truly belonged to him now; because he shot the junkie in the alley, shot him dead, and ran to Icarus to escape, only to find that his numb flight was not a flight from anything, but the beginning of a nightmare.

Play Twisted Kicks.

I will.

TWO

CHAPTER TWO

Within a Grove of Buddies: 1

Waking, for a moment Lang did not know where he was. Late afternoon light came seeping dimly through the cracks in the curtains.
Then he saw Johanna's letter, and everything returned to him.

Lighting a cigarette to clear his head, Lang sat up on the couch,
and thought of what she had written. He didn't need to look at the
letter. He had read it over and over again last night, before finally—
unwillingly—turning out the lamp on the table to lie awake in the
dark for what had seemed like hours, and even now he knew its every
word, down to her quick but still-neat scrawl on the back of the
envelope: *Myra, please forward to wherever the hell he is now—if
you know.*

Or care, Lang added to himself. He had not expected to hear
from her again. Since the night he walked out of a party at Erica's
house, three months before he left, and found Johanna crying on the
curb for a reason she would not tell him, and which he did not find
out all that night, or ever for that matter; and took her home even
so—suddenly he did not want to remember the rest of it. They
hadn't been able to be friends, afterwards. No one ever could, Johanna least of all, not in Icarus, where one-night stands meant just

as much as a tortured affair that lasted a year, and sometimes could
mean more. She always called it the night she was unfaithful to herself, and he always called it the time he almost found love; and maybe
that was one of the ten thousand reasons why she went South, and
he went North, and they both left Icarus to sort out its destiny without them. He hadn't seen her again before his departure—he hadn't
heard a word from her since.

As you will see from the envelope I have finally quit Icarus. I'm
DJing at a radio station down here—AM twaddle of which I'm sure
you would disapprove, but I want to see you anyway. Please come
visit me—I am starting to think that I— This last was crossed out: in
its place was an innocuous and anonymous paragraph assuring him
of her seriousness, and a dry signature without any valedictory above.
That was all: no explanations—she had always been that way. He
didn't even have any idea of how long ago she had written it. There
was no date on the letter, and the postmark was smudged.

It was insane to even think of her, Lang told himself as he
looked at the envelope on the table. What had they ever had together?
A high-school classmate—part of that same class that had produced
Richard, Brewer, Lorraine, and Carmel (Erica and Odell were a class
behind); a few vague hints of flirtation and caring in an intermittent
friendship across the years; one night together; and an ache in his
heart whenever he thought of her name. Nothing more. She was the
one part of Icarus he wanted to remember. Which meant exactly that
she was the one part he had to forget.

Lang put the letter away and went upstairs. Andrew Hoffentlich
was sitting in the living room, staring heavily at nothing, an unlit pipe
in his mouth. His large, thickly-haired arms hung down. The gray
light from the window behind him mapped the scars on his bald head.

"Hello, Daniel," he said placidly, as if they had only said goodbye the night before. His voice was deep and resonant, all out of
proportion to its surroundings. "I'm glad to see you. I may not seem
that way, because I'm a little under the weather, but I'm very happy
you're here."

"It's good to see you too. You're looking good."

Andrew gave a buried chuckle. It came from deep inside him,
and racked his frame as it rose. "No, I'm not," he said. "Go on and
say hello to Myra. We can talk later."

Lang went on into the kitchen. Myra, coffee at her right hand,
cigarettes at her left, was reading a tabloid. "Feel privileged," she
said, looking up. "He spoke to you. He hasn't said a word—he's been

sitting there all morning. But then he always liked you."

Lang poured himself some coffee. Myra turned a page of the newspaper.

"Look at these pictures from England," she said. "They're disgusting. Those kids with the safety pins and the holes in their clothes. I can't stand it."

Lang looked over her shoulder. "Oh, yeah. That's Johnny Rotten. He's great."

Myra glanced up at him. "Don't tell me you're involved with all that—they have them in New York, too, don't they? Or do they?"

"You're wonderful, Myra," Lang said. "The only thing you bother to know about anybody is their private lives."

"What else is there?" Myra answered, turning another page.

Lang was looking at the high-school yearbook lying on the stove. It was opened to a portrait of Alice, Myra's daughter, dressed in black and staring directly into the camera. Her eyes were cool and impatient and withdrawn; her baby fat, instead of melting away, had coalesced into the hard-edged, determined bluntness of a hooker's dead pan.

Is she still doing acid?

No, downers, Carmel had answered. *Downers are very big these days.*

"Well," Myra said, putting down her paper with a snap, "now that you're here, Lang, what are you going to do with yourself?"

Taken aback, Lang looked up from the yearbook. "I don't know yet."

"If you didn't come back here because of Erica, what did you come for? There has to be a reason."

"Why?"

"Why what?"

"Why does there have to be a reason?" Lang said.

"Maybe there doesn't. Even though nobody would ever come back here just for a vacation. But I am curious to know just how you're planning to spend your time."

"I don't know," Lang said, sipping his coffee. "Maybe just hang out for a while, see some people. Find out—"

"Yes?"

"What's going on," Lang finished. The cup was hot between his hands. Did Myra really expect him to play detective, and sift for hidden signs in the debris of Erica's death? He was not even remotely curious about the hows and whys of it, or even the melodrama and gossip of it; and his lack of curiosity didn't surprise him in the least. The only thing Lang wanted to know was what happened next, and he was still too full of fear to confront that question mark head on.

"I think I'll go see Richard," he said, standing up. "Maybe check out that new girlfriend of his—fourteen years old, didn't you say?"

"That's what I heard. What do you want? Sloppy seconds?"

Lang grinned. "You never know. It'll kill some time anyway."

"Here. Don't walk. It's a long way. Take Andrew's car—he never uses it unless he runs out of booze . . ."

Lang looked down at the keys she had put on the table. Then he walked into the living room.

"Andrew?" he said. "Is it okay if I borrow your car for a couple of hours?"

Andrew took his pipe out of his mouth. "Of course, Daniel," he said slowly. "Feel free."

"Thanks." Lang went back and got the keys from the table. Myra looked irritated.

"Just whose side are you on?" she asked harshly.

"Who's talking about sides? I'm not on anybody's side."

"Good luck in this house, then," she told him.

Outside—driving down the streets which called the roll of all the old, familiar names, lost to him for so long—Icarus flooded him. Now it was New York that was unreal. For months he had lost Icarus in a world defined and dominated by performances, by endless rehearsals, by sound checks, equipment hassles, money hassles, by the labor of constructing a fresh façade and a life lived entirely in the present tense. But that was all gone, as if it had never been. Instinctively he fought the pull of the buildings, the streets, the names, as real as gravity. If he let go he would drown in it. But the only alternative he could offer was the pinched face, the baiting, begging voice of that one member of the audience, at that last show. Oh, are you looking for some kicks, kid? Well, we got 'em, just for you. Here they come now. Here they are.

And what, after all, would Johanna make of that? *That* would be a bitch to explain, Lang thought suddenly, and he didn't even mind, as he laughed, that his laughter was fraying at the edges. "Well, there was this junkie, see—" he began to say aloud. But then he stopped.

His hands tightened at the wheel of the car as if the gun were back in his hands. It was too close. "You have to keep control—you have to work this out," he told himself fiercely. But he felt as blank and empty as the moon.

Fifteen minutes later, when he opened the door and saw Lang standing there, Richard gave a casual smile. Among many people, his apathy passed for self-control; once Lang had admired him for it. But he had finally come to realize that the only reason Richard kept his feelings so carefully in check was for his own protection. Out in the open, they would not be convincing—they did not have the strength to stand up to air.

"Hi, man," Richard said, taking advantage of the open door to flip his cigarette into the yard. "I heard you were around."

"You going to let me in, or not?"

"Shit. You want an invitation? People come, people go, come in, stay out, sit in the trees, I don't give a fuck." The eyes in his handsome face seemed to wobble, as if they couldn't focus in sunlight. "Help yourself." He let Lang through and kicked the door shut. "I've just been sitting here, getting off on the game shows. You ever watch 'em?"

"No." The room was cramped and shabby; ugly Venetian blinds cut off all light from outside. Only the TV set, hung above the couch like an intravenous feeder, gave a little life.

"Great stuff," Richard said, sprawling on the couch." "Aaah," he yelled at one of the contestants, whose wife had just lost five thousand dollars, "get rid of the sleazy bitch—she's got no room in the life of an ambitious man like you."

He pawed through the clutter on the floor for his cigarettes. "So here you are," he said to Lang. "I guess New York turned out to be too tough for you, huh?"

Lang smiled at the note of hope in Richard's voice. "No."

Richard stood up again, and walked around, scratching his head. He managed to look both restless and indolent at the same time. "No, huh? Well, that's good. I guess that's good . . ."

"I wanted to thank you for calling to tell me about Erica," Lang said.

Richard paused, his hand still up in the air. "Oh. Yeah. Well, sure. I thought you'd want to know."

"I wasn't that surprised."

Richard's cigarette glowed in the dimness. "No, I guess not. Wanna beer?"

"Sure."

The apathy seemed genuine. It had always been just for show, before. Richard acted like a man with his mind somewhere else; but there was nowhere else.

"So you're doing all right in New York, then."

"I'm still alive." Lang shrugged.

"Punk rock, huh? I know all about it. It's such shit. I mean,"
Richard grinned, "nothing against you, Lang, but it's swill. Most of
it. That tape you sent me was okay."

The grin gave a faint echo of Richard's old charm. That charm
had carried him long after faith, and trust, and belief had all been
gone. But it was only an echo, and it faded quickly. Ever since Lang
could remember Richard had been able to ingratiate himself into any
company, and dazzle any girl by his looks and spark. It was all he'd
had left, and now it was gone too. Standing there, in the barren
room, Richard could have been anyone.

"What I mean," Richard went on, taking a long swig of beer,
"is that they don't know fuck about rock 'n' roll. The real stuff, the
great people. Like the Who or the Stones or Dylan. They just shit on
it, and who the hell are *they*? I was really surprised to hear you were
into it . . . even though that tape was okay, like I said, but—oh, man,
remember how it used to be? Like the Rock N Roll Theater. Remember that? That would have been great. . . . I mean, I'm still going
to do it, of course. And when I do, I'll blow those fucking punks off
the map. I'm gonna bring back the Sixties, man, you watch me."

"That was ten years ago," Lang said.

"I know," Richard said. "And we missed it. We missed it." His
voice grew bitter. "I still can't get over thinking about how I missed it."

"We'd be old, by now."

"Bullshit."

Lang shrugged. It was no use arguing.

"You'll see—you'll see, when I tell you about the Rock N Roll
Theater . . ."

"You're still talking about that," Lang said. "You were talking
about that when we were still drinking 3.2."

"Well, I've been setting it up, that takes a long time. But I've
been talking to some people, and they dig the idea. And you know I
can do it. Just get a stage, get some money, work up some songs—I
was going to write you and ask you if you could give me some help
with that—I can always find musicians, actors, all that kind of stuff—
and wham! Just really lay it on these people. Show 'em what it's
really like. It'll be a gas."

Lang thought of the two hundred bands in New York, scrambling for rehearsal space, picking up any kind of job to stay alive,

working for months before they even got an audition. He knew of one girl, lead singer for a new band, who'd danced in a topless place for a month to get the money for their amps. He himself had worked bar in a Mafia joint down on Hudson Street while he was putting his own people together. And all for the chance of an hour on stage in that crowded, noisy little club on the Bowery.

"It's too bad Erica's gone," Richard said. "She would have been perfect for it."

"Oh, come on, man," Lang said, turning away in disgust.

"No—it would have been good for her. You don't have any idea of how bad she was at the end. I was meaning to call her up and ask her—you know, I really wanted to help her—" Sincerity overflowed in his voice. There was that old eagerness, the need to please—but now it sounded grotesque.

"I heard you were making it with a fourteen-year-old," Lang said.

"She doesn't look fourteen. And she doesn't act fourteen. No, man, she's really sensitive, and she fucks like a bunny. You'd like her. Matter of fact, you can meet her. She's coming over soon."

"It's been going on, then."

"Oh, yeah. Forever. I mean she really is the chick for me. I finally found one."

"What about Erica?" Lang asked, and wished he hadn't—it was like slapping a baby.

Richard sucked his lower lip in under his teeth. "Well . . . I guess it helps to have been in love before," he said, "I don't make as many mistakes."

Lang stared at him. At first he thought that Richard must be putting him on. But Richard was looking back at him with a pained, somewhat puzzled sincerity.

"—Erica, Jesus," he said. "That was over for months—months before she got around to offing herself."

"You still called me."

"Just to let you know. I thought it'd probably still matter to you. For me, it was finished a long time ago." Richard winced. Maybe it was the smoke from his cigarette.

"You know Odell?" he demanded suddenly. "Odell really had her number. He told me—told me years ago—that she was just a cunt, and not to go near her." His attempt at anger was querulous and pathetic. "I should have listened to Odell."

"Odell was always an asshole. He was our token asshole."

"Yeah, but he was right, wasn't he? She was a cunt."

Richard's voice was almost pleading. He turned in relief as the doorknob rattled.

"Ah. I bet that's my foxy lady here now." He rolled off the couch. Walking to the door, he moved sluggishly but stiffly, like an arthritic. Lang got it suddenly: the room smelled like a cheap hospital. An old childhood fear, that to go among invalids was to risk becoming one, remembered itself in a suddenly-sensed heaviness in Lang's arms, his legs.

Richard was right; his chick didn't look fourteen. She looked twelve. Flat-chested, mousy-faced—her mouth dripped down like sludge beneath leaden green eyes which looked at him suspiciously for a full ten seconds before she blurted, "H'lo," as if she were taken aback by her own eloquence.

A little boy was with her. Round-eyed, he glanced around the room, as if looking for an exit. But he stood absolutely still.

"This is my old buddy Dan Lang," Richard said to the girl. "Lang, this's Christy. And her brother, Jim. She's babysitting."

She still looked at him. She was still sullen. It seemed to be her only face. "You got a smoke?" she asked Richard.

He flipped her a cigarette. She broke it in two, and dropped it on the floor.

"I meant a smoke," she said.

"Oh. Oh, sure," Richard said. He got a large wooden matchbox from under the couch. Inside was a cheap corncob pipe and a plastic bag of dope. "Come on over," he said to Christy. "You don't get it for free."

"Oh," she said. "Kissy, kissy." She cast an odd look at Lang—as if they were both parents putting up with an errant child. She walked over to Richard; without changing her expression, she put her mouth up to his. Lang listened to them grind, and felt embarrassed, not for himself, but for Richard—and then not even for him.

Richard shoved a hand at the place where her breasts would have been if she'd had any. She jerked back. "You got no manners," She told him.

"But baby," Richard answered, with his old smile, "we're in love, remember?"

Christy sniffed. "Oh, yeah."

"Yeah," Richard said. "Hey, Jimmy, come here."

"What for?" the little boy asked, clinging to the doorknob.

"Just come on."

Hesitantly, the boy went. Richard put one arm around Christy, and maneuvered Jimmy with the other to a spot in front of them. The pipe was between his teeth. He looked up at Lang, and grinned.

"There," he said. "Don't we look just like a family?"

Christy rubbed her nose with her sleeve.

"You're fulla shit," she said, slipping out from under his arm. "I dunno where you get these sick ideas. Let me fill the pipe, huh?"

She took it from him and began to fill it. Her face grew quiet and absorbed as she rolled the grains between her fingers. Jimmy stood beside her, observing her intently.

"Can I have some?" he asked.

"No."

"Richard said last time I could."

"He was lying."

"Come on. You promised. You both promised." He grabbed for the pipe, and she slapped his hand.

Richard turned to Lang. "Always the same routine, right? When I was a kid, it was my parents' liquor I was after, but I was just as greedy."

"Yeah," Christy said, looking up from the pipe. "And now you're all grown up."

She wasn't stupid, Lang found himself thinking.

"I've gotta go, man," he said to Richard.

"Oh, no. Come on. It's not like you to turn down good dope."

Jimmy had begun to cry.

"Shut up," Christy told him.

"No, I really have to go," Lang said. "But I'll be around."

"Maybe I'll see you then," Richard said.

"Sure."

Lang was at the door when Richard said, "Wait a minute, will you?" He went into the bedroom, and came back holding a tambourine in his hand. "Recognize it?"

"No."

"It's Erica's," Richard said. "You gave it to her, a long time ago. I thought you might want it."

"What would I do with it?"

"I don't know." A look of misery, mingled with bewilderment, washed up in Richard's eyes. "I wish you'd take it," he said. "To tell the truth, it gives me the fucking willies, having it around—but I can't just throw it away. . . ."

"All right," Lang said reluctantly.

The sadness, deeper now, came back to Richard's face. "I'll see you," he said abruptly, and shut the door.

A tangible artifact. As Lang walked back out into the sun, he glanced back at the building he had just left, and then at the object in his hands.

Richard and Erica had been going together for a week when he gave her the tambourine. That was before the trouble started—before she began to sleep with other people and Richard, in his turn, started doing more drugs, in a kind of contest to see which of them was stronger. Erica had still been shy about being with Richard, then; she had accepted the gift with a small, uneven smile, not knowing why Lang had given it to her.

But Johanna had. She had watched the whole affair with an amused look on her lovely face, and teased him about it afterwards: "You see? You really are a romantic after all," she said mischievously, pinching his arm. "I promise not to tell anyone."

Lang was a little disgusted with the memory; he wished he hadn't taken the tambourine. It made everything too real.

What had happened to all of them, in that bloody year since he left Icarus?

Richard used to walk so cocky, sauntering down the street with his hands always propped on his hips, so cool, so sure.

Going out to the car, Lang gave the tambourine a tentative shake.

CHAPTER THREE

Richard: 1

On the evening of the day that Dan Lang first left for New York, a year before, Richard came slowly out of a blue and loaded sleep, feeling wasted. Still dazed, not quite alive, he stared at the mirror hung above his bed.

With waking came an iron depression, heavy in his chest, pinning him to the mattress. He looked at the mirror, and thought of Erica. It wasn't just knowing he had lost her that weighed on him so much as the chore of having to know it again and again, like new, every time he woke up. But he was used to that by now. Soon it would lift far enough to let him get to his feet. Waiting for it to lift, he reached out and hit the power button on the stereo. A nearly empty can of beer stood on the bedside table; he tried to drink it without raising his head. Some dripped over his chin. He rubbed his neck dry with a handful of his T-shirt and sat up. It almost made him sick: his brain slid too far forward and bumped into the front of his skull.

He jacked his turntable to automatic, and gingerly, as the tone arm hooked over above the spinning record, he stood up. The arm went down. The electric clock read nine P.M.; a guitar chord crashed and flipped into a drumbeat. Richard pulled on a clean shirt, and

hopped on one foot as he climbed into his jeans. Somebody began to
sing. Carefully, Richard put on his boots, pulling down the cuffs of
the jeans so they wouldn't bunch, stamping on the heels once or
twice to the beat of the music. Since Erica had left him, he had no
real taste for such niceties, but it was a habit. *"I don't say much"*—
Richard zipped and buttoned his jeans, leaned over to adjust the
treble on the amp—*"but I make"*—and buckled his belt—*"a big
noise . . ."*

It was a Friday night; people would be heading over to Hoffentlichs', gathering themselves for the leap into the weekend. Richard
wasn't really satisfied with the Hoffentlich scene. There he was forced
to be no more than his surroundings, and that grated on his pride.
But now empty spaces had returned to his life and he had to fill them
somehow. He felt a need to fly, to forge new armor for himself—he
only had to recuperate first, then he would begin. Begin for real this
time. He promised himself.

He picked the car keys off their nail, and put on his denim jacket.

Before leaving, he checked the humidor of pot on his desk. It
was getting low. Carmel sometimes stopped by at Hoffentlichs';
Richard made a mental note to put in an order. Beneath the humidor
was a disorderly stack of scribbled papers. He avoided noticing them
as he reached to shut off the light.

Alice Hoffentlich was in the living room when Richard came in,
a bottle of beer sitting on one side of her and some jock she'd picked
up on the other. A white wire ran from the jock's waist to a wall
socket behind him. "Heating pad," Alice explained. "He ruptured
himself, or something."

The jock dug into his crotch and came out with a control console. He flipped through its buttons sarcastically for Richard's benefit.

"I never saw one with lights on it before," Richard said. "When
you push the right button, does it get bigger?"

"No," he heard Brewer say behind him, "it just gets hotter."

No matter what was going on around him, Brewer always seemed
to speak out of a deep silence. He was sitting in a chair against the
wall, his round mournful face cast in its usual mold of apathetic anguish. The slump of his body suggested that suffering was an arduous
physical labor, like rock-breaking. His trunk was thick and flaccid
with gloom, and beneath it he stretched a pair of legs so angular and
thin that you doubted he would ever rise from his chair.

"Get yourself a beer, Richard." It was Myra, Alice's mother, emerging from the stairwell.

"I brought my own."

"That's rare," Myra said, shuffling across the room like a large distracted insect, her hair in her face, a cigarette dangling from her lower lip. "That's almost an occasion."

"Did you hear that Lang left town?" Brewer asked.

"What do you mean, left?"

"He took off," Myra said, "for New York."

"He didn't tell me."

"He didn't tell anybody."

A small sorrow, no larger than a pebble, turned inside Richard. Richard had seen Lang last—and then for the first time in many weeks —on the final night with Erica at Uncle Lou's . . . Lang had been distant, drinking in silence while the rest of them babbled on—with his queer, almost ugly pride, that so many people mistook for sullenness, that had been growing more and more total and removed, as if some cold force had taken up permanent residence in his head, until even Richard, especially Richard, should have guessed that something was going on. But he hadn't, and he felt hurt—hurt most of all that Lang had dismissed their friendship, along with everything else, by the arrogant silence of his departure.

Lorraine came in. Brewer gave her a despairing glance. She didn't bother to notice. She was dressed for dancing, and her dark hair glowed with heat. Striding cleanly to accentuate the line of her high-waisted slacks against her thighs, she swept over to Richard and perched on the arm of his chair. "You look depressed," she congratulated him.

"Ugh."

"You're cute when you're depressed."

"Fuck off, bitch."

She giggled. "Watch your manners."

"I'd rather watch yours," Richard told her. She put her face up close to his, and continued to giggle. He was silent. He knew that Lorraine wouldn't mind. Her attraction to him had nothing to do with his moods—it had always been that way. Richard knew he was attractive, so much so that he rarely even bothered to think about it. He accepted his shell; what frustrated and confused him was that being as good-looking as he was was somehow always at odds with the noble, introspective image of himself which he privately cherished— just as sexy, but more meaningful. Only Erica had ever recognized it. But she must have seen it from the wrong angle, for she had finally rejected it, and him too, and that would have been impossible if she had really understood.

Basking in the light that Lorraine turned on him, Richard brooded, as he often did, on whether that true self would ever leap out of his soul's walls and reveal him to the world. Lorraine, he thought, could never appreciate such a desire; going to bed with her would be a surrender. Richard liked moral questions. At once he felt cheered.

"Fuck off, bitch," Brewer repeated, his head lolled back. "I wish I had said that."

"You're starting early tonight," Richard told him.

"Wide world of sports," Brewer said. "The agony of victory, the thrill of defeat."

"Well," Lorraine interrupted him, "are we going someplace? I want to dance, I feel like moving. Brewer, you want to go out, don't you?"

Brewer's fingers trailed through the air, playing an invisible piano. "Why not? Seek truth. Discover reality instead. Find one righteous man, and this disco will be saved."

"He's hopeless when he's being philosophical," Lorraine said.

"I had no idea you knew such big words," Brewer answered. Even when he was being insulting, he still managed to show pain. It was a nice trick, but Richard felt suddenly oppressed. At times he wanted to make some declaration, tilt a lance against their endless artful talk; but you couldn't tell them anything about themselves that would surprise them. They had all been analyzing themselves for so long, and with so little perspective—"When was the last time you noticed your own breathing?" Erica said once—that they were prepared to accept any possibility. He had used up all his rage on the past, and besides, whenever he tried to express it, it always came out like posturing—he tried his best, even roughened his voice and chose his words to bite, but he never achieved true nausea.

He heard the back door open and Andrew's heavy step, then paper tearing, crashing glass. "Oh fuck," Alice said, "Daddy"; and untangling herself from the jock's wire, she went into the kitchen. "You slob," she said.

"The bag was wet," Andrew answered slowly, "it soaked through, I couldn't help it—don't insult me . . ."

"Sure it was wet. Two sixes and a bottle of gin," she called to Myra. "He's probably been drooling into it since he put it in the car. Somebody come help me, there's beer all over the floor."

"What about the gin?" Richard asked, getting up.

"Oh, he caught it in mid-flight," Alice said.

Andrew Hoffentlich stood in the kitchen with his shoulders sloping, his face sagging, arms hanging, trying to kneel. His broad naked head, gleaming in the light, slumped down on his neck. Alice was mopping the beer from a couple of broken bottles, and stacking the rest on the table with practiced hands.

Andrew peered at Richard. He tried to smile in greeting, failed, and said, "Welcome, Richard, how be you?" with a surreal courtesy.

"Just fine."

Alice straightened up, holding the wet rag. "You're too late," she told Richard. "It's all over." Andrew was staring at his dangling hands as if mesmerized by their uselessness. Alice guided him back to the vertical with a firm grip on his bicep. "Everything's all right, Daddy," she said, "it's all picked up. Go on to bed."

"I want to taste the company in the living room," Andrew answered. "I am not so low, or so soused, that I cannot perform the duties of the host. Get outa my way."

"I'm trying to keep you from falling."

"I can stay erect on my own," Andrew said gravely.

"It's through that door," Alice directed him.

"Once I led troops through the Khyber Pass," Andrew mumbled. "A covert operation, of course." He plodded out with his heavy step, like an animal who finds its own shell an impossible burden.

"We is stoned," a lilting voice declared from outside the door, hard on Andrew's exit. "We is oh so wasted."

"Austin and Veronica," Alice said.

Austin came in first. He was tall, with a loose detachment in his moves, and a voice which caressed every word it spoke. He was dressed all in black; Veronica completed him in white, down to the mouthpiece of her cigarette holder. She was a short pudgy girl with electric hair and a mouth that moved even when she wasn't talking. "Isn't it wonderfully slinky?" she said, displaying the holder. "I had to buy it, or rather, Austin had to buy it for me, but he's sweet, and he never complains."

"It is execrably difficult to drive in this wasted condition," Austin complained, swaying slightly, his hands dancing with each other. "Something akin to taking a piss with a hard-on. Accuracy is sacrificed."

"We were just on our way to Sunset," Veronica said with a flourish, "and we decided to stop and see what all you lovely people were doing."

"And of course to check to see if you wanted to come along," Austin added, looking at Richard.

Richard grinned, not bothering to answer. Sunset was the most ornate and expensive gay bar in Suffragette City, a carnival of mirrors, thick rugs, and watered drinks. ("The only place around that hasn't been ruined by the tourists," Austin said.) Austin and Veronica were regulars there. They would arrive together, and part to seek their separate pleasures, and drive back home together in a fine romantic glow, as dawn paled the sky. They were now in the process of gearing up their psyches.

In a way, Austin and Veronica sickened Richard. They were both so jaded that soon the only thing left for them to be jaded about would be the drabness of their own jadedness. Still, he didn't dislike them. They were about the only truly contented couple he knew.

Austin tweezed a chain out from under his shirt with soft and delicate fingers. A small vial hung from the chain, with a tiny spoon attached on a separate leash. It was the monogrammed coke kit that Veronica had given him for Valentine's Day.

"Carmel's finest," Austin remarked, opening the vial and filling the spoon. "Very nice stuff." He put it to his nostril and inhaled deeply. "Do you want a hit, Richard?"

"What about me?" Veronica whined.

"Don't be piggish. Don't conceal that you just had a whiff in the car." Austin held out the spoon, and Richard took it. Because the chain was still around Austin's neck, they had to stand in a virtual embrace. Richard, leaning down to the single curl of hair peeking out of Austin's shirt, felt a tingle of discomfort. Andrew's voice burbled up indistinctly from the next room, followed by Myra's in rebuttal; Richard sucked the powder into his nose, and backed off, wheezing.

"We have a line," Veronica said, "that Austin was born with a silver spoon up his nose."

Austin offered the spoon to Alice. She shook her head. "I'm on a diet."

The rush was beginning to hit Richard, clean and cold, burning every passage. It almost burned away his frustration, but some brave island of his mind held out against the current.

"Brewer was just telling us about his sex life," Myra greeted them, as they trooped into the living room.

"Thirty seconds of great talk," Brewer added.

"Thirty seconds over Tokyo," Andrew said suddenly, lifting his thick forearms into wings.

"Sit up, Andrew," Myra said.

"Boom, boom."

"Shut up, Andrew," Myra said.

"Tweeeoo," Andrew said. "Vroom."

"I was just wondering where you were," Lorraine said to Richard in a small voice.

"So was I."

"Austin's selfish," she pouted.

"He's just selective. What do you want, him to do a loaves and fishes number on the stash?"

"Damn," Lorraine said, "that reminds me, I promised my father I'd go to church this week."

They were interrupted by an explosion on their right. Andrew, sprawled in his chair, was making a series of broken strangled sounds from the pit of his belly. After a moment, Richard realized that Andrew was laughing. Myra glanced hastily around the room, to disavow any kinship with him.

"Lorraine, I love your outfit," Veronica said carnivorously.

"Yes," Austin drawled, "isn't she cute?"

"You know," Myra said, "in that blouse, Lorraine, in that light, you remind me of the wife of that flier, you know, Andrew, the king's goofy cousin, in Damascus . . ." She waited for Andrew to respond. Andrew did not respond. He seemed too preoccupied with the sound of his own breathing to notice anything exterior. Myra shrugged with her cigarette, and went on: "He was a crazy son of a bitch . . . During the coup, he tried to bomb the palace and damn near blew up our house. Came in just over the trees, dropping bombs left and right in zero visibility, the whole town on fire under his wings and him thinking it was the greatest thing in the world . . . I gave him hell for that at the Ambassador's party, the week after. He just simpered and said Meezez Hoffentlich, wit' so much explosive in town, is it not better to be bombed by your friends?"

"You know what the Arabs say," Andrew grunted. "One minute in your hand, the next minute up your ass."

Austin looked offended.

"Of course," Myra said, rolling her eyes, "Andrew thinks that it's best to get bombed by yourself."

Andrew looked at her with dull, inert anger. Myra quickly shifted gears, her cigarette cocked for a signal. "Three guys were in a

whorehouse," she began, "looking for a blow job. The madam said,
we've got the regular, the special, and the super . . ."

"Richard," Lorraine whispered.

"What?"

"—The first takes the regular, and comes back satisfied, you
know, it was pretty good. The second takes the special . . ."

"Aren't I going to get a chance to talk to you?"

"What about?"

"I don't know," Lorraine said brightly. "Things." She touched
his arm; talking was never just talk to her, but choreography.

"—He comes back radiant, it was fantastic, indredible. So the
third guy, right?" Myra cackled. "The third, now, hey, I go for the
super—now, he's gone for a long time. When he comes back—"

"Why don't you ever whisper intimately to me?" Brewer asked
Lorraine. "You only whisper to me when you want someone to
overhear."

"—he's doubled over, he's in agony, they say what happened?
He says, well! She took it out, and she washed it off, and she put
whipped cream on it, and cherries, and almonds, and chocolate sauce,
and—well, what? What? He says, It looked so good, I ate it myself."

Everyone laughed. Lorraine put in a perfunctory giggle.

"Myra," Andrew said, "you are a scummy slut."

"Oh, shut up! Just go to bed. Just shut up."

"You think I should shut up? Why doesn't everyone else shut
up? Why does everyone insist on talking, when they don't have a
thing to say and would conceal it if they did? Answer me that. Don't
tell me to shut up." His eyes were slits, the lids puffy under the beet-
ling brows. He began to speak in a guttural tongue that Richard
didn't recognize.

"Arabic," Alice explained. "He always starts talking Arabic when
he's this far gone."

"Flawlessly," Myra put in sourly. "He does it to prove that he's
still got a brain."

Andrew turned to Myra and grunted a single syllable.

"That means 'pig' in Arabic," Alice said mirthfully, white teeth
flashing over the mouth of her bottle.

Alice's jock, playing with his console, looked bemused. Lorraine
repressed her discomfort under a stiff smile. Richard knew that her
apprehension was only social. His went deeper—he was developing
habits of mind in which anything could be an omen. At least it
stopped him from being bored.

"In Damascus they were always pleased at how well he spoke," Myra remembered. She had apparently decided that Andrew wasn't in the room. "It was paying them a compliment."

"Yet the Arabs have style," Andrew rumbled. "They understood thousands of years ago that life is the process of accumulating vices, and their whole civilization is designed to enhance them, decorating them with curtains, rituals, and perfume." The sonority of the words seemed to give him a foggy pleasure as they rolled from his lips.

"We decorate our vices too," Brewer said. "With sweat, spit, and used condoms."

"We used to call them Tidal Basin trout," Myra said. "When I was young, I remember, the Moonlight Cruise on the old Wilson line, it left the wharf at eight-thirty, going up the river to Mount Vernon—you'd be sitting on the deck under the moon with your boy's arm around you, looking down at the water, and watching the garbage, the dead fish, and the rubbers float by . . ."

"Dalliance," Andrew said. "The painful beauty, the beautiful pain, of young love . . ." His eyes wandered mistily around the room. They came to rest on Richard at the end of the circle, and Andrew gave a loud fart—"Took the words right out of my mouth," he managed to say. Then he slowly toppled forward, his blunt head leading the way as his arms, legs, chest, belly rose and then his head sent an ashtray flying and he crashed on the rug, his hand grappling for the edge of the table. He vomited, quietly, his eyes wide open, staring up in baffled terror at the ceiling.

Lorraine jumped to her feet, jerking away. "Oh, poor Andrew!" she said. "He's staining the rug."

Brewer nodded placidly, as if this was what he'd expected all along. Austin and Veronica, holding hands, gazed upon Andrew with fascinated repugnance. He had abruptly become as strange to them as a visitor from another planet.

"Get him up," Myra said to Alice.

"Oh, let him lie there."

"No, he might choke on it. You better get him up."

"I'll get him," Richard volunteered; anything, to be rescued from his thoughts. He caught hold of Andrew's shoulders and tried to pry him up from the floor. The weight was immense. The muscles in Richard's back shuddered; he was uncomfortably aware of everyone looking on. He heaved again, fingers slipping and catching on the fabric of Andrew's shirt. Andrew lumbered, swayed, and was finally up, wiping vaguely at the yellow spool of vomit on his chest.

Alice was already coming with the rag.

"Andrew, you cut your head."

"I know."

"The first aid kit's in the bathroom downstairs, can you make it?"

"I know where the fucking first aid kit is."

"You should. Anyway, hurry up, you're going to bleed to death."

"It's all alcohol, anyway," Alice said. She was down on her knees, cleaning the rug. Andrew aimed a halfhearted kick at her, lurched, and almost fell. Then he started toward the stairs. At the first step, he paused. Turning, his face impassive, he raised his hand above his head, palm outward, and moved it around several times in a tight circle.

"What's that mean?" Lorraine asked.

"It's an old cavalry signal," Myra said. "It means to fight on foot. You know, like Custer's Last Stand."

"He always used to do it when we were going to someplace new—like getting us together before we went on the plane, you know," Alice said. "When I was a kid. We were always getting on planes . . ."

Meanwhile, Andrew had continued on down the stairs. It was painful to listen to his slow, crippled progress. When he finally tripped at the bottom, everyone looked somehow relieved.

Richard's hands were clammy with Andrew's sweat, mingled with his own. The thick dank smell of Andrew's body, like the smell of a closed cave, still filled his nostrils. He wiped his palms quickly on his jeans.

"Blot, don't scrub," Lorraine told Alice, with the quick embarrassed insistence of engraved habit.

"And when I think that Andrew used to be so thin," Myra said, "I mean, so smart. Do you know what he was doing when I met him? He was working for his second Master's—his second, mind you." Her cigarette twitched expressively as she spoke.

"Mommy," Alice said, slapping the wet rag against her thigh, "you met him when he was trying to stop you from dancing the can-can without any underwear on, at a party."

"I meant what he was doing with his mind . . ."

"Oh that."

"Decay is in the bones of the beholder," Brewer said, to no one in particular.

He had to find some alchemy, Richard thought, or a scheme, something to unravel the truth behind this petty art. Once, he had believed that Erica was the connection. Now he no longer knew what to believe. Still, something had to happen, he didn't care if it was good or bad, or what it let loose. . . . He looked down. Austin was lying on the floor, collapsed onto one elbow, his knees jutting up, as if he'd just been shot and had fallen here haphazardly in his death. Richard remembered a faded photograph of the Union casualties at Cold Harbor, sepia faces cast up above their tumbled visors, in a dream of absolute stillness—they had charged the Rebel line with their names and addresses pinned to the backs of their jackets, for they knew that none of them would come back alive, and the European observers telegraphed back to their capitals that they had never seen such bravery before. . . . Austin rolled over to touch Veronica's braceleted ankle, and said, "Love, we really must get to Sunset—it's rush hour there now."

"Whores abnature a vacuum," Richard said aloud; but his words went suddenly unheard in a howl of metal and brakes, slowly fading into a sob, from beyond the walls.

"It's a wreck," Veronica said, peering through the curtains, her tongue darting over her lips.

"They always take that turn too fast," Myra complained.

"This one looks bad . . . Oh! There's someone coming out of the car."

"Is he all right?"

"No, he's on fire."

In the room, everyone was on their feet. Without knowing why, they all clustered toward the door. They spilled down the steps and onto the front lawn, Myra last, like a dowager queen, her wine glass held aloft. In the center of the circle, wavering in the abrupt deep-blue night, Richard felt queasy and alone.

A crowd had gathered from up and down the street; the red light of the police car flashed over their faces as an ambulance's siren keened across the horizon. A few stray flames still licked at the wreck. It had come, apparently, spinning around the corner, gone out of control, and slammed into a telephone pole. The pole lay across the road like an amputated limb, its wood shattered, its ripped wires tangled in their brackets.

"Let's not go up too close," Austin said delicately.

"It stinks here," Lorraine said, "it smells awful."

"Burnt flesh," Austin explained, in the same delicate voice.

"Oh!" Lorraine yipped. "Is that it?" She clapped both hands to her nostrils, as if to keep out the smell.

The ambulance arrived, its blue light circling in counterpoint to the police car's red. Their duel bathed the crowd in red and blue, blue and red, and threw leaping red-blue arcs all along the street. It reminded Richard of the light shows he would watch at high-school dances.

"Oh, this is going to ruin me at Sunset tonight," Austin said. "I have such bad memories of fire—do you remember, Veronica? That girl we knew who burned herself to death in her basement, about a month ago?"

"It was the same night as the Bette Midler concert. That would make it two months, about," Veronica said. "She was a sexy kid, too."

"Really," Austin went on, "if you make up your mind to die, burning's still the most painful way, I think. If it were left up to me, I'd just take an overdose and go to sleep."

"I'd use a shotgun," Brewer said dreamily. "I wouldn't want to just go to sleep. I'd want to be all over the landscape . . ."

"Oh, stop," Lorraine said, "you're being too morbid. Let's not stay here. I don't like this. Aren't we going to go dancing?"

"I heard that Erica was singing somewhere in town tonight," Brewer said. "We could go there."

"But Richard wouldn't like that."

Automatically, Richard stiffened. He wanted to keep the pain of Erica inside him, not lose her again to a meaningless conversation. The thought made the pain real again. The others were beginning to drift back toward the house, but Richard didn't move.

"Come on," Lorraine called. "We're going dancing."

"In a minute," he answered over his shoulder. With sudden resolution he started forward. He wanted to see the wreck up close. It had suddenly become important to confront the spectacle. He made his way easily through the thinning crowd, slowed only by confusion at his own desire.

The burned boy, wrapped in a blanket, was being lifted into the ambulance. Richard caught a glimpse of shocked white circles staring out of a charred face, a hand like a claw on the ribbing of the stretcher. His belly clenched with sickness. He had to summon up all his courage to keep from breaking away.

The car had been smashed by almost half its length; broken bottles and long slicks of glistening liquid were spilled for forty feet along the pavement, gleaming in the circling, flashing lights. A couple of cops were prying at the twisted metal with crowbars; a bloody hand was sticking up through the shards of the windshield.

Erica was singing somewhere tonight. He heard their laughter, Austin's, Veronica's, Brewer's, and Lorraine's, rising through the flame-filled air, painting itself across the canvas of the sky until it cracked apart and dissolved into the fire. . . . They had managed to extricate the other body from the wreck. It turned out to be a girl, fairly young, with a nice body, and no face. Richard didn't see any more than that, because the blue light flashed directly into his eyes and blinded him.

He longed for a bomb to plant in his heart and explode the pressure there—he wished that he could borrow some fire from the wreck. His eyes cleared, and he looked at the gutted car, wanting suddenly to see her, to stroke her face and reassure himself that she was still there. But she wasn't, not for him, not any more. . . .

The jagged hole where the girl's hand had broken through stared back at him. Richard turned away from its call and began walking toward the house. He'd go out dancing with Lorraine; maybe that would save him, for a while.

CHAPTER FOUR

Odell: 1

Odell's unrequited love affair with the Devil began at the end of the summer after his sophomore year in high school. Looking back, he took pride at having been a pioneer of suicide long before it got to be fashionable. While vomiting up the overdose of pills he had taken into the aluminum basin held between his nurse's broad red hands, he had discovered the rottenness at the root of all human relations, and it thrilled him; he promptly decided to embark on a journey into decadence. When he returned to school that fall, he showed the first plumage of a leather jacket, stovepipe jeans, and mirror shades; he had begun smoking thumb-sized cigars.

The shades were prescription, but no one ever knew. People only wondered why he kept them on after dark. When he was twelve, Odell had begun an interest in philosophy; for years he had honed his taste on the gloomy acolytes of rage, madness, and despair, poring over their books alone in his bed on Saturday nights. Nietzsche's syphilis became Odell's syphilis, and Schopenhauer's woman-hating was like a cool drink of water on a hot summer day. His suicide attempt, Odell thought, was the natural culmination of that life and the beginning of a new one. For his next birthday, he had his parents buy him a stereo and twenty-five rock 'n' roll records.

But Erica had been there before all that. They met in the ninth grade, when Odell was still innocent, a boy who had seen too little in too many years. His hunch that he was going to be an intellectual had already been confirmed by his experiences in gym class; she was writing her first poems. A long time later, Odell showed one of them to Richard:

> Some phrase of swirling music returns
> me to the bed where you crawled that night
> (I thought I had forgotten, but memory burns
> with the copulating gutter of old candle-light)
> you said you'd never go back to that bitch
> and you needed loving hands to caress
> you; but I knew that you needed a witch
> to soothe with her body what words could not bless.
> Like the carnal scream of ancient birds
> replacing present with past tense
> Wizard, you raped me with a phallus of words
> and tore the socket of my innocence.
> (I recall how I held you on my burning breast
> in time's cold waste. You know the rest.)

"What's it called?" Richard asked.

"The Wizard," Odell told him. "Don't you see what it says about her?"

"She was old for her age. So what?"

Odell, in the bloom of new toughness, puffed smoke energetically from his little cigar. "That's not what I mean at all. That poem is the product of a warped mind."

"Yours?"

"No, listen, Richard, she's sick. I mean genuinely sick. She's evil," Odell said, desperately.

"Our neuroses complement each other."

Angrily, nervously, Odell admired, as he had so many times, Richard's ability to make glib incomprehension more sophisticated and cool than his own frantic but real perceptions. His intellect, he decided, was always doomed to rage in cellars and seek out combat with the shadows flitting in their depths. He paced the room dynamically, twin trails of smoke spreading from the tips of his taut mouth like wings, his thoughts darting, missionaries to his nerves.

"You're going to wreck yourself," Odell pronounced, prophet

for a day. "I'm going to the bathroom."

Heartened by the masculine sibilance of his pissing, the firm-planted authority of his booted feet bracketing the bowl, Odell mused savagely on the impossibility of communicating the complexity of his vision; especially to Richard, Richard who was then Odell's hero, for that was when Richard had only begun to fall in love with Erica and was still triumphant, gorgeous, his every move a premonition of the victories slumbering in wait for him. Benumbed with a crystalline grace, Richard was the knob of that social constellation which had come to its maturity just as Odell was sliding into the long depression that would end in the emergency ward of Icarus Redeemer Hospital. In their senior year in high school, and for a time afterwards, Richard and his kind had been a revolving pantheon to the town, their various successes only showcases to their style; Richard, the actor, the writer and director of two plays before he graduated, was the brightest of them all, and Odell could not help but hunger after his effortless floating in the social winds, the gaudy embroidered caravan of his personality, so dramatically the antithesis of his, Odell's, grim dark explorations into brutal solitude, under his own thumb.

It was inevitable that Erica should eventually have looked to Richard. But when Odell first knew her, there had been no hint of that, of the red and rotting witchery sunk deep within her soul. Odell could kick himself sometimes for not having had any premonitions, or at least a touch of foreboding—still, he couldn't really blame himself. She had been skinny and close to blind, hidden in ambush behind huge fierce glasses, and she never spoke except in harsh criticism of whatever went on in class, in a voice that seemed to fight its way out of her throat. Who ever could have guessed that she would grow up to become the pinnacle of a dark and fearsome hierarchy of slithering decadence incarnate?

No one, not even lookout Odell. He and Erica became friends, the kind of friends who recognize each other by the books they both have read. They would have long, intense conversations; they would throw talk across the silences of the long autumn afternoons, and when the afternoons grew shorter, they talked deep into the night.

She made tea, but he never tried to touch her. Each thought the other physically ugly, and anyway they were both too intensely conscious of their futures to think of such a mundane practicality. What a fool he had been! If he had only realized what was going on, he could have saved her from her downfall; he could maybe have lost his virginity to her, instead of to that awful lump-faced girl, always picking the scabs on her cheeks, whose hips slid down to mid-thigh and who had been so ugly as to make a face when he suggested that she go down on him.

He didn't like remembering that girl (chick, he mentally corrected himself); she was an artifact of the time when he and Erica began to drift apart. In the course of the year after they met, Odell grew increasingly moody, hoping to be thought of as demonic but achieving only a dubious eccentricity; Erica was exploring new connections, and turning herself into a prime number.

"The day she discovered that she had a cunt was the day it was all over for her and me," Odell told Richard, some time after he finally returned from the bathroom.

"You know, your voice goes all funny when you say a word like 'cunt,'" Richard remarked absently. Behind the artillery of his cigar, Odell winced. There were still chinks in his toughness, hangovers from the nice boy who read too much. He knew that his sensitivity was supremely delicate, to put it bluntly, a fragile silver fish swimming in limpid pools of perception; but he had to make himself hard. Hard! He would be hard then. He would even be brutal, if circumstances indicated that to be necessary. The black cap of his Bic protruded with an evil gleam from the tight pocket of his close-clinging jeans.

He had told Richard that it ended on the day that she discovered her social potential, but in truth he had been allowed to linger for a few months after that, sitting on the edge of her life while she sported with her latest conquest. Only when he swallowed every pill he could find in his house one mellow-yellow August afternoon, and spent three days in the hospital, did she cut him off completely. She had no understanding of suicide—she told him that his reasons weren't good enough. "Well, fuck her," Odell said one night in bed, clutching a fistful of pillow, amazed and giddy at his daring. From that moment he dated his resurrection; from then on, as far as Erica was concerned, his heart would be made of unbreakable stone.

"Maybe she knew even then that I was going to become her enemy, because she always knew where she was going—she would have known about me too . . ."

"I don't think she thinks of you as being much of anything," Richard said, "if she thinks of you at all."

"Maybe she doesn't want to admit it," Odell said, jabbing a hole in the air with his cigar. "But she knows. Deep inside. I'm trying to tell you something about her. She's a monster. If you're really going to fall in love with her, it's something you should know."

"I don't think it's something I should know."

"You don't want to know."

"No, I just don't think it's worth knowing."

Why didn't anybody take him seriously? He spent so much time working on his insights, he knew they had to be good. The last time he and Erica had met, he played her a Rolling Stones album. He asked her to listen to it carefully, but she didn't. If she had only understood the Stones, their love might have survived—but when the side was done, she only looked up and said, "So?"

In those days after he first put on a leather jacket, the Rolling Stones became Odell's gods. They understood; they spoke to his silences. Keef's sinuously canted hips curved to the snaking contours of Odell's thought; with Mick he shook and smacked his lips at the taste of fire. Confronting his image as he squeezed a pimple in the bathroom mirror, he would whisper softly, "Well, ya heard about the midnight rambler . . ." and thus give coherence to his blurred reflection. Since his intent was to explore darkness, it was only natural that he should come under the shadow of rock.

While Odell plunged and pawed through the turf of decadence like a rabid puppy, revelations clanging like gongs, epiphanies every other week, calling up Satanic forces every time he whacked off, Erica was becoming a power. People formed themselves through her. For a time she was seen with one of Carmel's rivals, a dealer who had made his reputation during the Great Cocaine Craze which hit Icarus in the year that she and Odell finished high school; then when he got shot in the face, and came out of the hospital with his nose where his ear used to be, she moved on to the glitter crowd. Even the jocks were added to Odell's inventory when she spent a couple of weeks with a basketball player whose habit it became to make drunken confessions to her lap. She was steeped in a study of the arts of sex, the tricks of the glory that lasts a night; she was getting ready to become a star.

Odell had known Richard before she did—it was always his burden to be a pathfinder. He had made himself an intimate of the whole salon that coalesced around Richard and Dan Lang; at their parties, he was always around to change the records on the stereo when everyone else was busy necking. They all had a succession of partners, who came and went in the house of their power without so much as shivering the curtains; the very anonymity of those brief mates, picked up for a week or an hour, only served to make the pantheon more sinister, vivid, and glamorous. Odell smothered pride and smiled when Lang would call him Richard's latest fling. Wheels of frustration turning inside him at each new scene, he could not help but love the performance, and yearn to be part of it almost as much as he yearned to see it destroyed. When the pantheon finally did come crashing down, it all came down on him.

Yeah! He was the real casualty, for none of them even wanted to talk about it, and their faces grew constipated when he tried to explain to them that they were an allegory of doom.

He had tried, for the first time, that night with Richard in his room, dynamic restless fingers tying knots in the smoke of his cigar— Richard laughed.

"I've got nothing against your ideas, Odell," he said, "but you wouldn't know real decadence if it was to squat down and take a shit on your carpet."

"At least you had the pleasure before you had the pain."

"Oh, come on! They're the same thing. I mean, are you trying to tell me that if I choose to fall in love with Erica, I turn into the Ancient Mariner, and no one dares to come near me?"

"Yes," Odell said. "That's exactly what I'm trying to tell you."

They were all damned, and dammit! none of them realized it. Every coil had turned back to Erica, and Odell should, must, have known it would. Carmel had introduced her to Richard one night after a Joni Mitchell concert, and she told him: "You shouldn't come on so strong. You're much more interesting when you don't."

"How could you fall for that?" Odell demanded. "It's such an obvious trick."

"You wish she'd tried it on you, don't you?" Richard asked with a charming, infuriating grin. "Obvious tricks are the closest that people like us can come to honesty. I like honesty."

Odell was close to despair. He was always close to despair, but now he was even closer than usual, and it dizzied him: he was like a young girl whose familiar boyfriend starts going further for the first time. He couldn't understand how Richard managed to stay blind to all of Erica's potential evil, so naked to his own head; he had known, then, from the beginning, that violence was in the air. The knowledge was not without its pleasure. Richard deserved it for not listening to him.

He followed the romance as it grew, as he followed everything: passionately, from outside the window. In those weeks Richard was always tense. His tension invariably left a flutter of titillated nerves in its wake, on those rare occasions when he chose to make an appearance at the Hoffentlichs', or Uncle Lou's. He was hers now, Odell thought—brutally, savagely, sardonically—wondering how long it could last.

"She's not faithful to you," he told Richard, when they met once by accident at Carmel's.

"Leave it alone," Richard answered, with an imperial, dismissing gesture which picked up his beer at the end of its sweep. "I wouldn't stay if I didn't want to, anyway," he added.

Odell expected the break to come soon. She never stayed for long with anybody. The only lasting thing about her was the scars she left on people, he thought, rubbing his own. He hung on the tower of his imagination, a scarred Thersites waiting for his visions to unfold. But nothing unfolded. Instead, to his horror, things began to improve. She quit playing the field: "I've stopped extracurriculars," she announced one night at Uncle Lou's. Richard went around with a happy smile, assuring everyone that she had changed.

Then they had their fight. Odell was there. Just before she left, she turned and smiled; she smiled right at Odell, and he knew that he had been right all along. Her face held no happiness, nor even pleasure, but only a serene and calculated triumph, for she had her victory, she had destroyed him.

After the break, things went into a lull. Each day sank into the next with the monotonous suck of quicksand. The nightly gathering up of the summer heat, formerly the spark to a parallel bunching of apprehension, passed without trauma each sunset. Odell felt drained and empty; in a sense, after all, he had been just as much a participant in the affair as either Erica or Richard, and it had taken a lot out of him. An increasing restlessness staled and stifled his nerves—they cried out for hot passions and rivers of darkness to sail on. He resolved to continue his search into the heart of evil by another path, for he was a truly indefatigable seeker. No mere reality could turn him from his goal.

It was then that he began what he would later think of as his wanderings. He journeyed like the heroes of the ancients amid the fleshpots and fevers of haunted nighttown Icarus in an unquenchable attempt to discover the core of the sickness that infested its streets, on weekend nights, when he could get the keys to the family car. He would drive in endless circles until the early hours of the morning, on the prowl for symbols, a cold sardonic gleam in his glasses and the tape deck turned up loud.

Ride on, baby. As his loneliness seeped deeper and deeper, dank as a sewer, his ideas would tumble in a colliding farrago of mysteries laid on mysteries, theories sledding and skidding in a wild chaotic race, until Icarus was built again inside the private chamber of his mind, walls piled into bridges, houses tilted to topple into streets paved with lava, staircases climbing into glowing fire. His thoughts mounted upon the lust of their own conceiving until he felt ready to blast off into eternity. Transfixed in a dream of gods in black leather, before the livid reflection of his self-created monsters, Odell thought: let them be what they will, I am just waiting for my time to come to me.

CHAPTER FIVE

Within a Grove of Buddies: 2

At the Hoffentlich house, an argument was underway in various tempos. Andrew sat swaying on a chair, his features thick and sour, but infused with a curious, tentative apprehension too, as if the right word would either lift him into understanding or else plunge him all the way down to death. Myra and Alice circled around him in a flurry of ashes and tongues, flagging and starting with the weariness of an act endlessly rehearsed, never performed to its last curtain.

"Where were you last night?" Myra was saying. "Where did you go?"

Andrew watched her, slit-eyed and glazed. "What difference does it make?" he answered in a slurred rumble. "You know it was a bar. What else do you need?"

"I need to know the names because sooner or later you're going to fart your final fart in one of them, and I'll have to come identify the asshole—is that all right? Is that enough of a reason? You drunken bastard."

"Christ! I won't die out there—I'll die here—I die right here every day . . ."

"Alice, go get your Polaroid " Myra said. "Show him what a pig he is."

"Oh, crap, Mommy," Alice said. "That never works. He just . . . *looks* at them. Then he burns them."

"Why, you little bitch." Andrew gave a thick, gurgling chuckle. "See how fat you've gotten, from sitting on your ass all day."

"You're fatter than me," Alice said. "And you're old." She leaned in close to his swollen, bloodshot face. "Do you want me to tell you something?"

"Oh yes. Tell me something."

"Then listen. I know you love me. I mean deep down inside, you love me." Alice paused. "And, deep down inside, I hate your guts."

Andrew's great liquid eyes gleamed very sharply, staring at her; then they blurred over again.

Lang came into the kitchen. Ignoring the argument, he went to the refrigerator and got a beer.

"Come on and hear this, Lang," Myra said.

"I heard it," Lang said. He shut the refrigerator door. "Having a good time, aren't you?" he added under his breath.

Andrew laughed. He gazed up at Lang with a broad smile on his face. "You hang around shit long enough, Daniel," he said, "and sooner or later some'll rub off on you."

Myra glared at them both. Lang uncapped his beer and left the kitchen. He went down to the rec room. There in the dim cool he lay down on the couch, his arm over his face. He could hear the fight still raging, through the floor.

He was waiting for Carmel. Carmel had called him, earlier that day, and asked him to come along on his regular rounds that evening. Mink, his partner, was busy elsewhere—"just setting up a few arrangements for me," Carmel said—and anyway he thought Lang might like to check out the scenery.

Alice had been intrigued when he told her what Carmel had said. "Wow," she remarked. "He *never* lets anyone come with him when he's making delivery. You must have something." Then she gave a wicked look. "You know, if I wasn't sure he was straight, I'd say he was flirting with you."

"I'm sure it's just physical," Lang said. But he was uneasy inside. It seemed Carmel had been after him constantly since his return; he had called Lang twice the day before, and now he was offering himself as a tour guide to Icarus—well, after all, who knew the town better? But it wasn't like Carmel to spend so much time on anybody unless he wanted something from them, and Lang couldn't imagine what he might have to offer. But he had accepted anyway. Caught between memory and guilt, he was ready to take anything as a sign.

"Are you looking for some kicks, kid?" Lang repeated to himself, his lips moving against his sleeve as he lay on the couch. Unconsciously, his hand moved to his neck, as it had to pull up the collar of his leather jacket on his way back from the club, that night in New York. He remembered the shot, and the sound of his own footsteps splashing in the puddles as he walked away. There had been an open fire hydrant at the edge of the alley, its thin stream of water flowing out to mingle with the rain and blood—blood that was not his, but belonged to him now, because there was no one else to remember it.

"Daniel? Are you down there? I can't see."

Lang sat up, quickly. Andrew came plodding down the stairs, fists jammed into his pockets, his pipe clenched in his mouth. "We seem to be having a family disagreement," he growled.

"Yeah, I figured."

"Are you going to talk back too? You want me to punch you?" Andrew swung his fist in the air, and hit the curtain of beads hanging in the doorway of the rec room; they swayed and clattered all around him. He gave an apologetic grin. "I'm sorry," he said, and heaved an enormous sigh. "Violence is deplorable," he muttered.

He came and sat down next to Lang. "It's a terrible thing, Daniel. I really don't want to hurt anyone . . . not even you." He shook his head: his features went through a set of rapid transformations. "I can't help what they make me do," he said.

He put a fresh match to his pipe. Lang reached for the cigarettes on the table, and Andrew passed him his light.

"What a bitch she is," he muttered.

"Yeah," Lang said. "She's a bitch. You're a rummy. I think your daughter is turning into a zombie. I think you're all made for each other."

Andrew chuckled. "Well, Daniel, all I can say is you picked some postcard for your vacation."

"I can't help it," Lang said; "I like you," and he laughed too.

But Andrew was growing irritable again. "Did you know," he said vehemently, "that in all our married life, Myra has not once gone out to buy groceries? I protect her from the world, and she throws it back in my face—as if she hadn't asked me, demanded of me, almost from the day we met, to do just that. When I think—she doesn't communicate, you see. Not really. She writes scripts. It doesn't matter if they contradict reality, or themselves, or . . . whatever . . .

and she gets mad if you don't follow them."

"Everybody does that."

"Oh, I know," Andrew said. "You've got your script, I've got mine. But you can't be surprised when they change on you—you can't afford that. Any dream where you let yourself play the hero is going to turn on you, because all those other people aren't going to enjoy being your servants—not at all. They won't be satisfied with that . . . God damn it! Fuck!" He turned, his shoulders bulging beneath his shirt, at some imaginary call to battle.

"I don't think you'd better go up there now."

"Don't tell me what to do in my own house." The reflexive, automatic belligerence rose in him, and then died down. "God, I'm tired," he said. "I'm so tired of things. I love Myra, Daniel—I think so, anyway, I remember that I do . . ." He passed a large, knobbed hand over the short bristling hairs at the back of his neck. "I love her, but she never keeps quiet long enough for me to say it." He sagged back on the couch; his pipe bowl lay on his chest. He glanced at Lang.

"Oh, no," he exclaimed, rolling his eyes. "Don't go getting all quiet and cagy on me. I've seen you do it before. Watching people. You owe me a little bit more than that."

The side of Lang's mouth curved into the side of his cheek. "Okay," he said.

"It's not polite."

"Okay."

"Would I like the music you play, Daniel?"

"Not much."

Andrew puffed his pipe, reflectively. "I don't know about that," he said. "Do you remember the phrase, in Psalms—I don't know all of it—'Make a joyful noise unto the Lord, all the earth; make a loud noise, and rejoice.' A joyful noise. You see? I don't ask for much."

He stood up, pulling down his shirt. "Give me a swig of your beer."

Lang passed him the bottle. Andrew took a long drink, and made for the stairs. At the curtain of beads, he paused. "A joyful noise," he repeated sternly. A hint of humor crinkled the corners of his eyes. He nodded, set the pipe firmly between his teeth, squared his shoulders, militarily, and left. Soon Lang heard the sound of his car in the driveway.

Rejoice, he thought. They had all grown up on rock 'n' roll, they had all met each other through rock 'n' roll—it was a common religion, the first drug. They took their cues from the songs on the

radio, and they scribbled lyrics to each other in high-school class-
rooms. The music taught them how to be lovers, and how to be
rebels too, and if it all ended in death or waste or simple hopeless-
ness, that was the gamble you took, that was the price of admission.
Because if rock 'n' roll could save your life, then rock 'n' roll could
also kill you—simple logic. Lang had never once denied that it all
made perfect sense.

In the song "The Map" he had written: *It's a gone dead ro-
mance/There's no chance/No chance/Take it* . . . "No chance," he
sang softly now, his breath whistling off the rim of the beer bottle
at his lips. "Take it." But the words felt alien to him; he had no
right to them any more.

Alice was calling him. "Carmel's here."

Lang got up, finishing the beer, and put on his leather jacket.
As Andrew had done, he squared his shoulders before going up the
stairs.

Alice stood by the stairs. "Enjoy yourself," she told him.

"Why not?" Lang said.

Carmel was in a good humor. As they drove off in the mail truck,
his face, behind its shades, relaxed into an easy, charming smile. He
drove with one hand, and moved the other like a director, shaping
the conversation. "It's a real privilege to take you around," he said
genially. "I've been telling everyone that you're back in town, and
they're all real excited."

"I'll bet they are," Lang said.

He was irritated; he was in no mood for Carmel's jokes, and behind Carmel's expert small talk, as smooth as a veteran diplomat's, he
sensed a mocking edge. Hunched up in his seat, he turned to the window and watched the town flow past. He felt like a man traveling
through an old battlefield, to view the trenches under their peacetime
beard of grass, and reconstruct the combat—he felt old. Colorless sunlight hummed and flickered on the streets.

The first place they came to was Richard's house. "I don't suppose you want to come in," Carmel said.

"No."

"I'll be back in a second."

It was as if he knew everything. Lang felt nervous; he wondered
again why he was doing this, and what Carmel had in mind. But the
only way to find out was to play along. He felt too weary—of Icarus,
of himself, of thinking—to make any decisions.

Carmel came out of the house. "Jesus," he said. "That guy

won't even look at his own shadow. I used to think he had something, but now . . ." He shook his head, and didn't say anything more.

Later, they passed an anonymous row of cheap motel cabins, and Carmel waved a casual hand—"That's the last place Erica lived. Before she killed herself, you know." Lang craned his head to look as they drove by. But those apartments hadn't even been built when he left Icarus—he couldn't feel a thing.

As they continued on Carmel's rounds, and the spangled green-gold sunset slowly gave way to night, Lang's depression grew steadily worse. For the town had truly changed. A few of the people they saw were vaguely familiar to him, but most were strangers. They didn't look the same as the old crowd, and they didn't act the same. A deep and complacent boredom was settled in their faces—all emotion, all action, were null and void to the design of their lives, as if Icarus had burned itself out with Erica's death, and nothing was left but this cool, contented brittleness. Disco music blared from portable radios in their dim rooms. "The mail's here," one of them said, poking his head back inside after opening the door, and it might as well have been for all the life he showed.

"It's a new generation," Carmel said at the end of the trip, as they ate a late meal on the outskirts of town. "You might as well get used to it."

"It makes me feel like everything that happened to us never happened at all," Lang murmured.

"Oh, they know all that stuff. It's like ancient history to them. They only respect me," Carmel said, "because they think I'm a survivor. Might be they're right, too. I always stayed away from all the really awful, you know? self-destructive end of it. I had to keep a clear head."

"You supplied the tools."

"That's exactly why," Carmel answered, taking a bite of salad, "I had to keep a clear head."

"You don't like to talk about yourself, much, do you?"

"Uh-uh." Carmel shook his head. "No percentage in it. People get bored. I'd rather talk about them, 'cause that's how you learn things. Just don't let it show that you understand them any better than they want you to, that's all."

Lang looked away. Once Erica had told him almost exactly the same thing. "I've got to stay one jump ahead of the game," she said. "I mean, do lightbulbs tell their secrets to the moths?" She giggled, then, and Lang saw another reason for her success: when she smiled, she looked exactly like James Dean.

When he and Carmel had finished eating, Lang was ready to go home. He was in a deep funk, and he had been drinking, too, all the way through dinner. But Carmel wanted to go to a place he knew in Suffragette City—drinking only mineral water while Lang drank gin, he had seemed to grow more lively as Lang became morose, and now he was vibrant with energy. "Come on," he said, "It'll do you good to see this joint."

So they drove across the river and into the city, and down its broad formal avenues with monuments to dead presidents on either side, given a feverish glow by the high-intensity streetlights installed the previous year to ward off crime. They parked on a side street, near the Americana Hotel, and Carmel led Lang up a flight of stairs to a garish little sweatbox of a Mexican restaurant. "Just walk straight through," he said. Lang walked down a peeling hallway until he came to a fire door. Carmel pushed it open. They climbed down the fire escape and wound their way through a poorly-lit alley to an unmarked door. "Spy stories," Carmel joked, indicating with a wave of the hand that Lang was to go in first.

He found himself facing a swarthy thin man in a silk shirt and beige leisure suit, a gold medallion dangling from his chest. The man looked him over suspiciously. "Anybody invite you in?" he asked.

"I'm with Carmel," Lang said.

The man glanced over his shoulder and saw Carmel standing behind him. "Okay," he said in a chopped voice. "Step inside."

The door shut behind them. They were in a large, dark room, with a bar running along one wall and small tables scattered at random all around it. A thin tube of violet neon hung on wires above the mirror behind the bar, casting an eerie light on the well-dressed, dark-skinned men and the overdrawn, blank-faced women who sat at the tables, drinking, or else drifted toward another door that Lang could see in the mirror. Music came from there; Lang caught a glimpse of a polished wooden dance floor dotted with elegant, bored-looking couples moving each other around. Carmel motioned Lang to a pair of stools at one end of the bar, and they both sat down.

"How'd you find this place?" Lang asked, turning from the mirror to look at it in the flesh.

Carmel smiled. "I didn't," he said. "I was brought. That's the only way you ever get in here."

"Then who brought you?" Lang asked, although he had an idea that he already knew. The tanned, immaculate young men in the room, in their tailored, conservative suits and black shoes polished to a high gleam, with their chiseled features that had the look of being rented for a high price, were familiar enough to him. They were the same in every city. In Lang's neighborhood in New York you never had to ask who they were, or what they did, because their cars, their clothes, and the respect they were given told you all you needed to know.

"It was right after Jacker Malone got totalled," Carmel answered obliquely. "I was just a beginner then—dealing loose joints on the street, meeting kids at McDonald's—you know that whole routine. The Jacker's connection called me and said that we might have some things to talk about. We talked about 'em in this room."

"Huh," Lang said. "I'm surprised they don't have their first dollar hung on the wall—along with the guy they got it from."

Carmel cautioned him with a look. "Be cool, okay?"

"Right," Lang drawled. The liquor he'd consumed was beginning to make him feel reckless. He was in that sweet state of invisibility where it is impossible to believe that anything you say or do can possibly have any consequences. He watched the odd aquarium movements of his face in the mirror. "Bloop, bloop," he said to his reflection.

The bartender—a very young girl in a black leotard, with high cheekbones and dark, Eurasian eyes—came over to them. "The same as always?" she asked Carmel.

"Please." Carmel turned to Lang. "Whatever you want."

"What you're having."

The girl went away, and brought them two tall glasses of grape-fruit juice. Lang tasted his, and cocked a questioning eyebrow at Carmel.

"Hardly anybody here really drinks," Carmel explained. "They save that for the visitors. They've got to stay alert, you know . . . This—" he picked up his glass—"is just for appearances, really."

"Oh."

"Sorry to disappoint you," Carmel said. "Let me buy you something else."

Lang pushed his glass back at the girl. "The same, with gin," he said.

Carmel was about to go on to another subject, when they were interrupted by a girl in a white dress who wiggled her way in between Lang and Carmel, and called out in a high-pitched, lisping voice, "Carmel, you look lovely. How are you?"

"Free and easy," Carmel answered. "How're things with you, Candy?"

"Oh, lovely." Candy's skin was tinted to the peculiar sallow shade of bleached blondes. She had thick lips and protruding eyes, but still Lang was thinking that she was not entirely unattractive when she spoke again in a put-on falsetto that was unmistakably masculine:

"I just came over to see if your pretty friend would dance with me."

"Sorry," Lang said. "My card is full."

Apparently this was very funny, for Candy shrieked with laughter. "His card is full! Did you hear that?" she demanded of Carmel. "I asked him to dance, and he said his card was full—isn't that just lovely? What's his name?"

"Hi," Lang said broadly, putting out his hand. "Name's Lang. I'm here recruiting for the Young Businessman's League. Glad to meetcha—like to talk to you about forming a women's auxiliary . . ."

Candy pulled away. "Hey," she said to Carmel in a cutting voice, now without female pretense at all, "I'm not sure I like your friend as much as I thought . . ." She flounced away, and Carmel shook his head wistfully.

"What's she doing here?" Lang asked. "I thought these guys were all good family men."

"They are," Carmel said. "Candy used to be somebody's nephew from Cleveland."

"Oh."

"Look," Carmel said. "I've got to go talk to a man. But you stay here, okay? Ask for whatever you want—they know you're with me."

"Right," Lang said. Carmel patted him on the shoulder and walked away. Lang watched him deferentially pull up a chair at a table where a fat man in expensive bad clothes sat alone. Lang swung back on his stool and ordered another gin from the almond-eyed girl behind the bar, his eyes fixed on the mirror. He felt chilled, and oddly soothed, by the cool violet hues of the light. The men passing by studied him carefully, to determine his rank. Lang made his face empty to look back at them. In New York, a hustler from some fly-by-night agency had taken the band to a private room in a place just like this, and laid down a line of cocaine on the table for each of them while he rattled on cheerfully about contracts and percentages. But he hadn't been able to show them anything concrete, and they took his coke and got out . . .

. . . Those inert and empty children he had seen in Icarus this afternoon, handing Carmel his money with one hand as they took their plastic bags, or vials, or tubes in the other, were just like the kids who had begun coming to the club in droves after the press first picked up on the New York scene. You could spot them right away, even when you were on stage. Some of them tried to come on like the real thing, ripping their leather and acting aggressive, but the strain in their faces always gave them away. "It's an American thing to do everything young—like, why wait until you're forty to be a failure?" Sally had said, watching them crowd the bar one night. They were lost and futile, those kids—his fans!—grasping desperately at any noise that would give them a sense of belonging. But they belonged to nothing and no one, and when they came to the club they had nothing to offer except pieces of the fear inside their hearts.

"Are you looking for some kicks, kid?" he had said.

Lang—walking back toward Prince Street with the night's take in his pocket, trying to calculate how much had been skimmed off by the owner for the sound system rental and the band's drinks, thinking of the new guitar break they had put in the third verse of "Don't Talk to Me About Love" and how Sally had jumped up and down in the aisle, yelling his name—had heard the words only as an echo, in the way that you might count the tolling of a clock backwards in your mind, through the curtain of the rain. Then he looked up from the street, and saw a shadow walking toward him out of the shadow between two buildings, repeating its question in a frail and taunting voice:

"Are you looking for some kicks, kid?"

Lang recognized him at the same time that he saw the gun. The hand that held it was shaking—but not that much.

"Looking for some twisted kicks, motherfucker?" the junkie said.

He had been very cool. It was as if he as a personality had ceased to exist, and all that was left was the mechanism of his brain, connections clicking in a raw electric hum. He had taken a step forward, never taking his eyes from the gun. . . . He had not even been able to begin the trip back to himself until hours later, back in the loft, when he lay stiff and sweaty on his bed while Sally, beside him, repeated over and over again "What's wrong? What happened? You better tell me Danny, because you're going to have to tell someone sooner or later—" and the face of the dead man dissolved into Erica's face, and back again, before his icy eyes.

The ultimate fan, Lang thought; rejoice, rejoice. Maybe he had just understood the music too well. With a sudden savage bitterness, Lang looked around at the pimps and dealers surrounding him. "Do I qualify as one of them now?" he thought. "Do I make the grade? Do I look enough like you?"

Carmel slipped into the next stool, and gave him a friendly smile. "Sorry to keep you waiting. Enjoying yourself?"

"Oh, yeah," Lang mumbled. "I got Candy to gimme a handjob."

"I'm sure Candy wouldn't mind," Carmel said.

"You get your talk done?"

"Yeah."

"Did you tell 'em about the Young Businessman's League? Damned if I'm going to leave here without making at least one convert."

Carmel didn't look amused. "There's something I want to talk to *you* about now," he said.

"Eight inches," Lang answered promptly. "Since you ask."

"Myra tells me you're going down to see Johanna."

"Myra," Lang said, draining the last of his drink and signalling for another, "has a great gift for invention."

"But it's true, isn't it?" Carmel said impatiently.

"Let's say it's possible. Not likely—possible." Lang felt a moment of trepidation—as if even that might be too much to say to Carmel.

"I think it would be a mistake. You belong in Icarus."

"I belong in New York," Lang said, masking the doubt that welled up in him at the words with a makeshift irritation.

"I'm not so sure about that. I can tell you don't want to go back there."

"There's no place for me here."

"There might be," Carmel said, cryptically. "You don't know. And anyway, Johanna doesn't have anything left to give you. She just makes it with the pots and pans now."

"You don't like her."

"She gave me a little trouble once. Nothing worth talking about."

Lang, in a fog, wondered what that trouble might be; since Johanna didn't even do drugs, and so far as he remembered, she barely knew Carmel—since if you didn't do drugs, there was no reason to know him. But a lot of things had changed since he had left, and you never could tell . . . He took another drink. He remembered what

Myra had told him, that Carmel was living with Lorraine now, and he was about to ask Carmel what the story behind that might be, just to keep things even; but you didn't ask Carmel about that kind of thing.

"You got a hurt, Lang?" Carmel asked abruptly. "You got something on your mind?"

"Why would I have anything on my mind?" Lang asked slowly. He was terrified; but the liquor saved him. Using his drunkenness as a shield, he gave Carmel a lazy drunk's grin. "Don't be silly."

"Well," Carmel said. "You don't look so happy, Lang, you know? It's my business to make people happy, so naturally I'm concerned . . ."

For one precious eyeball-rolling moment, Lang was ready to tell him everything; but he stopped himself just in time—realizing that a confession to Carmel would be no confession at all, but a lever which would give Carmel total power over him. He didn't want to make that surrender, not just yet. So he only smiled at Carmel, and drawled, "I'm *home,* man—how could I not be happy?"

Carmel looked at him narrowly, but apparently decided to let the subject die—and that danger was safely over, for the moment at least. Lang felt the tension ebb inside him, leaving only emptiness in its wake. But Carmel was still onto something. He would have to watch out for Carmel from now on.

"Why did you bring me here, anyway?" he asked.

"Oh," Carmel said. "I just wanted to show you a good time, that's all. How do you like the place?"

"You know that's not it." Lang shook his head. He was spinning wheels; there was something terribly out of key about the whole episode, but he couldn't put his finger on where it was. There was only one thing certain, and that was that Carmel never did anything without having his reasons.

"Then just say I'm interested in you." Airily, Carmel lit a cigarette, and exhaled smoke toward the ceiling. He looked at Lang over the burning match. "Maybe I think," he said, "that you and I have a little bit more in common than you realize."

"Then tell me . . ."

"Tell you what?"

"Tell me what happened between you and Johanna."

Carmel looked surprised. "Well," he said easily, "you *are* interested in her, aren't you?"

"Well?"

"Nothing. It was just a question of money."

"Are you sure?"

"What do you mean? Yes, I'm sure. I'd tell you if it was anything more than that."

Lang didn't know if he believed him; but his mind couldn't function, he couldn't go on. His brain was racing, and yet he felt close to stupor.

"But what do you want from me, then?" he demanded, thickly, trying to keep going; knowing, somehow, that he had to pry a clue from Carmel. A clue to what? No matter. He would know when he found it.

"This isn't the time to talk about it," Carmel decided. He was almost tender. "You're wasted," he said. "Let's go home."

Lang stumbled after him out the door, and down the alley to the stairs, not even pausing to look at Candy, her white dress glowing, on her knees in a darkened doorway, her face turned away and a pair of big-veined hands locked in the roots of her bleached hair. They drove back to Icarus without saying anything—Carmel seemed suddenly impatient to be rid of him. But when they arrived at Hoffentlichs' he gave his most charming smile as they said goodnight: "I'm glad you're home," he said. "You know, maybe we could use you here."

Lang was too exhausted to think about what that might mean. He went inside as Carmel pulled out of the driveway. The house was dark. Everybody was asleep—except Alice, who came out of her bedroom to see who was there, headphones around her neck and swaying softly to the beat. Lang thought that she was about to speak to him, but after looking down at him for a second, she turned and went silently back into her room.

CHAPTER SIX

Richard: 2

Once, just before the end, Erica had asked him to take her shopping, and at a place in Suffragette City she had bought herself some boots. That seemed to put her in a good mood; she took his hand and showed off the boots with a pirouette on the street outside the store. The hot and cold fear which had gripped him constantly whenever he saw her in those last days, corroding his reflexes and shackling every word he spoke, ebbed into a tentative calm. But it flared again on the way home to Icarus, when she sat against the far window with her knees pressed up against the dashboard, and lapsed into her silence again. He had come to dread that silence. They were crossing the bridge when she asked him to turn the radio to another station.

"No," Richard said. "I like this song."

"You see? We don't even like the same music."

"What?"

"I said we'll never make it," Erica cried, "because we don't like the same music."

It was on the night of that same day that she walked out on him at Uncle Lou's Pub, in front of everyone. Richard still ached with the memory of how he had turned to find all of them watching, waiting, silent, as the door swung shut behind her. She was gone, and there he was, naked, pinned to a wall of air by helpless and humiliated love, for all of them to see.

Now, in his blue-walled room, alone, with the stereo on to keep the darkness outside his window at bay, Richard sat at his desk and felt his mind being pulled back toward Erica like a steel bearing sliding on its track. He had nothing left to think about; he could only contemplate the image of her, as if the engines of his life had jammed around her absence, and all he could do was wait for them to unlock.

He lit a cigarette and got to his feet. In the first despair of realizing how much loving Erica was going to cost him, he had begun to form a vision. With each new reversal at her hands, it had slowly gathered shape and density, riding on the music's flow. He had given it a name: the Rock N Roll Theater, and he murmured the title now, letting its incantation echo in the private echo chamber of his head. He put himself up on that imaginary stage, neck craned to his reflection in the mirror overhead, one hip cocked, lips moving silently in the shapes of words yet unwritten.

"A theater for us," he explained it to Carmel, the next time Carmel came by on the rounds of his regular customers.

"I know a dude who might be able to give you some help with putting it together," Carmel said. "If you're serious."

"Who? Seastrom?" Richard asked.

Carmel had been forced to quit his old place over some hassle with a client, and he was staying at the Seastrom house—"Just for a few days," he explained, "until I find a new office. Anyway Regina, the daughter, is one fine mellow-thigh chick like the Bowie song says, and we've been getting along, getting it on, so I guess I don't mind."

"I've heard of them," Richard said. "But I don't know any of them at all."

"Her father's very into theater. I'll tell him about this—he'd be interested. And I'm sure he could give you a hand with financing the deal."

Richard wasn't sure he liked the idea. Seastrom was well past forty, a businessman, president of an electronics company contracted to the government. To have someone like Seastrom involved didn't fit with the vengeful iconoclasm he had wanted to achieve. Besides, he was apprehensive at the prospect of having to translate his hazy grand visions of the night into hard actuality, giving his fancy a face to match its name. It would be real, it would no longer be his. "I don't want to sell out," he told Carmel.

"Before you worry about that, you better check to make sure that somebody's buying."

Richard tried a different tack. "I don't know if I'm ready."

"Hey," Carmel said softly. "This would be a chance to do something. You do want to do something, don't you?" with one of his cool appraising stares. "Just try it. See what happens."

So, a few days later, Richard drove with Carmel and Regina over to her father's house. Regina had a mystery. She moved and spoke in a style utterly cut off from her surroundings, as if she lived on her own separate level of existence, feeding off the barrage of her perceptions like an army living off the land. Her voice had the most unsettling combination of accents. It would shift from Boston to Tidewater in the space of a breath between sentences. When Carmel introduced her to Richard, she said: "My name sounds almost like yours. I don't think there'll be any trouble, though. We don't look much alike."

Right then, Richard felt he wanted to chip away that distance in her voice and find out what was underneath. She was as transparently impenetrable as a figure cut from glass. But he couldn't let himself think about it now. He fought the desire into silence, and listened instead to Carmel. Carmel was talking shoptalk:

"These up and comers," he said. "They don't know the protocol, they don't know what they're doing. The way I see it is this: when you're selling something that can wrap the inside of somebody's head around their little finger, you ought to have some pride in your work—you shouldn't take it lightly."

Regina said: "You have one advantage, at least. My house, I think, is the best front that anyone could ask for."

"*So* respectable," Carmel agreed, amused. "Yeah."

"My parents would no doubt be upset if they found out."

"Why? I think we're considerate as hell—about everything. We don't even fuck until we know they're asleep," he told Richard.

"It would disturb my father," Regina said. "He has very poor nerves."

"Use a silencer," Richard said.

They both laughed, but not at the joke. They were holding themselves a little apart; they had aristocracy's confidence that it was privy to secrets that others didn't even know existed. Again the desire to penetrate that calm hard reserve passed through Richard, quick as fire, and again he put it away from him.

Seastrom was sitting on the porch of his house. That was the first dislocation. Houses in Icarus didn't have porches, not like this one, with creaking weather-warped boards and big wooden chairs, and a hanging lamp—the porch, and the massive cantilevered house behind it, emerged suddenly from the gloom, like a leftover from the old and half-forgotten South before the war—Richard was entranced.

"Beautiful place," he said to Carmel.

"It's falling apart," Carmel answered. "But don't tell Seastrom I said so."

Seastrom had gotten out of his chair, and stood framed in multiple overlapping squares of shadow and light from the hallway behind him. His glasses caught the sunset as he came forward, and flashed briefly red before the wind stirred a branch to block the glare.

"*Patron,*" Carmel said. "This is Richard."

"The artist," Regina added. Richard couldn't tell if she was mocking him or not. He didn't think she knew him well enough to mock him, but it was impossible to be sure of her.

"Pleased to meet you, Richard," Seastrom said. He had a gentle deep voice. It would have been cuddling in its softness, if not for the depth. "I understand that we're to talk some business, if I follow Carmel correctly, which I don't, always." His hand, when Richard took it, was large and meaty, but peculiarly lacking in force.

"I was just watching the sunset," Seastrom said. "It's—not the best part of the day, maybe—but the nicest. Don't you agree?"

"Dawn," Richard offered.

Seastrom gave a pleased smile, and put his hands in his pockets. Richard could hear keys jangling inside. "Dawn's like everything else that's new," he said. "Loud, and too sure of itself." He smiled again, bunching his pink cheeks. "They wanted me to sell this place, so they could build an apartment complex on the land—but I couldn't give up the sunsets. Well, come now—come inside."

A smell of cigars hung in the air, all the more noticeable because it seemed perpetually on the verge of vanishing. Regina arranged her body on a chair, giving up nothing of herself. Seastrom sat on a couch, filling most of it, and waved Richard to a hassock nearby. "Would you like a drink?" he asked. "Regina, would you . . .?"

Richard asked for a beer; Carmel asked for a gin and tonic. "I know what you want," Regina said to her father on her way out. Her silver-studded denims waved like a flag to challenge the becalmed domesticity of the room. Richard, unable to help it, thought of Erica; how her pride or arrogance came from inside and was hardly visible unless you looked at her by a certain light, so different from Regina's pride or arrogance—or perhaps only boredom in her case—which was stapled across her face like a sliding bolt. He wondered which was worse. Perhaps both were in the end only ceremonial.

She brought the drinks back on a tray, and served them around —Richard watched the band of her panties make a ridge beneath her jeans as she bent over Carmel. Unconsciously, he had been waiting for her to come back before he started to talk.

He had expected that even if Seastrom liked the idea, they would keep to the financial and logistic side of the enterprise. But Seastrom kept asking instead for details of color and action, more details than Richard had; he seemed to derive a huge private enjoyment from them. Richard would describe a passage meant to be shocking and intense, and Seastrom's face would quiver with jovial amusement: "Oh, that's a jolly one, isn't it?" he would say, nodding benignly to include the rest of the room in the circle of his approval. Richard, snared by a rising uncertainty, was spinning around. Seastrom's giggles and winks mixed badly with his expectations.

Carmel didn't seem at all perturbed. From the relaxation of his body as he reached for a cigarette, Richard knew that he thought it was going well. For a bad minute he had the notion that Carmel had designed this encounter only to ridicule him. Hired a ventriloquist's dummy to impersonate Seastrom, a hooker to play Regina. . . . Increasingly he was pushing his words in her direction, but she only spoke once, without interest: "I don't see why people should pay to watch in a theater what they can watch for free on any Saturday night at Uncle Lou's."

"That's just it," Richard told her, although he wasn't sure it was. "They've totally lost awareness. If they ever had it to begin with. When they see it all together on a stage, with music, they'll have to look at it in a new way."

"Let him talk, Regina," Seastrom said. "I think that this is all very interesting." He leered at Carmel, who smiled back, as if the leer were no more than a nod.

Richard was about to go on when Mrs. Seastrom came in. "Please don't let me interrupt you," she said. She was a small blonde woman, determined to keep her serenity: there was aggression in her calm. She stayed for fifteen minutes, listening with a fixed expression and an occasional neutral comment. But whenever Carmel spoke, she looked away, and a twinge of disgust crossed her placid face. Richard hadn't seen any likeness to Regina before, but he thought he saw it then, just for a moment, before her face became her own again.

When she got up to leave, she said, "You know, Carmel, you may think that your music sounds best at three A.M., but some of us enjoy our sleep—could you give it a rest tonight?" Her voice was so cold that Richard was startled. Carmel ignored the words, but not the coldness; he waved his hand like a wand to dispel it.

Seastrom excused himself shortly afterward. "She can't get to sleep unless I'm there," he told Richard. "You must come again. I like this." In Richard's mind the conversation was already evaporating. It occurred to him that they hadn't spoken at all about financing. That bothered him. His relief bothered him more.

Regina was out in the kitchen. Carmel came back from there. "Come down to the office," he said.

They walked together down a winding flight of stairs.

"She doesn't like you, does she?"

"Regina?"

"Her mother."

Carmel snickered. "She's just burned at me for corrupting her daughter. As if that girl needed any help. I desecrate the house, you see."

"Must make it hard to stay."

"Shit," Carmel said, hitting the light switch at the bottom of the stairs, "she's nothing. I can always count on Mr. S. to take my side in a crunch. . . . It's just personal, anyway. The way things are now, she's got to come down to me, not me to her."

The front room of the basement, where they stood, was a clutter of leather-bound books, dusty magazines, old records, family albums, postcards, lamps, statuettes, the silt of generations. There was a faded photograph of some skeletons sitting at a poker table. An old saber hung over the door that led to Carmel's room.

"I've got some new uppers. Great stuff. I'm passing out samples to my regular friends."

"Not tonight."

"Ah, man! Come on. You're my one-man market research team."

The back room was completely Carmel's. Monastic and spare, it was as functional as a piece of machinery. His stereo sat on an altar in the center of a blood red rug patterned in concentric circles. Carmel pointed to a filing cabinet in the far corner.

"A lot of narcs would cut off a ball to get hold of that thing," he said. He walked over to the cabinet. "I keep my samples here. Enough to put me away for a thousand years . . . dammit, where— here we are."

"That's prescription," Richard said.

"Uh huh. I know a guy who works in a pharmacist's, and I also know that he was involved in that business of the girl who got chain-whipped outside the tennis club—remember? last year—and I know some cops who would be very happy to know all these things that I know. However, I also know that he can get me things I can't get anywhere else. We worked something out."

"If he's passing stuff to you, they could bust him for a lot worse than the other."

"Yeah. But I know one more thing which I forgot to mention. The dude is stupid. Sure you don't want some?"

"Not now."

Carmel popped a pill into his mouth and shrugged. "Keeps me alive," he said, putting the pills away.

Richard was looking at a diamond-shaped piece of wood hung on the wall. On it was mounted a varnished photograph out of Scott Fitzgerald, a pair from the Twenties: the man wore a bow tie and a wool cap slung low over one eye, and gazed thin-lipped at the camera; his lady had a fur boa around her neck, a big floppy hat on her head, and was looking off into the distance, radiant with expectation.

"It's nice, isn't it?" Carmel said. "I found it in a junk shop. The best part of it is that I don't know who they are—I don't want to."

"They look like a couple of ghosts," Richard said.

Carmel was busy putting a record on the turntable. His fingers darted among the knobs and dials. A jaunty melody came tripping from the speakers, muted to a murmur. Carmel bounced to its rhythm as he walked over to Richard.

"So you've got a thing for Regina, huh?" he asked pleasantly.

"What?"

"It's all right, man. I talked to her. She doesn't mind."

"Just like that."

"Why not?" Carmel smiled. "Fill your heart with love today," he sang with the record, moving around the room in a sardonic little dance, the piano bouncing merrily away behind him. "Don't play the game of time . . . Well," he said, "are you going to go up? I mean she's waiting."

"I'm supposed to go up there now?"

"No," Carmel said, still dancing, "wait for the next election. Of course, now."

"But ah—" Richard hesitated, not sure how to put it—"won't you get lonely?"

"Boogie," Carmel said, whisking a long scarf in front of Richard's nose. "Would you rather spend the time with me? Would ya? I didn't think so. So . . ."

Regina would be waiting for him. She had not spoken two dozen words to him, but still she would be waiting, with that same bored scorn she had been wearing all night for perfume. Richard, climbing the stairs, tried to make himself remember that Erica was gone and done and didn't matter any more. Desire and betrayal raced in alternating currents through his blood. He was charged and wired, plugging in to the mystery at the top of the steps.

"In here," Regina called from the living room. She was drinking something pale, and Richard sat down beside her, on the couch that Seastrom had occupied earlier.

"Well," she said, putting down her glass.

Richard touched a strand of dark hair cutting across her temple. "And what about your father's nerves?" he asked.

"Oh, that. That's just something to say."

"And he actually knows everything that goes on."

"I'll tell you," Regina said, "if you don't pass it on to Carmel. One night last week, we were in his room, and in the middle of things, I heard somebody breathing, which was okay, except it wasn't me and it wasn't Carmel. I looked over his shoulder, out into the front room— you know, where we keep all the family trash—pretending to keep my eyes shut, as if I were being very passionate, and I saw somebody standing there; light from the room reflected on his glasses. It was my father. He stood there until we were done. Carmel must have thought I was frigid that night, because of course I could hardly keep my mind on the job . . . And then while we were going through post-coital remorse, or whatever, getting dressed, I heard him go upstairs. Carmel never noticed."

"And he never said anything about it? Your father."

"No. It was all quite puzzling, really, but ah, you know . . ."

"What about your mother?"

"She only notices what she wants to."

"Then she must want to notice Carmel. Because she notices him, all right."

"There's a lot of things in this house," Regina said, "that never get explained." She leaned forward. "You know," she said, "you're not bad-looking."

When she took off her clothes, Richard looked at her and did not know whether to be amused or depressed. The rest of her body looked just as bored as her face. He bent down and gave her a kiss on the left nipple, to get himself started. As they worked their moves into a rhythm, he found himself wondering whether she was doing this for him, or he for her. The ambiguity slowed him down a little, but as it turned out, that was all right. The guilt that rode his shoulder was the only thing he felt, slowing his heart as it whipped his body; Regina was only another battlefield, and he didn't touch her at all.

She stood up, and put her clothes back on, and swallowed the last of her drink.

"Can't we talk awhile?" Richard asked.

He wanted some clue to place her, a key that the performance hadn't given him.

Regina smiled. Royally. "No," she said; "no, you see, I have to go back down to Carmel. But I will show you to the door, if you want."

Driving back to his room on the empty road, Richard sifted a restless catalogue: Seastrom's bluff joviality; the disgust on Mrs. Seastrom's face; Regina, who would remain a horizon no matter how far he traveled to reach her. Erica's ghost was the shadow hanging over it all. The images filtered like smoke through his mind until he reached the picture on Carmel's wall, two long-dead faces fixed in an eternal transience of luminous and vanished joy.

CHAPTER SEVEN

Within a Grove of Buddies: 3

Icarus dislocated everything; you always felt too large or too small, never proportionate. And yet the town had its own logic, Lang knew, as formal as a game of chess; now he too was part of it, another gambit on the board. So many pictures, so many remembered voices, were crowding his head that all feeling and caring had been crushed out, casual as a spent cigarette, quick as a random fuck, and only pure animal will kept him from going up in smoke.

He had always imagined that guilt like sorrow would be another grand gesture—like singing a song on stage. When you were performing, every moment was a pretty little apocalypse, and you tasted your victory or took your defeat and stopped living until the next show. But now there wasn't anything left to go on to. He was trapped, mired in torpor and too sluggish to act. Guilt was only another kind of drudgery, because nothing could change you afterwards—nothing would ever be quite as real to him again as the sound of that gunshot, the knowing of blood.

Maybe Erica was this way at the end, Lang thought—maybe no longer thinking of beauty or romance or the love that led her to throw her passion clear across the sky, but only sick of everything and driven

to self-murder just to keep herself separate from the muddy earth
below. But he couldn't follow her there—oh, he had thought of it,
dreamed of razor blades as a sweet deliverance in steel—but no, the
price of the act was to remember it, in reverse rehearsals, in bits of
mute and broken time, and he had to pay the price, he couldn't stop
the machine. After his night with Carmel he had taken Johanna's
letter and shoved it all the way down to the bottom of his duffel bag,
alongside Erica's tambourine, and he had tried not to think of her
any more; but of course he couldn't stop thinking about her. The
vision of her grew more lovely and harder to resist the further it fled
from him. He lay awake that night and longed for her in a pure agony
of regret.

Johanna continued to haunt him all through the next day; she
haunted him still that night, when he sat with Myra in the living room,
and they talked. A thin whisper of music came to them from Alice's
room. In the rec room downstairs, Andrew snored on Lang's couch,
his racking breath like the hum of a ship's motors in the night, lulling
its passengers to sleep. But Myra couldn't sleep; she and Lang sat
awake and talked through the dwindling hours—as they had done on
so many nights, so many summers before, when it had been ten of
them in the room instead of two and the talking and the drinking had
gone on, gone all the way to dawn sometimes, when the Ex-Prodigy
Club had been in its glory and the conversation was ripe with heat.
But that time was dead to Lang, deader than if it had never existed,
and returning to Icarus had not brought it back for him. It only made
him remember the loss. When was the past history, and when was it
only death? Sweat itched him like rust, while Myra's voice wound on
across the night.

There was a bottle of wine on the table between them. Myra
was in a melancholy mood. "God, I feel like hell," she said. "Talking
to you, now, takes me back—to when everybody used to come over
here. But hell, that's all over with, you know that. I feel like I don't
know any of the old crowd any more. And I'm not even sure I want
to." She chuckled, dourly.

"You don't. Believe me, you don't."

"You're probably right." Myra sighed. "Still, we had some
times . . . You know," she said suddenly, "you've changed, too. Just
like everybody else."

"Sure," Lang said. "I got older."

"Not that. Sure, that's true, but I don't mean that part. You
know, Lang, you've turned into a little bit of a cold fish. You don't

give out much."

"How did I use to be?"

"Nicer."

"Does that bother you? That I changed?"

"Would it matter to you?"

"Not much." Lang hesitated. "It's not that I don't like you," he said. "It's just—"

"That you don't care what people think any more."

"Maybe I don't," Lang said.

"That's what I mean. You would have cared once."

"I can't help that."

"I didn't say you could. It doesn't make that much difference."

"It doesn't."

Myra swirled the wine in her glass. "You're in some kind of trouble, up North, aren't you?"

"Yes."

Myra nodded. "I thought so."

There was an awkward pause. This wasn't the kind of conversation they were used to. They had known each other for so many years, and they had never said anything to each other that mattered at all. Lang felt tense, enervated. He had no idea what would come next. Like a man in the grip of an obsession, there was only one subject he wanted to talk about; but he couldn't bear to talk about it, he didn't dare to, and this was frighteningly close.

But Myra apparently decided that it was too close for her too. "I feel like hell," she repeated. "I don't know, I'm bored and I'm depressed and I'm bored and it's getting so I can't tell which is which any more . . ."

"Why don't you have an affair?"

"I used to. Believe me, I used to—it just got to be too much of a drag putting on all that makeup, but even so, I could tell you romances . . ."

"Let me imagine them." She had reminded him of Erica.

"Andrew's gotten worse, hasn't he," Myra said abruptly. "Since the last time around."

"What do you mean, worse?"

"I mean the drinking. I mean the fights. I mean the fact that everybody in this house is constantly at war with each other. Oh, shit, you know what I mean."

"It's not just Andrew." Lang said. "I don't see how you even have the energy to fight any more. I don't know why you bother."

Myra grinned like a pirate. "Oh, we don't really need much energy," she said. "It's just a reflex action now. We don't even need anything to fight about—we just get straight into the personal abuse."

She dragged on her cigarette. "I suppose it was always like that," she said, "but it didn't use to matter, when I was young—when we were young—Andrew was young, once. Oh, let me tell you, Lang, you think you've seen some wild times. You should have seen the gang we had in Damascus in fifty-three . . . Everybody was always drunk—everybody was a spy for us or for them or both or even just for themselves, and we all knew each other, then. That was our first post—right after Andrew and I got married."

"What was it like?"

Myra laughed broadly. A hint of gold gleamed in her mouth. "Oh, Christ, it was crazy. Once—Andrew and his Russian counterpart knew about each other, of course, they usually do—once, at a party, they both got so soused that they took out their pistols and marched through the house shooting out every light bulb they could find."

"Didn't that wake up the army—or anybody?"

"No. Of course not," Myra said. "Both pistols had silencers on."

"Oh."

"Imagine me! I was an Arlington princess with a father in real estate, and all my old beaus are high-school coaches by now, or dead. Enter Andrew, with his seven languages, and all that noise clicking away in his brain. . . . My father thought he was a drug dealer at first. Then he decided he was a thief, which made Andrew happy. He said he'd rather be a thief than a dealer . . ." She shook her head. "God, he was beautiful then—believe it or not—and he could be so romantic when he wanted to be. I guess I made it worth his while to be, then." She grinned again. "One night, I was in his room at Georgetown, and it was late, for me, then, it was late, and I looked at the clock and said, My God, I've got to go. He didn't say a word. He took out an African machete—you can imagine where he got it—and smashed the clock in two. He told me, Now you don't have to worry about the time. And he poured me a drink."

"And turned out the lights."

"No," Myra said, "no." She turned her glass between her fingers. "That was when he asked me to marry him," she said.

She grew moody, looking down at the cigarette-scarred table.

"Do you know why Andrew left the Agency?" she asked.

"I heard it was medical."

"Yeah. Medical. He had a breakdown. There was a man in

Europe who was ready to come over to us—Andrew had known him
in the Middle East, and he insisted that Andrew make the contact,
even though it was dangerous because they knew who he was, and
something went wrong somewhere. He got the man out safe, but he
barely got out himself. He was juggling three different identities with
half a dozen different groups, and he cracked. He lost himself somewhere in there. By the time he got back he was a basket case. He hid
under the bed, and he didn't recognize me."

"Wow," Lang said.

"Yeah. Well, they're used to that sort of thing—at the Agency.
They have a place of their own for when it happens to their people.
And when he got well, they retired him. Do you know he's bitter
about it? A year behind cork-lined walls, and he wanted to dive back
in headlong. It was his gift—it was what he wanted for his life. A
special breed—a special kind of man, I'll tell you, Lang."

"Yes."

"You like it, don't you? It appeals to you."

"A little bit. I like Andrew."

"Well, look what he's come to. What we've all come to. You
know sometimes I think—I think that maybe it just comes to people
younger now. . . . Everybody fell apart so quickly. Richard, Brewer—
Erica—all of them . . . And just a couple of years ago, they thought
they were going to be on top of the world."

"That was always such horseshit," Lang said.

"How can you say that? Remember, Lang, when you were in
high school, you were famous."

"Oh, come on."

"It was your whole crowd—you were all special. Or at least you
thought you were."

"And we all fell apart . . ."

"Except you, Lang," Myra said. "You're different from the rest
of them. Because you were smart enough to get out, and go up to
New York, and say you were going to make it, that you were really
going to make it—do you know how people down here talked about
you? God, everyone just thought it was fantastic . . ."

"Maybe they were wrong."

"There's just one thing I don't understand," Myra said thoughtfully. "Why you came back at all . . ."

A new, unexpected pain took him over at her words. Abruptly,
everything he had lost was real to him again. Struggling, fighting to
break through, to win . . . all that was gone now. Worthless: less than

worthless. He had been amputated from all that, and he couldn't look back. And then he thought he understood why, choosing flight, he had chosen Icarus: he had been looking for oblivion. He had come to take his rightful place among the has-beens and never-weres, to claim his berth in the mothball fleet. They had all failed, Myra said. Well, he could play that game; he would be the last, the biggest failure of them all. He felt that with this understanding, Icarus was opened to him at last; and yet he couldn't make himself take the final step. He couldn't say yes to all of it yet.

"Andrew used to say that you would be the only one to get out. But I'm beginning to think you're just like him instead. Ever since you got back you haven't done a thing but get drunk and slop around like a corpse. . . . Why, Lang? I want to know . . ."

There was nothing he could say. As with Carmel, but a dozen times stronger now, the desire to bellow out what he had done was like lava inside him; it was only with a huge effort that he fought himself under control. *Not yet, not yet. I can't do that yet. There's no turning back from that.*

Lang stood up, almost knocking over his wineglass. He paced the room on bony legs, one hand up ruffling his hair. The other was a fist hanging down at his side.

"Are you going to go see Johanna?" Myra asked.

"No," Lang said. "I can't. I don't know."

"There's nobody else left," Myra said. "Besides, she wants you. She always did."

"Oh, Myra, she's been gone a long time."

He was thinking that Johanna had always been ambiguous. He couldn't know her completely. Even the morning after their night together, she had refused to give him any sign, of love or hate or even indifference; she was a stranger, not only to him, but to the girl who had sobbed against him, a few short hours before. Now she was lost to him, and he would never know, not ever. But somehow, insanely, he still had hope of winning her—and at that realization he was ready to laugh. It was such a megalomaniac's pride, to think there might still be some chance there.

Then, almost in the same moment, he was seized by a bizarre fantasy, a flash of pure, grotesque desire: he would pull off his jeans, and moon out on the couch, and Myra's broad red mouth would dive down on him; he would roll and fuck with her right here on the rug, smacking her aging flesh with his palm, feeding on her fat and royal rump like some monstrous rite of passage. He was startled by the desire, and excited by it too—for a second it was unbearably vivid to him. Then it passed, and he felt sick inside.

Myra was looking at him thoughtfully—for a mad moment he was convinced that she had read his mind, and that it was no fantasy at all, but only the simple truth of what had passed between them in the silence which followed his last words. But then he saw only a tired, middle-aged woman, watching him with mistrustful eyes, and there was nothing between them at all.

Finally she spoke.

"This trouble that you're in, up there," she said. "It's something serious. That's why you don't want to go see Johanna."

"Look. I'm not going. I don't want to explain it. What does it matter?"

"It matters because I want to know."

"Well, I'm not going to tell you. I'm really not, Myra."

"But now I'm curious." Myra's face spread in a crafty grin—that look he knew so well, a look that said everything could be reduced to gossip, everything was cheap, and nothing was exempt. "Oh, come on, Lang, you always used to tell me everything."

"I've changed—you told me so."

"You want to tell me," she said, complacently. "You're just being coy."

"No, I'm not," Lang snapped. "Look, it just doesn't belong to you, don't you understand? It's nothing to do with you. You don't have any right to it. It happened somewhere else—don't you see?"

"It can't be that bad."

"Well, it is," Lang said. "You don't understand—there are some things that you just can't turn into your gossip, you know? It's not that easy." He knew he was babbling, but he couldn't stop. He hated it too much to stop. "I mean everybody else, okay, that's just a sick joke, it just uses up the time, you can tell all the stories and it doesn't make any difference to them, because they don't give a fuck anyway, you know what I mean? But this is way beyond you—I'm not going to turn myself into one of your stupid fucking stories, all right?"

"Lower your voice," Myra said. Suddenly, she looked sad, and old. "Oh, Lang, what happened?" she said. "I don't mean you. I mean everything."

He felt chastened. He had been right on the edge. He felt sorry for Myra. It was his fault, for coming here in the first place. He was the one who didn't have any right. And yet he could still feel his awakened anger stifling his blood, pleading for release.

"It's such a mess," Myra said.

"It's getting late. You'd better go to bed."

She shook her head vaguely. "No. I can't sleep." She reached for the bottle of wine, but it was empty. "Lang?" she said.

"What?"

"We did have some good times here once, didn't we?"

Lang didn't answer. Outside the window, it was growing light. He stood with his hands on his hips and looked at the sky. Behind him, Myra sat lapsed and quiet, staring down at the rug.

Stray visions of twisted kicks slid softly down the generations. That odd, perilous belief that they were all of them a special breed, meant for wild and glorious things, had ended in a dim half-world of emptiness and loss, where nothing was certain, and ego slept uneasily with decay. Yes, he thought: everything done here had been done a thousand times before, in endlessly repeated circles, and you could not avoid them no matter how you tried, even though they grew as monotonous as the rain that had, once again, begun to fall outside the window. If Erica had not died, she would have ended like Myra—half-drunk and alone in this barren room, telling off the beads of her days with no one left to listen or care; maybe the pantomine of her seasons was only the echo of a journey Myra had made two decades before. And Andrew, a spook turned into a ghost, with his past held in the palm of his mind like a ball of dust, might foretell them all, Richard, Brewer, Odell, Lorraine, Carmel and Alice, Lang.

Johanna, too.

He wanted to smash every clock in Icarus for her.

CHAPTER EIGHT

Brewer: 1

Somebody was getting beaten up in the parking lot outside Uncle Lou's. The scrape of leather on asphalt, the clatter of a rolling beer-can, followed Brewer like a breeze as he got out of his car and went inside. Then he shut the door and the other, interior atmosphere caught him up, enveloping him as he pushed his way through a gaggle of motorcyclists and their riders, hair whipping over sunburnt shoulders, breasts thrusting loose like blades beneath denim.

Carmel was in his booth at the back, lazy in a blue blazer, a beach-colored shirt stiffening his chest, a cigarette shifting from one hand to the other. There was a girl sitting opposite him; then she was Lorraine, her head lolling, her body liquid. She was wasted. She reached out to fondle Carmel's hair, and he flinched before regaining his composure and returning his cigarette to an upright position. Brewer, ordering a draft at the bar, wondered what she was saying, but there was too much smoke in the air to tell.

Now Carmel leaned forward and talked, and Lorraine listened. She seemed to have to catch her head with her neck to keep it from falling. She looked away; Carmel's face twitched with boredom. Brewer, holding his chilled mug like a shield, threaded his way to them.

Carmel glanced up at him with amusement. "This man, now," he drawled, "he used to be one of my best friends, but now I'm starting to think he's shopping somewhere else, 'cause he don't come around no more."

"No," Lorraine said, her voice all rubbery, "He's only moved on to another vice. It's cute. He's nice." She giggled. "I rhyme."

"Yeah. Why don't you sit down, or is there someone after you?"

"There's someone after someone," Brewer said, "outside."

"Oh, him! He was just in here," Lorraine said giddily. "He walked up to Carmel and asked him if he wanted to buy some mesc, just like that, can you believe it—to Carmel! Mink and the bouncer were at the jukebox, and Carmel said, with this lovely redneck accent —it was really good, Carmel—no, but I hear those two boys over there were into that, why don't you try them? So . . ."

Carmel winced. "Let's change the subject."

"But it was so funny—the look on his face when they dragged him out . . ."

Carmel smiled at Brewer apologetically. "I've been meaning to give you a call, man, but I haven't had the time. What you been up to?"

"Brewer's never up to anything," Lorraine sniffed, doodling on the wet table. "He never—"

"I was worried when you didn't come to see me," Carmel went blandly on. "I thought maybe you were buying from somebody else."

"I wouldn't do that," Brewer said. "I'm just not buying, that's all."

"His mother probably took away his allowance," Lorraine whispered conspiratorially. "She's like that. His mother disapproves of—of *everything.*"

Brewer, uneasy under Carmel's eyes, tried to shift their focus. "I wash my ego in the blood of others," he proclaimed. "If God had meant Time to fly, he would have given it wings. But what is time? We steal time from the dead. Drive carefully. The womb you return to may be your own."

"He doesn't believe in it anymore," Lorraine explained to Carmel. "Not since he went away and cracked. He wanted to leave, just like Dan Lang, but he went crack like an ice cube when you take it out of the tray and then he had to come home. Did you ever tell Carmel how you went crack like an ice cube, Brewer—"

"Shut up," Carmel told her, pleasantly. She took it as a sign that he liked her—for if he did not, her logic, Brewer knew, would run, how could he ever say such a thing?—and subsided, gazing on his blond inert face with brimming mute fondness.

"Why don't you sit down?" Carmel said to Brewer.

But Brewer was too queasy. He tried to go on, grasping at words by moments, in thicks and flurries, words that only led him on to more words, without pattern or logic, without a destination. "There's a little bit of deus ex machina in all of us, you know—" But before he could get anything to coalesce, he was interrupted. A kid, stroking his dawning beard like it was a puppy, knelt by Carmel's chair and began to speak to him with an unintelligible and private intensity. Carmel turned to listen, wearing the studied bored concentration of a priest hearing confession from an accountant. Brewer and Lorraine looked at each other, but their eyes had nothing to talk about.

Cracked like an ice cube when you take it out of the tray. Yes, marvelous, Lorraine. A gift. Never content to rest, she was always fertile with new damage to have you forgive her for. Hating, he had already forgiven her. He knew he would forgive her more.

Four months it had taken. Less. He had thought of it at the time as a fresh start: away from Suffragette City, cradled by red hills. *A small, isolated, yet liberal environment,* the catalogue had said. The last three weeks he had been in the undergraduate infirmary. An institution within an institution. How oddly much like his mind life was. He still thought of Anita often. After he went back to Icarus she wrote him every week for a while, but he had not been sure enough of himself to answer. Didn't even know where she was now.

"Well," Carmel said, "can't you tell him to do it through Quinn? No . . . Quinn's reliable—well, he's no use to us if this is his idea of a secondary market. Tell him to do it my way or forget it."

"But Carmel, man, he's a very big dude, you can't—"

"Look," Carmel said wearily. "I deal, but I don't make deals. You tell your dude that."

"He's not my dude."

"Who's your dude, then?"

"You are."

Carmel grinned. He looked very boyish. "I'd scratch you behind the ears," he said, bringing his cigarette to a Roosevelt tilt, "but I just painted my nails. You run that message, okay? I'll be here."

"Ah—right. Right." The beard backed away. Carmel turned to Lorraine.

"He was very disappointed I didn't ask him to join us—he was very taken with you."

"Was he?" Lorraine said, pleased. "I thought he was cute. What did he say?"

"He asked me, Does she fuck?"

"What did you answer?" Brewer asked. Shameful, to enjoy this, by proxy.

"I said that girls like Lorraine don't fuck. They have sexual intercourse. There's a difference."

"You didn't," Lorraine exclaimed damply.

"No . . . and neither did he." Suddenly preoccupied, Carmel lit another cigarette. Brewer realized that he had been smoking them almost nonstop. His glass was close to full; all four of Lorraine's were empty. "That boy that Mink took outside," he said thoughtfully. "He wasn't working independent. He was sent. As a challenge. I just wish I knew if they were serious this time, or only playing games. It's just barely possible, you see," he explained to Brewer, "that my business could be bought out very soon."

"He's silly, isn't he?" Lorraine murmured. "Someone should tell him he's silly." Suddenly she seemed totally disconnected from them.

Carmel was tapping his ring, Myra's false eye, against his glass. "Shouldn't you all be going on someplace?" he asked abruptly. "I don't want to be keeping you."

"I'm not going anywhere," Lorraine said, in a bright stupor of good cheer. "I want to talk to you. We were having such a good time, before . . ." Catching herself, she floundered. Her position was so obvious that there was no way for her to express it.

"I think you'd better go home," Carmel said. "Brewer can take you."

Don't do me any favors, Brewer thought; but Carmel was obviously elsewhere.

Lorraine stood up, tugging at her slacks. "I have to pay for my drinks . . ." she counted silently with her finger, moving her lips, with an air of surprise . . . "*all* my drinks."

"I'll pay for them," Carmel said with patient impatience. "You can't even count them."

She blew him a slurred kiss as she followed Brewer down the aisle, but he was staring vacantly at nothing, as if he wanted to seize the air before him and mold it into shapes. The false eye stared too, through the smoke uncurling around Carmel's hand.

The parking lot was empty now. A signet moon printed its pale seal on the page of the night's deep blue. "Don't take me home," Lorraine said, collapsing against the front seat of Brewer's car. "Just drive, drive fast, someplace, I want to feel like I'm moving."

"All right."

He pointed the car away from Icarus, and away from the pale halo of light hanging over Suffragette City, four miles away across the river. He turned down a road that wound through the shapeless darkness of the back country to reach the airport highway. Somewhere out there, twenty miles from the city, was the new international air terminal, a gleaming spire of curved white light. He wanted to see it rising up out of the earth.

The trees whipped past, fragments of moonlight trapped in their branches; Lorraine sat motionless, as if posing for a photograph. Her black hair was spread out on the seat, her small budlike mouth pressed itself tight. Brewer's headlights jousted with the white line running from his wheels. Richard had told him how, when he was still with Erica, he would often come to drive this highway, alone, in the fragile hour before dawn.

"I'm so sad," Lorraine said, "No, I'm so drunk. I mean, I get so sad when I'm drunk."

"You wanted to stay with Carmel, didn't you?"

"Who? Oh. No. I don't know. I don't think he likes me much. I don't think he likes anybody."

"He doesn't have to."

"I think . . ." her words slid on oil, lost their way, then returned —"I think he must be very lonely; or why else would he pick a business where he's so involved with people?"

"I talked to Richard today," Brewer said.

"How was he? Don't tell me. I don't want to know. I don't want to think about him . . . I don't ever want to think about anyone again."

Her voice was distorted, like a face behind glass; a trancelike sensation of palpable space had settled between them, buoyed by the night's onflowing haste. Brewer fixed his eyes on the speedometer. The needle quivered, potent with undisclosed power, as if its silent glide up the row of hatched numerals was a moving hieroglyph—one from which an entire civilization could be deduced, if the code could only be broken. The needle climbed steadily; his foot pressed steadily on the accelerator. He was removed from it, observing without emotion as it climbed to sixty-five, to seventy.

"I know it's pointless," Lorraine said. "It's worse than that, it's hopeless, and I have to stop, I know I have to stop—I'm just as smart as Erica is, and I'm certainly prettier, not to praise myself over my head but everything is relative you know, and she doesn't have any reticence, manners at all. . . . If he had gone with me, he wouldn't have been ashamed to be seen in public. What good could she have done him? She'll screw with anybody . . . anybody," Lorraine repeated. "I'm not a Puritan, but at least I pick and choose a bit."

"But she isn't with Richard any more."

"Yes," Lorraine said. "Of course . . ."

Brewer was back in a pastel afternoon of his last high school spring, in Lorraine's empty house, where he and she had gone to get a prop for a rehearsal. The shelves of her room held photographs of her from different plays she'd acted in—a dozen costumes, a dozen poses. Only her expression stayed the same. He had been watching Lorraine rub the dust from one of them with a finger that wasn't getting any dirtier; a bright new pain had risen in his chest, signalling new love, and he had known that from then on the name he gave his pain would be hers. Since that day, the pain hadn't changed. He could call it up at will. But it was not important now. What was important was the needle of the speedometer, moving up to eighty.

"Everything's gotten so sad and complicated," she went on. "I'll bet Richard was depressed, when you talked to him." Then her voice grew soft, cushioned with memory: "Oh, but Brewer, do you remember how lovely it all used to be? Before everybody got so wasted? When we'd drive into Suffragette on Saturday night, and just float down the streets, all of us dressed like kings and queens, and they knew us everywhere—don't you remember, how the piano player at the Pillar of Salt would play 'These Foolish Things' whenever he saw me come in? Richard had that embroidered jacket with the firebird on the back, he looked like a wizard and he'd always bow when he took me out on the floor to dance—"

"I'm sure he was the same for Erica," Brewer said, to cut her off.

"No," Lorraine said. "She's not like us. She never was. She just pretends. Deep down she's onto something completely different —I think that what she really wants is to blow it all up, and never go out dancing again."

Discomfort pinched Brewer; he was always uneasy with Erica for just the same reason. It was impossible to make dreams out of her. She existed too much in reality. She was all there, immediate, undeniable. He grappled hungrily for the next turn of his thought; then grew frightened, then cold, and turned his attention back to the rising needle. He must concentrate on that. Surreptitiously he pressed the accelerator—just a little bit more—eighty-four, eighty-five.

"She could be right, you know," he said.

"She wrecks things. She wrecked Richard. I went with him to Austin's last week, and he wouldn't talk to me at all. He just kept on talking about her."

"Usually he won't."

"He was awfully stoned. That's something else I've got against her—I mean I don't care about being wasted, but it makes me nervous when people do it for a reason."

"You were really in love with him, weren't you?"

Masochist, he thought.

Eighty-seven.

"Love?" Lorraine said, confused; her light had gone out and now quick darkness would rush in: "What's that got to do with it?"

"I'm in love with you," Brewer said. "If that means anything to you." His voice was limp and drained of conviction. "I don't know if it means anything to me," he added.

Lorraine passed her hand vaguely in front of her face, as if to clear a path for her thoughts. "That's sweet of you," she murmured, "but Brewer . . ."

He had broken the unspoken agreement, the tacit everyday sacrifice. But he couldn't believe that anything definite had been said, for he knew that nothing would come of it. The words had been empty of meaning before they left his mouth.

"But Brewer," she went on, surprise and injury in her tone, "you're my friend. I thought I could count on you . . . Do you think I'm stupid? I couldn't go to bed with you," she said. "It means too much to you."

"That's my business," Brewer answered, keeping his eyes on the road.

"No, it's not." She sounded drugged. "It's not—because it would still affect me. I need you too much as a friend to risk it."

"I don't impose the way I think on people," Brewer said. "I can't. I'll never have it the way I want it—I've learned to take what I can get."

"It would poison everything."

Silence: but her words did not, could not, frighten him. They lifted his soul to a feverish, uncertain anticipation.

"You don't have to agree with everyone you sleep with," he argued. "Not necessarily. Not completely."

"I do . . ."

"Why couldn't you just let it mean to me what I want it to,

and mean to you what you want it to . . ."

"Because then," she told him, "I might as well play with myself."

She must be even drunker than he'd thought. But he couldn't tell whether the truth faltering in her dazed voice, sluggish in its claustrophobic heat, was indeed truth, or only a fresh evasion. He felt excited and uneasy. He didn't know what would happen; he couldn't hold on to anything.

"I want to try," he said. "I have to know." But even that might be a lie. If he went to bed with her, his obsession would die; it might be that he wanted her mystery more than he could ever want her. He could already hear his heart cry out in panic at the prospect of having to knit and close around yet another answered question. To save himself, he began to push the car up to ninety miles an hour.

The terminal came into view on the horizon, its curving lines and sheer glass falls inevitably suggesting flight from the surrounding darkness, from the prison of its own earthbound concrete and steel. He hurled the car toward its gleaming purity as a rocket flings its fire across the void in search of a star.

"I can't, I can't . . . Why did you have to *say* it?" she cried out in frustration. "Everything was fine—I mean, I know you've been miserable, but you should be used to it by now, and anyway— let me just forget it. I wouldn't be able to talk to you again otherwise."

"It's all right with me to forget it." It made no difference. He couldn't care. A pent lethargy threatened to burst and swamp him under its warm waves of oblivion.

"Maybe it won't matter," she said hopefully. "If we really try, we can make it not matter."

He had been reaching for a catalyst; but if he had really believed that one was possible, he never would have spoken. Turn, and turn, all aching and barren; he wondered if he would ever crack the spiral of his self-deception, and end his endless conversion of what was not into what could never be, and make it back, ever, far enough to touch a human hand.

Lorraine might be only the first in a whole long gallery of impossibilities.

A pair of eyes suddenly glowed red in his headlights: some scuttling animal, trapped in the beam. Lorraine screamed. Brewer twisted the wheel and hit the brakes. Now terror rose again with its shouts and claws, and he was caught in its grip as the car went bucking and slamming a hundred yards down the highway, skidding wildly from side to side. The tires jerked and swayed beneath him; the whole frame shook. They were about to go into the ditch when he got control of the wheel. The car slewed all the way around a long careening curve until they came to rest, tilted at an angle in the thick scrubby grass of the divider. A stink of rubber and gas smoked the air.

"You could have killed me," Lorraine moaned, gasping.

Before them, the terminal gleamed, lucid, imperceptible, on the dark horizon.

What a prison she had condemned him to.

CHAPTER NINE

Richard: 3

She would be singing, weekend nights, at some cheap bar or high-school dance, and during the time they were together Richard would almost always be in the audience. When she was whirling under the lights, and saw him standing at the foot of the stage, lit by her reflection, her sea-green eyes would light too with a harsh, frightened anguish, as if he were violating some final privacy by his simple presence. But as he remembered it he could not be certain, there might have been nothing in her eyes at all; had she even looked at him, at all?

As a singer Erica had a curious style. She could not ingratiate herself with an audience to save her life—if she wouldn't play the clean-scrubbed and sexless doll for them, neither would she plead for mercy like a Joplin and give her shouts and screams away for free. Her voice was a runaway horse of pure anger held under a whip of icy control, leaving sweetness and sensuality and even despair finally behind, in a cold fire of absolute tension stretched beyond the breaking point. Her frail, thin-hipped body moved with the clean grace of a switchblade filed to razor sharpness; her whole being was a blade, her voice soared, fighting for flight above the storm of guitars, the relentlessness of drums. Her greatest love was to take an innocuous

pop song and convert it by the force of her fury into some final trea-
tise on the uses of power, a cool gleam of contempt in her eye for the
pretenses of prettiness and smooth art. It wasn't particularly subtle,
or even all that pleasant if the truth be told; her will was too steely
to surrender an inch of ground. People who saw her once rarely went
to see her again.

But Richard did. He never loved her so much as in those hours
when she stood on a stage and cried out her arrogance and disgust,
because he was feeding on her power, it all came back on him. When
they were together, he never made any distinctions: her rage, her love,
her faithless desirability, were all one. She made his life real—that was
the price she extracted for her love. His character became a landscape
which he had to cross to reach her. Now her memory caged him still,
and all he could do was rattle the gates, try to fix her in space by
counting her moods, and weave her voice through the interstices of
the wire:

"You don't need me. You just need me to love you. Don't you
see that leaves me with no choice?"

Three months after she had left him, he could still feel nothing
but her loss. He clung to it: it signalled that he was still alive. Driving
to Seastroms' in the fading summer, as the road began to rise and
twist and narrow and fall beneath him, under the evening filtering
down between the leaves, Richard would try to believe that he was
near escaping her, just as she had offered him an escape from his own
history; and always he was pulled back down inside the cage with
only his desire to keep him company.

Supposedly he came to talk to Seastrom about the Rock N Roll
Theater; but they rarely even pretended to care a damn about that
any more. Both of them had become spectators at another show.

The tension between Carmel and Mrs. Seastrom had the red
breath of the bullring to it now. "How's your househunting going,
Carmel?" she would say, with the innocent gleam of a child dowsing
an anthill with kerosene. Or else: "Why don't you and Regina set up
an apartment together?" Carmel would tilt his head to one side, blow
smoke, and answer:

"Why, would you like to move in with us?"

Seastrom, ensconced in his heavy chair, flung back his head and
said, "Oh, yes! She'd love that, a ménage à trois—you'd adore that,
wouldn't you?"

"No, but you would," she told him cheerfully. "Why don't you
try it?"

"Carmel won't have me," Seastrom said.

"Is that true, Carmel?"

"I think you're all sick. I'm going to go downstairs and shoot up so I won't have to think about it."

"Oh," Seastrom said, "I've never seen that . . . do you mind if I watch?"

"All he ever wants to do is watch," Mrs. Seastrom said, putting on a pout.

"Baby unhappy."

"Baby bored," Mrs. Seastrom said, still pouting.

Behind the smoke, a war was going on. Sometimes Richard was sure that it was all in his head. Sometimes he wished it was: it would be a lot easier to deal with, then.

Carmel was wandering around the house, a damp towel loosely knotted about his hips, wet hair hanging in his face, a cigarette dripping ash to mark his trail, muttering snatches of song under his breath and cursing every time the phone rang. Seastrom came in carrying his first after-dinner drink, and stood in the front hall, joking with Carmel and Richard in his soft courteous manner. He seemed in great high spirits. At one point he slapped Carmel on the back, causing Carmel to almost lose his towel.

"Oh, no!" Seastrom cried ebulliently, grabbing for it and yanking it back up into place. "Can't have that. Shock the ladies." He turned to Richard. "Who knows what it might lead to, eh?" He became aware that he was still holding Carmel's towel; he took his hand away and went into the living room. Regina sniffed in the corner as Richard followed. She had been having trouble with her nose. Richard asked her if she had a cold, and she sniffed again, scornfully.

Seastrom sat in his favorite chair, setting his drink before him. "I do hope you're taking notes on all of us," he said to Richard, "for your Theater."

"Should I be?"

Seastrom shook his head. "Just a suggestion." Richard puzzled briefly over that, but grew bored with it and went out to the front porch. It was night: a smell of mustiness and age flowed up to him from the earth. The air was very still. He turned, at a sound of creaking wood, and saw Regina coming out the door. She leaned on the rail and looked out at the night.

"Do you want to make it again sometime?" she asked him without preamble.

"Do you?"

She shrugged. "Carmel told me to ask you. I thought that meant you had asked him."

"I wouldn't have asked him."

Regina gave a muffled, skeptical snicker. Richard had the eerie feeling that she was laughing for Carmel, by proxy.

He had run into Erica, a few nights earlier, in the city; she had been coming out of a bar as he was going in. She had been with somebody he didn't recognize, and as she went by, the realization came to him that they would never make love again. He looked at Regina now, trying to remember what she was like, but his memory gave back a dull mist, nothing more.

"Well," she said, "I just wanted to know . . ."

A car slid to a halt in front of the house. Carmel, dressed, appeared in the doorway behind Regina. "Tommy the Spy's car," he said. "Business, children."

Tommy the Spy came up to the porch, scanning the gloom. He had a habit of moving his head from side to side, and only speaking at the end of each sweep. "You've got a new store," he said, looking South. "You're gonna lose your customers," he added, looking North. "Thought you was retired, or something."

"Nah," Carmel said. "Makin' it better than ever." He was slurring his words, speaking slowly and jerkily, adapting himself to Tommy's style.

"Heard you had some okay Mexican," Tommy the Spy said, looking South. "I could use a dime. And I need some reds, if you got any."

"I got," Carmel said. "Come on down."

He led Tommy the Spy inside. Tommy the Spy managed to look both ways simultaneously without once looking at Richard. Richard, in reply, looked pointedly away, and was rewarded when he heard Tommy the Spy ask Carmel, "That dude outside . . . Is he cool?"

Regina was silent as their footsteps faded. Richard wouldn't have noticed, except that her silence was more intense than usual. "Do you know him?" she asked.

"Who, Tommy? Sort of. I see him in Suffragette City sometimes. I wonder what he's doing on this side of the river."

"Did you know he was my brother?" Regina asked.

Richard parted his lips to laugh, but she never made jokes; he could only look bewildered instead.

"I haven't seen him in two years," she added, carelessly.

"He didn't even recognize you."

"My father's not the only good actor in the family." Regina peeled a chip of cracking paint from the rail. Her face grew opaque.

"You're too good at that," Richard complained.

"Don't tell Carmel," she said. "He—"

Carmel and Tommy the Spy were coming back. "Okay," Carmel was saying, "Mink'll get it to you in the morning."

"You sure it's g-g-good?" When Tommy grew excited, he had a tendency to stutter.

"It's good," Carmel told him in an indifferent voice. "What do you want, ten days' try-out money back?"

"Okay," Tommy the Spy said, descending the steps backwards, "okay." Midway down, he stopped. "Man," he said. "Life's weird. I was tripped out once in a house like this . . ."

"Yeah," Carmel said, "keep cool."

"Yeah, cool," Tommy the Spy said.

His car leaped away in a spray of gravel. Carmel watched its lights wink out of sight. "And to think it's people like that who make my ends meet," he sighed. He turned to Regina. "I have to say I don't see much of a family resemblance," he told her.

It was the only time Richard ever saw Regina look startled.

"I'm going to Uncle Lou's," Carmel said. "You staying here?"

"No, I'm going home," Richard said. He wouldn't have known what to do if he stayed.

Back between blue walls, he tried to extinguish his thoughts by putting out his cigarette, and only lit another. "You try to be on top of things," Erica said to him once, "and you always end up so out of it. You're like a kid, wondering where the circus went."

"And you like that, don't you?"

"Sometimes," she answered, stroking his hair; then still stroking his hair, she added, "Except when you stop."

"And that's when you go off with some other guy."

"That's a shitty thing to say."

"It's true."

"But that's—lie down—that's what *you* like."

"I don't want to lie down. And you know I don't like it."

"Yes, you do," she said slowly. "Sometimes you want me to be vicious, so you can be a martyr, only without doing anything for it. . ."

"I don't want you to be anything."

"Except horizontal," Erica said. Her red scarf glowed in the sunset. She laughed merrily, as if she had said nothing at all.

"Don't make fun of me," Richard said.

"I'm not," she said, "I can't make fun of you without making fun of me. Richard . . ." Then, in a moment, she was turning to place herself beneath him, and he pulled the blankets up over his shoulder and tried, lying in the harbor of her flesh, to forget the hours hemming them in on all sides. Such was her talent that she could open doors and then close them before you were sure of what you'd seen. As the cigarette burned down to his knuckles, he tried again, desperately, to recapture the smell of her skin against rough wool, the fragility of her features from only an inch away, and her eyes, as he sank down, traveling up beyond his face like a lifting veil, but the images broke and tore even as he touched them.

The cigarette's burning cherry touched his fingers and at the same time the telephone rang. It was Lorraine; there was a party on at Austin's, would he like to go? His room had become unbearable. He ignored the predatory gleam in her voice, and told her he'd be by.

She came bouncing out her door, and nestled close to him in the car. Her fingers danced on the dashboard as she sang along with the radio. "You're sad," she said, "I worry about you."

"I don't," he said, resisting an urge to stiff-arm her through the windshield.

"I mean it's just very obvious that you've been going through some bad times—I wish I could help you."

"You wanna jump in the back seat with me?"

"It's too small," Lorraine said.

We hang the lies we tell like nets beneath a tightrope. He liked to think that losing Erica had weathered him. And yet his armor was so fragile that he felt threatened whenever anyone tested it, even Lorraine who didn't know it was there.

"I used to think about you all the time. But I've almost gotten rid of it," she assured him. "Now it's only when I don't have anything better to do."

Richard decided to make a statement. "Shit," he said. "Why doesn't anybody ever just come out and say anything?"

"I've always been honest with you," she answered. He understood that for the time it took to speak the words, she believed them.

"I try to be honest with everybody," Lorraine said, "and when you think of how different everybody is, that's not easy."

They arrived. They found Austin sitting in the middle of a bright-patterned rug, near the door; he lifted two fingers, and moved them, as a greeting, in the sign of the cross. "Nobody!" someone shouted across the room. "Nobody, since Janis died! Shit on that noise." He was obviously flying, and somebody else reached out and pulled him down. A flashlight's beam shoved its way through the darkness. "Get a clip," a girl said in a spaced-out voice, "I don't want to be frantic, but somebody please get a clip . . . I don't want to burn to death . . ."

"Hi, Lorraine," Veronica said, giving her a wink. Lorraine smiled back politely. Veronica knelt down next to Austin. "Darling," she said, "we have a problem."

"Yes, angel?" Austin groaned. He looked close to passing out.

"We've run out of salt for the Margaritas."

"This is getting too domestic—all those dudes with hickies on their thumbs—"

A hand reached up from the shadows and offered Richard a joint. "Keep it, man."

"Thanks."

The room was a tangle of limbs in neutral, bodies spread like cushions. The music flaring from the speakers was the only thing to prevent them from dissolving completely: they clung like spiders on webs of sound. *"Stop! In the na-a-a-me of love; Bee-fore you break my heart . . ."* Richard moved along, joint in hand, nodding to fuzzily familiar faces as they rose and fell in the fog. He felt tremendous good-will. The roach had gone out, and absently he swallowed it. It echoed satisfyingly as it hit the bottom of his stomach. Somebody passed him another. "You *are* sweet," Richard said, kissing the lifted hand.

"Are you having a good time?" Lorraine asked, suddenly beside him.

"Wonderful."

Lorraine's mouth twisted down. A freak shoved a long chocolate stick between them. His eyes were so red in their sockets that they looked like he'd changed his mind halfway through gouging them out. Sweat glistened dewlike in his beard. "Do ya want this?" he asked. "I bought it for my buddy, but he's speeding, he can't take it . . . It's *ice cream,* man," he explained excitedly. "Vanilla ice cream with cherry sauce down the middle. They call it a cherry bomb—it's pretty far out . . ." He wandered away, the stick held out before him like a talisman.

"I'm not having such a good time," Lorraine said. "Do you want to go somewhere else?"

"Not yet."

"Please?"

"If you're so bored, why don't you go take Veronica up on it for once? She wouldn't mind."

"Maybe I'll do that," Lorraine said, and walked away.

Another voice called out to him: "Hey, man, I heard you were gone away . . ."

"Not me," Richard said. "I turned narc. I'm going to turn you all in."

He giggled. Everyone seemed to be standing about six inches off the ground. The rug undulated erotically. He wouldn't ever exhale again. He'd just get fuller and fuller of smoke until the night opened over his head and he floated away . . . a gweat big surfin' BIRD. . . . The red lights were softly attenuated to a sweet safe rose, pale and calm, and he felt himself wrapped up in its haze. The bathroom door was locked, he knocked, there was light from underneath. "Come in," Austin cooed.

"Shit," Richard said.

Somebody else giggled: a girl, sitting in the hallway, decked out in beads and feathers which only partly concealed the spread of her hips under her jeans. She was playing with a yo-yo; she gave him a considering look, licked her lips, and said, "Yo-yo."

"Nookie," Richard answered.

"Yo-yo," she repeated.

"Nookie."

"Yo-yo."

"Lord, what is this white trash?" Austin asked, emerging from the bathroom, reaching around behind to zip up his pants. They both ignored him.

"What's your name?"

"Amy. Yo-yo. I know yours."

Richard offered her his joint. "Thank you," she said, rolling her yo-yo up into her palm with a neat, precise thud.

"What's with all the Motown? Sixth grade," she said.

Richard shrugged. "Queers."

"There you are," Lorraine said, sounding harried. "Do you want to go yet?"

Amy passed the joint back to Richard, jerked her thumb at Lorraine, and asked, "Yo-yo?" in a puzzled voice.

"Nookie," Richard answered.

"Richard?" Lorraine said impatiently.

Richard looked up at her and giggled. "Yo-yo," he said.

"Oh, you're impossible!"

"She's pissed at you," Amy remarked, watching her go.

"Not really. Not so long as she could make an exit . . . Where's that joint?"

Through the sweet smoke he studied her face, and decided that she was sweet. She had no angles, she flowed smoothly. Her hair flowed smoothly around the roundness of her face. He felt a lifting which was not love, but close enough to let him feel loving. How nice pot was to you, he thought, promising you sex without danger. He reached out and flipped a playful finger across her nose.

"I like you," she said.

"I like you too." I guess. Why not? He didn't think he *dis*liked her, anyway.

She took the joint from his hand. "Then why don't you do something about it?"

"All right," Richard said. He uncoiled his many legs and glided down the hall. Low lights throbbed in one eye and out the other. He found Austin at the bar: Austin opened up the eyes in the back of his head. Richard soon guessed that he had actually turned around. "Can I help you?" Austin asked.

"Yeah. Do you have a room I can use?"

Austin laid a jeweled hand on Richard's shoulder. "Richard," he said. "I am going to give you some advice because I am your true friend and brother. More than you know. Don't do this to me."

"I'll let you watch," Richard said, thinking of Seastrom. Austin merged into Seastrom as he thought. He wouldn't mind if both of them watched.

"She's too fat." Austin sighed. "All right. If you must. Use my room." He turned back to his drink. "My mother didn't raise me to be a pimp," he said.

"What did she raise you to be?"

Austin smiled teasingly. "Promise not to tell," he answered, fingering the ornaments around his neck.

Richard went back, and found Amy trying to hypnotize herself with her yo-yo. She kept on losing control of the string. He held out his hand. They floated up the stairs.

"Turn out the lights," she said. "I'm shy."

In the morning Richard woke, and found himself staring into a writhing immensity of darkness. After a while he realized that the sheets on Austin's bed were black, and he was lying with his face buried in them. He rolled over and saw the heaped clothes, dirty in the light. His mouth heaved. Amy's hair cascaded over the pillow. Her mouth was open, her hand curling toward it as if to hold back an exclamation. Warmth found its way like water through the crevices of his headache. He touched a tentative finger to the breast poking out of the covers. He stroked her cheek, puffy with sleep like a child's.

Erica drifted into view, but he felt no threat from her. Even as memory stirred his senses until her body vied with Amy's for the attention of his mind's eye, and his hand would touch softness where it expected hard planes, and slopes instead of curves, he still felt a warm, sleepy daring, enough to challenge her—oh, to have done with ghosts and images, and go back to simple flesh. This time he could make it, he was sure. He could kill her at last. She was hung on the wall like a portrait; she was flat, lifeless, she had no substance. He stared at the portrait, and said to it aloud, "You see? You couldn't keep me after all."

"If you're going to talk to someone," Amy said, "why don't you talk to me?" She was up on one elbow, peering at him through the parting curtains of her sleep. "I'm the only one here," she said.

But she wasn't; she wasn't, and he had to look away.

CHAPTER TEN

Within a Grove of Buddies: 4

That morning, there had been a call for Lang from New York.

"What is that place," Billy said, "a shooting gallery? You're talking like a junkie again."

"Just tell me why you called." He was curt—it was the only way to keep control. The hard plastic curve of the telephone took on an intense, minute reality in his hand; by contrast, Billy's voice sounded unrecognizable, alien. A quick and lurid heaviness tilted like a tightrope in his belly, over the abyss between sleep and waking.

A little stiffly, Billy said that the A and R had called from the last company to hear the demo, and they were interested, they were expected to offer a deal in a few days.

"Well," Lang said vaguely, unable to concentrate, "They're good people there . . . We talked to them before. Good marketing . . . good distribution . . ."

"Yes, I know," Billy said patiently. "We've been talking about them for months."

"Well—uh . . ."

"You have to come back."

Fear gripped him like a steel brace, making everything cold. "I can't," he said.

"Lang, are you thinking of getting out for good?"

"No," Lang said, "I'm not. But I can't come back now."

The thought of going back to New York and being the young, ambitious artist—as if nothing had happened—sickened him. He felt like a laboratory animal hooked up to electrodes and made to feel nausea at the whim of an image.

Billy started to argue, and Lang told him, "Look. When they're ready to sign, and the time is set—call me then."

"You'll come back then."

"I'll think about it then. Goodbye, Billy."

"What was all that about?" Myra asked him. "You look like you just saw a ghost."

He didn't answer. He moved across the kitchen, shaking his head to sweep a stray strand of hair from his eyes, tapping his fist restlessly against his palm.

"There isn't any band without you," Billy had said. But there wasn't any of himself left either, not for them, not for that—he had used it all up. He had asked Alice, yesterday afternoon, if he could borrow her guitar, but he hadn't been able to do anything: he tried to play one of his old songs—one he had written when he first got to New York, all loose and kicking and overwhelmed by freedom, "Don't Talk To Me About Love"—but it disintegrated, beneath his hands, into random chords which fell away and scattered even as he played. He wondered if he had lost music for good. But he couldn't make himself care. He even considered that it might be for the best; it was too much luggage to carry around with him any more.

And yet he came back to it—walked into the living room now, where the guitar was propped against a closet door, and grimly picked it up again, to play until his fingers were numb from the pressure of the strings. He slapped at the guitar without rhythm or grace. He didn't know whether he was trying to salvage some shattered fragment from the wreckage, or taking pleasure in the wreckage itself. Either way, he was just making noise. But that, too, gave some satisfaction.

He was still playing when the phone rang again, and Myra called him back to the kitchen. "You're popular today," she said dourly, handing him the phone. "It's Lorraine."

"Lorraine?"

"Uh huh."

"Well, what do you know? And here I always thought she hated me." He took the phone from Myra's hand.

"Danny? Hi, Danny—welcome home . . ."

Lang rolled his eyes. "Yeah," he said. "What's goin' on, Lorraine?"

Well, she had heard that he was in town. Of course she was delighted that he had come back, and she couldn't wait to see him—since they had been such good friends, once. Why didn't he, in fact, come out to the dinner theater where she worked, this very afternoon, and they would go out for a drink? Wouldn't that be nice? Her voice went through the motions of gaiety and affection with an exquisitely calibrated sincerity. He couldn't help thinking that she was reading from a script. He couldn't remember ever hearing a single word from her that sounded even remotely human. But her dislike of him had been real enough—it dated from her first infatuation with Richard. Richard had been vaguely tempted (this was before Erica, naturally), but Lang had said to him, "Oh, man, turn queer, ball dogs, or do anything, but don't do that," and Brewer, in one of his more masochistic, therefore sadistic, moods that day, had repeated it to her. He couldn't guess why she wanted to see him now.

"Do you suppose that after all this time, she's just now decided that she's got to have a taste of the savage tool before she dies?" he said to Myra as he hung up the phone.

"The savage what? Oh, no. She couldn't. She's with Carmel now, remember?"

Myra gave him a ride out. The theater was nestled between the hills and the highway at the edge of town, near the diner where he had eaten with Carmel two days before. Its entrance was done up in fake Greek columns, with plastic masks of Comedy and Tragedy on either side of the door that vibrated when Lang touched them. Painted knives and forks were crossed beneath each mask; a bowing plaster statue displayed the dinner menu in one hand and the program for the after-dinner play in the other.

Inside, however, everything was spare and functional. The furniture was made of metal, and hidden lights gave the wall paneling a glassy sheen. Lang walked through a double door into the performance auditorium. They had just finished a rehearsal in there. Busboys were setting places at long tables around the small, bright-lit stage, where actors and technicians stood chatting in separate groups, surrounded by fragments of cheap scenery.

Lorraine was sitting at a table right under the stage, dressed in a pink satin flapper's dress with frilly lace at the knee. Her hair was pulled tightly up on her head, and bright spots of rouge decorated her cheeks. She was absently turning a long pink feather, attached to some kind of headdress, between her fingers. Lang pulled up a chair and sat down across from her, his long legs splayed out on the red linoleum floor.

"Hello, Lorraine," he said.

Her smile flashed, automatically, as she looked up. "Danny," she said in her best voice. "It's so good to see you."

"Oh, it's good to see you too," Lang said. "You look—you know, Lorraine, you just look more like you than you ever did before."

Whenever Lorraine was confused, she acted coy; she cocked her head to one side and peeked up at him. "Well, we all missed you, Danny, for sure," she said. "Where have you been all this time?"

"Around the corner, buying cigarettes."

"Oh," Lorraine said. "You're cute. I know we'll have a good time together this afternoon." She said this with the firmness of a general asking his men to volunteer for a kamikaze raid. "I want to take you to this wonderful new place called The Zone . . . It's a bar in the afternoon, and a disco at night. Austin told me about it."

"You don't go to Uncle Lou's any more."

Lorraine shook her head vigorously. "No. Never. It's too depressing. It's full of losers, and I'm sorry, Danny—" she raised her eyes, beneath their dark, full lashes, to look at Lang, and smiled again, regretfully—"but I just don't like to waste my time."

"Well, if you don't like losers, who's left to see?"

"Carmel, I guess." Lorraine had a trick of seeming to blush when she wasn't blushing at all. "I'm friends with some of the other actors here."

"Yeah," Lang said. Then he asked her the question she wanted to hear. "What're you doing in that outfit, anyway? Myra said you were an usherette."

"I was," Lorraine said, as if recalling an unnecessarily vicious episode from a previous life. "But the director—" she dimpled— "likes me, you know, and he gave me a little part in this show. We're doing *Cabaret*. He said the next part would be bigger."

"What did you do? Rent a casting couch?"

Lorraine debated whether or not to get angry. Then she laughed easily. "Oh, it's nothing like that," she said. "Everything's real modern here. But you ought to know what it's like. You're in show business, too." Then, with a look that was almost conspiratorial, she said an odd thing: "Carmel doesn't care about that kind of stuff much, anyway."

"Lucky for you . . . Lucky for him."

Lorraine began to look very distracted, and Lang knew he had irritated her. He hadn't meant to; but his mood was more sour than he'd thought, and it was almost a reflex action with Lorraine, any-way. Always had been. Amazing how fast you could slip back into old habits.

"We'd better go," she said. "I have to be back here by seven—for the performance. Just let me go scrub off some of my face."

She could of course have taken off her makeup before he arrived; but then she wouldn't have been able to advertise her status in full theatrical regalia when he walked in the door. He expected that she would keep him waiting. But she came back only a few minutes later, dressed in street clothes that managed to be at once more conventional and more garish than her stage costume.

Outside, as they walked to the car, he was able to study her more closely. He saw that she had not changed; she had only become more complete. The hard ambition in her face, present there only as one among many possibilities before, was now firmly and definitively set—as if all her decisions had been made, and she was only waiting for the right moment to realize them. She walked, he thought, as if her cunt were destiny itself on the move.

"The last time I ever went to Uncle Lou's," she said, picking her way across the asphalt in her high-heels as delicately as if she had been barefoot, "was the night Erica totalled herself, and it was pretty dull, believe me. No one could think of a thing to say." She laughed. "At least the bit with Erica livened things up, a little."

Lang tried to still the quick anger that flicked open in him at her words. He knew that Lorraine cared nothing at all about Erica, never had, and, anxious to prick him, had only picked up her name as a handy tool. Lorraine didn't matter, he told himself. It wasn't worth throwing away any anger on her. But already she had managed to shift his mood from sour to ugly, and that felt like paying cash he didn't have.

She noticed, of course. Her beauty forced her to have that much intelligence. "I'm sorry, Danny," she said, slipping on her shades as she started the car, "but I've got nothing to gain by being sad about it. I didn't like her, you know that, and anyway, what's past is past, isn't it?"

"Yeah. Except when it's not."

"You're just upset." The sunset drew a bone-white line down the calf of her leg—he wondered if she polished them. "I forgot she was a friend of yours. It's funny, Brewer acted the same way—and they never even knew each other, really. Ever since it happened, he hasn't called me, or come by. I don't think he likes me, these days."

"I can see how much that hurts."

"Well, it does. In a way. But it's probably better for him. I just wonder what I did to change him."

"You don't know it was you that did it."

"Who else would it have been?" Lorraine said, placidly. "Once, when he was out on pills, he said he needed me to save him. I couldn't do that—I wasn't even sure exactly what he meant, for one thing. I could have slept with him, but I don't know what else I could have done. He would just have held me back."

"Maybe he doesn't need that, any more."

"No. And he doesn't need me." Lorraine put on a tragic face, with compassionate overtones.

"You wouldn't have slept with him, anyway," Lang said.

Lorraine, behind her shades, glanced over at him.

"Probably not," she agreed, as they stopped for a red light. "I just always imagined it would be like sleeping with a corpse."

Lang smiled.

"For both of you," he told her.

The light turned green. Lorraine was angry. "I don't think that's very funny," she said.

"I'm sorry," Lang said, almost meaning it, because it wasn't Lorraine. It wasn't her at all. But there wasn't anyone else there.

"It bothers me when you're nasty to me," Lorraine said carefully; her mood had changed, as if she had suddenly remembered her lessons. "And even when we were in high school, you always were so mean. Because I think we could be friends."

There might be a place, Carmel had said. Lang still didn't know what it might be, but he was beginning to realize that it was going to be somewhere in Carmel's version of Icarus, not his own. What a burial that would be. But he might have no place in New York either. Perhaps the real oblivion was to remain always here, suspended between two lives.

"You said on the phone that we *were* friends," Lang reminded her.

Lorraine shrugged. "People can say anything on the phone. But I really think we should try."

They were on the main street of town. A frieze of supermarkets, drugstores, gas stations and fast-food joints flowed past. Lang saw the sign outside Uncle Lou's, neon looking dead in daylight, from the corner of his eye.

"Oh, Lorraine," he answered almost without thinking. "Why

do we have to call everything by a name?"

She leaned toward him, imperceptibly, sniffing a confession. Lorraine knew all about confessions. But Lang caught himself again: he saw her game exactly. She was Carmel's girl, so she wanted to turn herself into a little Carmel, with only the vaguest notion of the stakes involved. She had her notions of glory, too.

"You're pretty ambitious," he said to her.

Lorraine smiled, gracefully. "Well, you know I am."

"That's not what I meant."

She tensed a little, but not much. "I'm no different from anybody else," she said.

"What I meant was, would you have so much as gone near Carmel if he wasn't the biggest dealer in the territory?"

Lorraine didn't say a word. Hunching forward, she nosed the car through the traffic, slowing down until she found a place to pull over. Her face was white and hard and absolutely empty of emotion. "Well, Danny," she said in a tight voice, "why don't you just walk home? It's not that far."

Lang grinned at her. "Are you throwing me out, Lorraine?"

"Yes. Get out. I don't care what he does to me. I just don't want you in my car."

"But what about that drink? You promised me a drink . . ."

"Get out," she repeated, with considerably less assurance in her voice.

"Okay."

She was silent as he opened the door.

"I'll see you around, Lorraine."

She still didn't say anything. He watched her car pull away. It was painted a gay and incongruous purple, with a white roof that bobbed in the traffic like a whitecap. Over him, the gray sky, heavy with purpose, moved threateningly above the roofs of the buildings. Dead leaves, blown by the wind, tumbled down the gutters as if pulled along by the backwash of the traffic.

Lang zipped up his leather jacket and stuck his hands deep in its pockets. He didn't want to go home just yet. There was a McDonald's around the corner, and he headed for it. He wanted to sit by a window, and watch the twilight and the passing cars.

At the bright counter he ordered a cup of coffee from a girl whose hair was damp beneath her paper hat and whose acne appeared to have congealed into armor, glowing fiercely under the tinsel-colored lights from the food racks. "I don't suppose you'd be interested in our special Picture Pitcher mug for twenty-five cents extra," she said.

"Ah . . . Who's on it this week?"

"Ulysses S. Grant."

"No—I don't think so. Not today anyway."

"You don't look like the type." The girl seemed full of a nameless disgust. "Jesus Christ," she muttered. "They won't even let us have the radio on in here."

Lang sat down at a table far from the door. Sloppy in his leather and scuffed boots, he must have looked a sight; the scrub-faced young teenagers in their painters' pants and touch-tone wristwatches gave him a wide berth as they went by, chattering with each other. From snatches of their conversation Lang gathered that they were returning from a game. They irritated him—they were too clean. Too many things irritated him too easily these days. He had an impulse to jump up, pour his coffee down the nearest girl's middy blouse, defecate on the floor, howl and scratch his armpit, anything to violate their smooth, effortless sterility. When he was in high school, he used to point out some particularly slick or glib-talking straight kid and remark that he would make a fine ad executive someday; but these fourteen, fifteen, sixteen-year-old kids were beyond even that—they looked more like they had grown up believing the ads. Lang couldn't imagine them caring about anything. Their sex, if they even bothered with it, would be as heatless as the nibble of an electric plug in a rubber socket.

But it wasn't so funny as all that. He felt like a soldier on a long march, who no longer thinks of the battles ahead, but instead is driven near-insane by the weight of the rifle on his back. What was it Lorraine had said? "I just imagine it would be like sleeping with a corpse." Lorraine could say that; Lorraine could survive in this atmosphere, she was made for it. How impatient she had always been with everyone else's nostalgia for meaning. No wonder she had wound up with Carmel instead of Richard—poor baffled Richard, who had started out caring about things because it was hip to care, and got so hurt when he found out that the fashion had shifted beneath his feet and people wouldn't adore you forever on the strength of fine sentiments and lofty intentions. And poor Brewer too—why not, as long as he was thinking about her? Brewer had wanted Lorraine so much, believing that her corruption would bring him to life, lift him from the lockstep revolutions of his eternally self-doubting head; but like all sentimental people, she was cruel when it came to sex . . .

There had been a night in Suffragette City; they had been sitting at the edge of the dance floor, watching Richard and Lorraine do the Hustle together. Brewer, abruptly, turned to him out of a silence, and said, *"Maybe I'm queer. Maybe I just want to fool around with little boys. Maybe that's the answer—that I just want to drown in it . . ."* and, laughing, giddy with the potency of unexpected self-revelation, had been about to go on, to go into God-knows-what kind of details, when Lang held up his hand and said, "You won't want me to remember this." He didn't know if he had done Brewer a favor, or only stopped him out of cowardice—who could say at what intersection of a life the exits were jammed, and decay began to set in? Not him, for sure; certainly not him.

Suddenly he felt naked. Even the casual glances of a passing teenage stranger were too much to bear. You couldn't maintain yourself with people constantly. Let these blank-faced kids look down at the dead man for a while. Let Lorraine. She had bitten deeper than he realized. Hunching his shoulders, he threw away his cup and walked quickly out the door.

When he arrived, back home, Alice was sitting by herself in the living room. The afternoon light, soft and luminous as a faded painting, made her face—that hard hooker's face Lang had seen in her yearbook photograph—look patient and old, careworn like a pioneer woman's. But when she turned to see who was there, there was something askew in her rhythm—something liquid and somnambulistic, as if her eyes obeyed a different law of motion that the rest of her head—and he realized that she was out on some kind of pill.

"Plant yourself," she said to him.

"I don't have a shovel."

"I mean sit down. People make me nervous on their feet."

Lang sat down. He didn't want to. He was frayed and worn, and he would much rather have been allowed to go down to the couch, to lie on it like a ship on the sea and let his sleepless thoughts float on the rhythm of the waves. But the atmosphere of the room had a deadweight pull—he didn't have the energy to leave.

"Mommy had to go get Daddy," Alice said. "He called her up from the Greyhound terminal in the city—he told her he'd decided to go back home to his parents. In Minnesota. They've both been dead for years. He was really wrecked, she said—even for him, he was wrecked."

"Why'd he call her at all? He blew his getaway."

Alice snickered. "He wanted her to come and tell him what time the bus left," she said, "because he couldn't read the schedule, and he felt too shy to ask a stranger. I mean he explained it all very reasonably. It just didn't make sense."

"So Myra went to collect him, huh?"

"Yeah. He's pulled this before—two or three times. I can't understand it. Minnesota sounds pretty boring, don't you think?"

She stretched out her plump legs to the floor, very slowly, as if she were underwater.

"Why do you look so bad, Lang?" she asked. "You look like you don't know whether you want to piss or throw up."

A memory stirred awake in him, of something Carmel had mentioned, the night he arrived—it seemed incredible that it had been only four days ago.

"Alice, why'd you quit doing acid?" he asked.

She laughed. "You mean why did I quit being a flower child? Maybe I just got bored."

"There's more to it than that."

"Oh, look," Alice said, "I was somebody else thirty seconds ago. Don't bother me."

There was a pause.

"I'll tell you," she said, "if you want to know. It's like—when you're tripping, you see all those pretty pictures, and they're really pretty pictures, you know? Then you wake up. Crash. It's gone. I didn't get tired of having it. I got tired of losing it."

She lay back on the couch, he would have said relaxed but for the dark alertness gleaming feline in her eye. Her chin was pressed against the plump flesh of her jaw by the angle of her head against the couch; her hand lay casually on her breast, fingers spread, miming piety. They looked at each other across the empty space.

"Carmel gave me a tab once," she went on, "and I put a cigarette on my arm. It burned all the way down. You can still see the mark, there." She pushed back her sleeve, and the bracelets on her wrist jangled brassily in the quiet. "That's something I can keep," she said. "So I used to be fucked-up and nice, and now I'm fucked-up and mean, and I'll tell you, I like it lots better this way. Does that bother you, Lang?" It was mocking enough, but there was a very different question in her face, one he recognized but didn't have time to catch hold of before her eyes grew veiled again.

"Not a bit," Lang said. "Why should it?"

"I thought you were asking 'cause you thought I was really messed up, and it . . . offended you."

"You're just an amateur. You're too young to be anything else."

"I'm not so young," she said. "I've been through a lot, since
you left."

"Sure you have."

"No, I mean it . . . Carmel promised me that the next time he
got some smack, he'd let me have a taste—I can handle that now. I
don't care what happens."

She had never seemed more like an adolescent. Yet he could not
dismiss her words, because in Icarus people usually did what they said
they would do. To think anything else was to be like one of those
cheerful people who greet threats of suicide with the capsule phrase
that those who talk about it never do it, only to wake up one morning to a smashed corpse outside the window and sirens howling on
the street. Erica, it was true, had never talked about it, but she hadn't
needed to; it was written on her face, carved in the air by every move
of her haunted, thin, feverish body, as if the fever had come from the
center of her and it was only a matter of time until the message
reached her skin. So Lang did not doubt Alice for a moment. He
only wondered why she was trying to impress him now—she didn't
need to prove a thing to him, after all.

"Did you ever do smack?" she asked.

"Yeah, for a while."

"Honest?"

"Yeah."

"Then you're not any different from me."

"Okay, I'm not." Lang took a breath. "Everybody thinks they
can talk to me," he thought irritably.

"I bet that's pretty easy to get into in New York," Alice said.
"Lots of kinky people there."

She was so incurably divided: half of her was a canny little princess on her own turf, ready to mock every outsider—and locked away
inside was a gaping girl who really wanted to know, who was ready to
clutch at any clue Lang could give her. Her face was smooth and impassive, but within its shadows her eyes were living brief lives and going off on private little explorations all their own.

"Yeah," Lang said. "It sure is dull coming home, after all that."

She ignored him. "Didn't you ever hang out with the kinky
people in New York, Lang?" she asked.

"Oh, sure. What kind do you want?"

"Did you do lots of drugs?"

"Lots."

Her expression grew crafty. "What about sex? Did you ever

get into the kinky sex, Lang?"

Lang made a point of smiling. "Why? Is that another one of the things you want to do?"

"No," she said unexpectedly. "That's another one of the things I do."

There was tension between them now.

"Just a little bit," Alice said casually. Her expression was anything but casual. "I never got into anything fancy. I just like to get tied up and slapped around and stuff. So I guess I'm an amateur at that too."

Suddenly she grinned. It made her look like a wicked child. "Mommy doesn't know," she said.

"Oh, Jesus, Alice," Lang said. "Why do you need it? You don't need it."

He was tired of her; he was tired of teasing. Now they were really like kids, he thought.

"I do, though. I mean, why not? It makes me feel like I'm not responsible for anything. Isn't that what everybody wants?"

"Maybe they shouldn't."

"Maybe they shouldn't, but they do—don't they?"

"I don't."

But he did. How far he had deteriorated, that this childish dirt could put him into such a fever. But the fever was there.

"Why, Danny?" she said. "Are you scared?"

"No."

"You never even wanted to try it?"

"No."

"I'll bet you're scared. I can tell."

The worst of it was that she was right. He was trapped by dread, dread and a high, keening excitement—but what riveted him there was anger that she should have brought this to him at all.

"Oh, Jesus Christ," Lang said. "I don't have time for this."

She stood up. In one fluid motion she undid her belt and slipped it out of the loops of her jeans. Looking up at him, she held out the belt, spread flat across her palms.

"Come on," she said. "Don't you think you have it in you to hurt me just a little bit?"

"I've never done that," Lang said. "I'm not going to start now."

"You see? You *are* scared . . ."

"Not of you."

She came closer to him, the belt still held between her hands, her sweet, amoral baby-hooker's face expressionless and teasing and utterly calm as it hovered over him.

"Are you afraid to hit me? You want to, you know that. I can see it in your face."

"That's not good enough."

"Keep on asking why," she said, "don't you know that doesn't have anything to do with it . . . Come on, Danny. It's all the same."

The air between them was as sharp as a blade.

Into the silence came a cry from the phone. Alice looked at Lang coolly, without moving. It rang a second time. Then again.

"Answer it," Lang said.

The phone rang a fourth time. Alice went into the kitchen. She cast a scornful, flirting look at him as she passed.

"Hello," she said. "Oh, it's you. What's going on? . . . Yes, I'm just about out of them, but I don't think I want to try any more of that stuff. It doesn't do a thing for me . . ."

As she spoke, Lang looked around the blank walls of the room. He was in a sweat. "If you do this," said a voice in his head, "then it's over. It's really over. No Johanna, no New York —none of it left . . ."

. . . His second month in New York, it had been, when he'd gone uptown and met the man, in a topless bar on 49th Street. They had taken a cab to an apartment on the Upper West Side. The black man's fingers were soft, almost motherly, as he rolled up Lang's sleeve and began to hunt for a vein. His blood spiraled upward in the tube, swaying like a most delicate cobra, and then it bloomed and the man pushed the plunger home.

The water from the fire hydrant caught the reflection of the streetlight on the edge of the alley, and its flow became a stream of silver as he watched.

Alice was still talking on the phone: ". . . Don't you have anything new and exciting? I need a little excitement in my life, you know . . ." She laughed, gaily. "Oh, that sounds good. Only how much? I can't afford too much. Yeah? I think I can swing, oh, twelve—at the end of the week. Tell Mink to come by then . . ."

When she hung up, Lang was standing behind her. He grabbed her shoulder and turned her around.

"What are you—"

For a second her eyes were as full of fear as a young forest animal's.

Then the fear dissolved. He pulled her back into the living room, his face set, and pushed her down on the couch.

"Oh," she said, "you know."

Lang stood by the couch, looking down at her.

"Come on, then," Alice said. "Come on! Oh, that's it," she said, beginning to laugh. "That's the way. You're getting it—you've got it now. You're going to figure it all out, you'll see—it's all right. Oh, you were just pretending before—you know what to do, all right!"

CHAPTER ELEVEN

Odell: 2

What can a poor boy do . . .? Solitude had lost its poetry after the first few nights. Odell's midnight rambles became only another grim device to force the hours to pass, and he would have liked to smash his fist against the car windshield in frustration, but he was afraid that it would crack the silence that he hated so much. Obstinately, his neuroses refused to resolve themselves into madness—like tenants not paying the rent . . . No one would be out at this hour. They had all retired into some velvet bower of imagined sex, getting laid behind the curtains of the night, while only Odell was escaped alone to tell them . . . tell them what? He prowled on outside the close warm circle of their heat.

They were all liars, and Erica was the biggest liar of them all. He didn't think so often, now, of the small lies she used to stitch her days together, the lies that were only social; the flint that scraped to spark his hate was the last, largest lie, the false promise of her body that she would one day belong to him. Beauty creates its own debts, without knowing it creates them, or that they even exist; but it would have been far beyond his ego's powers of recuperation to even think of admitting that he was wrong, that he was not, after all, the chosen and anointed one, who lived closest to her secret breath, who could capture the castle of her soul. He could not accept her innocence: no. No way. She must have done it on purpose, she must have known all along.

All he had ever wanted was for her to see him as he saw himself, only leaving out the bad parts.

He was getting spooked. The racking sobs of the streetlights skewed into a long moan. Loneliness hugged fear for company while the empty road spoke awful menaces to his turning heart. Beasts made of paper and glass rose up around him, hanging with hot breath over the back seat, squatting primitive on the radio's green and glowing dial . . . Odell's brakes screamed as he skidded to the shoulder of the road. The hitchhiker backed away a couple of steps before recovering and advancing toward the door which Odell flung open.

"Jesus, am I glad to see you," Odell said, briefly forgetting his cool in the simple and unheroic relief of finding a living thing.

The hitchhiker hooked an eyebrow at Odell from under a wan flow of blond hair. "Hmp," he said, not committing himself.

"Where can I take you, man?"

Go with the *zeitgeist.* He always went with the *zeitgeist,* when he could find one. The hitchhiker was going to a house on the far side of town. When Odell said, "Fine," he showed no surprise; he nodded, and sucked in one cheek, thoughtfully. Odell was mystified.

"Why are you wearing sunglasses after dark?" the hitchhiker asked.

"Am I?" Odell reached up nervously and knocked them into his lap, then, remembering he was blind without them, hastily fumbled them back on again. "There's just been too many heavy things going on today," he declared, with aggressive joviality.

The hitchhiker didn't rise to the bait. He said nothing. Odell grew panicky at the prospect of simply driving him home, without extracting anything dramatic or significant from the encounter. "You live alone?" he asked.

The hitchhiker turned and studied him.

"No, it's just curiosity," Odell explained quickly.

"Oh. No. I live with my band."

"You got a band?" Odell asked, perking up.

"Yeah. Been together for a while now. I play lead guitar."

"What type a stuff do ya play?"

"Stones, mostly."

"Yeah," Odell said. "I like the Stones." This was even better than he'd bargained for.

"That's the real music. That's music that says something to you." The guitar player nodded, profoundly.

"What do you like best?"

"Dunno. It's all great. Like most people are really into the Middle Period. *Aftermath* through *Sticky Fingers,* say. Okay, that's the Stones. Leaving out *Satanic Majesties.*"

"It's like *Troilus and Cressida,*" Odell agreed. "No one knows where to put it."

The guitar player hesitated. But his obsession got the better of his doubt, and he moved on. "A lot of people are very down on the Later Period. But *Exile on Main Street,* that's a heavy album. You can't deny that it's a very heavy album."

"I like it."

"It makes a statement. That's what the Stones do best. Make statements. But lately I've been going back to the roots. The Oldham era. Pre-*High Tides.* Blues. That Chuck Berry riff. Lot more in that than most people think."

"The Stones are very important to me," Odell said. "Did you know that 'Sympathy for the Devil' is based on Nietzsche's concept of the eternal recurrence?"

"Nietzsche," the guitar player said. "Jagger quotes Nietzsche. In *Performance.*"

"You know Nietzsche?"

"Not personally. I was told he's dead. I had this friend who was into him. 'Nothing is true, everything is permitted.' I dug that. That could be a lyric." He was silent for a moment. "Listen," he said. "Come on in the house with me. I got a tape of the last time they played here—you see that gig?"

"Ah—no. I had a ticket, but I was too strung out to go—I had been given some bad acid . . ." Actually, he hadn't wanted to go. His embrace of the Stones' mystery had always taken place behind closed psychic doors; the thought of seeing them stark and real, mere objects, his own spirit lost far back in row on row of screaming, swaying anonymity, had infused him with a strange, light fear. He could be closer to their essence, he thought, if he kept them inside.

"I saw them," the guitar player said. "Every time. Since '66. I was only a kid, but I said, yeah. That Keith Richard. With his shark tooth earring. Bill Wyman chewing gum. It hasn't been the same since Brian went in the pool."

"Yeah, Brian."

"Brian was great. It didn't matter what he did so much, he was great."

"Of all of them," Odell said, "he was the one who really took the image to its extreme. Committing suicide is the ultimate Stones song. The culmination of the ethic."

"I said: he was great."

He would have to be careful. He had to learn a new language. He couldn't help it if his thoughts were more complex than most people's.

"You got to feel the Stones," the guitar player explained. "You can't think them."

"But you have to think to understand."

The guitar player shrugged with his mouth, and looked away.

"We got a new chick singer," he said. "She's not into the Stones. Doesn't understand it. Says we gotta do something new. The bass player brought her in. He's hung up on her. But none of us can sing—like Jagger says, it's not what you want, it's what you need."

Mate.

He had gone through all his searching to come back to her. His need would not be extinguished until he had seen her, tasted her with his eyes. Now, silent, pinned prisoner to his seat—the guitar player silent too, and not asking the silence any questions—he would, he was on his way to her. The red eye of a stereo shot ruby into Odell's eye through a window, as they walked up to the house.

"Shit," the boy who opened the door said. "I thought you were Mink."

"No," the guitar player said.

"Fucking Carmel. Mink was supposed to make a delivery day before yesterday." He jerked the door open violently. "We got nothing but nigger beer," he muttered, turning away.

"That's the drummer," the guitar player said helpfully.

"Oh," Odell said. He was looking past the stereo now, past the jutting amplifiers, the wires and headphones hooked over mike stands, the stacked instruments, the two bearded shapes who stood in the shadows, as if his eye were traveling down a gallery painted with portraits of his ancestors, all the way to the end of the room where a slice of light fell from an open door and a girl sat in an armchair, waiting for him.

"Hello," she said. "You're not supposed to be here."

"I know," Odell said. "That's why I am."

Erica stretched out her legs, crossed at the ankles, and flung her hands wide before bringing them back to lie clasped between her breasts. She was already enjoying the joke.

"Well," she said lazily. "How's tricks?"

THREE

CHAPTER TWELVE

Richard: 4

Amy was already in bed when Richard got home from the party. The light was still burning, and she had left a note, saying how she had waited up for him, which he didn't bother to read to the end. She lay flat on her back, gorged, ripe with sleep. Richard propped an ashtray in his lap and reached for a cigarette. He liked to watch the smoke turn blue as it passed through the lamplight. Some ash fell onto Amy's bare thigh, and he brushed it away with nervous haste. She stirred, but didn't wake.

They had been together for a month. Still he kept her separate from the rest of his life, partly out of shame and partly because asking her to share it would make him share more of himself than he wanted to. Once she had insisted on going to Uncle Lou's, and Brewer had been there with Lorraine. When they saw Amy, Richard felt as if he'd been caught masturbating. After that he was more careful. If they had any social life at all, it was with her friends, not his. Since they were her friends, they could hardly put him down for hanging out with her, he thought; his own indifference was close enough to their bemused apathy that they had no trouble accepting him. Among them, he felt like a king, traveling incognito.

With them, with her, he had no past. She didn't even know who Erica was—sometimes he repeated that to himself with wonder, she didn't know who Erica was. He hardly did himself, anymore; Erica had become a mnemonic button to punch whenever he wished to make his mood melancholy, as if she were a song he played. Still, she was closer to Richard than the girl beside him. Even in their love-making, when he would try like a wizard to sink the blades of his loneliness into Amy's flesh, she took the act for its own sake without asking questions. She accepted everything; that was why he couldn't bring himself to accept her entirely.

That afternoon, in a spasm of irritation, he had asked her: "Why do you like me, anyway?"

She looked puzzled. "I like you, that's all. I never bothered to figure out why. Why do you like me?"

He hadn't been able to answer, and realizing that he wasn't able to answer only worsened his mood. When they had begun together, he had been looking for an escape from his world. But now he condemned her for being so utterly ignorant of it, for flirting at its edges without noticing or caring. If just once she had shown a sign of anguish, he would have felt at home; but she never did.

She left the room, and for an hour he pored aimlessly over his notes for the Rock N Roll Theater. They were a chaos of fragments, scraps in a void, pointless and stale. Now he turned to them mostly as a pretext for avoiding Amy. She could be a pestering little bitch when it came to love, but the concept of creativity filled her with awe.

She came back, and nestled against him, and murmured "Yo-yo?" in his ear. It was a prelude to sex: the nonsense syllables by which they had come to know each other had evolved into the private language of their affair. He had never let it bother him earlier; after all, it was no sillier than some other codes he had known, with Erica, and before. Now, with the thought that not only the terms but the substance of their relationship could be reduced to that vacuous mumble, he felt a diluted but definite anger. Quickly, he tried to stiffen the anger into rage, but it wouldn't come. He rose from his chair instead, and slid into Amy's arms. What a way, he thought, what a way to spend your time. . . . When he gave in at last, it was with a rare force which delighted her, for she thought it was love and not dread that fired his desire.

He couldn't ever get as angry as he wanted to with Amy. The softness that surrounded her, so thick that at times it had more substance than her body, held him—he could never get clear. His times

with Amy melted into one another; no landmarks stood to separate
the crawling hours. Each time he left her he had to invent himself all
over again, and wipe himself clean of her clinging. These days his life
was running on double tracks, hot and cold, soft and sharp, as he
shunted back and forth between Amy and Carmel.

Certain moments and scenes at Seastroms' now lived in his memory almost before they lived in his mind, like the hallucinatory seconds
fractured by the flashing of a strobe light. In the center of it all, Carmel sat enthroned. He had pulled off one of the most difficult ma-
neuvers of his career. Mrs. Seastrom liked him now.

It had begun one night when she and her husband were having
an argument, an argument that progressed not so much by words as
by a series of brittle silences. Carmel had wandered into that loaded
atmosphere, sing-songing a snatch of something by Bowie; Mrs. Seastrom shifted irritably in her seat and asked, "What is that music that
you like so much? I hear it all the time through the floor."

"You hear it," Carmel answered, "but you probably never listened to it. Why don't you come on down, and I'll play some for you?"

Mrs. Seastrom shook her head; but some tremor in her refusal
must have clued Carmel that here was a crack to be mined, for he repeated the invitation several times in the next few days. "You don't
know what you're missing," he'd say. Finally, one night, she stood up
from the living-room couch, and said, "Oh, for Lord's sake, since you
insist so much," with broadly exaggerated good humor. Carmel bowed
her on her way and she went tripping down the stairs like a bride.

An hour later, when Regina came to the door of Carmel's room
to tell him that a client was on the phone, she was still there, sitting
on Carmel's bed. Carmel was in the middle of a performance:

". . . Cause his *ass* is so sore, you see," he exclaimed, throwing
his knees wide to do a duckwalk. "Why once, once! we were in a bar
in the city, and Austin had picked up on a dude. He came back to
our table and just stood there, a-mincin' and a-grinnin'—swallow a
canary! He probably had. Somebody said why don't ya sit down,
and he strokes his tush—" Carmel's hand caressed the air above his
buttocks—" and says, *Honey,* I'm too sore. So Erica gave him a Tam-
pax out of her purse and told him, Try this on for size."

Mrs. Seastrom bent forward to laugh, her gold hair catching the
light as it fell, her eyes moist and alive. "Oh, that's awful, awful!
What did he say?"

"Oh!" Carmel cried out. Although his body and voice were completely submerged into the act, he was measuring her by glances,

gauging her reactions as coolly as an agent in the back row. "He was shocked, of course," Carmel said. "Poor taste."

"Well, it is."

"But that's the whole point, woman! . . . Do you want to hear some more music?"

"Why not?"

"That's my girl." Carmel browsed abstractedly through the record rack, a finger to his lips. He was murmuring softly to himself. "Did you want something, Regina?" he asked suddenly, without looking up.

"It can wait," Regina said. Going up the stairs, she caught a glimpse of her father sitting in the living room. Carmel's and Mrs. Seastrom's voices were clearly audible, then they were drowned by music. "That was the funny part," Regina told Richard the next day. "Daddy looked like if anybody had swallowed a canary, it was him."

Richard, sitting in bed, smoke circling around him on its invisible axis, thought that would do for the beginning. It was no less real to him for not having witnessed it. His imagination could fill in the gaps; there in peace, he could tease the scene to leisurely horror. Lit matches, as he dropped them into the ashtray, set the crushed butts back on fire, and made a smoldering little blaze inside the circle.

With the precision of a composer bringing new instruments into play, with the confidence of a general committing fresh troops to battle, Carmel moved to consolidate his opening. A week after Mrs. Seastrom first went down to his room, he began to invite people over to the house: his clients and their hangers-on, camp followers and loyal citizens of Icarus. He started infiltrating them on a small scale, and gradually stepped up the operation until on a weekend night you could find a dozen people there, out on the porch, in the living room, in the kitchen, in Carmel's headquarters downstairs, where he gave out free samples and played music that penetrated into every nerve of the house.

At first Mrs. Seastrom was very reserved around Carmel's friends, but he soon guided her to find them interesting. It became not at all strange to see her deep in conversation with a couple of freaks in tank-tops, hair, and heavy boots, her socialite's patter intertwining with their snuffling, twitching grins, her cocktail gestures coupling with their swaying hips and shuffling feet. There was an utter sham in her acting the ingenue this way, but she was so oblivious to its being sham that you couldn't really hold her responsible.

Carmel, conscious of the effect he had created, conscious of everything, made a speech on the porch one night: "See what we've done to your beautiful house? We've turned it into a den of vice and depravity. . . . Any true-blooded American would take a knife to these degenerates!"

"That's right," Mrs. Seastrom said cheerfully, "you're corrupting us."

"I'm trying to. Give me time."

"Ask me for anything but time," Seastrom murmured from his chair. "Napoleon," he explained, to Richard's questioning look.

They were Carmel's army; but Carmel, Richard noticed, was not particularly intimate with any of them. Once things were set in motion for the night, he would usually retire to the porch and observe Mrs. Seastrom's promenades among them, ams folded, enigmatic and watchful.

"You're not being very nice to your friends," Richard said to him one night.

"Don't call them that," Carmel said, with an amused grimace.

"You don't like them."

"Not much." Carmel shook his head. "To tell you the truth, freaks bore me. Green smoke is the only character they've got."

"But the only reason they come here is you."

"Yeah. What I think isn't important. What other people think, now, that might be important." He gave a wry smile. "Look on it as a marriage of convenience," he said, and walked away.

Richard turned, and saw Mrs. Seastrom chatting with a diabolically bearded dude who stroked his chin in time to the movements of her mouth. Behind them, just below the level of their waists, Seastrom was watching from his chair, with a look of calm pleasure on his face. Richard knew it was the same look that Regina must have seen, the night Carmel first played his music for Seastrom's wife.

Seastrom treated the whole scene with the same urbane courtesy he employed for every social occasion. He adjusted so effortlessly to the new order that it seemed like no adjustment at all. Yet there was a curious slyness at the heart of his acceptance. Another moment, juxtaposed with the first in Richard's mental cinema: he was talking with Seastrom in the kitchen when she came in, wearing a pair of high-waisted black bellbottoms and a ruffled shirt with a silkscreen eye in the center of its back. "Don't I look new?" she asked, with a gaiety that became forced only as she took stock of their reaction. The clothes looked strangely false, but Richard didn't know why until she turned: then he realized that they were Carmel's. They fit surprisingly well.

"I got tired of looking so much like myself all the time," she said, "so Carmel offered these to me . . ."

Seastrom's eyes twinkled. "Oh," he said, "I thought maybe you'd just gotten them mixed up—when one's in a hurry, you know?" He winked at Richard with a complicity that Richard didn't want.

"There wasn't any need for you to say that," she told him. "Even as a joke."

"Darling, if we only said what needed to be said, there'd be an awful lot of dull silence in the world, wouldn't there? I didn't," he added with a wave of the hand, "mean to offend."

Mrs. Seastrom turned to Richard. "How do *you* think I look?" she challenged him.

Richard cleared his throat. "Nice."

The images shuttled in and out like trains in his brain; Erica would slip in as easily as if she had always belonged there. Even when he was with Amy now, he couldn't shut them off completely. They broke in on every interlude, jarring even that mindless momentary physical relief, the only gift from Amy that he could accept.

In his dissatisfaction he would tell himself, with a conviction that grew more firm with each new telling, that what he really wanted most of all was to find one person who hadn't been damaged yet, for whom sex was more than just the small change by which you paid your way, with whom love would be something other than torture and yet remain interesting. He wanted it pure, he thought; an angel to come down and lift him on her wings, and a cherry bomb to eat.

Richard started a new cigarette, and looked down at Amy, sunk in the rich warm immobility of her slumber. He couldn't imagine what she might find to dream about. She could never be his angel; if he had explained it to her, she probably would have done her best, but she simply did not look the part. Until tonight, she had been no more than a useful substitute; now, after what had happened at the dealers' party, he no longer had any desire to allow her even that much.

Carmel had greeted him late that afternoon outside the A.B.C. store, paper bags full of bottles under both arms. "Hey," Carmel said. "I was going to call you. Come over to the mansion tonight."

"I was probably going over anyway."

"I know, but I wanted to be sure. I'm not going to tell you what's going down, but you have to be there—you're going to observe. You want to play artist, I'll give you the chance. Make it around eight," he called over his shoulder, loading the bottles into Seastrom's car.

Richard went over to Brewer's for dinner. Brewer made a few perfunctory jokes about Amy, but for the most part he was despondent, as if Richard's visit only served to deepen his solitude. He only perked up a bit when Richard mentioned that he was going over to Seastroms'. Brewer grinned: "You know," he said, "Carmel is getting a lot of publicity off that show. Everybody at Uncle Lou's talks about it. The other night, Odell said that if Carmel had been in Germany he would have run a concentration camp—Alice Hoffentlich was there, and she said no, there's no profit in that: Carmel would have been president of the company that manufactured the gas . . ." Brewer laughed. "Don't you think that's pretty good?"

When Richard arrived at the house, the driveway was blocked with cars he didn't recognize. Carmel stood on the porch, one hand braced against the rail, the other hooked into his belt, looking like a young duke surveying his estates. He wore a purple velvet jacket over a flowing shirt, a rainbow of stripes and scrolls, translucent and shining. His belt had an oval mirror for its buckle; the false eye mounted on his ring clicked against the rim of the mirror, gleaming long and short in the sunset, flashing a message in code. Some aura of old-world elegance transmuted came off his clothes—and then was cut off by the clean American line of his jaw above the purple collar, the rectitude in the part of his blonde hair. He was dazzling.

"You're dressed to kill," Richard said.

"It's a night for killing." Carmel took Richard's arm in a proprietary way. "Still wondering what it's about?"

"Well, yes," Richard admitted.

"Every dealer in the territory is downstairs. We're having a party—a meeting of the inner circle."

"What's the occasion?"

"No occasion. We get together once in a while, just the dudes and their current lady friends. Tomorrow we'll be back in business and trying to cut each other's throats, but that's tomorrow. . . . You'll have to be careful. You're the only outsider, and some of them might get tense."

"I'll hide my face," Richard promised. He followed Carmel down the stairs. Anticipation tightened his chest as Carmel opened the door.

In the front room, all the old clutter had been pushed out of the way and heaped in the corners, covered with draped cloth. The lights were low, filtering through heavy smoke; the music coursed steadily, softly through the air. The dealers were arranged in small groups around

the room, dressed in the midnight finery they could never wear at
their work. The girls scattered among them wore uniform looks of
half-lidded disdain. Elegant arms passed pipes with careless grace.
There were carved meerschaums from Turkey, and hookahs, and intricate Bongs like coiled snakes of clear plastic. On a table was a gal-
lon bottle of red wine bucketed in ice, a bowl filled with loose pot,
and a small brass tray of E-Z rolling papers.

Here were the new aristocrats, the subterranean nobility of
Icarus. But if the setting was for pleasure, and if the girls were spread
around the room like bored flowers, the lords and dukes of this new
order showed no signs of letting go. They were professionals; their
voices were low and careful as they discussed their business among
themselves, filled with the quiet confidence of shared superiority.
There was none of the blurred, giddy confusion that marked the
usual Icarus party—it was the difference between the raucous floor
of a political convention and the quiet room where the decisions were
made, and Richard realized just how deep Carmel's contempt must
have been for the people he had been inviting to the house. They
were the greasy, grubby proletariat of this society, tolerated only because they were the fuel that turned the wheels. These guests were
Carmel's true equals, and he moved among them with a lithe assurance,
granting favors with a nod of the head, a quick and casual touch.

Yet the mask was not complete. For all the careful elegance of
the scene, once your eyes got used to the gloom you saw that the
grim purposeful faces still bore fading tracks of acne, that the hair
was lank and tangled, that the beards were not as full as they could
be, that the fingernails were gnawed and black-rimmed, and the teeth
had a greenish tint. Buried in the gravity of the mood was a memory
of the senior class play: at any moment one of the participants might
break character and wink past the footlights. But the new aristocrats
were deadly serious and close to dutiful in their role. That seriousness
was their pride, and they wouldn't let it be violated.

Richard poured himself some wine and began to circulate. Carmel was far away, talking to Regina under a huge photograph of Frank
Sinatra. Two young lords were bending over a girl nearby, holding
pipes to her face.

"Try some of this. It's prime. Nothing like it seen in this area
before."

"Don't listen to the man. He handles shit. Now this of mine is
beautiful—two hits and you're gone for a week . . ."

Further on, a tall, intense, gloomy-voiced peer was holding forth:

"That whole zone's gone to hell," he said. "You've got to take twenty, maybe even eighteen, and I'm talking quality shit. A man used to be able to cop twenty-five without moving. It's bad news."

"I'm still getting twenty-five," another answered. "In just that same territory."

Their ladies stood by with authoritative ennui, playing a duet with the smoke from their cigarettes.

"Oh, you can get it, but you got to take risks—even go to the *street!* Shit on that!"

Another pair were sitting by the wall, framed between an amplifier and Carmel's file cabinet. One, wearing a short black cape and boots, was dragging hard on a pipe. His face went briefly expressionless as he held down the smoke; then he exhaled, turned to his partner who was maintaining a studied cool, and said, "Pretty good. Where'd you get it?"

"One of Herman's people. They were being watched, and they had to get rid of it fast."

"Herman's? I'm surprised, man, I'm truly surprised. I don't do business with them—that last batch of stuff had word out on it to make you hold your nose. I bought some acid off them, and it had been cut with, you know, really awful shit."

"You have to be careful, yeah—" a girl wandered by, and he snatched the pipe, saying to her, "Hey, love, give me an opinion on this . . ."

In the doorway between the two rooms, three of them were in conference. The conference was going slowly, because they were all sampling each other's dope while they talked.

"Well," a plump, pudgy earl was saying judiciously, balancing a Bong between his hands like a saxophone, "it seems to me that downers are definitely on the rise. Especially in the fourteen-through-seventeeners, that's where you'll make your big sales. But it's always hard to predict what people are going to want tomorrow . . ."

"Yeah," the third drawled, "tomorrow they might want Jesus," and everyone laughed.

"Coke is pretty steady," a lady remarked. "People always want coke."

"Yeah, but a lot of them can't pay for it, and besides once in a while the distribution gets rough . . ."

Richard was becoming paranoid. Besides the wine, he'd been offered a few hits, but he hadn't gotten high. Instead the drugs had chilled and spiked his nerves, so that the most casual gesture was

invested with weird and frightening significance. Sounds struck his
ear with abnormal clarity, and reverberated inside, and collided with
the images vibrating off his eyes. He had switched back to wine, to
bring himself down, but so far it hadn't had any effect.

The caped peer advanced on him, offering a thumbs-up handshake. "Don't know you, man," he said. "What territory do you
work?"

"I move around," Richard told him. "Schoolyards, mostly.
Playgrounds."

"Yeah? Like where?"

Richard named a couple of elementary schools in the area.

"Doesn't touch me, anyway," the caped peer said. "It's pretty
risky, though . . . What do you deal? Anything besides grass?"

"Oh, some smack," Richard said airily.

The caped peer stared at him. "Shit! Kids that age don't have
that kind of money, do they?"

"Well, I don't always ask for money . . . Man, you give 'em a
taste and some of those little cuties will do *any*thing for more, you
follow me?" Richard opened his eyes wide and leered, nonchalantly.

The caped peer backed a step. "That's sick, man. I mean, I'm
cool, I don't pass moral judgments, but that's really sick." He walked
away, his cape stiff with indignation.

"You ever tried it?" Richard called out. His voice jumped as he
spoke, and hot sweat coursed down his ribs. Carmel was putting *Dia-
mond Dogs* on the stereo. One of the ladies was throwing pills up in
the air and trying to catch them in her mouth on the way down. Another girl crouched on her knees picking up the fallen pills. "That is
so *nouveau riche,*" said the tall, intense lord, turning away in disgust.

Richard became distantly aware of a commotion at the far end
of the room. Regina was speaking to Carmel, in a shrill voice which
Richard had never heard from her before—she looked very drunk, and
that was even more unexpected. She raised her hand to slap Carmel.
He caught her wrist midway through its arc and slowly pulled it down
until it touched his cheek with only the gentlest caress. "Be nice,
darling," Richard heard him say, ". . . Does anyone want to put her
to bed?"

Richard felt his mind starting to go, and tensed his muscles to
hold it back. Whenever a person moved, he could feel every vein jump
under their skin. His hand grappled for an anchor, and wound up
gripping his arm.

Carmel cut toward him, leading a girl by the hand. Carmel was laughing; fascinated, Richard watched his lips pull back from his teeth, the knit skin stretching like painted canvas over his jaw.

"Hello, Richard," Mrs. Seastrom said. She was the girl with Carmel. Carmel put his arm around her.

"Hello," Richard said. "What the hell are you doing here?"

"Why," Mrs. Seastrom said, "I'm just joining the party."

"Carmel!" the plump lord cried, emerging from the murk like a pale balloon. "Is this the lady you've been talking up to us?"

"None other."

"I'm happy to meet you," the plump lord said, bending too low over Mrs. Seastrom's fluttering hand. "If you'll permit me to say so, you sound like one foxy chick."

Mrs. Seastrom dazzled in reply. "Thank you. But call me Laura."

"Laura," said another, extending a complex Bong, "will you nave a hit?"

"Surely," she said. "Very kind of you." She handled the Bong with ease. That vicious bastard, grinning Carmel, must have taught her . . . memories of traumatic adolescence, how did the damned thing work? Smoke, smoke everywhere. Richard began to sulk.

In fact, he was close to being totally out of control. His paranoia was growing, gathering strength, sprouting horns, while his body grew weaker until it was on the verge of vanishing. The room, the walls, the ceiling, the people were disappearing too; all that remained was the music, climbing until it burst like blood, and fell like rain, onto his damp white forehead.

Meanwhile, the party, undisturbed, flowed on. Carmel's lady was the hit of the night. Everyone offered her samples. Regina had disappeared, but Carmel didn't seem much concerned about it. His face was sharp with a quiet pride as he led Laura from conversation to conversation.

"Laura, I'd like to have you try this . . ."

She did, and handed the pipe back to the caped peer. "Not bad," she said.

"Not bad! Why, woman, that's the best in town!"

"Bullshit," Carmel said. "The best in town is right here in my pocket."

He noticed Richard sitting in a nearby chair, head held tightly between his hands. "You all right?" he asked.

"I hate you, Carmel," Richard said. "I just realized it. I had to tell you—"

Carmel laughed. "If that's what you want to do, go ahead,"

he said easily.

"You're not going?" Richard said. His voice was panicky. He actually did hate Carmel at the moment, but even so he wanted someone to talk to.

"You'll get some company soon enough," Carmel said, and drifted away. Richard stared after him with catatonic apprehension. He couldn't guess what further turn Carmel might have plotted, and he didn't want to know.

He found out soon after. A bubbling laugh he recognized too well came bouncing down the stairs. Amy followed a few steps behind it. She saw him right away. "There you are!" she said, in a voice so loud it tore the air. She planted a kiss on the cheek he turned, and said, "Oh, c'mon, give me a real one," falling into his lap. "Carmel! Didn't you tell him I was coming?"

"It must have slipped my mind."

"I don't believe I know you," Mrs. Seastrom said.

"This is Richard's lady . . ."

"Why do you look so down?" Amy asked Richard. "Aren't you glad to see me?"

"Let me up. I'm going to get a drink."

She followed him to the bar. "I didn't think you and Carmel knew each other," he said, pouring the wine.

"Everybody knows Carmel—or maybe it's Carmel who knows everybody. He called me around dinnertime. I wish you wouldn't act so pissed off."

He felt as if everyone was listening; standing around, mocking them, him. "I'm just thinking," he said.

"You're not going to be any fun. I'm going to find some people who're fun."

"Yeah, do that." He went back to his chair, his armor clanking, his vision clotted with unfocussed rage. Amy was making sounds, talking to people, and her presence sliced at his nerves like a scalpel cutting away the insulation from a wire. He was ready to scream with fury, but he felt too weak to move.

It must have been some time later when he went to refill his glass, and ran into a group of people surrounding Carmel. "You weren't jiving us about your lady," the plump lord was telling him, in the breathless voice of a convert. "She's cool."

"I jive nobody," Carmel said.

"You jive me," Richard muttered. Carmel heard him, and turned.

"I thought you knew, man," he said.

"Does he know?" Richard asked, louder than he'd meant to. "Does Seastrom know?"

"You're in pretty bad shape," Carmel warned him. "Take it easy."

Before he could get back to his chair, where he was safe, Amy was on him, clutching thick-fingered and blind: "Have you cheered up yet?"

"No."

"I don't want to stay here much longer. These people are okay, but all they can talk about is dope. I mean," she giggled, "it's one thing to smoke it, but I think they get higher by talking about it."

He wished she were gone. He wanted to be alone, to brood without interruptions.

"Richard," she said, "let's go home."

"Why?"

"I want to get you out of your bad mood."

"No. I like my bad moods. They're fun. We're right for each other. It's a romance. Leave us alone."

"What the fuck is the matter with you?" she said.

The temptation was irresistible. "You," he said.

Her expression tilted back and forth. She took a breath. "All right," she said. "I'm leaving. If that's what you want."

"That's what I want."

Her eyes tried to decide whether to plead or not; then she broke for the stairs. Watching her go, Richard felt good. It was too bad about Amy, but it had done wonders for his self-esteem. Besides, it would be easy to make her blame herself for the fight.

He looked around for the first time in what felt like hours. Carmel and Laura Seastrom were standing in front of the bedroom door, the lords and ladies gathered around them. Laura's eyes were closed, and her hand stroked Carmel's pale hair as they embraced. Richard, glazed and stupid, with the overwhelming confidence of a mind that had stopped functioning long before, sauntered over to them and tapped his knuckles on Carmel's velvet back.

"Hey," he said. "I mean look. If you're gonna have a go, why don'cha lean back and let everybody have a go?"

Carmel turned. His face was very cold. "You'd better go look for Amy," he suggested.

Richard, about to answer, could not. The lords and ladies pressed in around him. He wasn't one of them, he was an interloper. He had no right to speak. He had to get out of here.

"Excuse me . . . excuse me . . ." He parted a path among them, hands out, aloft, unseeing. Near the stairs, he passed the caped peer, who glared at him with pot-maddened eyes. "Child rapist," the caped peer hissed.

Carmel and his lady were waving a royal farewell before retiring to their chamber. Richard gestured in Carmel's direction, inconclusively. "Not me," Richard said. "He's the fucking child rapist."

He thought to find Regina, and cool his head on her icy skin; but no, she had left, he had seen her, how long ago? He fought to recapture time, and mobilize the great gaps where it had stood still; but the trick eluded him. The connections of his mind were collapsing like the houses of a city on fire.

There was a bathroom off the kitchen, and he went to it, less to quell the unease of his stomach than in the hope that the mirror there might at least give the illusion of order. The door was open a crack, and he pushed it wide. "Hello, there!" Seastrom said merrily.

He was sitting on the toilet with his pants loose around his hips, and his hand dreaming down between his thighs. "Ah," he said, "caught in the act. You know, it's been so long that I've almost forgotten how. Don't leave! I want to talk to you. They're down there, together, aren't they?"

Richard nodded.

"I would have liked to see it," Seastrom said, "but my presence might have been a touch inhibiting."

"To tell you the truth, I don't think they'd notice."

"Possibly." Seastrom seemed to wander from thought to thought without trying to choose among them. "He's some lad, isn't he? Our boy. I mean Carmel."

"Shouldn't you be upset?" Richard asked hesitantly. "I mean, he is stealing your wife, and . . . well, you know."

"Not steal," Seastrom protested, "how can you steal what's given away? Sure, I gave him Laura, I gave him Regina too, and why not? The way I see it, I'm the benefactor—I have to admit I'm grateful to him. He's brought sunshine back into this house."

There was something awry in his logic, but the atmosphere was so fragile that Richard didn't dare disturb it. He still felt panicky, but now with a new calm: he had finally found a situation equal to his mood. Seastrom gave off the enthusiasm of a man enjoying a hearty meal. Warming to his subject, he continued:

"Our pleasures in this life are so poor, Richard, can you blame us for wanting to jazz them a touch? Why, when Laura—" he pronounced the name with the richest tenderness—"and I were married, there were noises in the air of romance and monogamy, but who believes that any more, I ask you, when you can stare up instead like the eye of the pig on the banquet table, and enjoy the spectacle of the court? I'm a captive audience to the world. All their twisting tricks do is prove to me each day that I was right to abandon the faculty of judging, and enjoy the show with all its separate little follies banging into each other. Don't worry your head," he added abruptly. "Look for a good time."

"But then you give up your responsibility."

"Why not? Everything is bad for everything else in the long run. I'm the only one who knows it, and I can sit back and play the spectator, because I've got the key to the secret and I know how it's going to turn out."

"How's it going to turn out?"

"We're all going to die," Seastrom said happily. "And nothing in our lives will make an iota of difference to history, so why try for the best? Try for the worst—it's all the same . . . Look. We dance the thin spittle of our hysteria along the lips of an enormous yawn. Good line, isn't it? Don't ask the beast's name. Catch the rhythm instead, so you can be a dancer too."

"But you have to judge," Richard said. "You can't help it." The words had a tinny, ineffectual ring to his ear; he felt like a bad actor. "I mean, it's how we are," he said, darting a covert glance at the mirror above the sink. But it was at such an angle that all he could see was Seastrom repeated.

"You still think that." Seastrom adjusted his weight on the seat, his pink hams wobbling. "All right, then, consider this little notion: trying to seek out the worst in yourself may be just as difficult and painful as trying for the best—catch that? Maybe more, because you go underground, and your path is lit by only a miner's lamp. None of that cold clean air of healthy ambition to brace you on your way. No. The air is thick, and dark, and the earth stings like salt as you go down, and you live in endless fear of the cave-in that could come at any moment. Think about it, Richard—who really gambles more, now?"

"But if you go to the bottom," Richard answered, "and then keep going—then you start to climb again, don't you? Is that what you're going to say?"

Seastrom shook his head. "Scratch a coward," he muttered, "and you'll find a sentimentalist every time. Damn Stevenson liberals. It's a nice idea, Richard, I grant you that, but no one ever gets that far. Because you see that at the center of the earth, gravity can paralyze you, and magnetism sucks." He clenched his fist. "Oh, yes! I've been waiting, wondering how long it would take you to figure out that all this was a joke, and you were the punchline. This little idea of yours, this scheme that brought you and I together—did you ever really think you could get to the truth of what goes on?"

"No," Richard said, unwillingly.

"You're learning," Seastrom approved him. "Forget categories— right and wrong mean no more than true and false, and true and false are one and the same." He paused, and added with a smile: "Because neither of them means a thing."

Richard suspected that this was only another performance. Nonetheless he was overflowing, Seastrom's voice was pouring into him like wine, and the temptation to agree was so sickeningly strong. If all that he had wanted to cherish for so long was false at the foundation, then goodbye, angel! and he might as well accept what Seastrom offered, find peace in blindness by calling it vision. He wanted to jump with all his heart, and only fear held him back.

"Carmel," Seastrom said, low-voiced, as if he had caught a whiff of that desire. "Everyone thinks that I'm the fool who pays the price of his foolishness, no more—even my own dear wife thinks so, bless her, and Regina has taken it for granted since the day he walked in the door. But my God! I couldn't love him more if he was my own creation, and sometimes I almost suspect that he is, in a way . . . No, Carmel didn't steal my life from me, I gave it freely, so that he could give it back renewed: a process of physics, you understand, Richard. I'm happier watching him than I've been in years. He's a lovely boy," Seastrom said, and his voice grew damp with sudden emotion.

A muscle in Richard's left leg began to twitch. He felt claustro- phobic; Seastrom's words were pressing in on him. He couldn't breathe.

Seastrom laughed heartily—the sound was as abrupt as a pistol shot. "It's marvelous," he said. "Everyone thought that Carmel was just cozying up to me so he could get to Laura, when actually it was the other way around. . . . You see, Carmel needs me. In purely prac- tical terms, he wants to expand his operations, and he needs my money—the money that was supposed to go to your Rock N Roll Theater. But it runs a lot deeper than that too. It's my chance for a new life—a real one, this time."

"You'll never get it," Richard said.

Seastrom grinned jovially: "And why?" he asked.

"You're too old."

Seastrom didn't act offended. "Maybe I shouldn't have talked to you," he said. "These are ideas I've carried inside for years, and when something spends that much time in the womb, it's apt to look pretty puny when it's first put under the light—haven't you ever noticed how . . ."

"I think I'd better go." His legs were caving in. He held himself up with an effort.

"What?" Seastrom chuckled, breathy with old intimacy. "But you can't. I haven't hardly started my seduction speech. *Now,* Richard . . ." He leaned forward, tense with a harsh energy which Richard would never have guessed at before. But Richard didn't see any more than that, because he backed out of the room and slammed the door.

He stood staring at the blank wood, as if waiting for his reflection to appear. He had carried his claustrophobia with him from the room. It was all smoke and madness filling his head—"Stare back into the eye of the pig," he said. Then he was out on the porch, alone. Music from the basement slithered out from the boards beneath his feet. From the bathroom he heard the sound of a loudly blown nose.

The sky hung above Richard's head, and its stars formed themselves into a giant question mark across the darkness. He had no answer for them. He was discovering that he had nothing left to give, nothing at all.

CHAPTER THIRTEEN

Within a Grove of Buddies: 5

Lang sat in the living room, Alice's guitar across his lap, a yellow legal pad on the coffee table in front of him. A rough chord progression had been scratched out across the top of the page. The rest was hatched and scored with deletions and arrows and phrases running like small trains up and down the margins. The beginning of the song had become the end, and then the beginning again. He couldn't tell if it worked either way.

If he went to see Johanna, she might be able to tell him.

His sickness had settled; it was part of him now. It had established its headquarters in his body, and was now slowly moving to fill out its living space, setting up a dominion over every nerve, every cell.

He had tried to call Brewer that morning. Seeing Lorraine the day before had put Brewer back in Lang's mind; but he had already been wondering why Brewer hadn't tried to get in touch with him. He must have known that Lang was back in town—like so many people who are silent as a means of preserving their character, Brewer loved to have information jangling in his pocket like loose change. Normally he would have called as soon as he'd heard. Lang thought of what Myra had said—*stick around, you'll find out*—*nobody sounds much like anybody these days.*

When he called, he'd gotten Brewer's mother on the phone. It was almost funny how the old sinking feeling had come back on him so quickly at her voice. She'd started right bang in on him, as if he'd never left—which as far as she was concerned, he hadn't, probably.

"Oh, Danny," she said breathlessly, "you have to talk to him. Someone has to talk some sense into him. My poor dear boy is talking about leaving home—about moving to some dreadful neighborhood full of Negro thieves across the river. Leaving his poor dear mother in this big house all alone. You have to try to convince him, Danny—you have to try to make him see, how wrong he is . . ."

Then Brewer had gotten on. "What do you want?" he said, sounding not at all friendly.

"Nothing," Lang said. "I'm just in town, and I wanted to say hello. What's with you? How come you didn't call me?"

"Oh. I thought that if you were staying, I'd probably see you around sooner or later. And if you were going to be leaving again, it probably wouldn't make any difference."

"Thank you," Lang said, but Brewer went right past him.

"Look, I'm sorry, but I'm very busy right now. Is there anything in particular that you want?"

"No," Lang answered, too baffled to argue.

He managed to keep Brewer on the line for a few minutes after that, but things didn't get any better. Brewer got quickly impatient with all of the old days that Lang was bringing up to keep the conversation going—"I don't know why you want to hear about all that," he kept saying, "that was all a long time ago." Yet he was hardly more forthcoming when Lang asked him if it was true he was moving to Suffragette City. "What do you mean, why? I'm of age. It doesn't really matter what my motives are."

"What are you going to do?"

"I'm not sure. Get a job, most likely. Pay the rent. I really don't care that much."

Finally, a little hesitantly, Lang had brought up Erica. He already knew that Brewer had been one of the people there the night she died. He didn't want to mention it, but it seemed like the only way to get across all the distance between them on the phone.

It got a reaction, but not the one he'd hoped for. Brewer's manner went from covertly hostile to downright angry. "Look, Lang," he said, "I don't want to talk about that. I don't want to talk about

any of that shit. It happened, yeah, she kicked, and that's all anybody can say about it. I mean, you know, you go away, you run off
to New York, and then you come back here and you start acting like
this was your life. If you decide to stay for a while this time, then
maybe we can get together and talk about something interesting. But
right now, I've got a lot of packing to do, and unless you've got something else to say, I'm going to get off."

"No," Lang said wearily, "I don't have anything else to say";
but the other end of the line had already gone dead. He stood, listening to the dial tone hum, for a long while before he hung up.

Since then, he had gone to call Brewer back three times, and
stopped each time. If that was what Brewer wanted, then that was
Brewer's scene, and fine. But his old habit—of caring about nothing
once he knew the reason why, and caring about everything until he
did—hadn't let him put the conversation out of his head.

He looked down once more at the paper before him.

So the dancers keep dancing

He wondered how the band was doing. Only a week ago that
contract had been the whole obsession of his life. He didn't know
how many hours he had spent mixing tapes, hustling labels, negotiat-
ing with the A and R men in those pseudo-intimate bars they preferred
for their business meetings. They kept their cool, it was their job to
do that. One even kept his when Lang, strung out and sleepless for
three days, screamed at him, "Die, you cheap fucker, you waste air
when you breathe . . ."

Lang had driven himself like a demon for the chance to make
that album. It seemed important, then, to get it all down, to give it
all some anchor outside his own mind. But now that seemed only
like the bullying of a childish pride. He had lost that part of ego, at
least; but he had found nothing to replace it with except the sickness,
and that gnawed at him more than emptiness ever could.

He would never capture it. Nothing was strong enough to hold
the blunt realism of an exploding gun, and he wanted to give up.
Everybody on the outside would only dismiss it as a sick, twisted
joke, anyway. But even though he was ripe for surrender, the pictures
in his head refused to stop. He let himself be buffeted by them as a
shipwreck victim gives himself over to the waves, finally wanting to
drown, and waiting only for dark water to flood his lungs.

and they feel no guilt

How artificial the city seemed now. New York was as practical
as a party girl cleaning herself out between tricks. Its life was dictated

by the hard logic of ambition, and it was the emptiest ones who made
the trip most easily. Put a band together. Get money. Make the connections. Bribe everyone with money, with art, with the hard cash of
your own desire. He had succeeded there by molding his shape to the
deep hole of its streets, but he couldn't do that now.

because the past was just what they dreamed

(repeat)

One night he had come in from a winter storm to a party at
Richard's old house. Walls of heat and music hit him hard upon the
raging cold outside. Erica was sitting alone in the kitchen, quietly
strumming a guitar. Lang sat down and unbuttoned his coat. She
made as if to stop—he motioned her to go on. "Please," he said. The
trample of voices and feet from the next room faded as she sang, without words, just letting her voice run lightly up and down the scale.
Lang listened.

"You like me, for right now, don't you?" she asked him.

"You're sweet when you sing."

Erica smiled inside her mouth. "You're sweet to believe it,"
she said.

For an answer, he plucked a string on her guitar. She understood, and started to play again, her gaze steady on him.

Richard came in from the living room. His walk was slurred,
and he looked wasted. "Ah," he said thickly, "betrayed by my own
good buddy. Sorry to break it up."

"Why don't you go fall down somewhere?" Erica said. "You
could use the experience."

"People wanna see you in the living room."

"Maybe I don't want to see them," Erica said, pushing his grasping hand away.

Richard leaned against the wall, rubbing his shirt, staring at her
resentfully.

"Can't you see," she said, "I just don't want to see people right
now?"

"You can see Lang."

She checked Lang out quickly, to see if enough of the old mood
was left for him to support her. "Lang's different. He doesn't ask me
for anything."

"I don't ask you for anything either." Richard was getting ugly.
Downers. "Except not to be a cunt—but that's already too much for
you . . . You gotta have your satisfaction . . ."

"I couldn't find it here. Not with you." Erica was angry. "Can't you just leave me alone? You all keep coming at me—can't you see I'm tired?"

"You ain't too tired to *fuck!* You're never too tired for that. Fuck your brains away. Fuck your heart out. Now, you gonna fuck her, Danny boy? Lemme tell you about Erica here. As you can see her fucking boobs aren't much to write home about, but that mouth of hers'll go anywhere you say—and she gets real good when she's on top—"

Lang stood up and grabbed Richard by the collar. Richard was limp and loose in his hands. Lang threw open the door. Cold air streamed in over them. Lang looked down at the mumbling, quivering bundle in his arms. Then he pitched Richard out. Richard yelled; then they heard a thud, just before Lang shut the door.

"See what happened to him," Erica whispered.

"He's passed out," Lang said, "in the snow."

"You'd better go claim him."

"No."

"Please, Lang. Just put him on his bed. He'll never know."

Lang went outside and somehow got Richard's huddled body upright. He half-dragged, half-carried him inside, not looking at Erica, or at the party when he passed the living room. He barely got Richard up the stairs. Richard flopped back on his bed, his clothes all tangled and damp. "Roses are red," he muttered as his eyes slid shut, "violets are blue . . . and some rhymes rhyme, and some don't."

Lang went back downstairs. Erica was looking at the window. Her guitar stood propped against the wall like a sentry. "Thanks," she said in a distant tone, one she might use for a servant.

"Erica?"

"What?"

Lang hesitated. "Let's go to my place," he said. He put his hands in his pockets.

"You know I can't," she told him softly.

Lang didn't answer.

"Are you sure he's all right—Richard . . ." her voice trailed off.

"I didn't mean it like the rest of them," Lang said.

"Oh? How do the rest of them mean it?" Then she put her hand on his arm. "Sorry. It might have been nice, but—"

"It's all right."

She was going to let her hand fall, but he caught it. Hastily, and half-unsure, he kissed her. Her lips tasted feverish, dry and hot. When they broke apart, they both looked sheepish, as if the very simplicity of such an act made it out of place.

"You know what I'm thinking," Erica said.

"What."

"I'm thinking that maybe we should join the party."

They both grinned; but as soon as they entered the next room, the intimacy was lost. Her weariness was betrayed by countless small signs, and yet she achieved a successful mask, she became the axis of the room. It was finally too depressing to watch her, and Lang left.

Back then it was easy to believe that his Erica was the true one; but he had come to see that the mannequin who danced the thousand dances for the thousand eyes of Icarus might be just as real, and he, too, would never know. If he had only seen her at the end, he might have known her for real. He lived with questions like a man in the ruins of a passionate marriage. He was afraid that when, if, he met Johanna, he would have nothing left to offer, no gifts saved from his trip.

but it's still just my passing fancy to say

Myra stood at the door, holding a newspaper. "The country's going to hell," she said. "Do you want to see?"

"I've got problems of my own."

Myra looked dour. "They could drop the bomb on this town, and do you know what would happen? No one here would notice."

"Maybe it's the other way around, and we're the last ones left alive."

"Huh? Oh, well. Better us than Cincinnati. You know? How's Brewer?"

"Beats me," Lang said. "Where'd Andrew go?"

"The library."

"What's that? A new bar?"

Myra looked up. "No. That's what we always called the Agency. He still goes over sometimes, to talk about old times. Don't worry—he'll get to a bar, soon enough. Or sooner, if he can find a friend."

"I wouldn't think he'd have many friends left there."

"Oh, yeah—that place is home to him. It's really all he's got." She said this utterly without self-consciousness.

"That why he got into it to begin with? I always wondered about that."

"That was part of it. But not really. You have to understand this about Andrew—he was absolutely patriotic. A real flag-waver, wanted to save his country. He really believed all that. Hard to believe now, isn't it?"

"Not that hard."

"I know . . ." Myra nodded. "It's funny—after we talked, the other day, I was talking about you with Andrew and I asked him how you'd do with the Agency. He said he thought you'd be pretty good."

"No."

"Yes! I laughed, and he said, No, truly, you'd be good. You had the right kind of character. You realize, of course," Myra said, "that he meant it as a compliment. How does the idea of being a spook grab you?"

Lang was about to answer, when the back door opened and Alice called out, "Mommy, look what followed me home."

She came into the room. Behind her came Odell. and another boy behind him. Odell was wearing leather pants, which clung in folds around his skinny legs, and high-heeled boots. A chain was wrapped around his waist. A black shirt was open nearly all the way to the chain, revealing a German cross on a pendant around his neck. A floppy leather cap slouched on his ragged hair, pulled rakishly over one ear. The boy with him was dressed in a discount version of the same outfit; his face was pasty and slack, and his eyes bounced in Odell's wake like two berries in dough.

Odell braced his hands on his hips. "Hello, Lang," he said portentously.

"Hiya, cutie," Lang answered.

Odell's lips tightened. The boy looked confused.

"His name's Randy," Alice explained.

"Right," Myra said. "It's nice to meet him. Now if you all will excuse me, it's time for my bath." She turned and ascended the stairs at a stately pace.

"I don't think she likes me," Randy said. He had a pinched, nasal voice.

Alice tittered. "You're right. She doesn't."

"It's her loss," Odell said without humor.

"You got that hash?" Randy asked Alice.

"Yes—why don't you go find it?" Odell said to her. "You go help her," he added to Randy. "Lang and I have some things to say to each other."

"Okay. What things do we have to say to each other?" Lang asked, when they were alone.

"I heard you were in town," Odell answered. "I thought you'd want to see me."

"I hadn't planned on it."

Odell chopped the air brusquely with his hand. "I know what you thought of me, back when we were friends. But I've changed a lot. I'm all right. I had to bleed a little for it, and go through some pretty rough times, but my shit's together now. You can probably see that."

His old desire for power—the power to face a mirror—had solidified into a grim and dutiful pompousness; curling around its edges like a ghost was a hint of the wheedling, ingratiating manner that had once been his shield and sole offering to the world. He was now cautiously testing his muscle for a battlefield that had long since been deserted.

"Let's face it, Lang," he said. "I used to look up to all your bunch—I thought that you were pretty hot. And I admit that we had some good times. But in the final analysis, it all turned out to be pretty meaningless shit, didn't it?"

"You're a better judge than me."

"It did," Odell said. "Erica proved it. Look at what she turned out to be—a sick, twisted little cocktease at the end. That makes me pretty sad. I don't know about you, but I felt sorry for her."

"I'm sure she'd do the same for you."

Odell paused; but he had decided to make a speech, and he wasn't going to let Lang get in his way.

"I'm a survivor," he declared. "No one else came through all right but me. Why Richard, Richard's going out with a girl who's even younger than *I* am." His eyes glittered. "And Brewer—"

"I don't want to hear a shopping list."

"I don't mean that. I'm just saying it's pretty depressing—when I look back, I wonder how I could ever have believed in any of you. I know that's pretty harsh, but I have to be honest. The night I finally gave in and went to bed with Erica, it was pretty awful—by that point, she really needed help, but I knew it would be wrong to be her crutch." He looked at Lang carefully. "But you must have known what that was like."

"No," Lang said, "I never found out."

"Fuck, man!" Odell said with gusto. "Then you were the only guy in town who didn't get it on with her." He laughed broadly. "Why, you poor bastard."

"Yeah. You must be proud, Odell."

"Not proud. It was more of a favor than anything else. . . . But so long as she was passing it around, why shouldn't I have gotten my share, you know? That was the way I saw it."

"So you got it."

"Well, I wasn't going to argue when it was offered."

Lang nodded, thoughtfully. "You know something?" he said. "What?"

"I'll bet you were such a hot crutch that the next morning she told you she never wanted to see you again."

Odell cleared his throat. "Well . . ." he looked down at the floor. "I think it's pretty low of you to say something like that," he said quietly. "Considering that she is dead, and so forth. I don't think it's really appropriate for you to indulge in sour grapes now."

Lang could have smashed his head in, but it wouldn't have done any good. Odell had convinced himself—he was far more sure of himself than Lang could be.

"The thing is," Odell said, "it's not going to be as easy for you to put me down as it used to be, Lang."

"Don't shit my pants for me, Odell. You can't handle the work."

"You're running scared," Odell said calmly. "You got kicked out of your band because you were too strung out to play, didn't you?"

"Where'd you hear that? No. Never mind. I know." A little bit from Richard, a little bit from Alice. Maybe Carmel had even decided to throw in a few touches of his own. "Anyway," Lang said, "it's not true."

"Prove it. You're in bad shape, and everyone in town knows it."

"But you still had to come all the way over here to pick a fight with me? That's pretty."

"I didn't come over here to pick a fight with you," Odell said. "I wanted to see you because you were always the one who had nothing but contempt for me, and I wanted to change that—because your opinion did use to matter to me, once. You've come down, Lang, and I've come up a lot—I think it's time that we were friends. Why," he smiled, putting his hand on Lang's shoulder affectionately, "I just came over here to welcome you home."

Lang knocked his hand away. Anger tightened Odell's face. They glared at each other. They were still glaring at each other when Alice and Randy came back from her room with the hash.

"We're going downstairs to smoke it, okay?" Alice said. "So Mommy won't be disturbed."

"Let's get high," Randy said, "oh, let's get high."

"You want to join us, Lang?" Odell asked.

"Why not?" They looked at each other coldly. "I mean,"

Lang went on, "let's find out if you're right."

Just so had Erica gone down. "Never get wasted with people you don't trust," she told Lang, but that was before she found that no one could be trusted. Instead she chose to make herself a lightning-rod to every crack of their thunder. He might as well follow.

In the rec room, Alice prepared the hash, rolling the ball deftly between her fingers. "Ah, ya got no music," Randy complained. "Ya need music."

"Ask Lang to play us a song," Alice said.

It was good hash, tarry, acrid, and strong. By the time it had gone three circles around, everyone was high. Things lost their moorings and turned to silhouettes thin as paper, thick as flour. There was comfort in the disordering of space. If you could only take one step further, then you, too, would be loose in the easy air.

"Somebody spiked this stuff," Alice murmured, holding the pipe. "I'm turnin' inside out and I'm growin' fingers in my stomach."

With all the accelerated tunings of insight the high could give, Lang knew that he had made a large mistake. He was unequal to the challenge. Even their positions attested to it. He sat on a chair, the other three faced him from the couch. The smoke from the pipe seemed to embrace them, and bind them into one; but as it turned to him it turned malignant, and bright with fear.

Randy, now, to his eyes, resembled nothing so much as a contented rat. The slick strands of dark hair angling across his forehead stood out like spikes through the gray gauze wrapping Lang's vision. Randy passed the pipe obsequiously to Odell . . . Reptilian smoothness of a glazed and lucid void. Lang lurched and reeled in the silence.

"Last month I swore off 'is," Randy said expansively, his voice molasses, slow dripping sludge. "I was out of my skull for three days at a great fuckin' party. They had every kind of high, I mean you could touch whatever you wanted without even moving. But it got to be too much. Out in the front room was a nude chick spread, and all the dudes too wasted to have a try. I'm telling you it was weird. They hadda unravel me from the bannister, I thought I was an angel. They stuck me inna bathroom with a box a Fig Newtons to come down. So I figured, man, you got to get off this—but you always come back, don'cha? You can't stay away from this jazz."

Transparent to the eye, solid to the touch. Reversals quick as a flipped card. The gun was in his hand. Then back to the other. Fear's other face turned, was hate.

". . . How much did this cost you, Alice?"

"Twenty-six. The market's up this week. Carmel's floating it, though, to the end of the month."

"He can afford to."

"Yeah, but most dealers wouldn't even think of it. Or of charging interest."

"'At Carmel's a pretty sharp dude," Randy said, his face suffused. "He's okay. He only muscled me one time, but that was special—some chick needed an abortion. Carmel'd just bought up a whole shitload of new stuff, and he didn't have any cash on hand. So he really had to put the screws on some people."

"Oh, yeah," Alice said. "I wondered what happened. That's really amazing, Carmel, of all people—he's so careful."

Lang was barely listening. He had fastened his attention on the power lines crisscrossing outside the window, cutting up the sky into puzzle-pieces.

"It was a real pain for him—you know, he didn't want to look bad, even though it was the chick's fault—like she refused to use anything. I met her once. A very weird chick."

"Who was she?" Alice asked.

"I don't know. She left town a couple of days later. You know Carmel likes to be pretty secretive about his chicks, just like he is about everything. I think it was just a one-night stand though, which was probably why he was so pissed off about it."

"What was her name?" Lang asked.

Randy looked up, as if he had forgotten Lang's existence, and disliked being reminded of it. "I said already, I dunno—what's the difference? She was just another kid." He turned back to Alice and Odell. "She sorta reminded me of that one I told you about, that night when I was in Baltimore—you remember, she . . ."

"What did you think?" Odell said impatiently to Lang. "Of course, it was Johanna."

". . . you know, she comes up to me in this redneck bar, and asks me if I want to dance, and I—"

Lang stood up, finding his legs with difficulty. He took a few tentative steps toward the window.

"What's with you, Lang?" Odell demanded jocularly. "You aren't deserting us now. Life's just starting to get good. Have another toke."

"Freakin' me out," Lang muttered, waving at the pipe. "You should have told me there was something else in there . . ."

The floor beneath him was a hydraulic lift, slowly rising to meet

ing. Lang rested his head against the cool glass of the window
lt its chill enter him, traveling the thousand miles to his feet.
power lines outside shifted and dissolved before his eyes. He
the cold white light, and felt the arctic silence. The glass was
np where Lang's forehead touched it.

Alice was beside him, angrily. "You don't even know what it's
like," she said. "You don't know enough about it to care."

But he did know, and Alice had missed it completely. It wasn't
the fact of the abortion, for in Icarus that just came with the psychic
territory, and had no moral value except as a kind of stopwatch for
one's sense of time. It wasn't even because Johanna had slept with
Carmel; that part of it was his problem alone. It was Johanna. That
violation, which for Alice or anybody else would be as casual as a
change of clothes—Sally had had two in the time since Lang met her,
and always came home smiling—to Johanna would be the one unbearable thing. To open herself to the world's dirty fingers brought her
down to the same ugliness as the rest of them, and she could no longer
set herself apart. That was why she had left Icarus, he knew; but why
had she chosen to sleep with Carmel in the first place? He tried to
explain it to Alice, or rather to that accusatory voice impinging on the
frontiers of his awareness, knowing beforehand that it would be hope-
lessly inadequate. "It's just," he said, "that she always valued her
privacy."

"I don't know what that word means," Alice said.

Lang stood huddled at the window, his arms wrapped tightly
around himself.

"He's pretty fucked up," Alice said.

"He should have known that he couldn't control it," Odell
answered.

"Jesus," Randy said in wonder. "That dude just can't maintain—
just can't maintain at all . . ."

CHAPTER FOURTEEN

Odell: 3

Every magic moment must have its magician, and seldom had Odell
felt such a sense of shamanistic immediacy as during the days that he
spent with Erica's band. Through the sullen wane of the summer their
gigs took them all over Icarus, then all over Fairfax County, random
pinpricks that gradually crisscrossed into the pattern of a map; the
map was Odell's, for he had immediately realized that the band was
a viable metaphor, and so from the first night on he clung to them.
They were like guerillas he thought, making their raids and then melting away under cover of the fires they had set—he was the war corre-
spondent along for the ride. Their truck slid uneasily through the
musky green of the summer nights, and there was never either wind
or rain.

Odell knew full well that it was the tense dark beauty of his own
visionary consciousness that gave the events of those weeks their
metaphysical bite. But he could never have done it without Erica.
She provided the spark, and Odell matched himself against her—the
comprehension of her designs, he realized, would require him to
achieve new horizons in intellectual heroism. He recognized it with
a delirious fascination so intense that he often felt like throwing up

from excitement. She wished, he saw, to capture all the members of the band, one by one, and thus assert her power by destroying them. It was chillingly, thrillingly evil. He himself could not have chosen a better microcosm.

They flowed in and out of her eyes as if they only came into existence when she saw them. Even the guitar player, in his monotonic way, seemed to grow nerves when she came near. Eventually, Odell thought, she would allow each one his flood tide, before they all ebbed back, when she was done, into being mere shades again. Odell could see it all in advance; he studied each new cog in her machinery like a recruit learning the nomenclature of a rifle, with the recruit's anxiety at knowing that someday he will have to assemble it blindfolded.

When he had confronted her with the design, not without pride at having discovered her so quickly (he had only been hanging out with the band for three days at the time), she had pretended amusement: "Now why didn't I think of that?" she said merrily. But Odell was not fooled. He knew that she knew that secretly he understood her far better than anyone ever had; he was yin to her yang, she was doomed to preserve the circle. Still, he was surprised at how much she seemed to enjoy it. Sometimes their banter would grow so easy that he almost forgot about the months of bitternesss since their friendship had ended, and even forgot he was her mortal enemy. Perhaps—perhaps she wished to corrupt him away from his insight, in order to keep herself safe; the idea made him feel dangerous, potent.

"Don't try to seduce me into believing in you," he told her.

Her mouth gaped. "Honest, Odell, the idea never occurred to me to seduce you, I swear to God. I mean it never even crossed my mind. I mean not in my wildest *dreams* did I ever . . ."

"All right, all right," Odell said irritably, puffing cigar smoke against the chimes of her laughter. "Drop it."

All her wit could not conceal her, not from Odell, who could take her most trivial action and jump it through the hoops of his mind until he was satisfied that it fit the pattern. He was proof against her; he was the spy who knew too much to be killed. That he might not be worth killing never crossed his mind. She needed him, that was all. By placing her at the center of a cosmos of indescribable depravity and violence, he gave meaning to her life.

"How long are you going to stay with the bass player?" he asked her.

They were sitting on the hill above the swimming pool at the Icarus tennis club. The band was playing on a makeshift stage next

to the diving board. They always did a short set by themselves before
Erica came on; it gave them a chance to do all the old numbers she
disliked. The set invariably closed with "Jumping Jack Flash"—they
were starting it now.

Erica looked down at the bass player, almost hidden from her
sight behind a wall of amplifiers, his eyes searching for her in the
blinding circle of multicolored kaleidoscopic lights which she had insisted on incorporating into the show. "How long do you think he
deserves?" she asked.

"I think you've just about finished it with him. He's going to
stop listening to you one of these days." Odell was on uppers at the
time, and it frayed the edges of his conversation. Erica had refused
to join him; she said she didn't trust him. The implied compliment
gave Odell a warm, pleasurable glow inside.

"You're probably right. He was awfully upset the first time I
slept with the drummer."

"He might have been less upset if he hadn't been speeding when
you told him. He started screaming that everyone was teeth and eyes,
comin' at him." Happily, Odell noted that he was becoming less self-
conscious about dropping his g's.

"My timing was off. It was a mistake."

"So the drummer's going to be the next one, then?"

"What?"

"The drummer's next."

"What makes you so sure that I'm going to stay with the band?
Or that he'll even want me?"

"I know he will. And so do you."

"Jumping Jack Flash" was in its final verse, and Erica stood up.
"I believe it's time to go," she said. "God, I hate that song."

"You should."

"Why?"

Odell shook his head. A few moments later, watching her stride
out onto the stage, the audience swayed by the flow of her legs, already beginning to clap and call out as she brought the band back to
her by the slap of her tambourine against her thigh, he figured out
the answer to her question; but he wouldn't tell her yet. His gaze
raptly on her as she quivered at the microphone like sound made physical, her tense quick fingers curling on the stand as her breasts shook
to the beat, he felt a tremor of ecstasy at the power of his own insight.
The Stones had confirmed him again. He rode their Olympian wave-
length once more.

"Can't you all cut that damn song?" Erica asked on the way home. They were all slumped together in Odell's speeding car, while the keyboards man in the truck behind skidded frantically to keep up.

"No," the guitar player said. "Not that one."

"But it's so fucking stupid."

"Forget it, Erica," the bass player said, trying to sound proprietary.

"Not that song," the guitar player said.

"I'm *miffed,*" Erica murmured, curling against the bass player to reassure him that she really did notice him sometimes. One of her gifts was that she never became strident.

"Okay, tell me why they're all so nutty about it," she asked Odell the next day. "You always have an explanation. Even for things that don't happen. In fact—"

"I'm going to wait until you're finished with the band."

"In fact," Erica went on, "your explanations for things that don't happen are a lot better than the ones for things that do. You know, I really resent being turned into a demonic figure sometimes."

"I'm just talking."

"Sure. You're an intellectual. You know what that is? Someone who talks all the time because he can't do anything else."

"You were an intellectual once upon a time."

"I'm not. I never was. I'm not an intellectual," she said, "I'm too smart," and she laughed. "I like that."

That same night she ditched the bass player. Odell was at the house. He and the guitar player sat in the living room, talking under the music:

Don't ya think we need a woman's touch,
to make it come alive. . . .?

"None of that Beatles shit," the guitar player was saying. "With their fucking medals from the Queen."

"John Lennon gave his back," Odell felt compelled to point out. Erica and the drummer were necking on the couch. She had baked him a cake for his birthday; they were sharing a piece between kisses.

"He did? Good going, John." The guitar player thought for a moment. "But why did he want it in the first place?"

"John Lennon's a complicated guy," Odell said, keeping his mind on the conversation with difficulty. He had just noticed the bass player coming in the door.

The bass player reached down and shook the drummer's shoulder. The drummer found his mouth long enough to smile at the bass player. The smile was weary, without triumph, as if he were the one defeated. Which he was, to Odell's understanding, but the bass player understood it differently and wanted to hit him. The guitar player stopped him, so he turned and kicked a leg out from under the stereo instead. The needle screamed in pain as the turntable slid down on one end, slow and final as a sinking ship, and then crashed. The turntable kept turning, with a low, sexual moan, even though the tone arm had broken off and the record was shattered, its fragments jaggered in the wreck of Erica's cake, which had been on the same table. The red eye of the receiver winked knowingly at Odell.

At the next gig, the bass player moved forward to sing "Jumping Jack Flash." The guitar player moved in close, throwing a loop of music over him like a commiserative arm, and the keyboards man bounced on his stool, nodding encouragement. Erica didn't ask Odell for an explanation. She watched the drummer, isolated behind his kit at the rear of the stage. He was large and fat, and trying with something like Kierkegaard's leap to grow a beard over his pimples.

"Lord," she said, "he really isn't much to look at, is he?"

Odell smiled—sardonically, he hoped—and she cleared her face to beam at the drummer, who flourished his sticks in response.

"The guitar player and the keyboards man don't like me," Erica went on. "The drummer had a thing for me ever since I joined the band, so I only went with him to make him happy, because he and the bass player were friends and he didn't like the illicit to be poisoning the atmosphere like it was. I took him because they both needed me but I couldn't answer to both, and the drummer needed me more. That's all. I didn't plan it. I'd have let the bass player down easier, if I'd planned it. Still think I'm demonic?"

Odell was always irritated at the casual way she spoke of her evil. It diluted the sense of doom which he was trying to impart to her. "You mean," he tried, "that you're not ready for the others yet, and the drummer was the easiest, so you might as well get him over with."

"Oh, come on," Erica said. "He's very sensitive, and very lonely, and—you know, all that stuff. Sometimes I feel like I'm running for President. Same goddamned speech at every stop."

"If I had a complexion like that, I'd be sensitive too."

"You don't need it," Erica said.

She didn't stay with the drummer very long. Less than a week later, she told Odell, "I feel ripped off. I thought—I hoped—there could be more to it than getting rid of his frustrations. But once I got rid of his frustrations, it turned out there wasn't anything else there.

I'm too old to keep on making that kind of mistake."

"It doesn't matter. Even if you couldn't destroy him on your terms, you destroyed him on his. Telling him to let you get on top 'cause you didn't want to suffocate."

"What does that have to do with it?"

In the brief time they had been together, the drummer had sucked in his stomach—she told him to lose weight—and shaved off his beard, so that his acne shone forth proudly under the lights. Now his belly sprawled again beneath his shirt, and the thin dirty fuzz reappeared on his cheeks. He moved his drum kit forward on the stage, the guitar player and the bass player flanking him, while the keyboards man was exiled to a corner. A special mike was set up, at the next gig, for the drummer to sing "Jumping Jack Flash."

No matter how they disposed themselves, when she came on Erica was always in front of them all. She controlled the moves, but showed no interest in their components; she did as she liked, and left it to the band to rearrange themselves behind her. "We're not playing like we used to," the guitar player said. "Everybody's decided to be Brian Jones all of a sudden. Too wrecked to gig."

He was right. Each of them was now missing cues he should have caught blindfolded, going out of synch on the simplest changes, as if they now had to translate for each other what once had been a common tongue. The strain showed nowhere more than in "Jumping Jack Flash." It wasn't even music any more.

"Jesus," Erica said one night behind the stage, as they wrenched out the chords. "They used to be so good."

"You're almost done now. You only have the guitar player left to go."

"I'm going to stay with the keyboards man. I like him, honest I do. We might even move in together, did I tell you that?"

"No," Odell said. ". . . the song's nearly over."

As it turned out, she didn't move in with the keyboards man. But they acted almost married. When she came into a room and he wasn't there, a worried look would cross her face. He played with her hand, absently, while talking to other people, and she sat beside him, still and content. This was during a time when the band was getting very few gigs, so Odell and everyone else had plenty of leisure to study them; Odell hung like a doll on the nail of the days, suspended in wonder, and sensed that he was not alone.

Perhaps he had only been playing games all along, making chains out of random circumstance and accident; perhaps Erica herself was only a circumstance, an accident. It was possible that he was a fool. This thought put him into a deep depression. Or was her sudden domesticity—this cheered him up—a last desperate subterfuge, to avoid the fate he had verbalized for her? He wanted to talk to her to find out if he was right, but she was too happy with the keyboards man to notice him.

One day he caught up to her as she was walking up the hill to the band's house. The air was sodden with summer heat, and she was alone. There was no one else with whom she could share her gaiety; for the first time in years, Odell wished that the past could be blotted away, and room made in her life for him again.

"Richard broke up with that girl—Amy?—that he was seeing," she told him, tossing her hair against the unaccustomed breeze which had sprung up. "Carmel said so."

"I was wondering why you looked so happy."

"It doesn't matter to me any more how Richard lives—how he spends his time. It used to, but it doesn't any more. I used to think just like everybody else, that he was going to do something wonderful, but it's obvious he's blown that—so he might as well enjoy himself."

"He had a good time with Amy. At least it looked like a good time."

"She didn't understand him. . . . He wants to be understood, because he thinks that's the same as love. But there's not much in him left to understand, now. He was more interesting when he didn't care."

The leaves turned red above their heads, and the sun was chased away by the new wind.

"And you understood him."

"He was different then. He didn't need to talk about his future—now it's caught up with him. Yes, I did understand him. Certainly better than you, you were just hero-worshipping. And you accused me of ruining him once."

"Well, you did."

"I'd have to stand in line," Erica said, "and he'd be way in front of me."

They had almost reached the top of the driveway. Odell turned to her, about to say that all was forgotten, all was redeemed, and he loved her still; but they were interrupted by the keyboards man, coming quickly through the front door—his urgency grew quickly casual when he saw Erica.

"What're you in such a hurry about?" she asked him, her voice already alert beneath its brightness.

"Oh, nothing really. Well, it's not important." The keyboards man kept looking away, using his hands to convey expression instead of his face. "Just that the guitar player took some bad acid last night, and he's sort of freaked out."

"Has he come down? How is he?"

"Oh, basically pretty good. It's just that he keeps screaming. You know. And, uh, he tried to total himself, but we got the knife away. He'll be okay soon."

"There's something you're not telling me," Erica said impatiently, "come *on*, now—"

The keyboards man twitched guiltily. "Ah shit. You know. It's not serious. He just keeps calling your name. He was begging us to let you get him out—like we were cops or something. But look, Erica, it's just that he's out of his head . . ."

"Oh, Christ!" Erica said angrily, pushing past him as if he had abruptly ceased to occupy space. The keyboards man fingered his mustache, trying to share his nonchalance with Odell, but Odell, at that moment, was seeing with Erica's eyes, and the keyboards man remained a phantom.

Leaves drifted across the concrete slab of the porch. The bass player and the drummer came out of the house. "She went right in there," the bass player said. "Right past us. For a second I thought she was tripping too. She looked wild."

"Shit. He should of told us that he'd never done acid before, that's all."

"Ya gave him too much."

"Oh, what's too much. You tell me what's too much."

"We had to put the chair up against the refrigerator," the bass player told Odell. "He kept on seeing dead people come out of it. The stuff really fucked him up."

"Acid can't fuck you up," the keyboards man said. "It just brings it out if you're already fucked up."

"Oh, man. I've been around acid for years, and I've never seen it do like it did for him."

The drummer scratched his belly. "Fuck this," he said. "I'm going down to Uncle Lou's. Let the two of them play house, man."

The bass player giggled edgily. "Oh, yeah."

"They can climb into the refrigerator together, man."

Odell had not realized until then just how much they hated her. Gradually, they began to move toward the truck. Odell did not go with them. They didn't ask him to, or even look at him as they shuffled away. He was on her side as far as they were concerned; how were they to know that he had been one of them, years before they ever saw Erica's face?

He sat on the porch and waited. By nightfall, Erica still hadn't come out. He would have waited longer, but the wind was blowing—it was getting too cold.

He didn't hear from any of them until, three days later, she called to tell him that the band would be playing in Icarus that night. He drove down to the place through a red and brown twilight; the weather had resolved itself into a chilly autumn, and Odell exchanged his leather jacket for a long dark-green cloak which had once belonged to his mother.

Climbing from his car, he saw that the show was already under-way. Erica was not on the stage. He found her on a concrete balcony at the far end of the auditorium, leaning on a railing painted a peeling black.

"Funny," she said to him. "This hall was where Richard was go-ing to put on the Rock N Roll Theater—that show of his. Remember?"

"Erica," Odell said impatiently. "What happened?"

"Oh, all right. I stayed with him for twelve hours. It took him a long time to come down. Then he started to cry, and I held him while he cried. When he was finished crying he wanted to fuck me. So I let him." She bowed her head, as if the exhaustion was only breaking over her now. "I went into his room," she said, "and he was sitting there with his guitar on his lap, but it was unplugged, and his eyes looked as if they went all the way to the back of his head. He didn't recognize me; and when he did, he just crumpled, like a paper bag . . ."

Odell was watching the band. The guitar player crouched over his instrument, tearing ragged chords from its strings, his face blood-less and shocked. The rest of them exploded in his wake, now white, now yellow, now blue, now green, now red in the wheeling, jagged lights. There was not even the illusion of unity. Each one rushed down the road of his private vengeance without care or awareness for anything exterior.

"Didn't you notice?" Erica said. "It was so obvious. I noticed, I knew. For a long time." The revolving lights gave her profile an eerie, chameleon edge. "From the way he'd look at me when I was with the others, the way he always put me down for being with them. I didn't want to, even though I knew, but that night it was just too much, I didn't have any choice." She glanced around at Odell, just as the red light struck her hair. "Of course you don't believe any of this."

Odell started to speak.

"I'm not sure I want you to," she added suddenly.

"Why aren't you down there?"

She seemed surprised that it had to be explained to him. "The next morning," she said, "he started acting as if it was all my fault—as if I had betrayed him. And today, when I showed up for rehearsal, they were all treating me like shit. Like little boys, showing off how tough they could be. I couldn't take it—I didn't feel like I could understand anything anymore—so I left."

Down on the stage, the band had just finished a song. Applause came weakly, sullenly back, mixed with scattered booing. The auditorium was close to empty. The guitar player stepped up to the mike—his gaunt, emotionless features twisted themselves with effort into a smirk. "And now," he said, ignoring the catcalls, "we'd like to do a number for a very good friend of us all who can't be here tonight."

As the familiar chords began their climb, Odell felt a confused elation. Unsure of his thoughts, he turned to Erica for guidance. The light carved her face into impenetrable stone; but it was strong enough to light up the half-moon slivers of moisture in her eyes. That satisfied him. It was not out of spite for her; now she was only a figure on a board, and his complacency came from hearing the click of the final move.

"Will you take me to the house?" she asked. "I mean home. My home."

Odell hesitated. He wanted to stay. Then he realized, quietly, that going with her was what he was supposed to do.

When they got to her house it was natural that he should get out and follow her. They both stepped carefully on their way, to avoid the memory of all the afternoons they had walked this path together, when they were young. But even so, Odell thought, all pent with excitement, the past was still leading them by the nose, up the steps, and through this door, and inside to that cloistered smell of armchairs and perfume, so vividly remembered. Once inside, he stood hovering on the wine-colored rug of her living room, too uncertain to move.

Erica settled herself on the couch, flinging her hair back in a fluid golden sweep, then curling up on herself with the same swift grace, only her eyes fixed on him. He was suddenly conscious of his boots, his studded belt, his cigar, as if they no longer fit him. But he pressed on: "You're done now," he said. "You've got them all."

"Why not say they all got me. In one way or another. Even the keyboards man . . . Did you know," she asked, "that I never slept with him?"

"I don't believe you."

"It's true. And I was happy because we didn't need it. But then he started treating me as if we had. That was why I was ready to go with the guitar player—but it would have killed him if I'd told him that. Even so," she went on, "I didn't chase him—I don't care what you think. I never chased anybody. They all came to me. Just like you."

"That's not why I'm here at all, and you know it," Odell said quickly.

Erica looked puzzled. "I meant a couple of years ago."

"Oh." After a pause, Odell continued: "But leaving me out of it," he said. "It's still not true. Look at Richard."

Erica gave a deceptively lazy smile. "Richard," she said. "Do you remember when Myra Hoffentlich bet him a bottle of bourbon that he'd go back to me inside a month; and when the month was up, they had a party and drank it?"

"I was there. Richard got wrecked enough to spend the night on their couch."

"That's what I'm trying to tell you. He didn't. He came and woke me up at four o'clock in the morning. He was so wasted he could barely talk—Carmel drove him—and he begged me to let him stay the night one last time . . ."

"So you let him."

"Of course I did. I used to love him . . . I didn't enjoy it, much, but I did it."

Odell was losing his relation to things. The room looked insubstantial; nothing felt valid. He shifted his weight back and forth, but gravity did not reassure him. He had the dreamer's terror that everything was focussing on him in the precise instant before he vanished.

"There was something you were going to explain to me. A couple of months ago, when all this was starting."

"What?" Odell asked, although he knew.

"That song. They dedicated it to me, after all." She gave a wry smile. "It's not every night a girl gets a song dedicated to her."

He was hardly hearing her words. She was in command, he thought; he was helpless. Stubbing out his dead cigar, he took out a new one, patting his pockets for matches frantically.

"Calm down," Erica told him, gently.

For the life of him he could not have determined, at that moment, which one of them she was humoring. Then the music started to come back to him. Odell felt it rising inside him, knotting his muscles into knots, into muscles: finger-snapping power cracked and swelled his joints. He found a matchbook. All right. Thumb locked on his low-slung belt, he did a strut before her. He wheeled, and put out his hand, palm up:

"What it's about—" he stopped. "What it's about—"

Then the last bond snapped in his chest like a rubber band. He felt free. She sat there, waiting for him.

"What it's about is how Dante got out of the Inferno. Remember? Or did you forget everything, once you quit reading? Lucifer is sitting buried up to the waist, in the last circle—in a lake of ice or fire, I don't remember which—and the only way out is through the bottom of the hole. So Dante climbs down by using the fur on Lucifer's chest for a ladder. That's how he gets out—that's how he gets to the next book. That's what the song's about."

"You've already lost me," Erica said; "but don't let that stop you. Come on, go on."

Odell sensed uneasily that her attention had very little to do with what he was saying. He couldn't help thinking how much easier all this would be if he was stoned. But the night was still gathered around them: if he stopped talking now, it would take control. So he made himself go on.

"The first thing you have to understand," he said, "is that none of them ever loved you."

"None of them?"

"None of them."

"Damn."

"No, let me talk. You said you wanted to hear this, so let me talk. They never loved you. They hated you." He held his breath, waiting for her to snicker. She didn't. He resumed. "—Hated every minute they had to spend with you. And hated you so much it felt like metal, tasted like metal, inside."

"Swell," she said. "They could have told me. Left a note in the bathroom, or something."

"Come on, listen. But it didn't have anything to do with you as a person. All you had to do was be there. All you were was an image, a challenge. But you know that. You *let* them," he said bitterly. "You knew they needed you for that. It didn't matter who you were. They knew they were going to lose—they knew that before any of it started, before they even knew it was going to be you—but they had to try, even so."

"Who did you want to win?" Erica asked suddenly. "Them or me?"

"Them, do you have to ask? But that's where the song comes in. Listen. It's a myth. Or at least it's what we have instead of one. Because none of the real ones fit anymore. *I was born in a crossfire hurricane.* That's where the hero starts out. Born at the tail end of the twentieth century, there, in the eye of the storm. No home, no parents, no past—no kind of history at all that he can call his own. The second coming has come and gone. The only thing he can hear is the sound of radios and TV sets buzzing all around him. Everything that can possibly happen has happened, and he's living in the ruins. He's born out of nothing and into chaos, and he doesn't even know he's an orphan. He's the child of the nightmare, and cut off from everything else; he doesn't have a thing to hold onto, and that's the way he wants it, do you see? Because he doesn't even know he's lost."

He was growing animated now, and all but oblivious to her presence, pacing up and down the length of the couch she sat on, moving with the liquid stutter of a marionette. He held his cigar poised before his chest, like it was a microphone.

"So chaos is his only inheritance, and his first education is betrayal. *I was raised by a two-faced bearded hag.* That's Janus, the two-headed god—Edith Hamilton, you remember, we had to read her in ninth grade—the beginning and the end in the same person, good and evil like a coin you flip; there isn't any difference between them. And it's Tiresias too, blind and half a woman and half a man, and who is able to see the future as compensation for being punished for telling the truth once in the present. You see? You can't separate. Everything connects. The hero learns that every truth is just its opposite in a mirror, because the ultimate in anything always turns into its opposite. But when he first sees that, it only makes him another victim, schooled with a strap across his back, and the only thing that comes out of it is more violence. Sympathy for the devil, yeah, right, sure."

Erica roused herself long enough to complain: "Don't switch songs."

Odell was annoyed at the interruption. He had been going along so well that for once he had not only believed what he was saying, but had even come close to feeling it. He made an abrupt, dismissive gesture.

"It was just a parenthesis. But that comes into it too. Wait, you'll see. I told you—everything connects. That's all the Stones do. They draw the lines from one thing to another. It doesn't matter if it's right or wrong, or not. Now, in the third verse—"

"Already?" Erica murmured. This time he did ignore her.

"—the third verse is where he turns it all around. He starts out as Ulysses, naked and bleeding and left for dead on the beach; left for dead, because you can't be resurrected without dying first, everybody knows that. But then he decides that being Ulysses isn't enough for him, he can do more than that, and so, in the next line, he switches to being Christ instead—because when history is already over, it doesn't matter who you are, or what name you choose for yourself; you can be anyone. He crowns and crucifies himself in the same moment—*with a spike right through my head.* Except it's Lucifer instead of Christ. Because maybe it's better to rule in hell and maybe it's not, but hell is the only place he knows, so he might as well start there. That's how he becomes free—not by choosing good or evil, but by saying there's no difference, and putting himself beyond both of them. He looks into the abyss and saves himself by loving the abyss. He creates himself out of nothing, he turns himself into Jumping Jack Flash, and celebrates himself; he's seen the twentieth century and beaten it at its own game, embraced the decadence and the brutality and the horror and all the rest of it, and made it his own by saying it's all great. Because when you're born in the heart, the center, of evil, the only way to save yourself is to master it, or else you just become another body in the nothing all around you. The only way to escape Lucifer is to be Lucifer," Odell declared violently. "That's what rock and roll is all about," he added.

Briny sweat soaked his armpits—he went slack. Emptied of all energy, he couldn't face her. "And you," he explained lifelessly, "you're the final evil, don't you see? You're the evil they have to destroy in order to surpass it. You're the last passion that has to be overcome, before they can set themselves free. Because they all want to be Jumping Jack Flash. That's why they hate you, because that's the only thing that can save them. They have to kill you to win. But they know they'll never be able to, and so they . . . uh, they . . ." He turned away, his throat quivering with effort, and shrugged. "I mean that's basically it," he said.

Behind him, he heard Erica stand up.

"And you want to believe that," she said.

"I do believe it," Odell said.

"You really want to believe that's the way things ought to be."

He couldn't look back. He was afraid that if he turned his face to her, she would be mocking him; even if she hadn't been before then.

"Well," she said unexpectedly, "maybe you're right."

Then he did turn around. Her voice had been flat, toneless. Her face was the same. She looked worn out, like a mother, and quite empty; even her green eyes, to him, now, looked gray. He felt an unmistakable thrill vibrate like a tuning fork in his stomach—starting there, and going down.

"Or maybe it just doesn't make any difference," she went on carelessly, "and you're still right."

He couldn't believe that he had actually won her over; he felt a flush of pride. And yet it was so unexpected that he could not find an expression for his face. His instinct had stopped when he stopped talking, and he had to look away again. *You have to leave while you're still you,* a part of him was saying. *Before it breaks down and you have to start being somebody else just to go on.*

"You want to be like that, too," she said. "You want to try, just like you said about them."

"Yes," Odell said; reluctantly now, and with a twinge of fear.

"And that means you want to go to bed with me, doesn't it? I mean, that's what all this was supposed to lead up to, wasn't it?"

"What do you want me to say? Yes."

He heard her sigh. "Well, troops," she said, "here we go again."

She was too close, he thought; too close. Too close, even though she was only a shadow, like him, even though neither of them was really here at all—it wasn't her hand on his arm—he couldn't remember her ever touching him before.

"Hey," she said. "Little boy." But her voice was soft: "Do you want to fool around?"

CHAPTER FIFTEEN

Richard: 5

They were over at Amy's place, and a few of Amy's friends had dropped by. Richard could never remember their names. They came and went, wraithlike and soporific, and one replaced another without any change in the room. At Richard's feet, one of them lay passed out on his back with his mouth open, the hairs of his beard curling inside his lips, as if in search of shelter.

"You don't love me no more," Amy said to his ear. She had been saying that all evening.

"I'm a romantic. I don't love anybody."

"Oh Christ," she told him, "you are so wasted."

"I'm all right."

"Sure," she said, "you're all right. You just talk and act funny."

Richard was watching her friends. Even when they moved, they were still. They might be crawling organisms on another planet, protozoa with loud voices, but his telescope wouldn't focus.

"Let's go to a dark room," Amy whispered.

"You go. I can't get up."

"Hey, Richard," a blurred voice insisted to his other ear. Richard switched channels:

"Yes, Jack."

"You want to come out to the car?"

"Commander Quaalude again."

"No—got some mesc."

"Oh, man . . . I'm seeing too much already."

"Amy?"

"Where's it from?"

"Carmel."

The name bothered him, though he couldn't think clearly why. He slumped catatonically in his seat.

"I'll be back," Amy told him.

People came up and talked at Richard. He tried to answer, without success. They didn't seem to mind. Some of them had first met him in the days when Carmel was using them as troops in the Seastrom campaign, and so they treated him with respect in spite of his incoherence, as an intimate of the only power they recognized.

A face positioned itself in front of him. Eventually he noticed it. It was distinctive in that it only observed him, without attempting to speak.

"Hello," Richard said.

"I was wondering if you were alive."

"Do I know you?"

"Maybe."

"Your name's Crissa."

"Christy. You were close."

"That's a nice name, Christy."

"It never did a thing for me."

After careful study, he was able to determine that she was very thin, with long slender wrists and veined hands; her eyes were a pale green, like Erica's the first time he looked, like her own the second, and like nothing at all by the third. A hint of sullenness fleshed the corners of her mouth. He thought that she must be very young; and the way she held her head cocked to one side, with her hands laid flat on her thighs as she knelt, confirmed him.

"I know I met you somewhere, but I can't think where."

"Maybe you met me nowhere."

He liked that. It sounded very existential. Really ought to find out more about that stuff. "You should see me when I get straight," he said, "I'll remember everybody."

He was about to say more, though he wasn't sure what, when Amy hurtled joyfully back into the room. "Behind my back, cocksucker!" she cried out gleefully.

"I wouldn't wanna be in the way," Christy said.

He didn't see her go, because Amy had seized his face and was kissing him. He wondered if she ever brushed her teeth.

Then there were more people, and soft lights going bright, and music. Richard felt a vague need for subtitles. Someone spilled a lit pipe in his lap; he looked on stupidly as hands brushed the sparks away.

Amy was leading him to her room. He crumpled onto the bed. She began to undress him. He lifted docile arms to her commands. "I've been here before," he muttered.

She worked her way into his nerveless grasp, she stretched out on the bed beside him. "Kiss me goodnight," she said.

Abruptly, without any decision on his part, they seemed to be fucking. He wondered how this had come about. Letting go, he was lost, moving without consciousness, one blue light burning to light the curve of Amy's cheek. Her body carried him, but she neither knew nor cared who he was. She was strung out of time and a million miles away, twisting to chemical visions and not to him at all.

She turned away from him and curled up tight into a motionless ball, only her eyes drifting wildly as if they had broken their moorings. He spoke to her. She didn't answer. He stood up. She didn't move. She had gone away completely. He wasn't there anymore. He put on his clothes and left.

The living room was empty; that startled him; he thought no time had passed since they had gone into Amy's room. Only the ashtrays, the piled records, the empty and half-empty beercans remained to say that human beings had once lived here.

Outside, in the cool darkness, he let the air out of his choked lungs. The sky was starless, the moon was only a smudged brown outline. Christy was sitting under a lamppost at the curb.

"What're you doing?"

"Waiting for you."

"How'd you know I'd come out?"

"I didn't."

"Oh."

"I love being alone at night," she went on in her flat voice. "You can wrap yourself up in the dark and pretend that everybody's dead."

"Nice work if you can get it," Richard said.

The lamplight made her look even younger. "Amy told me you were working on a show. Some kind of rock show."

"Nah," Richard said. "Just talking."

"I never really got into that artistic kind of stuff."

"Smart girl."

"That sounds condescending."

"It wasn't meant to."

"That doesn't make any difference. I'm very sensitive about my age. It's how it sounds, not what you mean. I need a ride home, by the way."

"All right," Richard said.

She stood up, narrow and angular, silhouetted against the street.

"It doesn't look like anybody's inside," Richard said, when they pulled up in front of her house.

She did an unexpected thing. She looked embarrassed. "Nobody is," she said, and waited for silence to follow her words. Then she went on: "Would you mind coming in for a minute? It scares me to walk into an empty house."

Richard had used up all his chivalry. The night had already lasted too long. "If there's a killer inside," he said, "he'll only get both of us."

"Oh, shit," she said. "Forget it."

"You don't have to if you don't want to," she told him, when they were halfway up the walk.

"It's all right."

They went into the living room. She sat beside him on the couch. "Do you want a beer or something?" she asked.

"God, no."

"Music?"

"If you want."

"I think music is something people use to fill pauses."

She could be so irritating sometimes. "Well, no, then," he said.

"You don't know me very well. There might be a lot of pauses."

"It's a challenge." Richard wasn't planning on staying long enough for there to be any pauses. "You don't know me either," he reminded her.

"Maybe I do—better than you think. I do a lot of sitting around, listening to people."

"So you know all my secrets."

Her lip curled scornfully. "Sure," she said. "All your big romances. At least from when people used to talk about you."

Richard let that one go. There was so much to let go these days. "What about you? Don't you have a love life? We ought to keep things even."

The scorn deepened. "No, I don't. I'm just a little girl."

"Oh, shit. How old are you, anyway?"

"Almost fifteen."

He had put her closer to sixteen, maybe older than that. He didn't know why his surprise should have such a delicious edge; he had no designs on her, none that he knew of. Still, fifteen—*almost* fifteen—hoo, man.

"That's too young to have a love life," she said primly, but her mouth flickered as she said it. "You don't think I'm serious," she accused him.

"Are you?"

She shrugged her skinny shoulders. "Two of my best friends have already had abortions. It makes me feel kind of left out."

"Feel lucky, they cost money."

"That's not what I meant." She picked at a cuticle. "It's probably kind of dumb. But you know, when you listen to everybody talk about their favorite lay, and you can't do anything but nod when you think you're supposed to, and try not to let it show that you don't have any contribution to make—it's a social thing."

Richard sank into being swayed by the arid melody of her voice, as it worked through its little kinks and knots. For the first time in months he was tasting the sweets of new possibility, nursing the vision that here at last was his angel. He was potent with rich, paternal warmth. He looked at her pallid face, and found freshness there; he saw a trembling innocence behind the calculation in her eyes. He was already beginning to make her up. But he was not conscious of that.

"I guess it's a silly thing to worry about," she said. "But it gets to you." She was pacing back and forth, speaking with solemn detachment. "Sometimes I think that there's maybe something wrong with me—something abnormal. You're bored."

"No, I'm not. Much less so than usual. Honest." She probably didn't realize how erotic was her stance as she stood before him.

"I get scared sometimes," she went on, still pacing. "It's bad at my age to feel like an outcast."

"But you don't need that. You don't need any of it."

"Crap," she said tightly. "If you don't, how can you get on to anything else? You have to need it. Okay? PGP—"

"PGP?"

"Peer group pressure. That's dull. But you still get so you can't sleep, it's like an obsession—you get confused, you think that just 'cause you're alone, that makes you special. Fuck that. Who wants to be special?"

"But you're fourteen years old—all right, almost fifteen, but—"

"I know. I should have gotten over all this a long time ago, huh?"

He wanted to explain that he had meant something very different, that what she thought of as a burden was as exotic and wonderful to him as some rare tropical bird. He had already decided to save her. Inevitably, he was willing to accept his destiny before knowing for sure that it was his.

He lifted his head to smile at her encouragingly, and discovered that she was standing directly in front of him, the buckle of her belt only a few inches from his nose. Her expression was harsh. "Look," she said, "do I have to spell it out for you?"

"Ah, no," Richard told her, sinking. "Oh, shit. No, really."

She sat down close to him, her urgent slender hand pressing his. "It won't make any difference to you," she said.

But it would make more of a difference to him than it ever could to her. She was only thinking of herself as a person. He had already, promiscuously, turned her into a symbol, and he couldn't bear to abandon it. He had so few of them left.

"I'm not asking for a commitment," she explained. "I'm just asking for a favor. I absolutely guarantee that it won't mean a thing."

Richard reached for his beer before remembering that he didn't have one.

"If I don't," he asked slowly, "you'll just find somebody who will, right?"

"What do you think?" Christy said in exasperation.

He could see it already. Purple lights, moiling confusion, his lovely Christy too drunk to protest, feebly muttering, the greasy pawings of some pimpled pig. . . . Yet that was certainly what would happen. He was ready to cry.

He might be better for the task; he might be able to preserve her. He might guide her away from the pain at the end of the road she was so determined to follow—was it only his imagination, or could he really feel her nipples against his arm? Once he realized that the act was noble, it was easy to accept. The decision came almost by accident:

"Well," he sighed. "All right."

She showed no particular pleasure at his words. "You understand," she remarked, "this isn't any romance. I'm not trying to take you away from Amy."

Richard thought of Amy, curled on her bed, lost in acrylic dreams. "Sure," he said. "I understand."

"Okay," Christy said.

The kiss went on—she knew more variations than she should have. She was the one who pulled away at the end. "You know," she said, "I think I'm going to like you."

They moved to her room. The light was shaded by a paper bowl printed with the heads of cartoon characters. Christy reached across the bed to shut it off; Richard followed her leaning body with his own until they were both horizontal. Just before their lips touched, she looked up at the ceiling, and said: "I suppose you're wondering why I picked you."

He hadn't, actually; he was a little disturbed that she even felt the need to tell him.

"I didn't plan on you specifically—but I wanted somebody older. Old enough to understand, or at least to do it right."

At the reminder of their ages, he grew uneasy. He had hoped for a word that would warm the clinical chill of the scene, but it was not her taste to make such pronouncements; his melancholy was left marooned in the cold. He kissed her again. His hands moved to her breasts.

"Hey . . . Try to understand this too. Don't go too fast."

It seemed that she wished to execute all the formalities. He had been hoping to get home before dawn. "All right," he said.

"You must have had somebody in your life," he said, a moment later.

"I did. We almost made it, too."

His hand moved carefully along the plateau of her belly, carrying the edge of her shirt before it like a battle-flag. "Tell me about it."

"All right." Deftly, she curled against him. He extricated his hand and began a new progress, up her side.

"He was a lot older than me—about your age. I took some acid, it was a bad trip, I was walking the streets completely strung out and crying. Some way or other I ended up in the parking lot outside the library. I was sitting there and Glen stopped his van and took me away until I came down."

"I didn't know you were into drugs."

"Who wasn't? I'm a lot straighter now than I used to be—never stuck a needle in my arm, but I did just about everything else. I was sort of crazy when I was young," Christy confided cheerfully. "Glen got me off the harder stuff, 'cause he only did hash and pot, you know, what's safe."

Her voice wrapped itself around him. It looked as if he would have no choice but to learn something new tonight.

"We sort of got into the habit of seeing each other. It wasn't a sex thing—we just talked. He was very philosophical, peaceful, you know . . . He always talked about how he wanted to rescue me. I never found out what it was I was going to be rescued from."

Richard sagged under a dull, embarrassed pain. He tried to shore up the timber of his desire against the carving knowledge in her voice.

"He wasn't good-looking. For a while I even thought he was gay. But I developed a real thing for him, you know? A physical thing. I kept it quiet, though, 'cause I didn't want to wreck the relationship. Then one night he flipped out on THC and tried to rape me."

Richard pulled back to look at her, even though he couldn't see her in the darkness. "How did he try?"

"There wasn't any doubt, if that's what you mean. He tore off my tube top, you know? He'd never done THC before. I jumped out of the car and ran. It was funny 'cause of course I wanted to, but not like that. He scared me. He really scared me. I don't like being scared. I didn't go near a guy for a month."

"Why do you say a *guy*, like that?" His hands were still moving over her. With grim satisfaction, he noted that her breathing was slightly more audible.

"Oh, I fooled around with a girl, a few times, after that."

"Uh-huh." His hands stopped moving.

"That was actually sort of funny, too. The first time we were both stoned, and we were arguing about the best way for a guy to make the moves—girl talk, you know?—and we wound up trying it on each other. Then a few days later, straight, we got a little more involved. We'd see each other maybe once a week . . ."

"What stopped it?" Richard asked, his stomach tight.

"She told one of the guys she was seeing at the time, and he suggested that the three of us get it on. I backed out. I mean, they were pretty heavily into it, and I was just as much of a virgin then as I am now. Don't worry," she went on, laughter bubbling up in her voice, "I'm not a *les*bian, or anything. It didn't even turn me on, much. It was just to pass the time." Her laughter broke loose, and she gave him a kiss.

Now he forced it to last. He worked his fingers around her shoulderblades, and lifted her to get her shirt off. He had to stop kissing her to pull it over her head; his mouth was reaching for hers again before the shirt was past her eyes. He was afraid that she would pull away, and start talking again.

In her bra she was tiny, stalklike and slender. Richard fixed his

lips to her collarbone and eased her down onto her back again. His
hand ran over her bra strap, looking for a clasp, and found nothing.

"It unfastens in front," she said gaily. "You wouldn't believe
how many people it's confused."

Glumly, while his mouth nuzzled the upper parts of her breasts,
his hand moved between them and found the clasp. He pushed the
cups apart and moved his face lower.

Her body shifted, and Richard looked up inquisitively.

"Nothing," she said. "Just the way you do things—it reminds me
of a guy I used to know."

Wearily, Richard bent to the task again. He tried to vary his style;
her words had made him tense, and he couldn't find an appropriate
rhythm.

"That's a funny thing."

Richard took his mouth off her navel long enough to ask: "What?"

"The differences in people's techniques. How you could be blindfolded and still recognize them."

"Never worries me."

"I always notice things like that. It's one of my habits."

Richard gave up. "Did two of your friends really have abortions?"
he asked her.

"Sure . . . I had to loan one of them the cash. Don't worry, by
the way. No chance at all here. I was very careful about picking the
time, believe me. Is that why you asked?"

"No."

Each new thing she said chipped another piece from his statue
of her. But he was almost ready just to let that go; what pissed him
off was that she was dominating the dialogue. After all, he had
traumas just as valid as hers, if not more so—and he, at least, knew
one when he saw one. She reduced hers to mere anecdotes, which
struck him as an awful waste.

But if he couldn't equal her in conversation, he could lead in
other ways. He began to undo her belt and loosen her pants, agoniz-
ingly conscious of his every move.

To his surprise she stopped talking, and rolling against him she
helped him get her pants down. Soon she was nearly naked, looking
more frail than ever. Her legs felt as thin as a child's when he pulled
them into position.

"You're not bad," she said.

It was no use, she had broken his rhythm again. He stopped.

"I mean you're pretty confident," she went on. "I like that.

There was one guy I used to see who was so neurotic. Always asking me how it was. You know, in the middle of fingerfucking me, before he even pulled it out. Finally he was about to go down on me and I said No, you're no good, before he even started."

"That must have done wonders for him."

"I was about ready to ditch him anyway. But guys are weird. They've got freaky notions. That girl I used to fool around with, remember? She always had a lot of guys on the string, and she thought everything was cool. Until one of them asked her if she was faithful. Those exact words. Faithful! She could have lied, but she was honest, she told him the truth, and he walked out the door and wouldn't go near her for three days. Do you know what she told me?"

"No. What did she tell you?"

The first time he had asked Erica if she were faithful, she had told the truth just like the other girl, and he had walked out too. He had come back, though; he had always come back, for as long as she let him, and he had stopped using the word "faithful" in front of her.

"She said once that sex was the closest she ever came to praying. I mean, was that a joke or something? She was actually pretty strange— that's another reason we didn't stay together. As far as I'm concerned, whatever you do is just what you do, you know—for fun. Right?"

"But there's a lot more to it than that," Richard protested, feeling outraged. "People go through all kinds of hell—"

"Oh, bullshit."

"Why don't you quit talking about things you don't know anything about?"

"Don't say that to me." Now they were both angry. Their bodies were rigid. "How was I supposed to know that you were insecure?" Christy said in an arch, infuriating voice.

"I'm not. I'm just old-fashioned," Richard said, and shoved his hand down inside her panties as roughly as he could.

She sat up, fast. Her small breasts wobbled. "Don't be a bastard," she said in a pale voice.

"I'm sorry."

She folded her arms tightly over her thin chest. "It would serve you right if I ended this right now," she said.

He seemed to remember that he hadn't been the one who'd started it, but that was a long way away. His mind was fraying, fragments colliding in the dark, blind man's furniture . . . and when she told him the truth, he walked out the door . . . He turned back to Christy out of a child's blind need for protection. She came easily

into his arms. "I'm glad you didn't keep *that* up, she said. "I mean, I
like you, and I wouldn't want to have to change my mind. But *do*
you get hung up on being faithful, and all that kind of crap?"

"I think it's nice when it's there."

"But you're here with me anyway."

"What does that have to do with it?"

"Well, Amy . . . Remember Amy? Are you going to tell her? I
think anything's all right, so long as you tell people."

"I'm not going to tell her."

"Why not? She told me she tells you everything."

"When'd she tell you that?"

"When I found out about Jack."

Only a few hours ago, the education would have been painful.
But now Amy was fading fast, and another figure was returning to the
center of the stage: and when she told him the truth . . .

"But he's as fat as a pig."

"She's no swizzle stick herself. No, I didn't mean to say that.
Look, they were wasted, it was nothing. '

"How'd you find out?"

"Cars have windows, even when it's dark, and it's kind of hard
to walk on by when you see this boot kicking rhythmically against
one of them."

"You did say you did a lot of watching and listening."

She stiffened under him. "Don't get shitty again."

He didn't say anything.

"I'm afraid of ugliness," she told him in her flat little voice. "I
hate vicious people."

When they turned to each other again, he finally got her panties
off, she was naked at last. He pressed against her, hunting for passion.

"I hate to point this out, but you've still got all your clothes on."

The truth was that he didn't want to take them off. He was already shivering. She didn't seem to feel the cold at all.

"Can't we get under a blanket, or something?"

"What's the matter? Don't you want to look at me?"

She was flirting with him. Richard was stunned. He would have
thought the occasion for that had passed long ago.

Propped on one elbow, she watched him undress. It seemed unfair that he could bare himself so easily to Christy, after all the time
it had taken to do the same for her. He lay down, naked, burrowing
like an animal for warmth. Their bodies tangled; when her head started
to slide down his chest, he let her go. Trying to relax, he reached down

to touch her hair. He imagined he could feel each separate spiky point as it brushed over his thighs. Just as he was beginning to loosen, she took her mouth away.

"Go on," Richard grunted.

She pushed her moist face against his shoulder. "You don't understand," she said. "That's not what I want. Don't get me wrong, I like it, it's nice, but I've done it before."

"I wasn't even close," he lied.

Christy made a muffled sound of amusement. "I just didn't want you to get too used to it," she said.

"Then why did you start?"

"Haven't you ever heard of foreplay?" she said irritably.

"Haven't you ever heard of cockteasing?" he said just as irritably.

"Don't call me that. Call me anything you like, but not that."

"Oh, shit," Richard said, "let's just do it, okay?"

And when she told him the truth—

"Now," Christy said.

Aching, he began to go through the preliminaries. It was no use. Nothing was left but the chill, the unyielding body which he touched and stroked and probed, hoping without hope to stir himself to action. As he crawled on top of her it felt like going up a cliff.

"That's it," she said.

But it wasn't. He was on the verge of going completely limp, and he was raw, aching too, from all the rehearsal. His first few jabs missed the mark, and he could feel his strength dissolving under him with each new failed attempt. Finally he had to use a fumbling hand to guide his way.

"That makes it less romantic, somehow."

Forced to urgency by her voice, and by the happy shouts of a hundred new-born ghosts struggling to breathe, the bells of dread clanging in his ears, Richard went back to the siege, and succeeded in finding a path. He gave a good hard push, hoping for a quick release.

"Ouch."

"You're so goddamn tight," Richard muttered, still swamped at the arena's gates.

"Remember," she said in a small, recalcitrant voice, "remember, I am only fourteen."

That tore it. He could feel himself ebbing, shrinking away from her. Horrified, he made a last lunging try at getting it in before it wilted completely. "What?" she said, clutching at his shoulder, "what's going on?" Sweat broke all down his spine. He molded his body against hers, trying to get himself alive again. He fell back, gasping.

"No," she said.

He twisted away from her and tried desperately to pump his life to stand again.

"Oh," Christy said in disgust, "don't do that."

Limp cock clutched in a dead man's fingers, an anguish finally pure recoiling all through him in frenzy, Richard howled, "Well, my God! I have to get it up somehow!"

Panic burst in his chest. It was all over. He pulled himself back onto her, and flung himself like surf upon her shores, many times. Nothing happened.

"This is hopeless," she decided.

Richard sagged against her, helpless, his last defenses broken. His head sank down between her breasts and he cried out, "Oh, please, please, oh please . . ." He did not know for what he was begging, to whom.

Perhaps it was his angel.

When his trembling passed, they were quiet for a while. "Oh, Jesus," Richard said, brokenly. Christy took it as her cue, and edged herself out from under him. Her body was silhouetted against the window as she stood.

"Well," she said, "I did my best"; and bent to put her panties on.

They dressed in silence. Richard stood in the middle of the room, wishing that he could just simply stop, pulse, heartbeat, brain, all. Whores abnature a vacuum: music, to fill a pause.

"That girl," Richard said, his voice scratchy as an old record. "The one you told me about—"

"What about her?"

"How did you meet her?"

"I met her at a concert. She was singing with a rock band. Why?"

There was one more question to ask, but he couldn't ask it, because he knew what Christy's answer would be. To know the answers, all you needed to know were the questions—and when she told him the truth, he walked out the door.

CHAPTER SIXTEEN

Within a Grove of Buddies: 6

Andrew lay on the lawn and stared up at the moving sky, his prone bulk looming white against the browning, uncut grass and its speckled rug of dead leaves. A few of the neighborhood kids had gathered on the sidewalk and were watching him curiously. He was immobile: only his deep liquid eyes, blinking restlessly, showed that he was alive. Occasionally, his lips would part to release a wet, gurgling chuckle, which soon faded into silence. The door of his car was open, and the engine was running.

That was what Carmel told Lang and Myra when he came into the kitchen. He had seen Andrew on his way into the house, and paused to shut off the car's engine. The children had backed off a little at his approach, but returned when they saw that he wasn't going to interrupt their show.

"He's done that before," Myra said moodily. "All the kids call him Gulliver. I suppose I should bring him in, but the truth is he's probably happier out there."

"Yeah. I didn't talk to him." Carmel turned to Lang. "I came to see if you wanted to go for a drive with me. One last visit. You want to?"

"Depends on where you're going," Lang said. He still hadn't

recovered from the hash session with Odell; his head was thick and listless, all its circuits dead. When he had seen Carmel jauntily approaching the house, he hadn't even been able to feel any hate for him. *This is the man who took Johanna away,* he told himself. But the words didn't connect to anything inside him.

"A cemetery," Carmel told him cheerfully. "I want to visit a cemetery."

"I thought she was cremated," Myra said.

"Oh, not her," Carmel said. "I wouldn't want to see her. No, this is something special—a trip I've been meaning to take for a long time."

He was wearing a belt with an oval mirror.

"Do you want to come with me?" Carmel repeated.

Lang shrugged. "If it makes you happy. It's all the same to me."

"It makes me happy."

"Have a good time," Myra said.

Andrew was still on the lawn. The children were still watching. They watched Lang and Carmel too.

"Let us cross the river," Andrew recited in his rich rumbling voice, "and rest under the shade of the trees."

"How's the weather?" Lang called to him.

"Fine," Andrew answered. "Lovely, Daniel."

When they were out on the highway, Carmel remarked: "That man is not long for this world."

"You just don't like it because he's out of your market. He's legal."

"Who says that makes him out of my market?" Carmel asked. "Huh. Myra talks about him stopping. But that's his whole identity, right there in that bottle, man. She takes that away, he won't be there at all."

They drove over a bridge that straddled the river and the highways flowing down to Suffragette City, and crossed the state line into Maryland. The sun sat like an abandoned toy on the edge of the horizon, where the clouds broke, and the thin slivers of its light splintered on the river's stately gray unrolling. Lang was mystified—this wasn't Carmel's territory.

"Are you really taking me to a graveyard?" he asked.

"Of course," Carmel said, grinning. "I'll never lie to you."

They arrived at the place soon enough. Dimly, through the blue haze of dusk, Lang made out clusters of tombstones beyond the gates, leaning together in the wet, thin grass.

"We're about ready to close," the caretaker told them.

"We won't be long," Carmel said.

Lang thought they must look more than a little strange: Carmel dressed for a ball, his belt buckle and Myra's false eye winking at the setting sun, a leather handbag over his shoulder; himself in a filthy black T-shirt, bluejeaned, booted, and unshaven. Both were equally out of place in the cemetery's aura of stolid, seedy respectability.

Carmel made his way with quick assurance along the winding paths between the stones, his cigarette jutting out like a periscope. Most of the graves were old, their markers cracked and stained with weather and age, the names close to illegible. They passed a latticed gazebo, a bit run down, like the graves, and turned a corner.

"Here," Carmel said.

Lang looked down at the place he indicated. There, on one square stone, was carved the name of the last American poet, and that of the woman who had been his victory, his defeat, his reward and his sentence all in one—both fading in the twilight.

"I didn't know they were buried here," Lang said.

"Most people don't. I didn't, for a long time. Richard told me."

Lang was silent; moved, in spite of himself, by the austere memory carved in the stone, growing dim in the fading light. He wanted to linger for a while, but Carmel's voice wouldn't let him. It pushed him forward into new connections, other links on the chain.

"Richard wanted to bring Erica here," he said, "right after they broke up. Can you picture it? A little tasteful necrophilia to get the romance going again. She wouldn't, though—she didn't want to take the risk."

"She wouldn't have come back to him, even for that. Richard was just being sentimental."

"That's what he's got—you play with what you've got." Carmel's voice had the hard-nosed decisiveness of a business transaction. "Like Andrew and his booze—or Erica, with love. Everybody's got a ticket."

He took a few stiff-legged steps around the rim of the grave. His fingers forked a cigarette—the smoke rose to touch the dusk. "Well," he said quietly. "How do you like it?"

The names on the stone stared up dully at Lang. He could not resurrect the brief life they had lit when he first saw them. Now they were only faint scratches on a slab of marble, and no more than that. Carmel leaned on the marker, and threw his cigarette away.

"You see," he said, "it's really so much bullshit, after all."

"Are you going to preach to me too, now?"

Carmel smiled—abruptly, he was at his most boyish again. "Maybe. Just a little bit. See, I brought you here for a reason—I want to talk to you about your future."

"My place in Icarus," Lang said, remembering.

"Yeah. Your place," Carmel answered. He resumed his restless pacing around the grave. "You know," he said, "I heard that tape you sent Richard—that you made with that band in New York. And I thought, wow. You really got it—you really got this town, you hit it dead on. But you fucked up, man. 'Cause underneath all that noise, you were still dreaming the same dreams that put this place on a death trip from the start. I mean, I could tell. You still wanted to believe that if you just took one step further than the rest of them, you could make it all good again—but it never was any good to begin with, you know that. And still you figure that if you could only fall in love, for once, for real, then you'll be saved."

"And you don't."

"No. 'Cause that just poisons you. Didn't you learn a thing, from all the time you did in Icarus? It's not love, not at all, man, it's connections. Connections and little wires, everywhere, you plug into me and I'll shoot you some juice, sell you enough power to cruise just one more time. You got to get those little wires to hum, that's the secret of the game—you think I deal for money? Shit. I deal because that's my finger in the pie. I got half the people in town, you know? and they wouldn't want the sun to shine if I didn't put it there."

Lang smiled. Carmel smiled, too.

"Yeah, it's funny. It has to be. Did you ever listen to the way those people laugh? Look at 'em. Pimply kids lookin' for the wild side. Little girls who think I'm such an ace stud they want to ball me on the highs I give 'em. Freaks in vans, lookin' for California, so laid back they could of died three days ago, and who would know? I swear you can get sick. Not to mention all the people I got to cozy on the inside, all that Junior League Mafia baggage, with the .32's up their armpit and the Kleenex in their crotch, and they'd kill me if they had the guts, but I'm too pretty. I'm a good businessman, you know—I got brown on my tongue and hate in my heart and I'm the string they've got to pull if they want the world to keep on turning. Yeah! You, and Richard, and Erica, and all the other fucking basket cases out there, you all thought you were artists—*I'm* the artist, man!"

Lang zipped up his leather jacket against the wind, and turned the collar. He understood, now, how so many others had come under Carmel's sway. He tried to resist the rush, but it was useless. He felt the same fearful exaltation he had known when he first saw the glow of the cauterized spike, and Carmel's words took hold of him like heroin.

"So why," he asked, "are you telling me all this?"

Carmel held up his ring hand, thumb and forefinger half an inch apart, and drew close to Lang. His face was warm with joy, but his voice was calm:

"I got a plan. I'm working it out now. It's taken me a long time, because it involves trusting some people I don't want to trust, and back-stabbing a whole lot more. And if any of them found out what I was really up to, well, I'd be balling Erica in the sky tomorrow. I been living under the gun for a year, and who the fuck else in town could do that? Suicide's easy, you understand. You set the terms. All Erica saved was her complexion. I took the dare, and now I'm about to make the last deal. And if it works, then no one will be able to touch me, because I will be the absolute, one and only, main man in the territory." He paused. "That's where you come in." He peered at Lang in the growing darkness.

"I'm still around," Lang said.

"I'm not going to ask you to get involved in the actual deal— that I have to do alone. But once I make it, then . . . I'm going to need some help."

"Why me?"

"You know the place. I mean you know how it works. It's in-side you, man. And I need someone like that with me, because it's going to be a big fucking complicated operation and I won't have time to watch over everything. You could be a lot of use to me, Lang," he said, an unaccustomed weariness in his voice. "You're the only one left. And it would be good for you too. I don't mean the money. I mean that this is a chance to cut right into the whole stinking heart of things, and know everything there is to know. You see, man, you don't have to wallow in this shit forever—you can come with me, and run the show instead."

Lang was kindled now. There in the dusk, he felt the fire crumbling his last walls. Back in the alley, he found the strength to move— unleashed by the junkie's finger tightening on the trigger, he dove sideways and down, throwing up one arm to knock the gun aside. The junkie's knees caved in on him, and the gun clattered against the raw bricks. Lang twisted and arched against him, slamming his elbow into the junkie's belly as he tumbled, and wrenched the gun away from the hand slick with sweat and rain. He backed away two steps and trained the sights on the crumpled body huddled against the wall. "Get up, motherfucker," he said.

"Tell me the plan," Lang said.

"I can't. It's not a question of trust."

"But you want me to trust you."

"You have to," Carmel said. "I'm all you've got."

The darkness was complete, and the names on the grave were now indecipherable. The two of them stood there silently, listening to the wind.

"You know what I dug about Gatsby?" Carmel asked suddenly, as if remembering where they were. "Yeah, I read that book. Some bullshit high school English class—you know, they asked me what the meaning was of those big eyes on the billboard, and I said, That they're open. No. Tell you what I dug about Gatsby. His effort, Jesus, his incredible effort. Like he built a mountain just to be closer to the sky. No holds barred, fuck 'em all, concentrate on the main chance. Fantastic." He flicked the ash on his cigarette. "Too bad it was all wasted on a girl," he said.

"That's what you think."

"Yeah," Carmel said, remotely. "You haven't given me an answer, yet."

"I can't tell you now."

"Take a couple of days, then. No more, though. I can't afford more."

"I'll tell you tomorrow."

"Good." Carmel grinned. "A toast," he said, "to our potential partnership. Or call it just a gesture of good will." He opened the mirror on his belt buckle, and removed a small, flat disc. "The best stuff, absolutely the best, on or off the market," he said, opening the disc. "It's already cut. Have some."

Lang dipped his finger and took a sniff. "Well," he said, "that's something."

"Told you so," Carmel said, taking some for himself. He replaced the disc. "You want to go? It's getting too dark."

"Don't tell me you're scared of being surrounded by dead people at night."

"Yes, I am," Carmel said, with some grimness. "It gets too close."

They started back through the tombstones. Lang was going to look back at the grave they had just left, but stopped himself—it was too dark to see now, anyway.

As they approached the gazebo, Carmel held up his hand. "Do you hear it?"

"What?"

"Listen!"

Beneath the faint singing of the birds, Lang heard a chorus of small mutterings and breathings, the sigh of loose clothes pushed aside. It came from the gazebo.

"Let's have a look," Carmel said. "Just a look."

Reaching into his handbag, he got out a small flashlight, cautioning Lang to keep quiet. They came up to the gazebo.

A high and almost childish voice spoke with sudden clarity above the small sounds: "Johnny, please hurry—get it over with, I gotta go . . ." Carmel twitched with silent mirth. Lang felt sick.

Carmel lifted the flashlight up to an opening cut in the latticework, switched it on, and barked: "Police! What's going on in there?"

"Oh, Jesus!"

There was a brief, mad scuffle inside. Out of the other side of the gazebo came two frantic, half-naked figures, stumbling in their sweaty panic, their clothes flying, jerky and fast as a silent comedy. They raced off wildly among the graves, looking like darting fireflies in the gloom until they finally disappeared, and the silence crept back into its place.

Carmel cupped his hands and bellowed after them:

"Hey! Kids! Can I sell you some dope?"

He came back to where Lang stood waiting. Lang saw that he was in a high state of nervous excitement. His fingers trembled as he replaced the flashlight, and there was a note of hysteria in his laughter. "For a minute," he said, "when I first heard 'em, I was sure one of the stiffs was walking—oh, man! Did you see them go?"

"I saw them."

Carmel danced a little victory jig, jerking one knee up in the air.

"The poor bastard won't be able to get it up for a week . . . And her! Her first time! In a cemetery, boy! No sense of propriety." His words came tumbling over each other. The coke had hit him hard. He was charged now, animated, shaking as he walked. He put his arm around Lang's shoulders, something he never did. "Hey!" he said teasingly, "Ain't you high?"

"No," Lang said. He had missed somewhere. He felt the chill, but that was all; the sight of the two kids, running away in terror, calling out to each other like frightened animals, had taken away the rest.

"One of the guards reported a disturbance," the caretaker said to them as they approached the gate. "You boys didn't see anything, did you?"

"Us, sir?" Carmel said. "No, sir. We're clean-cut young American lads." Oddly enough, as he said it, it could have been true; his face shone like milk, and his blond hair gleamed in the twilight with all the purity of the Midwestern fields. "Only came out here for some of Mom's apple pie—she died a year ago today and . . ."

"Shut up, Carmel," Lang said, pushing him toward the car as the caretaker began to rise from his chair.

Driving home, Carmel handled the wheel with such assurance that it was as if he'd never been high at all. As for Lang, the cocaine had finally begun to reach him, but in a bad way. He was suspended above the emptiness of his own mood, his heart.

They arrived at the house. Carmel tapped him on the shoulder. "Remember," he said. "You decide tomorrow."

"Don't worry. I will."

Lang got out of the car. Some memory of the grave behind him—of all the graves—teased his skin with heat as he crossed the yard. He felt dread crawling inside. The price of freedom was to accept the gift Carmel had offered—oh, he could lose it all there—even the sight of the dead man, his grasping hands stiffened into claws as he lay on the asphalt with his blood caking around the hole Lang's bullet had made in his heart, and the soft rain falling on his sightless eyes.

Lang entered the house. Both cars were gone, and no one was home. Quickly he moved through the rooms, turning on all the lights. When he came back to the kitchen, he saw an envelope lying on the table, addressed in Johanna's handwriting. At first he thought it was his own, but that letter was downstairs in his duffel bag, folded inside Erica's tambourine, and the address on this was to the Hoffentlich family, no other name. Lang picked it up and opened it. Inside was a formal card, engraved and stiff to his touch. It was the announcement of Johanna's engagement, for a wedding three months from now, to a man named Ron Bridgeport, in that small Southern town where she had disappeared after escaping from Icarus, some time before.

CHAPTER SEVENTEEN

Brewer: 2

Brewer stood in his living room and watched himself grow solid in the picture window, by the yellow light of the living-room lamps, as an afternoon thunder threw its dark scarves across the sky. He turned away, then turned again, to rehearse himself once more, caught in three-quarter profile above his own slanting shoulder.

It wasn't love, he thought. Not love that held him here. Revolted fascination—fascinated revolt—bunched and twisting like a worm on a hook. Worms love the hook: their purpose in life. O pierce me.

If he could ever break free long enough to sink into anyone as deep as he sank into himself, it would have to be love. Nothing less— he told himself—would chase him from his hole, out into the shadow-less light. Where then?

Deliver me from reasons why you'd rather fly, I'd rather cry.

Brewer discovered he was in a sweat. He had been fevered by his mind, and not the weather, which lay bleak and cool under the clouds, as if waiting. We breathe in what the earth breathes out, Brewer thought. He pressed back an urge to wipe his reflection away.

I could keep this up forever, you know.

He picked up a bronze rose from the table—a souvenir from his mother's honeymoon. Its petals gave off a tinny twang when he plucked them. Silence bloomed from the sound and filled him like helium.

The rose had been lying across a book bound in imitation leather, stamped with his name in imitation gold. It was a chronicle of his childhood, bought blank at his birth from a stationery store that also sold Bibles and adding machines, and filled in by his mother in a hand that got increasingly ragged from year to year, until it finally ceased entirely in a creamy mire of empty pages. Brewer lifted the cover, and then let the book fall shut without looking at it.

But his name was still there. The sight of it, staring up from the table like a brained fish, never failed to make him uneasy. Yet he undoubtedly belonged to it. Perhaps it was when he first learned the distance between his name and what went on inside that he had begun to live with the notion that every fact is only the understudy to an ambiguity—or live beside it, as one lives by a river.

When the front bell clanged, hours later, he was sure, for no reason, that it was Richard. Erica was standing there instead. Brewer backed a step, to retrieve his thoughts. Under the gray thunderheads, her face was as sharply outlined as if it had been cut from a magazine. Her eyes glowed deep in their hollows—her colorless skin was pulled tight as a sail over her bones.

"Let me come in, at least," she said.

Brewer shut the door behind her and told her to go into the living room. Alone, he stood quietly in the vestibule, tight with panic. She had never come to him alone before. He felt as if he had been cut open like a pie, by a pale and frightening stranger—for she was finally just that, to him.

When he got brave enough to enter the room, she glanced at him over her shoulder, but did not speak. She stood in the middle of the room, hugging her belly. The silence reassured him. He could still be neutral. If that was anywhere.

"I brought back the books you lent me," she said, jerking her head toward the couch. "I figured you thought you'd never see any of them again."

Brewer looked down. There, dog-eared, *Nightwood. The Iceman Cometh. Hollywood Babylon. An American Dream.* And two Pogo books.

"Did you ever read them?"

She shrugged. "I read the Pogo. I never had time for the rest. But I was clearing out my room today, and I thought you might want it all back."

"Something's wrong," Brewer said, unwillingly.

Her wince stopped halfway. "I suppose I ought to apologize for coming," she said. "But you were the only one I could think of. It's funny that I trust you. There's not too many I do."

"It's only because I'm not dangerous."

"Huh," she said. "You rate yourself pretty high, don't you? If you want to be an angel, you'd give me a drink. Wine, if you have any. I know you're not supposed to do that . . . I'm all in," she said as if they were friends.

When he brought it he was struck again by how unhealthy she looked. Her face was luminous, like fever. She looked as lifeless as something he had fantasized. Again he was afraid. It came back like a memory. He wanted to be alone, where things were unbearable, again. She was sitting on the couch, next to the books, her body knotted, looking out the window, at the clouds waiting so patiently for the rain.

Then Erica turned around. "But you're wrong, you know," she said. "About being dangerous. Because when that much hate builds up inside for so long—never lets go—never speaks—people like that can explode, sometimes, and then it's all over before anyone has a chance to see."

She took the wine, looking up at his retreating hand. It must look so soft to her, Brewer thought. "You're so tense," she said, ". . . what are you waiting for?"

"Why did you come here?" Brewer cried. "I never did anything to you."

"I told you. You were the only one."

"I've never been that."

"Attrition," Erica said. "Everybody's at*trit*ing like crazy. I woke up this morning and decided everybody was gone. Really gone. Maybe I'll have forgotten about it tomorrow. Hope so. Have to function, anyhow."

She drank with both hands around the glass—the ice was like a small pale ghost in the red lights of the wine. She set it down, then picked it up again. She was suddenly fretful—her lips twisted before she spoke:

"Have you seen Richard, at all? Recently, I mean."

"I didn't think you'd care," Brewer said.

Erica nodded. "Oh, right. I forgot, I destroyed him. I ought to tie a string around my finger. Odell's been telling me all about how I destroyed him for more than a month now—"

"Odell?" Brewer said, surprised into practicality. "I didn't know you were talking to him."

"Oh, we're talking. That's just what we're doing—talking." She hesitated, trying to decide whether or not to pause. "Or were doing. But you didn't answer my question."

"Richard?"

"Uh huh."

"I saw him. Two days ago. Maybe three."

She wouldn't take her eyes off the floor. "How was he?"

Brewer felt displaced. Richard's name didn't seem to belong here. It was outside, like the weather.

"The same as ever." He decided to try out something else. "Pretty bad."

"But acting like he hadn't noticed it."

"Yes, if you want to put it that way."

She sighed, looking out the window again. "God, that's him," she said. "He never notices these things. He'll just go on, waiting for things to be pretty again ... When they don't have any right to be, anymore."

"You ought to know."

"You really do believe that, don't you? You, and every other dumb motherfucker in the joint. You don't understand it at all." She shrugged again. It was more like a tic. "That's all right. I'm tired of people who think they understand me. What I want for Christmas is a blank. A nice big cozy blank I can talk at. How does that suit you, Blank? Do you think you can manage that?"

There was a quality in her of not caring anymore what she said, or where it hit. It was letting go, not out of exhaustion or abandon, but with a cold, rich, and deliberated pleasure in the sweets that letting go might offer. It made her seem invincible. That was much scarier.

"Do you really hate me that much?" Brewer asked. There was no anger in his own voice; only a tone of earnestly wanting to know.

Erica smiled. It began at the center of her shut lips and curved off to one side of her mouth like an arrow. "What if I told you," she said, "that it's the other way around? C'mon, don't bother to say it's not true, people use too much up that way. I recognized you once—at a place where I was singing, years ago. Mostly I don't see any audience at all when I'm up there, but I saw you. All of a sudden, I was certain you were going to kill me. No, listen. I could see it in your eyes. I was in the middle of a song, and it went through me like a telegram, he's got a gun. Very strange feeling. I was so sure of it. Then when I looked again you were gone. Even so, I had to find somebody to take home with me that night. I wish we were still young enough to sleep with night-lights—it's a lot cheaper."

Brewer looked for a reaction. Until he found one, he asked, "Is that why you came here? Just to tell me that?"

"It may have had something to do with it. Oh, let it go. I came here for absolutely no reason at all. Will that do?" Then to belie her words she got to her feet, the wine-glass in her hand, and prowled the room around him like a camera, until she lit on the bronze rose on the table. She picked it up, and turned back to him.

"Who died?" she asked gaily, twirling the rose before her face.

He took it from her, and laid it back on the table.

"Oh, all right," she said like a girl.

Brewer watched her circle the room. It was no respite. He kept thinking of her power, of how she could make men act in ways that contradicted their whole character. They could eat themselves up inside trying to discover what she wanted; the answer wasn't in them, but it happened anyway. Even he could feel it now. But the tension was all his. She was calm and somber, all removed, one finger stroking her lower lip.

Brewer thought then of a night when they had gotten lost in Suffragette City, and ended up in a bar in a neighborhood where none of them had ever been before. The place was packed—nobody in the car had remembered it was Memorial Day—and after fifteen minutes of trying to get through the press, Richard said maybe they should just give up. But Erica—Brewer remembered it—told them all to wait; she went up to the bartender, tapped his arm, and said, "If I show you a boob, will you give us a free drink?"

Back against the wall, they couldn't hear a word; all they saw was the bartender do a take, and then nod, and then Erica, quicker than thought, unbuttoning three buttons on her shirt, and expressionlessly cupping her pale white tit for him for a moment before putting it away again. Then the bartender shouted that he was giving everybody in the bar a drink. There must have been a hundred of them, haw-hawing and glancing over at Erica after they got the news. She never bothered to look back.

Richard kept telling her how wonderful he thought it was, and even Lang gave one of his tight smiles; Brewer had been frightened. There was chaos in everything she did, a tearing of order that yawned in front of him like a hole torn in the air. He kept thinking of what would have happened if even one of them had taken her up on it. He got so rattled, in fact, that he had to let her take the wheel for the drive back home.

"Erica," he interrupted the silence now. "What makes you do the things you do?"

She looked amused. "If I knew that, what on earth makes you think I'd go on doing them?"

"No, I mean it," he said, "I really want to know," asking it less of her than to feel the borders of his fear. He thought she saw that he was serious. Even so, her answer made no sense to him.

"I don't do anything," Erica said.

"I don't understand you," he said.

"It was all him—it was all all of them. They invented somebody, and I just happened to be around to pour it into. They put all the things in me that they don't want to take the blame for, all the chances they don't want to take. Come on," she said, with a sudden laugh, "do you think that even if I tried to, I could have made myself up? I'm a cathedral—ten thousand people built me. Whoops, boom, another stonecutter just met his. Well, don't just stand there—get somebody else carving on that buttress. You, with the cape and the funny-looking cigars. Just kidding. No, I'm not. Come to think of it."

Brewer felt resentful. How could she be so proud as to think she had a monopoly on the edge? When all she had was a knack for the theatrics of doing it in public. But in the end he only said, "I don't know how you can say that. With all the things you've done."

"The things I do I do for me—not for them. What they make of it, that's their business, not mine." At his face, she grew mocking. "Oh, I know—I know I look like a death trip, and ooze decay, and smell like—like an oil slick burning," she said, "but I can't help thinking that no one's ever going to get to the end of anything who doesn't live the way I do, isn't that awful?" She laughed again, the ice rattling in her glass. "Oh, Jesus, they're stupid. I spend half my time forgiving people when I don't even think they're worth it."

"Like Richard."

"No. Not him." She was silent. "I thought he was worth it."

"What," Brewer asked, "what gives you the right to forgive anybody?"

"Because I'm better than they are," she snapped. "And anyway— it's a dirty job, but somebody's got to do it, right? Or else you might as well just lie down and let everybody have their way."

"Most people in town think you're already doing that."

"Oh, they can think what they like. No, fuck it, they can't. God, let Lorraine play that part—she's so much more of a slut than I am. I mean, I sleep with people, I sleep with a lot of people, but she—"

Erica's mouth went thin with scorn—"she tells them that she loves them! A new one every full moon! And then they're in for it. Richard's been coasting on that offer of hers for so long—he's totally in debt to her, she bought him time. But she's going to call in the bill, pretty soon now—you just watch . . ."

Brewer felt a real anger rise inside him. It was not sound so much as motion, involuntary and brief, but it caught her ear.

"What?"

"You're still in love with him," he accused her.

" . . ."

"No, I'm not. But it wouldn't matter if I was. That's over." Brewer had no sense that she was arguing with herself. She might have been regretful, but it was only in passing; as if she were behind a desk telling you that a certain thing was not done here.

But by then his anger had gone back to its usual place. He felt as if he were groping along a ledge. Without his knowing where the line had been drawn, things had gone along until they had become strange. But strange felt familiar. He might have been alone with this cardboard face. Outside, the sky was still waiting patiently for the rain.

"No, it's not," he said. "Not so long as you're still thinking about it."

"Maybe that's true for you. Me, the only time I ever think about anything is when it's over. Before, I just don't have the time."

"Anyway," Brewer said, wondering how malice would fit him, like a shirt, "he's over you."

"You talk like there was something left of him," Erica said. "Don't you see, that's why it doesn't matter how I feel about him, because he's not there anymore. They say it was me who did it . . . All I ever was was unfaithful," she said, "if you want to call it that. But he was my knight, and he betrayed me."

It hurt Brewer like a cigarette tightness in his lungs to have to talk about Richard with her. His mind resisted the name. But then, like a salmon coming over the last spill, he knew he had to know. He had never asked Richard; no one ever had who wanted to go on liking him, somehow.

"What happened the night you broke up? The night at Uncle Lou's?"

The flickering private smile played over her face. All over again he was aware of how apart she was.

"Do you really want to know?" she said. 'I never told anyone. Not even," she added as an afterthought, "him."

"Yes, I do. I mean, I'm not sure if I do, but if I don't I won't ever be sure."

He could see her tongue lolling in the inside of her mouth. "Okay," she said, "that's not bad." She took a deep breath, and then laughed as if to cancel the breath. "It wasn't anything that happened there. That's where everybody screwed up. But earlier, we were having dinner, at my place. We had run out of things to talk about on the outside—" and from the way she said *on the outside,* Brewer knew it must have been one of their expressions. That carved at him.

"—and he asked me what I wanted to be in five years. Just the sort of thing he loved to ask to fill the chinks. And that bothered me, but I looked at him and said, 'Well, a lot of things, but one of them is to be married to you.'"

Brewer burst out laughing. "You did that? You told him he was going to marry you? That's wonderful, that's fantastic." He could taste the sudden relief of vindictiveness at the heart of his laughter. But then Erica laughed too, and for that one moment it felt like they were partners in crime.

"Well, he didn't say anything, but even so, I didn't figure anything was wrong. So I thought, okay, I'll play, and said, 'Why, what do you want to be?' It was like I'd hit the fast forward. I don't remember exactly what he said, but it was a lot of stuff about how he hated to lock himself in, and he felt like he had so many burdens on him already that he wanted to keep himself free ... He was like somebody trying to talk their way out of a parking ticket. But I didn't realize how angry I was until we got to Uncle Lou's, and I watched him come on the way he always does, you know, like wow, we're all so boho. Then I saw something in him that I just couldn't stomach, really."

"That he was scared?"

"That it was all such bullshit," Erica cried out. "Come on, Brewer, *imagine* Richard talking about all the responsibilities on him, about wanting to stay free. What a fucking joke! He didn't understand—he'd never understood. All the things he wanted were just cheap tricks—not the real thing at all. He thought it was all just to look cool, and that was as far as it went. He didn't want any more."

She laughed. "Because, God," she said, "if he had wanted adventure ... Spending the rest of his life with me would have been an *adventure.*"

Then she got bitter again, down in herself, so deep that Brewer didn't want to follow. "But it wasn't just that. Not just selfish. Or maybe it was all selfish, I'm not the one to say. But just that if he of all people didn't know it was all for something more, that it was all for a reason, that meant he was just one more fucking person standing there to say that it was all wasted."

"I don't think that there is anything more," Brewer said after a while. "I used to, all the time, but then I quit."

They sat there in the gray light. From upstairs he heard the static from his mother's clock radio.

Now the memory that came to fill the space was of a night when he had gone over to Hoffentlichs' alone, so gone, and babbled on for hours. They thought he had passed out, and Myra said to Alice, "You know, he's going to kill himself someday." And Alice's lip curled and she answered, "Are you kidding? He'll still be working on the note when he dies of old age."

That may be sooner than you think, he had wanted to say, from the depths of their couch.

The big sleep. The maximized sleep.

He got up, stood up, and went to look out the window. The rain was still not falling.

"Then why do you go on with it?" the voice behind him said. "You know you're just as much a part of it as me."

"I can't do anything else."

This time there was enough silence to go around. Then she said: "Did you ever even try?"

"Once," Brewer said.

In his room she had been there, white on white sheets. He was coming back from class in the red sunset, under the red-gold hills, from postcard to postcard down the leaf-spangled blossoming concrete, to his dorm. *He wanted to leave, just like Dan Lang, but he went crack like an ice cube when you take it out of the tray and then he had to come home.*

Anita was in American Studies. Brewer, on the lookout for a new life, took the course because he'd heard it was a gut. She saw him outside the lecture hall; they learned to talk. She came from Roanoke and nothing bad had ever happened to her. He was endlessly amazed at how little of a past she needed to get through her life. That he had to make room on his maps for someone so unmarked. He couldn't explain it to Anita: there was no word in her language for most of what went on in his mind. It just had to go on stewing away by itself, living in stop-time, when he was with her.

It was in November that time started again. He unlocked his room, and touched the light-switch, and she flashed on in his sight as suddenly as if she had been the bulb itself, sitting on his bed with her eyes the only darkness—orphaned, by all that white.

Life's little ironies . . . Oh, fuck that.

I can't, he'd said.

She thought it was what he'd wanted. For him, she wanted to be more than she was. He turned the lights back off. It was easier to remember her in the dark.

You don't understand, he tried to tell her. His head was bowed down between her rigid breasts. The words ground out. *I'm ugly—so ugly—you don't want to know—*

She didn't understand. She told him she loved him. He was maddened by her stupidity.

You don't know enough to tell anybody that. You don't have the right. You don't know anything.

Tentatively, she reached out her hand and laid it on the inside of his leg, high up. He jerked back as if he'd been caressed by dry ice.

Don't do that, he hissed.

He heard a rustle, felt weight lifting from his bed. *Wait,* he said— *wait, where are you going?*

"Leaving," she had said.

The next time he saw her, walking across the campus between classes, he hit her in the face. He only missed the first time. When he woke up he was in the infirmary. They'd given him a shot. He sat in his bed for three weeks, staring at the wall as if it was all the books he'd ever written. Then his mother drove down and took him home.

"Once?" Erica said. "Didn't try very hard, did you?"

Brewer was annoyed. He still didn't know why she had come. She didn't have any right to come here, and make him think of things he didn't want to think of, things she couldn't know. "You're talking in circles," he said. "It can't matter to you." That didn't seem to be enough. "Maybe I am part of it like you say," he went on. "But I'm not like you. I don't—"

"Not like me?" Erica murmured. "Is that the best all of you can do?"

"It's true."

But she had already gotten to her feet. Flowing up, like a waterfall in reverse. She came toward him.

"Not at all like me?" she asked.

Involuntarily he cast a look at the rose on the table.

"Don't do this, Erica," he said.

"Oh, I'm going to do it, all right," she assured him. Her hawk's profile sliced the distance between them. So close by then he could feel her breath flow back and forth in the words. Trade route aroma, musk and tang and silvery silk, salt ships.

The room was pressing in on him. Barometer dropping, always thought it was from fear when you read that in the paper, fear of storms, dropping for shelter. Her circling fingers played a precision scale on the soft roll of flesh at the back of his neck. The warm hole of her mouth was next to his cheek.

"Not even a little bit like me, Blank?"

The chicken run. *Hee hee... Where's Buzz?* Erica's other hand drifted, eddied, riffed up his denimed thigh. He felt himself going into shock. At this sign of yielding, she snickered softly. Nipped his ear. "Well, you know," she whispered, "you can say what you want, can't you? Just let me take it all over... You know I could do you just like a man." She brought up her leg, letting it slide along his on the way, and started to hook it across the back of his knee. It was like being inside one of those clocks whose casing is made of glass. He couldn't stay there.

"—bitch," Brewer said, "get away from me."

Three steps from where his jerk backwards had flung her, she caught her balance. She stood there laughing at him. "Oh, Brewer," she said, "you ought to see it. Your fucking face."

"You *are* insane," Brewer said. "What makes you think you can treat people like that—like channels you switch when you get bored..."

Erica made a gesture of indifference.

"You can do to people whatever you can do to them," she said. "They don't know it. The walls are so thin. How much dirt they'll come running to lay at your feet if you so much as hint you're interested... And they all act so grateful for the chance. I hate it," she said. "I really do. And since when was calling somebody crazy a putdown to you, Brewer? You wouldn't have said that if you hadn't been awfully scared."

He knew that she could see that one go all the way in. She was telling him he didn't have the courage of his convictions, didn't truly believe in his own craziness. When it came to that topic, the two of them had always been like a couple of people running for assistant D.A. But it seemed so unfair to ask him to live up to everything, all the time—it wasn't supposed to be for her, but she made you feel that way. She commandeered everyone else's life.

"Well, are you going now?" he said. "You got what you wanted."

"No, I didn't. Not yet. I told you—that was the easy part."

"For you."

"All right," she conceded, "for me."

"Then what *do* you want?"

That made her restless. She fidgeted with her glass a bit, stood up, sat down again. "I'm not sure," she said at last. "I'm just—I'm just trying to decide, what the next thing is going to be. You know all of this is over. But I'm too tired to stop now ... Did it ever occur to you that the secret of life might be nothing more than good timing?" She turned away. Then she was not speaking to him at all. "If I was wrong," she said, "then I want to go now."

Then she was with him a little more; but she was still removed, her voice liquid, liquid and weightless, oddly serene. "I've got to work it out—I don't have much time." Her hand tightened on the glass, a bloodless shellshocked claw. "Danny, he knew—he understood. How scared is the only instinct you can't trust. How you have to make yourself go deeper than anybody, just to keep from drowning, and sometimes you come back with gold, and sometimes you don't come back at all." She laughed. "Oh, yeah. But you have to do it anyway, because you hate them. Don't forget how much you hate them. Because there's more truth on the edge than there is in the middle, and everybody spends their life running away from knowing that. Do you know what Lorraine said to me once, the funniest thing, I could have shot her for it, 'Well, Erica, all that's fine for you, but you don't have to carry living by extremes to excess, you know.'"

She shook her head. "Oh, Jesus, Brewer—what will they say about us a hundred years from now? How strange we were? Will they listen to the records, and look at the Valium and the spike-heel boots, and say, What a joke? Or will they say anything at all?"

Brewer said nothing.

"I mean, suppose—" she was already off on another tack. Her voice had taken on a ragged, rambling quality, as if she were seeing many different roads at once and any one of them might take her to her destination. "Suppose, that when we all started out, or began, or whatever you want to call it, we all had one mind—soul, if you want— and then something happened, and it got broken up into a hundred million pieces . . . and everything we call love, or friendship, and maybe hate too—everything we think is for other people—is really only trying to paste it all back together, with whatever glue we can find . . . They say the world began when the universe exploded, so why not us too, like that, from thin air?"

Then something seemed to die in her face, leaving her features with nothing underneath them.

"I suppose, you know, that this is what I mean: what do people who turn sex into a religion do, Brewer, when they get told that God is dead?"

Brewer was beginning to suspect that something was actually going to happen.

"Erica, what are you going to do?" he asked, not wanting to know.

"Try to take some of it with me."

"What do you—"

"—This." She clenched her fist and the wine-glass shattered. Shards and drops glittered as they fell through the air.

She let out a small cry; whether of fright or triumph, Brewer couldn't tell.

"Are you hurt?"

"No," she murmured, standing as he bent to pick up the pieces of the glass. ". . . It was almost empty anyway."

Brewer held the last ice cube in his palm, feeling it melt as he held it: like small, gray teeth decaying. He collected the broken glass and put it on the table, next to the rose. A few slivers still gleamed in the rug.

"I'm sorry," she muttered. "Freaked you, didn't I? It's what I'm good at, the boys say . . ."

"Erica?"

"What?"

"Why me? Why bring me into all this?" He didn't know the difference between honor and fear anymore. His belly quailed; he wasn't the one to ask for absolution.

"If it happens—if it happens, then I want someone to be there. To know. A witness, if you want to call it that. To say it wasn't that I gave up—that I was scared."

"If? It's your choice."

"It's not," she said. "I told you I don't do anything."

He knew he ought to have some words inside him, ought to make the gesture, at least, of telling her that what she was doing was wrong; nothing would come. She was so complete. She had already crossed the frontier—but she had always lived there. *My God,* Brewer thought, *we were all so out of it. So absolutely irrelevant. She was just being kind to let us think we had anything to do with the part that mattered. It couldn't have looked like more than traffic to her. But she still wants someone to know. Not us. Not me. She wants Lang to remember her. That's the only thing it can be.*

"But what about the rest of us?" he said aloud. "What will we do?"

"Do what you want," Erica said.

He laughed unhappily. "I don't know what that means."

"Brewer, look at me," Erica said.

He tried to.

"What you *want*," she insisted. "Even if it leaves you more fucked up than you were before. That's the only way anybody ever knows anything. Knows it for real. You have to try."

Then, at her words, he had the temptation to let go, to go into all of it—he wanted to come clean for her, in a way he never had for anyone before. Then, with mingled regret and relief, he realized that there was no need.

"Give me a little credit, at least," she was saying. "It is one of the things I've had some experience of. Don't fight it anymore. . . . Sometimes it takes more to give in."

"I don't know if I can go it alone," Brewer said.

"That's the only way you can do it," Erica said.

Then she smiled a little shakily.

"Okay," she said. "Now, I'll leave."

She looked down at the fragments of glass on the table, and held up her finger. "When this you see . . ."

It wasn't until the door shut behind her that it all sank in on Brewer. He stood before the window, watching her walk, straight-backed and slender, down the darkening driveway.

Suddenly he was seized by fury. Her arrogance. Her monstrous arrogance. How could she put this on him? He thought of what she had said, about seeing him in the audience at her show. It bothered him a little that she had been right.

Well, this time, he might prove her wrong. Just as he had stuck to his guns, against all the odds, and proved Anita wrong. That was the location of his pride.

He scooped the broken glass off the table and into his open hand. Then he carried the fragments, gingerly, out to the kitchen, and threw them in the trash. He could hear the engine of her car gunning, and then fading away; and then suddenly, the sound of rain—

Outside, the weather had arrived.

CHAPTER EIGHTEEN

Odell: 4

Fat bright-jacketed books bricked his room in ascending columns, leaning toward each other at their heights like the houses of an Elizabethan street; the barbed wire of their titles seemed to watch him as he sat. Often, typing messages to himself in the dead of night, Odell would turn in fear to a murderer hovering at his back, only to discover that it was his own looming library that had terrified him.

Even when his mind was empty, and what few thoughts came drifted like lonely sails across his horizon, Odell hated to be interrupted. "What do you want?" he snarled into the intercom, clicking it reluctantly back to LISTEN.

Another click echoed from the other end. "I have asked you not to use that accent to the family," his mother said. "Anyway, darling, I've got a class in the studio and they say your music bothers them, they can't concentrate, can you turn it down?"

Click. "Let them listen to it," Odell said, looking moodily at the prancing Jagger on his wall. "Maybe it'll change their lives." Click.

Click. "—their what?—"

Click. "—lives." Click.

"—Ha, ha."

Click. "All right! I'll turn it down."

Three days a week his mother taught painting to a gaggle of house-wives, based on a system she herself invented of interlocking patterns and lines upon which the colors were laid. She called it the Structured Palette, and had been trying to get it patented for years. Once Odell had shown Dan Lang her studio.

"Why didn't you tell me that she taught painting by the numbers?" Lang asked.

Shortly afterward, Odell's mother had given him to understand that Lang was not welcome in their house. So he had severed all connections with Lang—that had been hard, he knew, on Lang, but this was no time to be sentimental. Ceremoniously, he traced with his finger the words typed on an index card above his desk. "Silence, exile, and cunning," it read. Underneath, in parentheses, was typed: "Joyce."

His father had come in while Odell was tacking it to the wall. "I can see the silence and exile, all right," he said, "but you seem to have forgotten about the cunning." His father had still been wiping the tears of laughter from his eyes at the dinner table, forty-five minutes later.

But it wasn't true, Odell thought furiously, clenching his fists. His angst was the real thing, he knew—no matter that in his leather jacket he felt like a bad actor, while a crew-necked sweater fit him like a straitjacket, like a charm. When his emotions were too secretly wholesome, he had to twist them to darkness by an act of will—but that wasn't hypocrisy. His desire for decadence was too desperate to be false.

"The will to power," Odell repeated musingly. "The will to—"

Click. His mother: "Dearest? You have to do me a favor. Congressman Alberta's car just pulled in to his driveway, and the vote on the school lunch bill is tomorrow. Will you run over there quick and ask him to vote against it, as a favor to me?" Click.

Click. "—he won't listen to me, mother."

Click. "—Never mind. He has a responsibility to his constituents. Please?"

Click. Odell sighed. Ever since she'd found out that their new house was next door to a Congressman's, his mother had been unable to get it out of her head that he belonged to them. She was forever giving him advice. It was one of her habits which they had grown used to. Whether Congressman Alberta had also grown used to it was anybody's guess.

On his way down the corridor his mother came out of her studio and stopped him. A streak of paint scarred her cheek, perpendicular to a falling lock of Indian-black hair.

"Never mind," she said. "You're wanted on the phone. Muriel will do it."

"All right."

"—and darling?"

"Yes."

A paint-brush was stuck like an arrow behind her ear, and she reached up nervously to adjust it. "Reggie's here," she said.

"Oh, God."

"Now listen, lovey, listen. You know that Muriel really likes this one—much more so than usual. So no matter what our private opinions may or may not be, we've got to put them in the back of our heads and be very polite and very, very charming, do you understand?"

Her tone was breathy with drama; she considered herself to be very emotional, and she tended to judge all others by their histrionic abilities. "Yes, Mother," Odell said, picking up the phone.

Carmel was on the line. "Mink says you're looking for some speed," he said.

Odell glanced covertly to see that his mother was safely back inside her studio. "Yes, that's right," he said.

"You're in luck. I just got in some fine stuff."

"How much?"

"Thirty-five."

"All right."

"Fine. Mink'll be by tomorrow afternoon . . . I might see you tonight, though," Carmel said. "At the Walden High auditorium."

"Why would I be there?"

"Erica's singing there tonight. Didn't you know?"

"I thought her band broke up."

"She got a new one."

"She would," Odell muttered.

"I thought you'd know. The story I heard is that you were like her favorite groupie these days."

"I don't know how that got started. I don't want to see Erica—I don't even think about Erica."

"My mistake." . . . Carmel laughed, faintly, and hung up.

Odell got himself under control and went back to his room. He stalked up and down between his rows of books, angry and blind. Erica! He was on the verge of shattering into tiny pieces when his sister interrupted him.

Click. "—it's your turn to set the table tonight."

Click. "—I'm busy," Odell snapped, still trembling. "Can't you do it?—" Click.

Click. "—fuck you! You're always trying to cop out. I'm going to tell mother that you haven't been doing your share—I'm so sick of you . . ."

"All right!" Odell snarled at the machine, but Muriel couldn't hear him, because her button was still on TALK.

"I mean really! You know what Mama says, that if we want to preserve the nuclear family we've all got to pull together, and you're not—"

"All right! All right!" Odell yelled, shunting his button back and forth between TALK and LISTEN; but he couldn't cut into her channel. He smacked his hand into the speaker grille, and its pattern scraped his palm.

"—and like yesterday, when you wouldn't put out your God-damned cigar—"

Cursing, Odell ran up the stairs to the kitchen. "Shut up!" he told her, somewhat out of breath.

"Well, at least I got you up here," Muriel said.

Odell was about to scream at her when he realized that she wasn't alone. "Hello, Reggie," he said.

Reggie nodded. Reggie was huge and black, and had no expression in his face. Odell always found it hard to separate his hugeness from his blackness. He had a quality of absolute motionlessness which often caused people to mistake him for a piece of furniture—he was intimidating, but only in the way that a fireplace or a heavy table can be intimidating.

"How ya been, man?" Odell said jocularly, offering a thumbs-up handshake. Reggie managed to return the grip and shrug at the same time. His eyes were glazed, and his hand felt like limp steel.

"Reggie's staying for dinner," Muriel said. "You remember I wanted him to come last week, when Aunt Phyllis was here—she'd have been so offended to see that I was having a passionate *affair* with someone who—well, someone like Reggie . . ." She was so thin that when she laughed her skull threatened to burst right through her face.

Reggie lifted his sullen eyes to her. "Shit on your Aunt Phyllis," he said.

There was a silence.

"You still ridin' that same bike of yours?" Odell asked him genially.

Reggie shook his head. "Total'," he said. "Plowed a van. Fuckin' redneck. Took the turn too slow. I wasted him. He waste my bike, I waste him. Ain't that how it works?" he added, menace gathering in the smooth emptiness of his face.

"Sure is," Odell said heartily. "Is Papa eating with us tonight?" he asked Muriel.

"I don't think so. He's indisposed."

"Indisposed, my ass," Reggie said. "Your Daddy's crazy, girl."

"Everybody's crazy," Odell said jovially, to change the subject. "Why," he went on, "I hear that you're the craziest man in town from people who don't even know you!"

It was too much to hope that Reggie would be amused. But Reggie didn't even try. "Is that right, now," he murmured. "Is that right."

Muriel bent her thin body toward him—it made her look like a diagram—and took his face between her hands. She turned it sideways and then up, and planted a kiss on his forehead. He stared at her without expression. She giggled. "Hi," she said. He continued to stare at her, without expression.

Odell set the table in the dining room to the tune of Muriel's chatter and Reggie's intermittent grunts. His imagination unfolded, to the clink of forks, a picture of Reggie's massive thighs clamping like rubber teeth over his sister's prostrate form . . . Reggie was only the latest chapter in a long succession of boys, men, studs, jocks, rednecks, freaks, geeks, apes, and other curiosities whom she had brought home and sought to domesticate. No two had been alike, and none had been able to stand it for more than ten days. Each new loss was followed with bouts of tears, hysteria, running away from home, and suicide threats. Odell, clicking knives, wondered if his sister would ever find happiness. It did not occur to him that she already had.

The table set, he went down the hall to his father's room. He stood there for several seconds, not wanting to go in. A painful tension teetered low inside him as his hand reached for the knob.

His father was sitting in a chair at the far end of the room, dressed in full combat uniform. His olive-drab fatigue pants were stuffed into gleaming parachute boots; the eyes of his webbed belt gleamed too, hooked with bulging cartridge pouches. The lamplight gleamed on his bald head. His field jacket was zipped up all the way to the silk scarf knotted around his neck. His eyes were hidden behind shining shades.

He didn't look up right away. He was busy loading a rubber-tipped dart into a plastic pistol which Odell recognized as belonging to his own childhood. The floor was covered with other memories: toy soldiers, set in ragged ranks, advancing across the rug toward the chair in which his father sat. Some had fallen; their end was marked by the spent darts lying beside them. On a nearby table were stacked bandoliers, canteens, packs, entrenching tools, bayonets, and various metal canisters painted olive drab.

"Hello, Papa," Odell said.

His father glanced up shyly, like a caught child. The shyness did not fit his patrician features, thick brows and furrowed cheeks. It was like seeing two different people in one face.

"I was looking for my old uniforms," he said softly, "and I found this stuff of yours, too, up in the attic. I don't know why you ever stopped. This is very—" he squeezed off a shot; a soldier went flying as the dart ricocheted against the wall—"relaxing."

"Well," Odell said, "your aim seems to be pretty good."

"You know how it is. An old soldier . . ." He gestured with his pistol at the stacked equipment. "Look at all this," he said. "It's a lot of fun to get it out—remember it all." He picked up one of the canisters. "Smoke bombs," he said. "I did a cost-efficiency study on them once. Marvelous things. They just blind everything around you." He gave his odd, whinnying chuckle. "So here I am. All dressed up and no place to go."

"I know what that's like," Odell said.

"Son, I've been thinking about you. I feel that you're not getting as much out of your adolescence as you ought to." He reloaded the pistol.

"I just came to ask if you were going to eat with us."

His father lifted an eyebrow above the rim of his shades. "Don't feel comfortable talking about it, eh? I can understand that. When I was your age," he added, "I had a girlfriend."

"No, it's just that it's dinnertime, that's all," Odell said. The tension inside him coiled in time to the spring inside the barrel of the gun.

"You know, son," his father went on, "it's occurred to me that we haven't communicated as much as we might have. And if the Pentagon renews my contract—" his voice cracked just slightly—"we're probably not going to have much chance to, in the future. What are your problems?"

"Oh, the usual ones," Odell said, nervously. He resisted an urge to raise his hand for permission to leave the room.

"Ah." His father nodded in satisfaction, and drew a bead on another toy soldier. Odell waited, but the subject seemed closed.

"Are you going to eat with us, Papa?" he asked.

"No. I don't think so, to tell you the truth. I have a lot of work to do. Have your sister bring me a tray."

"It's just that you haven't left the room in three days. Mother's getting worried."

His father grinned. "Oh, you're wrong about that . . . I sneak out sometimes, when the rest of you are gone. You see, son—you don't mind if I call you son?—I must be about my work, and much as I'd like to see you all, it's just not feasible right now . . ." Savagely, he pulled the trigger, and gave a grunt of pleasure as another soldier fell. "Please express my regrets to Reggie," he added. Odell left.

Odell had been brought up from the age of reason on to admire his father's intellect. It was certainly an intellect to be admired. The rest Odell found somewhat frightening. Often he wondered why his father had chosen to spend his genius in the role of a weapons-system analyst for the Government, and still more why he seemed to enjoy it so much. When the Pentagon was having an off season, and there were no new weapons systems to analyze, Odell's father grew thorny and unpredictable—as now—and the family anxiously read the papers until a new budget was announced.

On his way to the table Odell met his mother. "Smile, for Lord's sake!" she hissed.

"Yes, Mother."

The unease he had been feeling since Carmel's phone call was returning by accumulating sections, like a series of quick clutching hands. The sight of Reggie, solidly entrenched behind the table, did nothing to stop his rising paranoia. The food was heaped on the plates, ominously, as if waiting to pounce.

"Dig in, everybody," Muriel said, raising her fork.

"You're forgetting something," her mother said. Muriel winced. Her mother saw the wince, understood it at once—not for nothing was she an artist—and turned to Reggie with a bright, handy laugh. "Prayers," she said gaily, "aren't they quaint? It's just one of our odd family habits. Please don't feel obligated to join in—unless you want to, of course."

Muriel looked ready for either end of a firing squad, and Odell felt embarassment crawl over his own face. This was just the sort of thing that cracked his cool at the edges. Still, he bowed his head along with Muriel, who mumbled something in a voice distinct only for its speed. Odell wished that he had some way of letting Reggie know that he was hip to the absurdity of the scene, but Reggie looked too bored to care.

As they began the meal, a new difficulty raised its head. Politics dictated that the conversation should center on Reggie, but he would not be drawn in. Whenever a comment was pointed his way, he would stare at the words hanging in the air until they lost all life, and then respond with stony silence or a stonier grunt. The rest of them floundered in blind search of a center, and the talk grew quietly hysterical beneath its increasingly incoherent façade. Sentence after sentence lost its way and disappeared into the oblivion behind Reggie's eyes.

Only Odell's mother refused to give up. The more awkward it got, the more animated she became, her hands cutting and slashing at the air. Her laughter stuttering like a machine gun, she would say, "As I'm sure you'll agree, Reggie ..." or, "Well, Reggie's opinion on that is probably more interesting than anything I could say ..." But soon even her resources failed her, and for lack of any other available weapon, she began to nag Muriel about the dinner. Muriel protested—Muriel's voice soared up the scale of violence as if it were taking flight. Seeing what was coming, her mother reversed her ground and tried to stave it off by saying lightly, "Oh, you're an impossible child. I don't know why any of us put up with you ..." She turned to Reggie:

"Why do *you* put up with her, Reggie?"

"Because she's white."

Odell and his mother both listened to the pause for a moment. Then she exploded into laughter. "Oh, that was clever," she said. Reggie looked puzzled.

None of them noticed that Muriel was getting ready to cry. They were all surprised when she jerked to her feet and ran, sobbing, out of the room.

"Why, that—" Odell's mother began. Then her face changed. "Oh, quick, Reggie, go and comfort her," she said in a broadly conspiratorial voice.

"No ma'am. I expect that she can comfort herself."

"Well, whatever you prefer, of course. You mustn't take any of this seriously. She's always been very high-strung—she gets it from me —but we all love her anyway, ha ha."

Reggie's lack of response to this was interrupted by Odell's father, who wandered in looking like a bear called out of hibernation. Still in full combat uniform, he had traded his pistol for a pair of pliers and a screwdriver. Odell's sense of unreality lurched into dazzling high gear.

"It's very noisy around here," his father said. "Noisy, and confused. It makes it hard to do one's work."

"What have you been doing?" Odell's mother asked.

"I've been going around to all the intercoms, and locking them on LISTEN. You see, when everyone is listening, no one can talk ..."

"Ah," Odell's mother said, turning to Reggie with uneasy good cheer. But she couldn't think of anything to say. She looked at him, her mouth gaping. "Ah."

"Well, well," Odell's father said, "I can't waste time kibitzing when there's work to be done, hey? Duty is duty. Especially when nothing else is."

As he went out, Reggie coughed. "Mrs. Odell," he said, "I've got to be going. Thank you for the dinner."

"But . . ." her hand fluttered uncertainly in the direction of Muriel's room.

Reggie grinned, and stood up, and suddenly loomed over them. "You tell her I said to say hello." Nodding all around, he walked gracefully out the door. Odell and his mother stared at each other across the table. Odell felt as if small animals were having meaningless sex inside his stomach.

"Well," she said to him, *"you* were certainly a big help."

"What?"

Muriel burst back into the room, the red around her eyes magnified to flame by her glasses. "Did he leave?" she asked.

Odell's mother nodded glumly.

"Christ! Why didn't you stop him?" She darted to the window, and then back. "His car's gone—oh, God! What am I gonna do? Every time I find somebody that I care about—that I really care about—my damn family fucks up . . ."

"Screws up, please, dear. I don't tolerate fucks. And I'm sure you can patch it up with Reggie. *We* certainly didn't . . ."

"Patch it up? Christ! I never want to see him again!"

"Well, that's all right, too. I must say I wasn't very impressed . . ."

"Will you just shut up, please, Mother?"

"Why is everybody shouting?" Odell's father inquired, peering around the banister.

"There you are. *You* certainly put in a contribution."

"What?"

"You're all awful!"

Odell tried to think of something to say. The situation was out of control, and besides, he felt ignored. In the absence of words, another force clicked into motion inside him, blanking out the surrounding storm, and slowly, he got to his feet. No one saw him leave.

First he paid a visit to his father's bedroom, and then he went to his own, and stripped off his clothes. He was filled with a cold, quiet calm. Thought fell away from him and he moved like a robot. The only thing in his mind now, beyond feeling, beyond will, was the need to complete the ritual, and bring the circle to its close.

When he reached the auditorium, the parking lot was filled with cars. A few kids were sitting around getting high under a bare flag-pole. Odell climbed out of his car and moved toward the door, spirit-shrouded in his long cloak, his jeans stuffed inside his boots. He started to light a cigar, then threw it away.

"Hey," one of the kids underneath the flagpole called out, swiveling his head in Odell's direction, "this isn't Hallowe'en, is it? I get so screwed up with dates," he added, turning his head back the other way.

Another boy snickered, but Odell couldn't see his face in the hurrying dusk; only a flash of pale blond hair, like glittering gold in a mineshaft. Ignoring them both, Odell stalked on, grim as a cop, up the steps and through the double doors into the lobby. He could hear the music throbbing, only a wall away.

He would have to hurry. Every wasted second cut into the mood he was trying to preserve. Pulling open the door, he stepped into the auditorium. There, far away, down endless ranks of dirty necks, grimy heads, lips lifting over gray teeth, was the stage. Odell heard the clatter of a beer bottle toll like a bell against the concrete walls.

Shafts of light speared and spread all around her as she turned and lifted the microphone's snaking cord to her face. The tambourine slammed jingle-jangle on her hip. Her new guitarist raised his axe over her head like a wand.

The song reached its climax and then broke in floods over the packed anonymous bodies in their rows. Erica bobbed in a bow, her cascading hair cutting her face in half under the lights. Odell stepped forward into her blinding glow.

He threw his cloak back over his shoulders. Underneath it, hooked on his belt, were the smoke bombs he had taken from his father. Some-one advanced toward him, hesitantly—the boy who had spoken to him outside. Odell drew the pistol and aimed the rubber dart directly be-tween his eyes.

"Don't try it," he said.

The boy faded back into the gloom. Odell unhooked two canis-ters from his belt. His whole being surged with power. He paused a moment; then he pulled the rings and threw the smoke bombs, one after the other, at the stage.

CHAPTER NINETEEN

Richard: 6

"Last call, last call . . ."

"Austin was getting tired of the scene, and he wanted to look for some fresh kicks he said—he went to the worst bar in Suffragette City, and tried to pick up some pretty boy . . ."

Richard, watching the ice melt at the bottom of his fifth drink, tried to light a cigarette, but he was striking the match against the blank side of the book. Veronica had to reorient his hold.

"Last call!"

"It turned out he was a lifer Marine, and he took Austin out and beat him up, stole his coke kit and left him to bleed." Sighing, Veronica winced at Richard's smoke. "It's made him question the whole meaning of his existence." She plucked the cherry from her glass and turned it like a globe between her long-nailed fingertips. "He's always so hard to live with," she said, "when he's questioning the meaning of his existence."

"Last call! If you want it, make it now."

"I'll bet Austin enjoyed it."

"You shouldn't say things like that, Richard," Veronica reproved him. "Even if—Austin thinks of you as a friend, and I like you, too."

"You don't have to like me if you don't want to," Richard muttered with sudden, alcoholic gloom.

Veronica, brisk and motherly, patted his wrist. "Come on, now. I'd rather have you be cheerful, even if you have to be nasty to do it."

"What's the difference?" He had trouble understanding her point of view. Happiness and sorrow, these days, came and went in him too quickly to take hold.

"Besides," Veronica went on, "you're supposed to be happy. I heard that you had a new romance."

"That's what they say."

"What's she like?"

"Oh, she's wonderful . . . Even when she's in the room, she's hardly there at all. You know?" Richard laughed, chokingly. He felt very brittle. It pleased him that he might be finally no more than a glass through which the world could peer.

Over Veronica's shoulder, he saw Lorraine and Carmel come in, and by reflex they saw him. Carmel directed Lorraine to the table with a word to her ear and a quick tap on the shoulder, and sauntered on down the bar. He was dressed for business; an uncharacteristic strain tightened his face as he bent to confer with Mink.

"Hello," Lorraine said. She looked a bit wobbly.

"Come sit with us," Veronica invited her.

"Oh, Richard doesn't want me to, I can tell. He—"

"Sit down," Richard said irritably.

"It's not directed specifically at you," Veronica explained. "He's been acting this way with everybody."

"Well, it's not hard to understand. Have you seen his new girl? Oops. Sorry, Richard, how are you?"

"Worse than I was."

"See? He doesn't want me."

"We all want you, Lorraine," Veronica purred soothingly. Lorraine was saved from the need to respond by Carmel, who suddenly got to his feet and hurried out, Mink in tow.

"He didn't even finish his drink," Richard said.

"I wonder what's going on," Veronica said.

"I wonder if anyone else is going to claim that drink," Richard said.

"Well," Lorraine said, "there goes my date for tonight."

The door opened again.

"Slam!" Richard cried. "And here's the substitute—how do you manage it?"

Lorraine had a few seconds' grace in which to look irritated before Brewer reached their table. They all shifted their elbows to welcome him.

"What's with Carmel?" he asked. "He ran right through me."

"We were just trying to figure that out."

"Some of us."

"He got a phone call from the White House," Brewer suggested. "The Man wants him to balance the ticket."

Richard was watching Brewer. He was carrying some knowledge inside him: his heaviness was sharp with purpose. Richard wanted to get away. He wanted to go back to his room and let his mind-movies roll. Images of heroism and blood, every sword its own dragon, bursting and flowing, to soothe him. He hated Brewer for breaking his frail peace.

Suddenly he noticed the silence. Everyone was sitting around with their mouths open but unmoving, blank, frozen by the awareness that they had nothing left to say. Richard had always wondered what would happen when such a moment came. He had no sense of discovery; his mood only dropped another notch. Who would break the silence? Richard began to make faces, and Lorraine laughed. Then he realized that he had imagined the whole thing.

"Erica asked me to find you," Brewer said to him abruptly. "I thought I'd find you here."

A sick throb, embryonic fear, kicked in his belly. "What does she want?"

"She asked me to tell you goodbye," Brewer said with a strange, abstract intensity which did not fit his face.

"I didn't know she was going anywhere," Lorraine said.

Richard and Brewer still looked at each other. "She isn't," Richard said.

"Look," Brewer told him, "I think we'd better go."

Richard shook his head. "I don't believe her," he said. "You go if you want."

"You saw her this afternoon."

"So what?" He rebelled at having this burden come back on him again. Sullenly, he refused to accept it; why should he be chosen?

"You saw Erica this afternoon?" Lorraine said. "What . . .?"

"We don't have a lot of time," Brewer said.

"I'm not going."

"What are you talking about?" Lorraine wanted to know.

"Brewer thinks that Erica's going to kill herself," Richard

said harshly.

Lorraine burst out laughing. When no one joined her, she grew flustered. "I thought you were joking," she explained.

"I'm not going to make you come," Brewer said, standing up, "but you know you have to."

Richard hesitated. It wasn't a question of making up his mind. The decision had already been made; he just didn't know whether he would obey it. He wanted to sink away into the night, and leave all this behind him.

"All right," he said, and added: "They're closing up here, anyway."

"Are you all really going?" Lorraine asked. "Can I come along?"

"Why?"

"Well, I don't have anything else to do, and—and besides, if she's really killing herself, I don't know—I might be able to help, or something."

Brewer didn't like it; Richard could tell that he was about to say no. Quickly, he turned to Lorraine and told her, "Of course, you can come. More the merrier, right, Brewer?"

Brewer didn't say anything. He stood watching Richard somberly. Richard hated him with a blind, impersonal fear.

"Count me out," Veronica said. "I get sick," she added apologetically. "The last time Austin tried it, I threw up all over the bed."

"We'd better get going," Brewer said.

"Hope to see you soon, Lorraine," Veronica called after them.

They all sat together in the front seat of Brewer's car. Lorraine stroked Richard's arm in a comforting way, even though Richard wasn't sure that he wanted her to comfort him. Erica dying, Erica possibly dead—she felt very far away; he didn't know what it had to do with him.

When she had told him, that afternoon, that she was going to do it, he had known that she was serious. But it would have cost him too much to believe her—he would have had to take action. He still didn't know how he was supposed to deal with it. He had put her out of his mind until the moment that Brewer came into Uncle Lou's.

Erica's door was unlocked. They went straight into her bedroom, Richard in the lead, only because Brewer pushed him into the lead. She was sitting on her unmade bed, her red scarf tied loosely around her neck. On all sides were scattered several empty bottles, a few pills loose in the folds of the blankets, and her tambourine; she looked up at them, with both fists full, and giggled.

"My latest stud," she said in a high-pitched, uneven voice. "When he saw what I was doing, he tried to stop me—then I waved a knife at him—and he left. Scared of a knife!" she snorted derisively. "And he said . . . good luck . . . on his way out . . ." She looked at Richard, her eyes bright and burning, and giggled again. "Hi, Richard . . . It was nice of you to come and say goodbye . . ."

He caught her wrist and twisted it, forcing her to loosen her grip. Her pills went flying across the patterned rug. When she realized what he was doing, her burning eyes grew wild with fear and then anger. Thrashing against him, she screamed, lunging for the pills as he held her back:

"No! No, you can't do it, it's unfair—you're breaking the rules, don't you see? . . . I won—I won the game—I was going to make it this time, really I was, you're cheating on me! Don't do it—don't you make me go back now . . . Oh, Richard, don't you do this to me . . ." She tried to bite his hand, and he pushed her head back. He heard Brewer's voice:

"Lorraine, call the rescue squad."

"What's their number? There isn't a phone book around here . . ."

"Get it from the operator," Brewer told her, meanwhile grabbing for Erica's legs, trying to hold them down as she kicked and flailed the air. She was still screaming, but only sounds now, not words, as they forced her down by brute strength.

"Hello, is this the rescue squad? It is. Oh, good. Hi. My name's Lorraine Carlton, and there's a girl here who's trying to kill herself . . ."

Erica stared up at the two of them bent over her, pinning her, their bodies rigid and trembling. "Go ahead, do whatever you want— go ahead, all of you, all of you—I'm not strong enough to fight . . ." Then she bucked and surged again, she rose like the sea. She screamed: "Oh, but I *will* fight you! I will! *I will!*"

"Lorraine," Brewer called out, his face shining with sweat, "how long did they say?"

"Only a couple of minutes," Lorraine answered. She came back and peered down at Erica, her fear barely concealing her curiosity. "Funny," she said, "I never thought she'd do it with pills—I always thought she'd use a razor."

At the sound of Lorraine's voice, Erica seemed to focus on her presence for the first time. For a moment her face was a mask of absolute bewilderment; then she began to laugh.

By the time the rescue squad came, she was much weaker. She still struggled, but without force. Her screams were cut to whispers, a faint, insistent repetition of the words "I will, I will." The two men in their sloppy jackets and bored faces picked her up and half-walked, half-carried her down the hallway and out to the blue bus parked at the curb. Richard, Brewer, and Lorraine followed in chorus. While they were lifting her into the bus, her scarf slipped off her neck and caught on a stanchion, and one of the men tore it loose and threw it out into the street.

The driver got in and started the motor, and Richard thought that would be the end: whether she lived or died, it was no longer in his hands. He felt a delirious, empty relief. Then the other man said to him, "There's room for one more inside."

"What?" he answered in a daze.

"To keep her company."

Richard turned pleadingly to Brewer. Brewer shook his head: "You better go. We'll follow you in the car."

Climbing into the bus, guided by the man's hand on his arm, Richard imagined that he was being arrested, and it frightened him. Erica, strapped down on a stretcher, looked like a ghost already. The man climbed in behind him, slammed the door shut, and rapped on the steel partition to signal the driver: "Okay, move it out."

"My name's Fred," he added conversationally, as the bus lurched into motion. "Here." He passed Richard a plastic vial, about two inches long. "Ammonia. Try to keep it under her nose—keep her awake."

Richard put the vial under Erica's nose. She jerked away. He followed her, and she jerked away again.

"Do you know how much she swallowed, or what it was?" Fred asked.

"No."

"Oh, well," Fred shrugged.

"Do you run this gig often?"

Fred's mouth twitched under his mustache. "Last night we had a kid on acid, he was so far gone, he'd taken a knife and cut half his damn dick off. We got him there all right, but shit, he wasn't worth saving."

Apparently this exhausted Fred's fund of small talk. He hid his mouth under his mustache and stared out the window, one arm braced against the rocking of the bus. Richard concentrated on keeping the vial under Erica's nose. The bus seemed to be going very fast, and he couldn't guess its direction. Everything swayed; only Erica was immobile, as if she were a piece of glowing ore and the world around her only a bouncing snow of atoms and electrons, products of her fission. For his greatest romance to end like this, riding a blue bus into unknown distances, under the swaying light, with Erica maybe dying beside him . . . Yet for all her force she was only a shadow, foreign and faintly repellent. She had been no more than a shadow, either, that afternoon, when he had opened his door and found her standing there. He had kept her frozen in his remembering for so long that to see her hot and breathing before him, in the raw present, was as much of a shock as if she had been indeed already dead, and then returned; to sit here, beside her wasting body, was at once jarring and relentlessly familiar.

Feeling pressure, he looked down, and saw that Erica's hand had locked on his, as if she meant to drag him into an embrace. He had no choice but to return her grip. He didn't know how long she had been holding him, or even if she knew she was doing it. Her sweat- and tear-streaked face was removed beyond distance or time, and he couldn't guess whether she were fighting to live, or fighting to die.

They reached the hospital. Fred and the driver struggled awkwardly with the stretcher, and Richard struggled alongside them, Erica still clasping him tight. As they carried her in, he had just time to notice that the bus had AMBULANCE printed across its hood, only the letters were backwards. He thought it was an illusion, and then he realized: of course—so the cars ahead could read it in their mirrors. Then they were inside. An attendant in a white gown, with what looked like mustard stains on its front, was untangling his fingers from Erica's, as if doing a trick with knots.

"There's a Coke machine in the lobby," Fred told him, with a familiar pat on the back, as Erica was wheeled away through a pair of rubber-edged doors marked OPERATING. Richard watched the doors swing shut behind her, and wondered what came next. He had, in a way, anticipated this scene, but his imagination had been swift and left him helpless to combat the ticking tedium of the clock. He could not tame his thoughts: he was too much in the middle of things, and yet he was nowhere at all.

A nurse at the desk called him over to get names and addresses, Erica's and his own.

"Do you know why she attempted to kill herself?"

"Is that on the form?"

"Uh-huh. Number nine. Motivation."

"I don't know," Richard told her.

While he was finishing with the nurse, Brewer and Lorraine came in. Brewer had lost all his authority; he was just Brewer again. Richard was relieved. Lorraine, though, was acting shy and edgy, as if he were the victim and she dared not get too close. Richard didn't dwell on it. The thought had just occurred to him that Christy was going to be pissed when he didn't show up tonight. The immediate situation should make such considerations void, but on the other hand he didn't want Christy pissed at him. He could phone her—but that would probably look bad; he would just have to face the consequences.

They waited in an alcove off the lobby. No one said very much. Brewer read a magazine.

A cop came up to them, and started asking questions. He asked Richard if he knew why Erica had tried it, and Richard said again that he didn't know.

"Either of the rest of you know?"

"Well," Lorraine offered, "she was awfully screwy."

They went back to waiting. An hour passed, silent and slow. Then Richard caught sight of Fred walking toward the door; Fred waved at him, and then came over.

"Shit," he said, "you still here? That chick you brought in's okay. It was close—about ten minutes more, and goodbye. But they pumped her stomach, and she's upstairs now. Don't worry," he told them cheerfully, "she'll make it, all right. They'll just keep her under observation for three days or so, and then give her back to you good as new."

"Will they let us see her?"

"Not until tomorrow. You might as well head on home. Those assholes at the desk must have forgotten you."

"Oh, good," Lorraine said, jumping to her feet.

"You did okay," Fred told Richard. "Anyway, I got to go—some kid just shot his brother through the head with a forty-four. Busy night, man," he grinned through his mustache, "busy night. Nice meeting you."

A silence grew to fill his wake.

"Is that all?" Richard asked uncertainly.

Lorraine was tugging at his sleeve. "Let's get out of here," she said.

"Let's go to my house," Brewer said, as they stopped for a red light on the way out of the hospital parking lot. "You probably don't want to be alone for a while."

"Sure," Richard agreed, almost without hearing. He felt very absent; he had to fill himself back up again. He couldn't face Christy in the shape he was in. Just to see her in his room, in his bed, would be too much. From a faraway place in his brain he heard a gunshot, echoing through the coils of a great vast distance. In the front seat, Brewer was humming a calm, indecipherable tune.

They came to the house. Brewer was first up the steps, bunched keys spilling softly from his fingers. Richard sprawled on the couch, his arms spread wide along the backrest. "Anything to drink?" he asked. "Or smoke, or swallow or sniff, or otherwise imbibe . . ."

"I saved some of Erica's pills, if that's what you want."

"Oh, don't talk about it," Lorraine said, "don't talk about her."

"Brewer, are you mad at me?"

"No, not really. . . . There's just something I was wondering about."

"What?"

"I thought that you might know what finally made her decide to do it, and you didn't tell anybody."

"Stop," Lorraine said, "I don't want to hear about it. Richard's just been through an emotional crisis, Brewer, don't you understand?"

"So what?" Brewer said.

"If I did know," Richard murmured, waves of weariness collecting and unfolding inside him, "and I told you, you wouldn't believe me. And if you wouldn't believe me, the cop and the nurse sure as hell wouldn't believe me." He tried to laugh. "I'm not sure I believe me."

"Then something did happen this afternoon?"

"I didn't say that."

Brewer was silent: he came to a decision. "It's nearly dawn. Why don't you crash here, and we can go see Erica, tomorrow."

"Erica?"

"I thought you'd want to see her. They'll let us see her tomorrow."

"Oh—sure . . ."

Richard sank down on the couch. Exhaustion flowed through him, blanking out the outside world, replacing all sensation, all thought, all feeling. "I'm so tired," he said, as if it were the only revelation he would ever have. But he couldn't sleep; he was lost in a high, hollow, feverish delirium of weariness. The moments were going by too quickly, out of sequence, and yet each moment by itself was as long as a breath of eternity.

Lorraine put on a record, and stood with arms folded in front of the stereo, her lips pursed soundlessly halfway between a hum and a whistle, swaying millimetrically to the beat while her feet did a kind of shuffle-in-place. Richard leafed through a book on the Civil War, lines of dim historical text deployed by ranks: *Pickett, where is Pickett's division?* and the answer: *I have no division, Sir.*

All three of them sagged in a kind of stupor, as if they had just emerged from a furnace and were still drugged with the heat. Richard let the book fall; his head was empty, his blood slow. Lorraine was drinking tea, hunched over, her shoulders sticking up. Brewer had gone into the next room and turned on the TV set. Richard could hear its muted electronic voices through the wall, frayed with static... He lost track of how much time had passed. He stood up, and went to see if Brewer knew. He found him lying on the floor, fast asleep and snoring. Lorraine came in behind, and peered over Richard's shoulder.

"Is he really out?"

"No," Richard mumbled, "I'm sure he's faking it."

She had something in her hands, he noticed—a metal flower, its petals molded in bronze. He wondered where she had found it. She laid the rose on Brewer's chest, and folded his hand symmetrically to cradle it. Rearing back on one knee, she examined her work. "You always knew I was religious," she said to Richard.

By a common instinct they returned to the living room. Still, she was holding herself apart, she affected to be alone, separate from him. Richard, in the blossoming of his fatigue, grew irritated; he couldn't understand why she was turning away now, after everything was already over. The irritation stole him some energy. He went to Lorraine, took her arm, and turned her to face him.

She brushed away, with an impatient lift of her chin, and walked over to the other side of the room.

Richard could hardly keep his feet. Every move he made tore at muscles pleading they could move no more; his bones were slowly disintegrating beneath him, like sand running through an hourglass. A manic giddiness flared and flickered in the dead center of his brain. He gathered up his body, all that old battered armor, and approached Lorraine again.

She was a little closer now. She let him kiss her, but she was tense in his arms, not opening to him at all. She was haggard and tight, not at all attractive.

"Don't you care about anything?" she asked him.

"No."

"Couldn't you have picked a better time?" she asked, practical as a shopper.

"No, it had to be tonight."

They were both thinking that she had been ready for months, and he had always refused her. A bleak metallic sourness edged the mood.

"It had to be tonight," Richard repeated.

Lorraine looked out the window.

"Today," she corrected him.

She began to yield, but she was still not complete; she was as harsh to his touch as a body emaciated by a wasting disease. He was sluggish, fumbling through the thickness of his exhaustion, going in and out of focus. They struggled against each other, wordless and grim, in the wan light seeping through the window.

"In Brewer's house," she said.

"There was a time," Richard answered, fighting to make the words come, "when you were ready to do it in Brewer's lap, and not give a damn."

She turned in the loose prison of his arms. "Maybe I've changed, too," she said sulkily.

"Not that much—never that much," he told her, praying that he was right. He was baffled by her resistance; everything was collapsing. The needle of the stereo bounced on a scratch, repeating in a monotonous exhortation: "Be true to your—be true to your—be true to your—"

"We'll have to go to another room," she said.

"Where?"

"His room. It's right down the hall."

"What if he comes looking for us?"

"He won't. If he wakes up, he'll know we're in there, and he'll stay where he is."

"Are you sure?"

"I know him," Lorraine said.

At the door she stopped, held in his arms. He stumbled, and only kept his balance by stepping on her foot.

"Sorry."

"You don't really want to do this," she said.

He didn't know any more if he wanted to or not. The question had no meaning for him. The fires in his head burned with a cold intensity; they were what forced his sapped, unwilling body to action. He held her numbly, without any sense of contact.

"It's wrong," Lorraine said. Her voice was petulant, ragged, close to a whine. "Don't you see? It's wrong . . ."

"What difference does that make?"

Reluctantly, in a swaying lockstep, they went into Brewer's room, impelled by a desire which neither of them wanted or cared about any longer. "Come on," Richard said, lugging her forward like a piece of furniture.

A damp towel lay tangled on Brewer's bed, in the center of a sea of tattered comic books. There were hundreds of comic books in the room; they covered the bed, and spilled onto the floor, and were stacked up in piles in the closet. Dirty clothes were heaped in a corner, on a mat of comic books. When Richard pulled Lorraine to the bed, they crackled under her, the slick covers and soft paper creasing and bending against her body, sliding over her skin like oil over a blade. The air was stale and heavy, clinging close. They rolled and clutched at each other in the thickness. Her arms and legs were arched like girders, her mouth was stale and gaping, her breath harsh on his. They did not meet. Each of them fought alone in the dark. He raged against her, wrenching lust out of the pit of his chest like a stump from a thicket, the cold fire licking through his veins. He was giving her Erica's death, he was pounding Erica's death into her. She wouldn't yield. His own body fell away from him, and he was light as fire, pure in the fire. He lunged, slammed, and was done, too soon, it was all too soon, and a cold wind went spilling through him, how many times, how many times had he impaled himself on this darkness? Breath sobbing rustily in his ears, he came to rest, and she turned, and let him slip out, and off, with a quick, volatile jerk of her loins.

The darkness was too great a distance for him to touch her: they did not speak. Filled with a fierce solitude, Richard curled up on his stillness. Then he was asleep.

Six hours later, he got out of bed, and walked shaky-legged across the room. He pushed a heap of dirty underwear off a chair by the window and sat. The blinds were down. He thought of raising them, but did not move. Lorraine's back was to him, and all he could see was a comic book mashed under her head, its pages fluttering in surrender, and a limp hand hanging over them like a drowning man's. He felt curiously serene. He hoped that Lorraine wouldn't wake up, and spoil it; he could only maintain his peace until the world began to exist again.

But she was already awake. She rolled over, and fixed him with a clear, empty stare. He looked back. Silence lay between them like a challenge.

"Nothing like last night ever happened to me before," she told him.

Richard lifted his eyebrows.

"It was awful," she said.

"Come on."

"No, awful," Lorraine insisted.

"You're serious."

"Did you think I was joking?"

"Yes," Richard admitted.

"I wasn't. I hardly slept. I've been thinking about it all night."

The image of her, eyes gleaming in the darkness next to his collapsed body, chilled him. "All right," Richard said. "You better talk."

"I already told you it was awful. I don't know what's to talk
about."

"Don't you see, you can't just say that—" Pure male pride animated him now; his last castle was being stolen away. His voice was
jumpy. "You have to give me something."

Lorraine sighed, cupping her chin in the blankets. "I guess you
know that I wanted to make it for a long time."

"Yes—that's why I—"

"But it wasn't because of you so much," Lorraine went on de-
terminedly. "I mean I thought you were good-looking, and all that,
but the real reason was Erica—she was my enemy, and she had you.
Then she didn't have you, and I should have lost interest, but you
know how it is, when you get into the habit of thinking about
someone."

"Yes."

"But when it happened, you were just a ghost, and I felt crummy.
I don't know when I've had such a depressing experience. It was a lot
better when I fantasized, I mean, I always enjoyed fantasizing about
you more than I enjoyed fantasizing about anyone else . . . I guess it
was false advertising . . . I felt like you were a fake." She shook her
head, wonderingly. "And do you know what the strangest part of it
is? I realized that I don't even think you're particularly attractive,
any more."

He was all used up; he had no reactions left. A flooding self-pity
seized him. It had all been a gigantic conspiracy, they were all in on
it from beginning to end, it had all been pointed at him, he was the
solitary victim, him! He discovered that he was kneading a pair of
Brewer's dirty shorts between his clenched fingers, and quickly
dropped them.

"Well?" Lorraine said.

"Well, what?"

"Aren't you going to leave?"

"What for?"

"So I can get dressed," she said, "for one thing."

Brewer was standing in the kitchen, wearing an apron and sipping a beer, waving a spatula over the burners of the oven, when Richard came down. Crackling smoke rose from the frying pan. "Be of good cheer," Brewer said, "the sun is singing, the birds are shining."

Richard sat down. "Why'd you pull that trick last night?" he asked. "Passing out like that."

"Things must have gone badly, or you wouldn't call it a trick. But I promise you I did it completely by accident."

"I don't believe you."

"You'd be surprised at the things a person can get used to."

"You wanted it to happen."

"I keep on telling myself, it's only a phase, damn! It's only a stage. But all the world's a stage." He began a speech, accompanying himself with the spatula. "Or else, I tell myself, all the world's a stooge. In which case I'm in good company. You look puzzled. You're not too fast off the mark this morning, are you? What I'm trying to say is that I needed love, but no one would give it to me. So I had to do it all myself. . . ." He waved the spatula merrily. "Good morning, Lorraine," he said.

She had come in behind Richard's back. She was playing the shy maiden; her steps were small, her manner demure.

"Sleep well?" Brewer asked.

"I like your comics," she told him, sitting down.

They ate in silence. Richard felt too fragile to breathe. What a pain it was, he thought, to explode your life into a thousand fragments by night, and wake up every morning to find it still there. Erica had tried to kill herself the night before. They had taken her to the hospital. He had ridden beside her in a blue bus. Brewer was going to make him go back there and see her again. He was saying that they would leave right after breakfast.

So they went to the hospital and heard the story of how Erica had managed, that morning, to barricade herself in the bathroom of the psycho ward; and had smashed the mirror, and slashed her wrists with one of the broken pieces; and was dead. The nurse at the desk told them in a quavering voice that no one was responsible.

Lorraine was the only one to cry. She sat on the couch in the alcove and cried as if her life had cracked in two and was pouring out across the rug. Richard walked out the door, into the soft gray day.

He could see the ambulances come and go, big and silent as moths.

"All right," Brewer said. "Now you can talk."

Richard hugged himself tightly. He felt nothing at all.

"When she came by to see me," he said, "she was in pretty bad shape. She wouldn't talk to me, not really, she kept on changing the subject. Then she asked me, out of the blue, what I thought of the two of us getting together again. I got up and put on a cassette—something Dan Lang had sent me from New York. I told her that was my answer. She knew the song—I'd played it for her before. She said that if that was my answer, there wasn't much else left for her to do. Maybe I should have argued with her, but I told her she was probably right. I hated her, absolutely."

Brewer said nothing.

"She killed herself because of a song," Richard went on. "See what I meant when I said you wouldn't believe me? And do you know something else? I only meant it as a joke. I really wanted to say yes, but I couldn't, and I couldn't make her see why."

A spasm of hysteria passed through him, and was gone, leaving him empty again.

Then he thought of the photograph on Carmel's wall, in that room at Seastrom's where Carmel had assembled his personality, where the rough materials were laid and the preliminary drafts discarded; he knew, at last, what the woman in the photograph was looking toward.

I am an ice-cream man—the men don't know, but the little girls understand.

"Why doesn't anybody laugh at my jokes?" Richard muttered.

Brewer reached out his hand. His expression was blank; he acted out of duty more than anything else. Richard waved him away.

"No," he said. "Don't come near. I can't explain, but I just don't want anybody to come near me now."

CHAPTER TWENTY

Within a Grove of Buddies: 7

Early in the evening, seven days after Lang's return, a power failure
struck Icarus and blacked out half the town. Myra discovered it when
she tried to turn on the living room lights at dusk, and nothing happened. "Go wake up Andrew," she told Lang. "He's the only one
who can understand the fusebox."

Lang looked out the window. "It's not just us," he said. "There're
no lights on anywhere up and down the street. And the streetlights
are out too."

"Shit," Myra said. "I'd better get out the candles."

"You don't need them yet."

"No. I want them now."

Lang sat in the soiled and fading light from the window and
watched the shadows deepen in the furniture, not feeling a thing, not
even fear or the need to move. The news of Johanna's engagement
had stolen whatever shreds were left of his energy. Earlier that afternoon, he had called Carmel at Lorraine's place to tell him that the
deal was on, he could go ahead.

"Well," Carmel said dryly, "I was sort of thinking of going ahead
anyway. But it is nice to have you along."

Lang was vaguely surprised at how easy it had been. The

conversation made clear what he had already suspected, that he was not even a particularly important cog in Carmel's scheme. It didn't bother him; if anything, he wanted it that way. "Just sit tight and listen to the radio," Carmel told him. "This part is all my show. I'll be in touch—don't worry." Lang wasn't worried. He was going to put a period to everything, and keep safe by calling it an end. All he had to do was believe it; and nothing, as he had learned from Richard, was easier to believe in than nothing.

Myra came back from the closet, breathing hard, her large body, in its shapeless clothes, passing by him like a wind. She set the candles in their places and struck a match to light them. The flame gleamed off her glass eye like the binnacle of a compass.

Alice came down. "My stereo's conked out . . . Oh, wow, everything's conked out," she said. Myra gave her a candle and she returned silently to her room, huge pitching shapes flickering over the walls behind her as she went.

Myra settled heavily into her chair. Surrounded by guttering golden spots of fire, bathed in their soft shadows, she looked regal, ageless. She struck a fresh match to light her cigarette.

"I heard something strange today," she said. "Do you know the Seastroms?"

"I never met them . . . I know them, yeah."

"Well, apparently their son left home and just vanished, for close to two years, had you heard that? He came back home for good last week, to play the prodigal son, only the family was gone. Their house had been sold to make room for an apartment complex. The parents were divorced, and the other child, a daughter, apparently went to California or someplace. Only the father was left—supposed to be living somewhere in town—but the kid couldn't find him. Isn't that strange? Think of it, nothing left . . ."

"Not so strange."

"Maybe not—just sad."

"Oh," Lang said, a little irritated, "nothing's just sad anymore, Myra."

He was thinking of how the club lights would dim just before they made their way down the narrow ramp from the dressing rooms, swinging up long-armed onto the stage, their silhouettes bobbing in the gloom, checking their equipment, plugging the guitars in to the whining amps. Clapping, yells, and the clink of bottles would come to them from the audience, a dark and vibrant mass out there, beyond the narrow circle of their sight—at once in an embrace as close and hot as sex, and utterly isolated from any other living thing. Bleak and crowded was the air as Lang stepped up to the mike with his guitar hanging on its strap, balancing the neck with his left hand: "Hello, the name of this band is The Image, and the name of this song is 'Twisted Kicks' . . . one . . . two . . . three . . . four—"

The music faded into Andrew's voice, thick with sleep, as he came down the stairs—"Is this a surprise party?" he asked. "For me? Myra—our anniversary? It's sweet of you to—"

"Don't be such an idiot."

"Why get angry? I think that this is sort of pleasant," Andrew answered good-naturedly. "Electricity hurts my eyes."

"Dinner's ruined," Myra said, "I had a roast in the oven, but it's no good now."

"That's a small price to pay for the beauty of the dark," Andrew said in his most sonorous voice. "Not to mention the beauty of the candles."

"Damn you, I don't want to hear that—I want to know what we're supposed to do about dinner."

"Well, it's not worth arguing about—"

"Andrew—will you take the car and go get us some hamburgers— or fried chicken—or something? I'd like to sit here in peace, as long as I have to sit here, and I really don't want to listen to you. All right?"

Andrew's neck, in the gloom, swelled like a bull's with anger. "*Fuck* the dinner!" he bellowed at the room, at her. "And fuck the dark. Fúck the candles, too," he added as an afterthought.

Lang started to move toward the door, to avoid the argument he saw coming. But Myra said nothing, and suddenly Andrew collapsed.

"All right," he said. "I'll go. Daniel can come along to keep me company."

"If he wants to go, I don't care," Myra said without interest. "Just go."

They went outside as the last light was fading on the horizon. The houses all around were dark, their blank windows gaping like the toothless mouths of blank old men. As they drove, they saw that all the streets were just as dark as their own. The silence was eerie. Without electricity, it was just as if there were no life. Lang saw a few kids out on the streets, but without light to identify them they were as frail as ghosts. The streets and the houses blended in with the trees, the earth, the deepening sky.

"Daniel," Andrew said—softly, as if he didn't want to disturb the silence—"why is she always coming after me?"

"Habit," Lang said.

"She treats me as if I'm drunk even when I'm not. You don't know how that feels—I don't mind when it's true. But you know I'm not drunk, right now, don't you?"

"Yes." Lang wasn't sure, but it didn't matter.

"I asked you to come with me because you looked as if you could use some time away from there. You've been looking like slow death all day, and I don't like to see that. What's on your mind?"

"Nothing."

"Daniel," Andrew said sharply, "I like to think that we're friends. Don't tell me it's nothing when I'm concerned about you. It insults me."

"Then I'll say that I can't tell you."

Andrew didn't answer, but he was hurt—Lang could tell. For the first time, he felt uncomfortable with his depression. He thought he was used to it, but now it no longer fit so snugly. He had tried to avoid the idea that by going over to Carmel, he was betraying anyone besides himself. For himself he had no regret, not much, he didn't think, but he didn't want to have consequences for others. He had given up just because he could no longer bear to live with consequences. He was furious at Andrew for not allowing him even so small an illusion of honor. Then that withered too, and he settled back into apathy. Everything was done. Andrew had no right to make him think about it now that it was done—or else it would be always.

They came onto the main street with its clutter of stores and signs. The traffic lights were out too, and swung inertly on their wires above the dividing line of the roadway. There was something deeply satisfying in the sight of Icarus as a bombed-out moonscape at last, so many storefronts left empty and dark, so many tubes of dead neon. Up ahead, past the last intersection, they could see the edge of the blackout territory, a bright line of light, as sharply defined as the Berlin Wall. Beyond it lay the whole brilliant horizon.

They had been driving in silence for some minutes; but now Andrew said, with a gruffness that might mask embarrassment, "Daniel, tell me. That bar that all of you talk about, where you always used to go—where is it?"

"Right up ahead, just where the lights start."

"Well—what do you say we drop by there? It's just about the only bar in town I've never been in. I'd sort of like to see it, just once."

"I don't know if you'd like it," Lang said. "It's not your

kind of crowd."

"How do you know? And how will I, unless I go?"

Andrew was obviously determined. Lang, unwilling, pointed out the sign that spelled out Uncle Lou's.

"Myra's going to wonder where we are," he said, as they parked.

"Screw Myra. No—I don't mean that, but just—let her be the uncertain one, for once."

Lang climbed out of the car. Andrew walked ahead of him through the door, his pipe braced imperturbably between his teeth. The kids along the bar stared as he cruised by. Lang stayed close behind him. Even the jukebox seemed to fade as Andrew went past.

When they were installed in the booth he had chosen, Andrew looked around, puffing his pipe, and asked, "How does one get service?"

"You don't. You go to the bar."

"That's ridiculous." Craning his head, Andrew caught the eye of one of the bartenders, waved his arm energetically, and called out, "Would you come over here and take our order, please?"

The bartender—a big, bearded pseudo-tough with dirty ginger hair—looked stunned. A half-dozen kids were watching him. He grinned at them to show he wasn't taking this seriously, and walked over to the booth.

"You order at the bar," he said.

"Well," Andrew said equably, "you don't seem to be at the bar now. And as long as you're here, it would be very good of you to bring us two double Scotches. Do you mind?"

The bartender let out his breath, slowly, and turned away. Midway to the bar, he paused, and asked wearily, "On the rocks?"

"That would be nice," Andrew said. "Thank you." He knocked the ashes from his pipe. "You know, Daniel," he explained, "once I was in Kashmir, and my host, a very distinguished old boy from the Empire days, took me to a formal reception at the residence of the local maharajah, one of the few still out there—maharajahs are three to a block in some parts of Delhi—and I put on my best etiquette for the occasion. Trouble was, my etiquette wasn't theirs. I made one gaffe after another. Thought I'd balled things up completely—and this was a man we needed, you follow me. Afterward, I was horrified. But my host told me, No, no, Andrew, you misunderstand. They were quite impressed. They knew that your code was different from theirs, but they could tell that you had a code—that was what was important to them, and that's what they saw."

"Is that meant to be advice?"

"Of course not. It's a story," Andrew said.

The bartender brought them their drinks. Andrew thanked him pleasantly, and lifted his glass. When it was midway to his lips, he paused. "Do you think I drink too much?" he asked suddenly.

"When you drink," Lang said.

"I don't drink that much."

"Well—if you worked at it, you could probably drink more. But you do pretty good for an amateur."

"Did you know what that word used to mean? Amateur."

"No."

"It meant a lover," Andrew said reflectively. Lang thought of Alice. What a distance was there . . . or had she known that, too?

"I told Myra that once," Andrew went on. "That I was a professional at everything else, but I was an amateur of her. Of course, she took it all wrong, the way I knew she would; she answered me, Well, you didn't act like one on our wedding night. And I loved her for that, she had such a marvelous literal mind, she could reduce whatever kind of bullshit to its root, and I adored that in her until the bullshit became more and more necessary to staying alive and I couldn't stand to have her cut away my only means of survival even if I wasn't sure that I deserved to survive. Because she no longer had any right—we had lost everything else by then, and she had no right to keep that. I had to go on." He took a swallow of Scotch.

"With a little help sometimes."

"Don't begrudge people their crutches," Andrew told him, "so often it's all they have to offer." He looked down at his glass. Pale swirls of Scotch undulated through the melting ice. "Myra and me," he said, "there's so much that's happened, and so much that's gone by, we wallow like a pair of animals in the muck, and we can't even talk much, because everything's been said. But I still love her, the strangest thing that's come to pass is that I love her, even though it's all congealed under so many layers of trash and stink that it might as well be lost. You see that's the most painful thing—whether we love each other or not doesn't make much difference in the way we spend our time."

"It makes a difference," Lang said, unwillingly.

"I know. And I hate it. Because if it wasn't for that, I'd be—you know, I'd be released. I'd be able to kneel down before Myra, and lay down my sword at her feet, and say, All right, I've had enough, you win. Awful, isn't it? It's not doing anybody much good." He looked at Lang very directly. "You've hardly touched your drink, Daniel."

"I'm saving it," Lang said. "Keep talking."

"Don't worry," Andrew said.

He told Lang of how he had met Myra, and what she had been like, and what he had been like, and then what they had been like, and of his work; work so mingled with Myra that its excitement and the excitement of her became one, as they flew from country to country on wings of expectation, knowing that around the corner of the next day something astonishingly beautiful was waiting for them; and the gradual dissipation of dreams into days, and then more days—"We found that a hangover is not much of a sacrifice to give the gods every morning," Andrew said—and then he told of how they had ended, beached and breathless, on the shores of Icarus.

"And do you know," he said, "I can't help thinking that it was right, somehow, for us to finish here. We thought we were unique . . . We went farther than the rest of the world, and still we didn't move at all. There was a time," he went on, "when Myra went in for cults and other things, all that religious jazz and vomit—oh, it poisoned her—and once, we were in the middle of an argument, and she looked up at me and whispered, Don't you know, don't you know that we're all one? And look, Daniel," he said, his fists clenched on the table, "what I really want to know is this: if we're all one, then who the hell is everybody? Because so many people have died, and so many others have wrecked their life, and you only get by by pretending that none of it matters, and there's even some people who will say that it's all a great joke, and they're not laughing at you, they're laughing with you. But there's got to be something more than that—there has to be—because too much happened. It must have been for something, meant something, and I tried to find out all my life what it was, I tried so hard, and I don't know, really, I don't know. But there has to be a reason, even when there's no logic—you see, I've come to the conclusion that the only way to do penance for our large and little sins is to go on fighting, simply that, do battle, even when belief and hope are both long gone and your nerves are begging for a chance to rest. And so I go on about my business, which is the art of dying, and I wait and I watch. And there's one last surrender that I'm not going to make. That's to say my fight was not worth making, that it was all meaningless, that my life and my death were all a fraud, and my love was all in vain."

They sat and looked at each other across the table. Behind them was the sound of the kids talking and laughing, and the dull steady throb of the jukebox coming up off the floor.

"We'd better go," Lang said.

"Why?"

"Because I have to get ready to leave."

Then all the pain he had collected left Andrew's face, and he smiled. He smiled in pure satisfaction. "You're going down to see Johanna, then."

"I don't want to talk about it."

"Take your drink," Andrew said.

Lang's hand was slick on the glass. He gulped it down unsteadily, afraid of dropping it.

"Well," he said a little sullenly, "I guess I have to find out what's down there, after all."

"It's nothing to be proud of," Andrew answered. "It's just what you do."

"Carmel—"

"Don't tell me a thing. Myra may like to pretend she doesn't know who he is, but I know. I've known Carmel all my life."

Then, for some reason, Lang thought of a particular night at the club in New York, back in the early days, their first headlining gig. He was on stage, in the middle of singing a song called "Did You Know That Was My Name?", when he saw, in the second row of tables, a small, pale face, the tense bitterness of the mouth offset and echoed by a pair of dark deep eyes, watching him with an edgy intensity, gnawing on a fingernail. Later, the sound engineer at the mixing board told Lang that it really had been him. "Him coming to see us," Lang said. "Man." The engineer grinned: "Yeah, he comes here a lot, to check out the new boys. I mean, he's the one who started it all, right?"

When they left Uncle Lou's, the lights were back on all over Icarus. They had been in there for nearly two hours. It was only when they were walking up the steps of the house that Lang realized that they had forgotten to bring any food.

Myra was sitting waiting for them, her eye on the clock and her cigarette aimed at the door. "I won't even ask where you've been," she said in a cold, tight voice. "It's not hard to tell how you—how the two of you—have been spending your time. I sent Alice out for some food, she's gone and come back, and we've eaten. But what about you?"

Andrew flapped his arms like some large, ungainly bird. "Daniel, explain to her—what I was telling you . . ."

"There isn't anything you can tell me," Myra said, "and there isn't anything Lang can tell me, either." She turned to Lang. "You went with him. How could you—"

Lang went out of the kitchen, toward the stairs. Alice was standing in the living room. She eyed him without sympathy.

"Did you come back together," she said, "or did you leave him somewhere?"

Lang tried to ignore her, but she went on: "Brewer called. While you were out. I had to tell him you were out getting wasted." Alice snickered.

Brewer. But there was no time to talk to him now. Lang went on down to the rec room. As he got his things together, he could hear them all still arguing upstairs. This, too, would be graceless; an awkward lurch into the new, all fumbling fingers and stumbling feet, no more.

"Best I can do."

Soon his duffel was packed, and he went up. They had lapsed into a stony and unforgiving silence, the three of them locked in the cage of each other's stares. None of them said a word as Lang passed through on his way to the door.

But when he was almost to the street, the door opened behind him. He turned. It was Andrew. They looked at each other. Then Lang waved. In reply, Andrew waved his hand in a tight circle, high above his head.

Fight on foot. Lang hoisted the bag over his shoulder, Erica's tambourine clinking dully inside, and began the long walk up the hill to the station. An hour later, he was on the bus.

As he rode down the main street of Icarus for the last time, Lang saw a dazed figure stumbling out of a telephone booth in one of the enormous, empty parking lots, under the night sky. He wandered with his arms flailing as his head turned incessantly from side to side, regular as a weathervane. Lang had to look again, quickly, before the bus turned to the Southern highway and cut off his vision forever, but he was right: it was Tommy the Spy, wondering where everyone, everyone, everyone had gone.

CHAPTER TWENTY-ONE

Carmel: 1

Carmel came back to Lorraine's place, an apartment building in a
new section of town, shortly after dark. She was sitting in the front
room, reading a magazine. Carmel waved at her with the hand that
held his cigarette, and walked on into the bedroom. "Are we going
out tonight?" she called after him, but her tone expected no answer
and so he gave her none. The magazine's slick pages flicked impatiently at the frontier of his hearing.

He looked down. Out of the ragged dark below the window,
plows, shovels, cranes reared immobile from the earth. A new devel-
opment was under construction out there. Some of it was being built
on Seastrom's old land. Carmel had driven past the house on his way
home; it now stood marooned in a field of raw upturned earth, all the
vegetation cleared away, the land leveled, and the new boundaries,
ghosts of future houses, marked with stakes and bits of cloth, waiting
for poured concrete and steel girders to convert them into reality. He
had expected feelings of loss, perhaps even regret—instead he felt in
serene balance, as if the house were now more his than ever.

"Did you know that Lang left town again?" Lorraine called out
to him.

"Where'd you hear that?"

"He just took off. Earlier tonight. Alice Hoffentlich told me. No one knows where. Are we going out or not?"

She leaned against the door, the magazine held at her hip like a fallen flag.

"Not just yet," Carmel told her. "I've got some business. I'm expecting one phone call. If I hear what I need to hear, then we can go wherever you want."

"And if you don't?"

"I'm not thinking about that."

Lorraine inspected a nail on her left forefinger. "I wish sometimes that you'd tell me what's going on," she complained.

"There's no point," Carmel said lightly, his mind elsewhere. Lang was gone. That changed his plans, but not by much, and he was suddenly glad to be alone. He felt no sorrow, only vague surprise—to have gone so quickly, backed out, like a thief too, without warning. Carmel would have thought Lang was braver than that. No need to ask Lorraine for any details. He had already assimilated Lang's departure into the situation. He felt like a general, moving his divisions on a map.

"At least you didn't tell me not to worry my pretty little head about it," Lorraine remarked. "Richard said that to me once."

"Don't talk about Richard," Carmel said, to make her happy. Richard first; then Lang. Neither had taken his dare. Saps, cowards, both of them, all of them. Yes, he was glad to be alone, to do it on his own.

That afternoon, when he had given the list to the police, he had been suddenly, unexpectedly jittery. But it didn't matter; the cops liked that, it shored up their authority when they knew you were nervous. Giving the first name on the list, he had to force the words from a numb mouth: "This is the beginning—Eric Love. The address is . . ." But as he went on, he was soothed by the simple rote monotony of the names, so that he no longer connected them with their faces; he grew so confident that he had to throttle back his voice, and fake the unease which had been genuine.

"The second dude is called Ricky Blaumann . . ."

"The third is Larry Daniels . . ."

"The fourth . . ."

He had close to a dozen names to give, and each one seemed to take a long time. When he hung up, his palms were slick—not apprehension anymore, but a thin, quivering excitement. In all the weeks of planning he had never given a thought to what the act itself might be like. The preliminaries, endlessly checking and rechecking when the various shipments were due so that all the dealers would be holding a sufficient amount of goods to build a solid case against them, making arrangements with the cops, with Mink, always careful to cover himself, all had been difficult, but it hadn't affected him that much. He could have pulled out whenever he wanted. Now the line was crossed, his hat was in the ring, and all he had to do was wait for the results to come in.

As soon as he was done, he went to another phone and called Tommy the Spy. "Did you talk to all the people I asked you to?"

"Why, sure, Carmel, of course I did. You kn-know you can count on me."

"What did you tell them?"

"Just what you said. That I n-needed to score, and I'd bring them the money tonight. But you know that I don't have the money, and there's no f-f-fucking way I can see them all tonight—you know that, Carmel . . ."

"I'm glad that you remember my name so well," Carmel said. He was on a pay phone, but still he was careful—it was a habit.

"What?"

"Never mind. Look, Tommy: I don't want you to see any of them."

"I don't understand."

"I just wanted to make sure they'd all be home," Carmel explained. "I'm having a party."

"Can I come?" Tommy the Spy asked forlornly.

"Oh, Tommy—I'd really like it if you could. But remember I asked you to go to Baltimore tonight."

"I could go tomorrow."

"No, it has to be tonight. I'm really sorry."

Carmel hung up and leaned back in the booth. Tommy might be a risk. But Carmel's friends in Baltimore could keep him high and happy until he had forgotten all about the party. And they'd never trace Tommy back to him—not for a good long while yet, anyway.

Even so, with that precaution, with all the other precautions he had taken, it would still be possible for one of the dudes to find him out. Carmel knew there'd be no qualms about having him taken care of. And even if it was never discovered how the trap had been sprung, his new monopoly in Icarus couldn't last very long. In a few months, perhaps only a few weeks, every other hustler in the territory would be trying to move in. But if he established himself quickly enough, he'd be able to handle that. When they came, whoever they were, they'd have to climb a long way to find him.

In a sense, he didn't care, right now, just how it came out; his pride, his power, was that he had declared himself, had taken up the challenge that no one else had the guts or the vision to take. And if the gamble worked, then maybe the restlessness inside him would be sated, if only for a time. Briefly he let himself see a network spreading all over the state, the country; of hundreds—no, thousands—of people, all his. After all, he was still young. He savored the image; then shut it off. His kind had no use for fables. Better to translate them into action, precious and bold.

He fought to keep himself from looking at his watch. He sat by the telephone in the big armchair in the bedroom. It took an effort not to get up and move around. He couldn't give in to even the smallest impulse.

Lorraine looked into the mirror, aggrieved. She turned to him. "Do you dislike me when my mascara runs?" she asked.

Carmel, fist to chin, surveyed her. "When you made it with Richard, the night Erica totalled herself," he asked slowly, "did you tell him you'd moved in with me?"

"No. Of course not."

"That's good. I guess he deserves a little amnesty."

"Him," Lorraine said, picking at a lash. "If an atom bomb was to go off, he'd think it was the sound of his own tears hitting the ground."

Carmel laughed. "You're a nice girl," he said. "But tell me something. If maybe the two of you had made a little spark instead of just drowning in all that dishwater—if that had happened—would you still have come back here?"

"You know I would have come back," Lorraine said.

She was about to go on—hoping, as she so often, so tiresomely did, to provoke his questions into signs of feeling—when the telephone rang. Carmel hesitated. "Do you want me to get it?" Lorraine asked.

"No," he said, his hand on the receiver. "Matter of fact, why don't you move to the other room, and start thinking about where you want to go."

She didn't look cheerful about it, but she went. Heart beating dryly, Carmel picked up the phone.

"Yeah," he said.

"Well, it's all over," Mink told him. "I just talked to the main man. He says they got them all."

"Were they holding?"

"Coming out their ass. Loaded."

"Good. How did the call go?"

"No problem. The phone you picked was right next to the bus station, so it looked okay for me to hang around."

"That's why I picked it. What about driving back?"

"Nobody tailed me. I made sure of that. And I was using another car, just for insurance." Mink sounded amused. "It belongs to Ricky Blaumann's girlfriend."

"What if they trace it?"

"When I brought it back, I told her I'd seen the cops at Ricky's. She knows how much stuff he had on him. She'll be in New York by morning."

"You're sure about that."

"She was packing when I left," Mink said. "Oh, by the way—I don't know how important this is—one of the dudes got shot. I don't know who. He realized what was going down, and tried to hold them 'til he flushed the stash. They decided he was resisting arrest."

"How bad was he hurt?"

"I don't know. I didn't exactly want to make conversation, if you follow me."

"All right," Carmel said. "You did good."

"Okay, man. It was a beautiful show."

Tomorrow, he would have to call the suppliers, and tell them the news, and suggest that they begin routing all their goods to him. And he would have to start getting some people together, because the operation would be too big, now, for he and Mink to handle alone anymore. But that was tomorrow. He wondered vaguely, as well, who had been shot, and whether he was dead; but that was tomorrow, too.

He stood up. Watching himself in the mirror, he took off his brown corduroy jacket, and threw it on the bed. Sitting down, his eyes still on his reflected eyes, he kicked off his boots while unbuttoning his work shirt. Then he took off his jeans and dropped them in a heap on the floor. Naked, he was still, enjoying the supple relaxation of his body. Peace passed over him like a soothing hand.

He crossed to the closet, took out a clean white shirt, French-cuffed, wide-collared, and slipped it on. The creamy material hugged snug against his skin. Inserting the cufflinks, he looked for a tie, and settled on a conservative red-black, regimental stripe. It went well with the charcoal gray three-piece suit which he next removed from the closet and put on, careful to leave the last button on the vest open. A pair of black, zippered ankle boots, freshly polished, completed him; he gave his hair—cut the day before—a quick combing in the mirror, and he was ready.

Last of all, he took the ring with Myra's false eye mounted as its stone off his finger and placed it in a box at the bottom of his chest of drawers. Then he went into the living room.

Lorraine looked up in surprise. "I've never seen you dressed like that," she said.

"You better get used to it," Carmel said. "You'll be seeing a lot like it from now on."

"I don't have to get used to it," Lorraine said, rising. "You're beautiful. I love it. And I love you." She reached for his embrace; after a fractional pause, he opened his arms. "You," she said to his ear, in a tender little voice.

"Where do you want to go?" he said. "We can go anywhere in the world."

"Oh, Carmel," she said, pressed tightly against him, "let's just stay in tonight. Just you and me. That's the best way to celebrate—whatever happened."

"No. I want to go out," Carmel said. But he didn't feel her body opening to him, or hear her murmured, soft acquiescence; he was looking over her shoulder, beyond her, and the window, and the night outside. His town was waiting for him.

FOUR

Some people like to go out dancing
And other people, like us, we gotta work
And there's even some evil mothers
Tell you life is full of dirt . . .
But anyone who ever had a heart
Wouldn't turn around and break it
Anyone who ever played a part
Wouldn't turn around and hate it
Sweet Jane.

—The Velvet Underground
"Sweet Jane"

CHAPTER TWENTY-TWO

Lang: 1

Let's go, now.

Johanna's town was still sleeping when Lang arrived, a few hours short of dawn. Two hundred years before, it had been a staging-ground for the new country's leaders, and a crossroads of the Revolution. Then time and the highways had passed it by; its old buildings grew dilapidated as its population shrank and the power moved North. It was only a generation ago that a covey of millionaires had put their money into restoring it, constructing a history like an artificial limb, and thrown a circle of grinning ramparts around the temple so that Americans could come to gawk at their new past.

Lang, getting off the bus, felt a peculiar and disassociated sense of remembered belonging. On too many hot and motionless summer afternoons in his childhood, he, like so many others, had been driven the two hundred miles from Suffragette City to this town, to wander down its crabbed colonial streets and peer through thick glass at ancient days he could not believe and did not want, dragging his feet on its shiny old stones. He had always hated it, then.

Johanna lived in a townhouse complex near the radio station where she worked. He could see the station's antenna, high on a hill, from the bus stop. There was an all-night coffeehouse nestled at the hill's base, and he went to it. Only a few people were inside; from their gesticulations, Lang guessed that they were political. Behind their heads, one of the colonial buildings filled a window, the long line of its wall lit from behind by an arc light buried deep in its lawn.

Lang drank coffee and watched the sky. The politicals were replaced by some veterans of an all-night celebration, talking loudly to keep themselves awake, their mouths smeared and uneven above their polished clothes. When they left, Lang left too. He knew Johanna would not wake for some hours yet, but he felt restless, and he had to move.

He found the house without trouble. It was still night, but the blue had taken on a cool, metallic quality, promising that dawn wasn't far away. Out of habit, Lang tried her door, and found it locked.

Then he noticed that one of the windows was slightly open. The crack was just a finger wide. Instinctively, he looked around to see if anyone was watching; then he laughed. He liked the idea of coming in like a thief. Cautiously, he worked both hands into the tiny space and put some pressure on the sash. It only gave by a couple of inches, but now he had some leverage. On the next push, the window lifted by more than a foot.

Lang parted the curtains and looked inside, making out her living room in the murkiest outline. He pushed the window up the rest of the way. Reaching back for his duffel bag, he lowered it carefully onto the floor inside. Then, gripping the sill with both hands, he tried to pull himself up over it, but his feet couldn't find a hold on the ragged brick, and he dropped down.

He wiped his hands on his jeans, grasped the sill again, and lunged. He hit his head on the sash, there was a second when he almost fell, his legs kicked the air, his palms hurt, but now he was up. His belly was cramped by the sill and his legs hung out behind. He wormed the rest of the way, arms stretched out blindly for the floor, and finally he was there, all of himself there.

Scrambling to his feet, he closed the window. The sun was breaking loose at the far end of the sky.

There was just enough light to get his bearings. One door opened onto the kitchen; right near his window was a staircase which must lead to Johanna's bedroom. On the knob of the bannister hung a coat which he recognized as hers. Lang felt very tired. He lay down on a couch, first dragging his duffel bag near, and fell asleep almost immediately, one arm over the bag.

When he woke up, Johanna filled his sight. She was less than a foot away, peering down at him. She hadn't realized yet that he was awake.

"Hello," Lang murmured, ". . . sweet Jane."

A smile broke over her lips. She didn't pull back. "You were always the only one who called me that," she said.

Lang sat up.

"No one else ever knew what it meant."

He was discovering her all over again. So far as Johanna was concerned, his memory had been a cold tool. If it had given her a more perfect beauty than she deserved, it had still left out the delicate lilac shadow on her eyelids, the smooth curve of her hair against her cheek, the frail gravity of her lips, all those physical ambiguities that made her something other, rarer than beautiful. And to see her so close now, looking down at him—he knew that if he reached up to kiss her, she wouldn't resist. She must have thought the same, for she moved her face closer by one tentative inch, and was about to move the next, when they both became aware of another presence in the room.

"Well, Johanna, are you going to introduce me to our visitor?"

He was wearing a pale beige-colored bathrobe, belted at the waist, his hands in its pockets. A lock of wispy blonde hair hung over his forehead, just touching the top of his wire-rims; he smiled at them both with an air of mussed waking bemusement which somehow didn't make him look the least bit vulnerable.

Johanna stood up. "Daniel, this is Ron Bridgeport. Ron, this is—"

"Dan Lang," Ron said in a friendly voice. "It must be. Johanna talks about you so much that it can't be anyone else. I'm glad we've finally met—I was beginning to think that Johanna had made you up."

"Oh, she did," Lang said.

Ron chuckled, and put his arm around her waist. "She mentioned to me that you might be coming to visit—but that was quite a long time ago, wasn't it? Or was it?"

"Yes, it was," Johanna said.

"Well, it's good of you to come at last, Dan, however unexpected," Ron said. He had an air of precise diplomacy, of fine-tuned concern for the well-placed gesture, that reminded Lang a little of Carmel. "Are you going to be here long?"

"I don't know yet."

"Well, you're certainly welcome for as long as you'd like to stay. We can show you the town," he said. "And you know, whatever you need, whatever you want—as I'm sure Johanna will tell you, it's her house, after all—why, I'm sure we can provide it."

Lang looked at him silently. "Have you got any cocaine?" he asked.

Ron's eyebrows arched into a pleasant smile. "Afraid not. We've got a little grass, of course, that we keep around for social occasions—but as for the rest, the best we can offer you is a rain check."

"We could offer you lunch instead," Johanna interposed.

"Lunch? I was thinking of breakfast."

Johanna freed herself from Ron's arm. "We never get up before one," she said, "isn't that awful? You'd better get dressed," she told Ron. "You're due at the station in twenty minutes."

"Why do you have to remind me of these things?" Ron complained, humorously. Johanna patted his back and kissed him on the cheek. "All right, all right," he said. "Sorry I can't stay for lunch—I'd have liked to talk to you, Dan."

He went up the stairs, humming. Johanna came and sat down beside Lang. "Do you want to go out for a walk after lunch?" she asked, not looking at him. Then she added, "Ron won't be back from the station until seven."

While they ate, they were both careful to keep the conversation irrelevant. Ron had left, but the house was still full of him; its walls contained every distance Johanna had crossed since Lang had known her. "The station's still pretty chaotic," she told him, "but it's nothing like it was. Ron started it all with no money, no anything, just a license and a generator. It was incredible how hard he worked—he's very ambitious. It's a pretty amazing accomplishment, when you think about it."

Lang heard the pride in her voice, reluctant but undeniably there, and to spare himself, he changed the subject. Later, though, when they were out in the air, strolling together down the streets toward the old colonial town, he put his restraint aside, and said to her: "Well. You've got some explaining to do."

"Do I? You know what I left."

"I left it too. But I didn't just hide in the first hole I found."

"Do you want to play it that way? No, Daniel, it wasn't just the first hole. There was a lot more to it than that."

The pavement beneath their feet turned to cobblestones. A trailing spittle of tourists hovered around them in all directions. Cameras gleamed like coins on their chests.

"It's not bad here," Johanna said, "it's not, really. Sure a lot of the people are atrocious, but you can always laugh at them, and the people at the station are good. They took me in, you know—they helped me. A lot of people back home didn't."

"So you found Ron instead."

"He's good to me . . . He's good for me. There's things in him that you could never begin to guess. And as for excitement, well, you know I had enough of that."

"Will you wear a white dress to the wedding? Will you honeymoon at Disney World?"

Johanna looked down at the cobblestones. "Getting married was Ron's idea. I'd have been happy just to go on the way we had been. I don't like putting locks on things."

"But you'll do it for him anyway."

"Maybe it'll be good for me. I was so scared all the time. . . . Oh, Daniel," she said, the melancholy in her voice suddenly rising, "I waited for you for months. Even before I wrote that letter—I couldn't get rid of the idea that someday you were going to show up. And when I sent that card to Hoffentlichs, I stopped. Part of the reason I sent it was so you wouldn't come. And I was just getting used to that when I came downstairs and found you, this morning. You were smiling in your sleep, you know . . ."

"Maybe I was thinking of you."

Somewhere a child began to wail. "I can't take this street," Lang said. "Isn't there someplace we could go?"

"I know a place. The garden, behind the old Governor's house. The tourists don't get to it. I used to go there by myself, all the time, when I first came here."

They left the street and went down a crooked path, behind one of the cottages. They followed it until it disappeared at the border of a barbed-wire fence. Lang lifted a strand for them both to step through. The garden was a small, uneven plot of ground, staked out by a row of trees at one end, and at the other by the square brick back of the Governor's mansion. No tourists could be seen. For all the hundreds of people just outside the frame, the two of them were alone.

They found a place beneath a tree, and sat down in the armchair of its roots. Johanna rested her head on Lang's shoulder; his chin just touched the part of her hair. He started to stroke her arm, but felt a tiny flinching beneath her skin, and stopped.

"I almost wish you hadn't come," she said. "You brought a lot of Icarus with you."

"I'm not making any claims—for it or for me."

"Yes, you are," she said. "Just by being here. Unless Icarus has changed a lot," she went on, "you heard about why I left."

"Yeah, I heard." Lang reached for a cigarette, then stopped, not wanting to break the mood.

"I just couldn't say I was different anymore. I had to leave then —to keep whatever was left."

"I know."

"Richard called to tell me about Erica."

"He must have called everybody."

"And he probably wasn't any more satisfied after he did," Johanna said. "Poor Richard. There really isn't anything else you can say about him, is there?"

"He gave me Erica's tambourine."

"The one you gave her, way back?—I remember." Johanna paused. "I was a lot more shook up by it than I expected," she said. "If I'd stayed in Icarus, I know I would have been just like her by the end—whatever the end was."

"Yes."

"Why did you go back there?"

"It wasn't just because of Erica—not the way you think. I can't tell you why."

"Can't, or don't want to?" She peered up at him, the sun on her face.

"Don't want to."

"Was it bad?"

"Yeah."

"A girl?"

"No. Look, I'll tell you sometime—but not now. It's too nice a day to tell you now."

"It is nice. . . . Nicer than I thought." In the calm, she was distant, and yet closer than she had been before.

"I miss Erica a lot sometimes," she said quietly.

"You were never friends."

"I know. But remember what I said, that I would have been just like her? It sounds strange, because I stayed away from all that—that always belonged to her. But I never knew which of us was right."

"I always liked you for staying out. I thought it took some guts."

"That was just what it didn't take. Look, there's Erica—when she was fifteen, she was already telling the world to come on. I always backed away. I could never face love when it wasn't permanent, knowing I'd have to hurt somebody or somebody would have to hurt me before it was over. I didn't want to get my hands dirty. So I missed all sorts of chances. I mean," she said, "fifteen is the time to be cruel. I wasn't, and I lost it for good. Everything you thought was strength was being scared, just that—so weak . . ."

"Oh, you were lucky."

"Then I didn't deserve to be. I paid for it. You pay for everything—you pay even more for refusing to accept the price." She stood up suddenly. "It's getting cold. And I have to fix dinner—" she stopped, and Lang finished the sentence:

"For Ron."

"Yes, for Ron. For you, too. And for me. Don't be that way."

"Why not?"

"Because you don't have to be," she said over her shoulder, walking away.

Back in the house, while she worked in the kitchen, Lang lay on the living-room floor, spinning records on her stereo like a disc jockey trying to put together a mood. Nothing held. All day, being with her, he had been elated and miserable, drunk with her presence and filled with an overwhelming sense of exile from her life—a threat always hovering, like the hidden danger you find sometimes in pot, when the high tips over the line into paranoia, and you realize that coming down will be a bottomless fall.

He felt stifled all through dinner. Ron was back, dressed in a jacket, a tie, and cuffed pinstripe bellbottoms, his briefcase propped against the table leg. Ron held the conversation with a long story about his meeting with an advertiser who was being boycotted by the blacks on the college campus—"I just told him that we wouldn't run the ads during our disco hours, that's all"—and by an endless flow of urbane anecdotes about money. At first Lang was only irritated. Then he understood that Ron was running scared; he was putting all his armor on display, in a show of force. The realization that this was indeed a battle buoyed and excited Lang, even though he didn't know, yet, what the stakes were, or whether he wanted to win.

Ron turned to him with courteous bonhomie. "I know this must be very dull for you—but you'll be able to meet some of the people I'm talking about at the party tomorrow night."

"I didn't know there was a party."

"Oh," Johanna said, "didn't I tell you? I—well, Ron and I—we're having a party for all the people at the station. Everyone is supposed to come dressed as their favorite song. Ron thought it up. It's . . . sort of a celebration." Automatically, she looked up at Ron at the end of the sentence, realizing too late that this would force her to smile.

"You're invited," Ron said to Lang, "of course."

Lang had hoped that he'd get to talk to Johanna again after dinner, but Ron had arranged for them all to meet some people at a bar. She was sealed off—it was impossible for him to reach her, with Ron wrapping the cloth of her life so tightly around her at every turn. He grew gloomy again, and silent, as they got into Ron's car.

The people waiting for them were from the station too, it turned out—they were all coming to the party tomorrow night. They were united by a common shagginess, as if they were all tented under one enormous wig; they talked about disco, and Quaaludes, and the L.A. sound, mired in a fellowship as smooth as wax and as hard to penetrate. When they spoke to Ron, however, all their mellowness faded, and they turned themselves on edge to him like playing cards. He was the power among them; they never lost sight of that, no matter how benignly he approved their games.

Lang saw that Johanna was being drawn in too, carried by the flow, and he slipped even deeper into his depression. But it was only an indulgence, curiously superficial. His mind had already made the decision that the real contest would come later. A tall, rangy kid with a Lincoln beard leaned forward and tapped him on the arm.

"Hey," he said, "I hear you sing in a band."

"Yeah."

"Well, you know the Allman Brothers Fillmore East album? The guy who yells out 'Whipping Post' just before they play it— that was me."

Lang looked at him. "Fantastic," he said.

The kid nodded, bashful and pleased. For the rest of the evening, he would look Lang's way occasionally, and give him a tentative grin: they shared a secret.

When they drove back to Johanna's house, Ron surprised Lang by saying: "Well, here you are, kids. It's home and sacking out for me."

"I thought he lived here," Lang said to Johanna, when they were in the living room, and the sound of Ron's car was fading behind them.

"He's got a place just a few blocks away. It's just that he manages to spend most of his nights here."

"Except when you go there."

"No," Johanna said vaguely, "his place depresses me." She was a little drunk, and vulnerable. Lang reached out to touch her hair.

"Isn't he—isn't he afraid, that someone might seduce you?"

"That's why he did it," Johanna said. "As a test. He thinks he won tonight."

"Did he?"

"No. I don't know. Don't ask me to say." She shook her head. Her eyes were filled with tears too tired to fall, her arms hung at her sides. "I can't let you," she said. "Kiss me goodnight, Daniel."

Lang stepped forward. He bent down to her. Their lips brushed without force.

"That won't do," he said.

"No."

"Try again?"

Even as he held out his arms she was coming to him. Just before their lips touched, he spoke, not to her—"Oh, can I," he said softly. Her mouth surged up with sudden speed; then they were in a strange, electric embrace, for she advanced and withdrew, pulled forward at the same time she was pulling back.

But she broke it off; she was afraid. "Goodnight," she whispered, and vanished up the stairs.

Lang sat awake long after she had gone, burning cigarette after cigarette, wearing out his thoughts like the tires of a car racing the circle of a track at ninety miles an hour. He kept the stereo going low; he no longer wanted to disturb her sleep.

The next day she and Ron were both on duty at the station, and that was bad for him. He almost turned on her show, but he didn't want to hear her voice that way, amputated by the airwaves, more lost to him than silence could ever make her. Through the long hours, he created and re-created fantastic, chaotic visions of her, wandering the town to pour all its faces and colors into the images filling his head. When she finally came back, early in the evening, to get ready for the party, and he saw her coming through the door, he felt almost betrayed—she seemed too small to carry the weight he had given her. At that moment she looked to him like any other girl.

Then she said, "I bought some new boots. Do you want to see them?"

"Sure."

She opened the box and rolled up her jeans to put them on. Her calves were soft and white, beautifully rounded, and something turned inside him at the sight. He thought of Sally in New York—Sally used to lie around the apartment wearing nothing but a gray T-shirt, and never aroused the smallest flicker of desire. His most vivid memory of their lovemaking was the wet sucking sound of their chests colliding as they heaved together. For a long time he had let himself believe that there wasn't anything more to sex than that—now, watching Johanna, there was.

She stood up, and did a turn for him, laughing. "Do you like them?" she asked. "Do you really?"

"Yes," he said; he didn't trust his voice. He knew, right then, that he was finally and truly in love with her, and there was no help for him anymore. She must have seen it: she stopped laughing, as abrupt as a needle being lifted from a turning record. Their gazes met, and he didn't know, for a second, if it was her eyes he looked back into, or his own.

She touched his arm. "I'm sorry, Daniel," she said. "There's still too much to remember. . . ." She took her hand away, but stayed close. He had never wanted anything more than he wanted her now. But still he felt no regret.

When she went upstairs to get ready, he stood in the living room, surveying the scenery. Everything had been prepared. Lang's duffel bag and everything else had been moved upstairs. The arm of the stereo was polished to a gleam. The records were stacked along the wall, ready to go. The rug was rolled back for dancing, and the icebox was filled with beer.

Ron arrived, spangled in yellow shafts and rays of light, the colors bursting from a crimson circle positioned directly over his stomach. "What are you?" Lang asked him.

"Don't let the sun go down on me."

"Ah?"

"Elton John, you know."

"Oh, right."

"You don't like me, much," Ron said.

Then he smiled a friendly smile. "But I like you all right, and we both like Johanna, so everything's all right, isn't it?"

"I'll see you at the party."

Johanna still hadn't come down when the guests arrived. Apparently it had been arranged for them to come all in a body. Ron, in his gold, stood near the door and played the master of ceremonies to every arrival. Lang stayed by the wall, and watched each one come on.

Blue suede shoes was there, and everybody needs somebody to love. Twist and shout, and turn, turn, turn—the room was a riot of rainbows, gaudy clothes and high-heeled boots. Lang saw faces painted into glittering masks and hideous scars, hand-lettered signals and drawn tattoos. All the songs mingled their notes, swayed, broke apart, collected in new groups, burst and disappeared. Music drowned everything, rushed on, tipped over, careened and rolled in the air.

Ron stood up on a stool.

"I just want to remind everybody to all stay in character."

A girl came up to Lang. She was dressed in a sailor suit and carrying semaphore flags, and a sign between her breasts said S.O.S. "You aren't wearing a costume," she blurted out. "Everyone's supposed to be dressed as their favorite song. Why aren't you dressed as your favorite song?"

"Because I am my favorite song."

"Oh, wow. Do you want to dance?"

"Sure."

They went to the floor. In the heaving, surging field, all distinctions blurred, all contradictions broke. There was only the heat, the noise, and the ceaseless movement, absorbing every part. Sweat stung Lang's eyes. His hair was slick and wild on his head. He danced with the girl for half an hour, until he lost her.

"You looked pretty good out there," Ron said to him. Ron was reclining in a large soft armchair, near the stereo. In one hand he held a drink; with the other he adjusted the dials on the amp.

"Yeah," Lang said, wet and out of breath, "you should try it."

"I can't. I never dance. I've tried to learn, but I'm just not very good at it."

"Oh, man," Lang said, "if you don't know how to dance then I can't even talk to you."

Ron didn't answer. Looking past Lang suddenly, he stood up. Lang turned. Johanna was coming down the stairs. He and Ron were one in their eyes; no one else saw her. Her hair was loose, and flowed to her shoulders, smooth as a river—her face was pale and perfect, carved and still. She was lovely and perfect and inhuman. She was wearing black pants which fell in an unbroken line from the silver chain around her waist to the toes of her new boots; she wore a long-sleeved shirt of the creamiest white, unbuttoned to the edge of a tight black leather vest. A single bracelet gleamed on her wrist. She paused, midway on the stairs, to look down at the carnival below.

"I don't know the song," Ron said. "Do you?"

"Yes," Lang said.

Johanna came down and picked her way across the room; she was swallowed up before she got to Lang. He pushed through the crush to find her. Suddenly the crowd parted.

"Sweet Jane," he said.

"Hello, Daniel."

Then some people came between them, and he was thrown back. He reached out and pulled her to him. "We have to talk," he said.

"Not now. Wait." She sank back into the crowd.

He waited for over an hour. He watched her making the rounds of the party, giving a few moments of conversation here, a quick laugh or a merry face there, graceful and easy, tossing her hair back over her shoulders as she talked. She was so completely one of them. He wasn't, he didn't want to be, but the desire to be with her was more powerful than any bonds of personality or belief. Torn between misery, anger, and love, he could find no outlet. He was ready to explode.

Johanna was sitting on the arm of Ron's chair, talking, her face bent down to his. Lang went over to them. "Let's go outside," he said.

Johanna looked from him to Ron and back again. "All right," she answered quietly.

They left the party. Out on the porch, it was cool and dark. The light above the door threw deep shadows on her face.

"I thought we could have a nice time together," she said. "But instead you want to force things. I'm tired of being forced, Lang."

"I'm sorry. I'm in a hurry. I don't have time to be nice, and it looks as if being nice wouldn't help things much anyway."

Johanna looked away. When she spoke, her voice was shaky with anger. "Did you ever wake up late at night, screaming—screaming just to make sure there wasn't anybody to hear you?" She stopped. "Forget that part. I didn't mean to say it."

"I don't want to forget it."

"No. . . . We've been through all that. A long time ago." She stirred restlessly. "You were going to tell me why you went back," she said.

"Yes, I was."

"Will you tell me now? Now it's not too nice to tell it."

Are you looking for some kicks, kid?

"Please?"

Lang felt his hands trembling. He had been waiting for this moment, but to stumble into it now, too quickly, without warning, left him dazed and lost, almost unable to speak. He went slowly at first, to get accustomed to the telling; then the words began to come more easily, but without stilling the furor in his heart. He told her all of it, even the details he had left out all the other times, all the times he had told it to himself. He remembered the grimy, unwashed junkie stench that had choked his nostrils when they wrestled for the gun—and the moment when they first looked at each other, and it would have been impossible to say whose eyes were more filled with fear. Then with a cry the junkie lunged toward him, made a wild grab for the gun, and Lang's body twisted, his muscles ached, as he pulled the trigger, and the other sat down suddenly with the blood already spilling out onto his shirt before he fell over. Lang remembered the last sight of his face, belly-white and bloated, scarred with traces of old acne, as he lay there in the rain.

When he was done, Johanna was shaking too. She passed her hand vaguely through the air, as if to clear her sight. Her voice was a whisper: "But wouldn't it be—wasn't it—what do they call it—self-defense . . ."

"Yeah," Lang said. "That's what the cops would call it. Only it wasn't. Because I wanted to. I *wanted* to."

"But why?"

"Because it was just like Carmel said. It was power. He was everybody I ever hated, right then—all the hate I had inside me went right out the barrel of that gun, and put a hole in his heart. I'd been holding it in, fighting it, for so long—I was blowing the whole world away right at that second, I could taste it. I had to do it. Because it wasn't self-defense, but when you get right down to it, it was just what they say—it was him or me. Either he had to die, or I did. And no matter what that means, I can't pretend it was anything else."

"Just like that."

"Yeah, just like that. I've got to live with it—that's enough of a price. Look, I could have killed myself afterwards, but if it was going to mean anything to me, I had to live, whether I liked it or not. You know that."

"Besides," Johanna said coldly, "someone else did it for you."

"Yeah. Maybe she did," Lang said. "For you too."

Johanna became very still. "It's not the same thing."

"It was for you—for you. And I know it."

"Don't."

"You slept with Carmel."

Into the silence she said slowly, "Yes. But I'm not sure . . . that it was his."

"It had to be his."

"Or yours," she said.

Lang let out his breath.

"You're so damned good at remembering things, Daniel, why don't you try remembering the last time I saw you, in Icarus? And I went to Carmel the next night—the very next night—because I was afraid that if I didn't I'd never let you go again. I had to prove that I didn't care, or else I couldn't have survived—because I couldn't face losing you, and I knew that you'd have to go. . . . That's why I can't hate you, no matter what you say you did. I want so much to hate you," she said hoarsely, "I was trying so hard to hate you, while you were telling me what happened—and then I thought of what I did to you without you ever knowing, and I . . . I don't know, I—"

Then she was in his arms. How she got there he didn't know. He stroked her hair, staring out at the night above her head, while she pressed against him, crying harshly.

"Will you leave here?" he asked softly. "Will you come with me?"

She pushed away from his grip, struggling, her face torn open as if by a blade. "No," she said, "no . . . No."

Then she went inside. Lang stood looking at the door. His heart beat out the empty seconds.

"Okay," he said.

He couldn't go back in there—not now. He turned and walked away down the street.

Over by the college campus, the frat houses were having their parties. The windows spilled out light and giddy noise. Lang drifted on past their perimeter.

The parties ebbed into inconsequence behind him as he came down into the old colonial town. It was hushed and stricken at this hour, like an empty hospital, without the teeming tourists to give its buildings life. Under the moon, the street looked as artificial as a movie set. Bell towers cut out of cardboard stood to prop up the stars; brick walls clenched themselves like fists. Solitude destroyed the illusion of realism, and the town looked suddenly pitiful; the gaudy reconstructions melted away, and the uncovered nerve-ends of the past begged for release like pleading voices from beneath the ground. Lang sat down on the steps of a tiny church, to let his aching body rest.

He had no right. Here, she could construct a shelter for herself— she could be another tourist here, and pretend that she was whole. He thought of all the tourists who came here every year, half-hopeful and half-resigned, wanting a true history but forced to invent one instead, by whatever gimcrack and improvised rigging came to hand. And Ron had all those virtues of kindliness and decency and quiet good manners that let Johanna and everyone slumber on in imaginary peace—but shove all that, Lang thought, the taste of fury rising on his tongue, he didn't have the time.

He thought, then, of the suicide note that Erica never got around to writing—because, remember, she was in a hurry too:

> so . . .
> if you can't make it ONE way
> you might as well MAKE it ANOTHER!!
> isn't that right Danny boy?

In those last moments, while Richard lay in a sleeping fever beside wide-awake Lorraine, and Brewer slumped alone in the room beneath, watching the dawn slice at the windows, and Odell got out of bed, reeling drunk, to play "Moonlight Mile" on the stereo one more time, and Carmel sat in Lorraine's apartment making his plans, and Myra argued with Andrew's corpse, and Tommy the Spy crossed the river from Suffragette to Virginia, a cold and serene joy arose in Erica's soul. She flirted with the intern on the hall—feeling a dry amusement at the thought that now, this last time, all the tricks she'd accumulated over the years were finally being put to good use—until he let her go to the women's room alone. He told her, with a lopsided grin, "Now, come back real soon, you hear?"

She heard. Barricaded inside the room, facing the mirror, she took stock of herself, switching thoughts on and off in her mind as if she were tuning all the channels on a radio. Then she knelt and wrenched the cap off the radiator. Hefting the smooth iron in her hand, she stood up, and threw it at the mirror with all her strength.

Johanna was wrong. Erica's death had not absolved him. He knew the music which had been wind to her sails as she navigated into death—he had heard it too. Crack those mournful saxophones, and let them rust—it was a trumpet-call, a gaudy blast to summon you to the last and grandest challenge, beyond the night. It had fallen to him to take her dare and carry it on. All right, then. He would fight.

Because after all, he thought, after all, being damned was only your fate if you chose to accept it.

Let's go! Let's go! Let's go! Dimly at first, and then with a gathering velocity like a plane lifting to fly straight into the red eye of the sun, Lang saw that all that had gone by, and all that he had been, was only an apprenticeship to the future, a future he now had to make his. The war was on again, and he was ready for it now. He felt suddenly in touch with the whole country through the stones beneath his feet.

"You're on," he said.

It was dawn when Lang came back to Johanna's house. He had expected that she would be asleep—he only wanted to get his duffel bag, and then walk back to the bus station. But she was sitting up waiting for him, in the darkened living room, the wreckage of the party scattered all around her. Her face was very calm, and did not change when he entered the room.

"Somebody called you from New York," she said. "I guess he got the number from the Hoffentlichs."

"It must have been Billy."

"That was the name. He said they're signing the contract tomorrow. The band is supposed to go into the studio in two weeks. That's if you go back. You will, won't you?"

'Yes, I will."

"I told Ron I wasn't going to marry him."

"How did he take it?"

"Well. He takes everything well. He said he was sure it was just temporary—that I was just letting remembering get the better of me—and maybe he's right . . . Oh, Daniel, I want to go with you, but I can't I can't just yet. You understand."

"I know."

"Your stuff's still upstairs."

"I'll go get it."

He went up, leaving her there, and found his duffel bag in her room. He was about to hoist it over his shoulder when he saw a brown manila envelope with his name on it lying on the bed. He picked it up and opened it. Inside was a photograph, blurred and faded and somewhat grainy. It had been taken the day his class graduated from high school, and all of them were there: Richard, and Brewer, and Lorraine, and Carmel standing off to one side, Austin and Veronica both mugging for the camera, Johanna—and Odell and Erica too, even though they were a class behind and would not graduate for another year. The only one missing was himself.

He had taken the picture.

Lang opened his duffel bag and put the photograph inside. Then he took out the tambourine. With a pen and a piece of paper borrowed from Johanna's desk, he wrote quickly:

> So the dancers keep dancing,
> and they feel no guilt,
> because the past was just what they dreamed.
> But it's still my passing
> fancy to say
> that all things may yet be redeemed.

He folded the paper inside the tambourine and left it on her bed.

When he went downstairs, Johanna was waiting for him by the door.

"Thanks for the gift," he said.

She smiled.

"I thought you might like something you could keep."

"I know," Lang said.

Now he was impatient to leave.

"There isn't much left to say, is there?" she asked. "To each other."

"No. Not now, anyway."

"Will you come back?"

"I don't know."

She nodded.

"Well, I'll be seeing you, Daniel."

"Sometime."

Lang opened the door. He was almost to the corner when he heard her call out behind him.

"Luck!"

TWISTED KICKS
by Dan Lang

Are you thinking how the scene has changed
how the pieces of your heart have gotten
rearranged
oh, don't it make you feel
just a little bit ravaged
oh, don't it make you, don't it make you
just a little bit savage?

And you wonder how it came to this
it seemed so long ago it started
with a kiss
oh, don't the girls on the street
look a little bit ravaged
oh, don't the cops on the beat
look just a little bit savage?

oh, oh, oh, oh, oh, oh
all your two-bit friends
with all their twisted kicks
you better keep on rockin'
you're gonna learn some
new tricks, new tricks, new tricks, yeah.

Are you thinking of the things I said
When you walk to the mirror, start to
see red
oh and your face in the frame
looks a little bit ravaged
oh and I know
that at night you-he-she-they and all
got a little bit savage

(repeat chorus)

we talk, we say that it began
before we ever, ever began
and so our hands were tied
but tell me, is the breath of life
the liar or the lie
So go on and be a dancer
keep your balance as you turn
but listen when I say to you
that this town must burn
oh and my life yes my life
was a little bit ravaged
and now it's all come back to me
just a little bit savage

(repeat chorus)

McLean, VA
New York, NY
1974/1978

TEN YEARS IN AN OPEN NECKED SHIRT

John Cooper Clarke

'In a vain attempt at bourgeois credibility, Lenny changed his name to John Cooper Clarke and under this title embarked on a polysyllabic excursion through Thrillsville, UK. Yes, it was be there or be square as, clad in the slum chic of the hipster, he issued the slang anthems of the zip age in the desperate esperanto of the bop. John Cooper Clarke: the name behind the hairstyle, the words walk in the grooves hacking through the hi-fi paradise of true luxury...'

This is the collected poetry of John Cooper Clarke – rock poet, story-teller and humorist – and publication is planned to tie in with the Channel 4 series of the same name. The book is brilliantly illustrated by Steve Maguire.

'One of our most gifted and poetic young writers'
JOHN FOWLES

THE AFFIRMATION
Christopher Priest

When Peter Sinclair loses his father, his lover and his job, he withdraws to a country cottage in an effort to rebuild his life. But the autobiography he begins to write turns into the story of another man in another, imagined, world whose insidious attraction draws him forever further in.

Christopher Priest was selected as a 'Best of Young British Novelist' for THE AFFIRMATION, his finest work to date.

'The atmosphere of solitude and mental disequilibrium ... is beautifully conveyed, suggesting too the void that underlies all our reality'
D.M. THOMAS

'Priest opposes madness and sanity, life and art, the elaborate narrative and the empty page – and then makes them interchangeable ... an original thriller, a study of schizophrenia set against questions of persona and plot'
New Statesman

'Original and haunting'
The Times

'Rich and provocative'
Times Literary Supplement

ARENA

'Magnificent ... Miss Tremain has fashioned the totality of one life – and conveyed the evanescence of all human existence'

Sunday Telegraph

THE CUPBOARD
Rose Tremain

At the age of eighty-seven, Erica March died in a cupboard. She wrapped her body in a chenille tablecloth, laid it out neatly under the few skirts and dresses that still hung on the clothes rail and put it to death very quietly, pill by pill. She left a note, but the note made no mention of her suicide, nor of the cupboard in which she had chosen to commit it. And she had known, of course, that it would be Ralph who would discover her body – and that when he found her he would do everything she had asked, exactly as she had asked it.

The Cupboard is an evocative, complex and imaginatively perceptive novel about freedom and the will to live by one of Britain's most highly acclaimed young writers. For another of her novels, *Letter to Sister Benedicta* (published by Arrow), Rose Tremain won a place among the 'Best of Young British Novelists' for 1983.

'Strongly constructed . . . highly relevant . . . thoroughly fascinating'
Sunday Times

'Deeply evocative . . . a book brimming with life . . . remarkable'
The Times

'A fascinating *danse macabre*'
Scotsman

ARENA

ARENA

COMING SOON!

'An absolutely remarkable book' *Los Angeles Times*

EASY TRAVEL TO OTHER PLANETS

Ted Mooney

The sound of human music, of song or instrument, will transfix and exhaust a dolphin by its load of alien information. And if a rude music finds you, it will tell you stories, or invade your skin, or make you forget things you have always remembered. This is always true of dolphins – and sometimes true of men and women as well.

EASY TRAVEL TO OTHER PLANETS

'In Ted Mooney's remarkable first novel there are so many twists of fantasy and apocalyptic leaps into the unknown regions of human/non-human communication that the effect is dazzling'
Daily Telegraph

'A novel of notable skill and sensitivity ... The quality of the prose, and the imagination behind it is unmistakable' *Observer*

'Remarkable ... riveting'
Guardian

'Fascinating ... arresting'
Yorkshire Post

ARENA

COMING SOON!

'There are images in this book that burn the mind'
Publishers Weekly

FAMILIARITY IS THE KINGDOM OF THE LOST

Dugmore Boetie

In time, place and deed, much of Dugmore Boetie's savage yet funny autobiography – the autobiography of a black con man in South Africa – never happened. But it is not always necessary to tell the truth in order to reveal the truth – and the fantasies of a man who will not let his angry dreams be killed can tell better than any factual document what life really is like when you are born into a world in which you can only lose.

FAMILIARITY IS THE KINGDOM OF THE LOST
The classic story of a black man in South Africa

'It is a flight of wild comic exaggeration and invention that is not only vibrantly funny but a more honest expression of the despair of black South Africans than any number of moralizing exhortations'   Joe Lelyveld, *The New York Times Book Review*

'FAMILIARITY IS THE KINGDOM OF THE LOST is the best factual account of black life to come out of South Africa. But even more than that, it is artful'
Book World

ARENA

'Wickedly amusing ... a new and original woman writer who could be the best bitter-sweet comedian since Beryl Bainbridge'
ROBERT NYE, *The Guardian*

THE NATURAL ORDER
Ursula Bentley

'The adolescent male is the nearest thing to primordial slime still to be found in its natural state' concludes Carlo at the end of her first day's teaching. Brought up with her friends, Damaris and Anne, in an unshakeable belief in a Brontë-esque destiny, little has prepared any of them for the eccentric, brutish masters and sweaty pupils of the Blessed Ambrose Carstairs Grammar School for Boys.

Only Shackleton, the Adonis of the Sixth, transcends that world of aggressive, adolescent yearnings and clumsy rebellion, but even he, the perfect golden boy, is more – and less – than he seems.

THE NATURAL ORDER has not only received wide critical acclaim but has also won Miss Bentley a place among the 'Best of Young British Novelists' for 1983.

'Excellent ... a novel of style, originality and wit'
Daily Telegraph

'Vivaciously misanthropic, cheerfully lascivious'
Sunday Telegraph

'A romping dorm-feast of a novel'
Observer

FOR FURTHER INFORMATION
ABOUT ARENA BOOKS,
PLEASE WRITE TO
Arena Books
17 Conway Street
London W1P 6JD

ARENA